Sophie is S

Best wishes
Trish

Joan Fallon

SOPHIE IS STILL MISSING

A Jacaranda Dunne Mystery

Sophie is Still Missing

The Scottish novelist Joan Fallon, currently lives and works in the south of Spain. She writes both contemporary and historical fiction, and almost all her books have a strong female protagonist. She is the author of:

FICTION:
Spanish Lavender
The House on the Beach
Loving Harry
Santiago Tales
The Only Blue Door
Palette of Secrets
The Thread That Binds Us
Love Is All

The al-Andalus series:
The Shining City (Book 1)
The Eye of the Falcon (Book 2)
The Ring of Flames (Book 3)

The City of Dreams series
The Apothecary (Book 1)
The Pirate (Book 2)
The Prisoner (Book 3)

NON-FICTION:
Daughters of Spain

(Available in paperback, audio and as ebooks)

JOAN FALLON

SOPHIE IS STILL MISSING

SCOTT PUBLISHING
(ESPAÑA)

Sophie is Still Missing

© Copyright 2021
Joan Fallon

The right of Joan Fallon to be identified as the author of this work has been asserted by her in accordance with the Copyright, Designs and Patents Act 1988

All Rights Reserved

No reproduction, copy or transmission of this publication may be made without written permission
No paragraph of this publication may be reproduced, copied or transmitted save with the written permission of the publisher, or in accordance with the provisions of the Copyright Act 1956 (as amended)

All characters and events in this book are purely fictitious, and any resemblance to actual persons, living or dead, is purely coincidental.

ISBN 978-84-09-34608-0
First published in 2021
Scott Publishing
España

Sophie is Still Missing

ACKNOWLEDGMENTS

My sincere thanks to my editor Sara Starbuck once again, to Angela Hagenow for her excellent proof reading and to Alex Allden for the cover. Their advice and support have, as always, been invaluable.

And to my dear husband, Ray, who for fifteen years tried to convince me to write a crime novel. Well, here it is now.

Sophie is Still Missing

Sophie is Still Missing

HOLY WEEK
March 2018

The old man unlocked the heavy wooden doors to the Brotherhood to which he'd belonged for most of his life. Jorge was wearing the clothes they always wore for the Holy Week processions: his best black cloak over a simple twill tunic tied at the waist with a belt of esparto. His *capirote* was tucked into his belt ready; he would pull that over his head once they were about to start. He sighed as he remembered that this was the last time he would be taking part in the procession, and a feeling of sadness overwhelmed him as he put his shoulder to the massive door and pushed it open. The heady smell of carnations came out to greet him as he stepped inside their gloomy headquarters. This year he had been honoured for his long years of devotion by being chosen to carry the Guiding Cross and lead the Brotherhood of the Virgin of Remorse on their slow, twelve-hour walk through the streets of Málaga. He hoped his gammy knee wouldn't let him down.

'Come on Jorge. Get a move on,' said one of the Brothers; it was Felipe, a young man who worked as a solicitor. Behind him were almost two hundred of the Brotherhood, all dressed in their traditional robes and some even had their *capirotes* already covering their faces. It was a special day for them all. The Virgin of Remorse only ventured out on this one day a year, and the men had been preparing for it for months. It was the moment when they could forget their humdrum lives as waiters or bank clerks, teachers or builders; this was when they could rise above it and carry the Virgin through the streets for everyone to see, the faithful and tourists alike.

Jorge stepped forward and pushed the doors as wide open as was possible, letting his companions into the room where the Virgin's enormous throne was kept. Some of them knelt in homage to her, others made the sign of the cross, while some of the young ones were too excited to do more than stare up at her sorrowful face. Jorge paused, the glint of sunlight on her gold halo dazzling him for a moment. He looked up at the throne, four tonnes of wood, steel and plaster covered in gold leaf and silver mouldings, and thought back to the first time he'd been allowed to be one of the *costaleros*; Jorge hadn't even left school at the time and he had almost collapsed from exhaustion by the time they'd finished carrying the Virgin through the streets. He had felt such love for her that day and was proud to have been one of the two-hundred *costaleros*. His feelings had never changed. But he couldn't carry that sort of weight any longer. Not anymore. Not at his age.

He paused. Something looked out of place. For a moment he puzzled over what it was. If only the other brothers could show more respect and maintain a dignified silence, but the atmosphere was electric; this was the moment when they would take their places as the Virgin's throne bearer and carry her through the streets to her church. He peered up at her again. Yes, something was wrong. Of course. He shouldn't be able to see her halo from here; it was normally obscured by a dark red, velvet canopy, decorated with gold and silver thread. This morning that canopy tilted wildly to the right, exposing her serene image to those below. How had that happened? Such a nuisance. Some of the younger members of the Brotherhood must have dislodged it. They were too boisterous; they still had to learn the seriousness of their task. The Virgin had been set on her throne a few days previously, and everything was supposed to be ready for them to collect her and start the procession this afternoon. With their tight timetable, there wasn't time for any mistakes; they would be walking for hours, until well after midnight. He muttered a short prayer to himself to try and quell his annoyance and restore his calm.

'Someone's knocked over the candles,' a voice behind him said. It was Juan, one of the newer members to the Brotherhood, and a baker from Churriana.

'I'll see to them,' said another Brother as he clambered up onto the throne. '*Santa Madre de Dios*,' he shouted. 'What in God's name is this? How has this happened?'

'What is it?'

'Ring the police. And hurry. There's a dead body up here.'

'What are you talking about?' asked Juan. 'Whose body?'

Jorge felt a chill down his back as though a cold wind had blown into the room. Then they all began clamouring at once.

'How can there be?'

'Did someone forget to lock up, last night?'

'Is it a joke?'

'A pretty poor one, if you ask me.'

'Who is it?'

'Who's dead?' The Brothers pushed and shoved, trying to see what had happened.

'It's a woman,' one of them exclaimed. 'She's covered in blood.'

'A young girl, more like,' said another. 'A scrap of a girl.'

'I think we'd better all move back,' said Jorge. 'Show a little respect. If it is a body, then the police won't want us disturbing it before they've seen it. Come on now, gentlemen. Move away, please.'

Sophie is Still Missing

Reluctantly the Brothers trooped outside to wait, but they didn't stop grumbling.

'We'll be late,' one said.

'I can't believe this is happening,' said another.

'I knew it was too good to be true. This was to be my first time,' said another, a youth of no more than eighteen. None of the Brothers appeared to give much thought to the person who had died.

Jorge made his way closer to the Virgin and climbed up the steps, silently praying that she had suffered no damage. He sighed with relief; she seemed as beautiful as ever, her painted porcelain face, framed by its golden crown, looking sadly down at the body of a young woman. The girl lay propped against the Virgin, her hands placed together as though in prayer. She was definitely dead; her face was as pale as the porcelain hands that supported her frail body. She looked undernourished and was dressed in a plain cotton dress. She had no shoes and her feet were bruised and cut. He stared at her, feeling an overwhelming sadness engulf him. Had she come in here herself and climbed up there to die in the arms of the Virgin Mary? It was a nice thought, but somehow he couldn't imagine that fragile creature climbing up onto the throne. And why would she scatter pink carnations over herself? A glint of gold attracted his eye. Something was caught in her hair. Instantly he recognised it. The poor girl hadn't got there alone. Someone had brought her here; someone who knew the *Cofradía* well. Jorge began to tremble with fear then he dropped to his knees and prayed for her soul.

SIX MONTHS LATER

CHAPTER 1

JD unlocked the door to her new office; she'd been working from there for almost two months but still considered it new. It was tucked down a narrow street behind the Bishop's Palace, right in the centre of the city, and very convenient. She'd been lucky to find it; vacant properties in the centre were rare. Tim had told her about it as soon as he saw it was to be advertised in the local paper. Yes, Tim had his uses sometimes.

She had no sooner shut the door and switched on the lights when her young computer assistant, Nacho, arrived, carrying a bundle of newspapers and a half-drunk cup of coffee.

'You're early,' he said. 'Couldn't you sleep?'

'Don't be cheeky.' JD sat down at her desk and switched on her computer.

'Guess what, JD,' said Nacho.

'What?'

'The police have closed the case.'

His boss looked at him.

'The murdered girl. The one who was found with the Virgin.'

'Have they found who murdered her, then?' she asked.

'No, I don't think so. Doesn't give much detail.' He opened one of the newspapers. 'They've tucked it away on page five, so it wouldn't draw too much attention.'

'I'm not surprised. Six months and they don't seem to have found anything,' said JD. 'I'm sure we could have done better.'

'It's her family I feel sorry for.'

'Do they mention her friend? The one who's still missing?'

'No. Nothing.' Nacho closed the paper and drank the rest of his coffee. 'So what have you got for me today? he asked, as he skilfully tossed the empty coffee cup into the waste paper bin.

'See if you can find out any more about that car. Señor Ramirez is very upset about it.'

'Well, it's his own fault, letting his son drive it when he was underage.'

'Maybe, but the other car could have stopped. There was a lot of damage and his insurance company won't pay out.'

'Actually, I have found something. A witness said he was sure the other car had foreign plates, but he couldn't say what they were,' said Nacho, checking his notes.

'That's good. Could he describe them?'

'Not really. All he said was they weren't in the usual format of four numbers followed by three letters, but it was too dark to make them out clearly.'

'Anything else?'

'Possibly black, or blue, as I said it was dark. Oh yes, and it was driving very fast.'

'Well, see if you can rake up anything else.'

She clicked onto her open cases folder. There wasn't a lot in there. All small stuff, the damaged car, a woman whose bracelet had been stolen and she wanted it back before her husband found out—that was unlikely to happen— two cases of missing dogs and one wayward husband. She'd get Linda to check up on the bracelet, and she'd try and talk to the husband. Where was Linda by the way? She wasn't usually late.

Sophie is Still Missing

She opened the file on the missing husband and stared at it. It seemed plain enough to her that the husband had done a bunk and wasn't coming back, but his wife wouldn't have it. What else could it be? He'd taken all his clothes with him and closed his bank account. Money troubles? Or was it another woman? She sighed. Her thoughts kept returning to the dead girl and her missing friend. Why weren't the police continuing with the investigation? Was it because the girls were foreigners? It wasn't the first time a teenage girl had disappeared in that area. Her mother had told her of a young Irish girl, no more than fifteen, who'd disappeared one New Year's Eve. Nobody had ever found out what had happened to her; they'd searched for a few months then given up. That was over ten years ago.

The door swung open. 'Morning all. You should get this sign put up, properly this time,' said Linda, brandishing JD's new door plaque at her. 'How are people going to know we're a detective agency if it doesn't say so?'

'Good morning to you. You're late.'

'Not much. I got fed up seeing that old plaque lying on top of the photocopier, so I took it to get it repaired, but it was beyond all hope. So I bought you a new one. Ahí tienes,' she said with a flourish. 'Nacho can put it up.'

'Oh, can he?' said Nacho, taking the plaque from her. 'Great job, Linda. I see it's in Spanish and English. That should be good for business.'

'Show me,' said JD. The new brass plaque was engraved with JD Detective Agency and underneath it said, Private Investigator and beneath that, *Investigador Privado*. 'Shouldn't it be *investigadora privada*?' she asked. 'I am female after all.'

'Technically yes, but I thought this might look more serious. Our clients aren't expecting a woman detective. You can see the

Sophie is Still Missing

surprise on their faces when you tell them you're the PI, and not the filing clerk. I think we'll get more clients this way.'

'Linda, you're a traitor to your sex. Get it changed.'

'Can't do that. They'd have to do a completely new one. I can tell you the price, if you want.' JD thought about their dwindling bank balance and shook her head. Most of their clients came by personal recommendation or through the internet, anyway; that's why she hadn't bothered to put the old sign up. 'Leave that for now. I want you to try to find out what's happened to that missing bracelet. Have there been any similar burglaries in the area? Has it really been stolen or is this an insurance scam?'

'Okay, JD.' Her tall, blonde assistant sat down, took a mirror from her handbag and repaired her lipstick, then she opened the file on her desk and began to work.

JD had discovered where the missing husband worked and was busy concocting an excuse to ring and speak to him, when her mobile rang. She sighed. It was Tim. He was becoming a bit of a pest lately. Didn't he have any work to do? Shouldn't reporters be out looking for stories, not ringing their friends all day?

'Hi, Tim. What can I do for you?' she said in her most neutral voice.

'Just thought I'd give you a heads up, JD. You know the police have closed the case of the Virgin Princess?'

She shuddered. That was the name the English press had given to the poor girl; it sounded like a cruise liner. 'Yes, I saw it in the paper.'

'Well, did you know that they've closed the case on her friend, too?'

'The one who disappeared at the same time?'

'Yes, and I've just had her mother in here. She's not happy, and she's determined to find her daughter. But guess what?'

'What?'

'She wants you to help her. I gave her your mobile number.'

'Not my private one, I hope.'

'Of course not. Your office one. Do you have a private one? I didn't know that; I don't have it.' He sounded peeved.

JD ignored him and said, 'Did she ask for me by name?'

'Well, actually, no. She asked me if I could recommend a private detective, and naturally I mentioned you.'

'Naturally. Well thank you, Tim. I've been ruminating over that case for a while. Pretty sure the police could have done more. There's something they aren't telling the public. Any idea what it might be? Anything to do with people trafficking?'

'If I knew anything, I'd tell you; you know that.'

'Mmmn. I hope so.'

'So, you'll speak to her?' he asked.

'Of course. Thanks again.'

'Hang on, JD. How about a drink tonight? By way of a thank you?' Tim asked.

'Nice idea, but I'll be very busy. Got to tie up some open cases before I can tackle anything new. You don't want me to delay the poor woman, do you?'

'No. Of course not. Another time, then.'

'Another time, Tim.' She hung up quickly before he could suggest an alternative.

'What was that all about?' asked Linda.

'Tim, with a new client for us,' JD said, with a big smile. That should help their bank balance.

She remembered reading about poor Julie at the time; it was all over the newspapers and on the tv. Her mother had been very upset about it, mainly because her friend's grandchildren went to the same school as the murdered girl. It was big news for a few days then suddenly it went quiet, buried in the coverage of the Holy Week processions. She had expected to hear more from the police once Easter was over, but apart from a couple of paragraphs stating that the Guardia Civil were continuing their investigations into her death, there was nothing. And now it seemed as though they'd given up.

CHAPTER 2

Jim and Beverley Anderson were right on time. Linda ushered them into the room at the back which they used for interviews and meetings; it was a bit on the small side, but it was at least private.

'Nice to meet you, Mr and Mrs Anderson,' JD said, shaking hands with them each in turn.

'It's good of you to see us,' said the husband. He was extremely thin and his face was puffy from either lack of sleep or an excess of alcohol; she wasn't sure which. What she was sure about however, was that these were two very unhappy people. They both stared at her with such longing in their eyes that she could hardly bear it. For once her confidence wavered. Why did they think she could find their daughter when the police had come up with nothing?

'You come highly recommended,' added his wife, a fragile woman who looked as though she would break in two in a stiff breeze. Despite the fact that the summer had only just ended, there was an unhealthy pallor about her skin, as though she spent all her days inside the house, which she most probably did.

The husband placed a large folder of newspaper cuttings on the table in front of him. 'I thought these might be useful,' he said.

'Thank you,' said JD. She desperately wanted to help this couple find their daughter, but in her heart she knew that the chances were slim. Too much time had passed. The police knew what they were doing when they closed the case; they could only spend so many resources searching for a missing girl. She understood this perfectly well, but she still thought they could have discovered more than they did.

'We didn't know what else to do,' said Sophie's mother.

'Well, you know I can't promise anything, Mrs Anderson, but it won't hurt to have a fresh pair of eyes look at the case.'

'Please call me Beverley,' the woman said, with a wan smile.

'And I'm Jim,' said her husband, pushing the pile of newspapers towards JD. 'I have to admit I thought we were meeting a man. The reporter called you JD.'

'Yes, everyone calls me that, well except my mother and a few close friends. I hope you're not disappointed.'

'No, no, no, not at all,' Beverley interrupted. 'Not at all.'

There was a tap on the door and Linda put her head round. She smiled and asked, 'Can I get anyone a coffee?'

'Yes, good idea, Linda. I think we're going to be quite a while.' They gave her assistant their orders and once she had left, JD asked, 'You don't mind if I tape our conversation? It helps when I'm going over it with my team.'

Both the Andersons shook their heads.

'Good, then why don't we start at the beginning. Tell me about the day Sophie went missing.' She pressed the record button on her phone and sat back.

Jim looked at his wife. 'I think you should start,' he said.

Beverley pulled out a tissue and blew her nose, then began to recount the last time she'd seen her daughter. 'It was August, last year. I remember it was a blisteringly hot day, and I suggested the girls go to the beach to cool down.'

'The girls?'

'Sophie and Julie. They spent all the summer together.'

'They were inseparable,' added Jim.

'Do you have any other children?' asked JD. She vaguely remembered reading something about some sons.

'Yes, two boys, they were sixteen and eighteen at the time.'

'So older than Sophie? Did they spend much time with their sister?'

'No, not much. Ricky used to go with them to the beach, but Zak, never.' She hesitated and her eyes filled with tears.

'What is it?'

'The girls didn't want to go to the beach, that day. They said it was too hot. They wanted to go to the cinema, so I told Ricky to go with them. I didn't approve of Sophie going to the cinema on her own. Of course he wasn't happy about that. He said it was time Zak took a turn and anyway, he was meeting his friends at the leisure centre, and wasn't going to babysit for two soppy girls.'

'So what happened?'

'I told him I'd stop his allowance if he couldn't put himself out just once in a while,' said Beverley.

'It was a bit harsh,' added Jim. 'Of course he didn't want to go with his sister. What teenage boy would?'

'And Zak?'

'He was just eighteen. He said he wouldn't be seen dead with them, and I couldn't blame him,' said his father.

JD could see where this was going, even if the parents hadn't at the time.

'Well then Sophie said they were going to see Spiderman, so Ricky reluctantly agreed to go with them.'

'And you never saw her again?'

'No. She said she might spend the night at Julie's, so I didn't worry when Ricky came home alone.'

'You didn't ring Julie's mum to see if they'd arrived safely?'

Beverley shook her head. 'No, they were always sleeping at each other's houses. It wasn't anything new.'

'So when did you realise she was missing?'

Beverley couldn't reply; tears were streaming down her face by now.

'It was about lunchtime the next day,' said Jim. 'Fiona, Julie's mum, rang to remind her daughter that they'd arranged to visit her aunt in the afternoon; she was staying in Benalmadena for a week's holiday. It turned out that Fiona hadn't seen them either. The girls hadn't gone there that night, so her mother assumed they'd decided to stay with us.'

'I don't know why she didn't phone to check with us?' Beverley wailed. 'We thought Sophie was safe.'

'What did Ricky say? Was he questioned by the police?'

'That boy. I'll never forgive him. Never,' she said. 'He never had any intention of going to the cinema with them.'

'So where did they go? Does he know?'

'Eventually he admitted that the girls had gone to see "My Little Pony." He said there was no way he was going to sit through that, and Sophie said they didn't want him to go with them, anyway; they preferred to be on their own. So he went off to join his friends.'

'Do you know which cinema it was?' asked JD. 'Was there any CCTV outside?'

'I think it was the one in the Plaza shopping centre. That's where we usually go. The police checked them all out, but nobody had seen them.'

JD noticed that Beverley was trembling. 'Are you feeling all right? Would you like a break?'

'I need a fag,' she said. 'I'll just pop out for a minute.' She leapt to her feet and almost ran out of the room, just as Linda arrived with three coffees.

'Thanks, Linda,' JD said, handing one to Jim and adding, 'Your wife is very upset.'

'Yes. She hasn't had a decent night's sleep since Sophie disappeared. She won't eat, just seems to exist on her endless cigarettes and glasses of white wine. She's killing herself. I tried to get her to go back to work, but she can't manage it.'

'What work does she do?'

'She works for me, luckily. I have a car hire business, and she works, or rather worked in the office. It was very successful, but now things are not so good. We're both finding it hard to keep things together and the company is failing because of it. I'm not sure how we'll live if things carry on like this.'

'How are your sons coping with it?'

'Well Ricky is in the Sixth Form now. His exam results weren't very good, but they're letting him continue. You know, in the circumstances. He's at the International School.'

'And the older one?'

'Zak. He's left school. Was supposed to be going to uni, but he's given that up. He's gone back to the UK, to stay with his grandmother. He took Sophie's disappearance very hard. She idolised him.'

Already JD could see that the ramifications of the girl's disappearance were wider than she'd realised. The Anderson's business was on the verge of bankruptcy, the sons' education had been affected and both parents were suffering both physically and mentally.

Jim drank some of his coffee, then added, 'I don't know if I can stay in Spain. We have to face up to the fact that we're never going to find Sophie. Even if you do manage to discover what happened to her, I know it won't be good news. I can feel it in my bones. I think we may have to sell the house and take Ricky back to the UK. The longer we stay here, the worse Bev gets. If I don't get her away from here, she'll drink herself to death. The doctor has already warned us about the state of her health; her heart is not good.'

JD thought he was going to add something, but just then Beverley returned, the odour of cigarettes clinging to her like a well worn scarf.

'So, did your daughter go to the cinema a lot?' JD asked.

'Once a week, I suppose,' Beverley replied.

'And was it always Ricky's job to go with her?'

'Lately. I used to take her and Julie; sometimes Fiona would take them.'

'Fiona?'

'Julie's mum.'

'So they were always accompanied by an adult?'

'Or Ricky.'

'Is that usual? I mean, they were both fourteen, why didn't you allow them to go with their friends?'

Beverley looked horrified. 'How can you say that? Look what's happened. That's exactly what I was trying to avoid. I'm a good mother. I didn't want anything bad to happen to my daughter, but it did anyway.' She began to sob uncontrollably.

'I'm sorry, Mrs Anderson. I wasn't criticising your parenting; I'm just trying to get a clear picture of the girls.'

'Well maybe you'd better speak to Julie's mum. She was always saying I was too strict with Sophie. And look what's happened to her daughter,' she snapped.

'Where else did Julie and Sophie go to enjoy themselves, besides the cinema?' JD asked.

Beverley looked at her blankly. 'Well they went to the beach a lot.'

'What about during term time?'

'Sophie didn't go out that much. In the term she had too much homework to do. She and Julie used to spend a lot of time at each other's houses, playing music and just being teenagers,' Mr Anderson said.

'How would you know? You were hardly ever home.' snapped Beverley.

'What about discos or parties?' asked JD.

'No. She wasn't into that sort of thing,' said her father.

'So she had never tried to run away before?'

'You're worse than that police woman. How many times do I have to say that Sophie hasn't run away; she's been kidnapped.' said Beverley.

'What makes you so sure?'

'Apart from the fact that I'm her mother? Well she didn't take any clothes with her, nor her makeup. And she didn't take her phone or the charger. She always takes them both when she goes to Julie's house. Always.'

'And when did you discover that?'

'When Fiona rang us and told us that the girls hadn't been there. She said she'd tried phoning Julie but there was no reply. It turned out that she'd left her mobile at home. So then I tried ringing Sophie and her phone was here, in her bedroom.' She began to cry again.

'Her mother's right; she wouldn't have even gone to Julie's without it.' Her father seemed bewildered.

'So nothing was missing? She took nothing with her?'

'Well, some of her winter school uniform has disappeared, but I can't think why she'd take that. She must have left it at Julie's house.'

JD switched off the recorder and said, 'I think that's probably enough for the moment, Beverley. I'll get in touch as soon as I have anything to report.'

The parents were right; it didn't sound as though the girls had run away. There was something else going on here.

CHAPTER 3

After the Andersons had left, JD handed the pile of newspaper cuttings to Linda. 'Go through these would you and see if there is anything useful in them.' She turned to Nacho and added, 'See what you can find online about the case. Concentrate on the early investigation and get the name of the officer in charge.'

'Okay, Boss. What about the dead girl?'

'Yes, anything about her as well. We're going to have to investigate both cases. The father says the two girls were inseparable, so the chances are they were together. We need to talk to their friends. Can you go to the school and make some enquiries, Linda. Were they planning to meet anyone in the cinema? Did either of them have a boyfriend?'

'Okay, I think all the schools are back now.'

'Did you get much from the parents?' Nacho asked.

'Not a lot. It's a bit strange that Sophie's mother didn't phone the Bennetts to see if her daughter was there. Is that normal, do you think, with a fourteen-year old girl?'

'No, I wouldn't have thought so. My mum still keeps a check on my movements, and my sisters definitely have to let her know where they're going. So it is a bit strange. But then she is a foreigner, maybe they are more lenient with their children. But why didn't she ring Julie on her mobile?'

'That's odd as well; the girls didn't take their phones with them. They left them at home.'

Sophie is Still Missing

'What teenage girl goes out without her mobile? It's like leaving her right hand at home,' said Linda.

'And I wouldn't say either of the parents were lenient with their kids, more on the strict side. In fact the mother seems to have been over-protective with Sophie.'

'So what are you going to do?' asked Linda.

'I'm going to ring my dear friend, Jacobo, to see what he knows. I have a feeling he did a television documentary on missing children and modern slavery some months ago.'

'So, you think they were kidnapped and sold as slaves?' asked Nacho.

'Well, if that's the case, we'll never find her,' said Linda. 'She'll be in the Middle East or Russia, by now.'

'But you're forgetting poor Julie. Remember the state of her, undernourished, barefoot and dressed in rags. And where had she been for the past six months? She was being held somewhere. But for what purpose?'

'Have the police said if she'd been sexually assaulted?' asked Nacho.

'I haven't read anything about that.'

'Want me to look?'

'Yes, see what you can find out. I'll ring Captain Rodriguez and see what he can tell me. He owes me a favour, or two.'

'I wondered when you would get around to adding him to your list of people to contact,' said Linda, with a broad smile.

'There's nothing between us. I've told you that a dozen times,' said JD, trying not to blush. Captain Federico Rodriguez Lopez was a senior officer in the Guardia Civil, and JD had first met him some years before, when she was working for the Met and had come to Spain trying to locate a missing woman. Since she'd been working as a private investigator their paths had crossed many times.

'I believe you. Thousands wouldn't,' said Linda with a laugh. 'What do you want me to do about the missing bracelet?'

'Keep looking. You might get lucky.'

JD sat down at her desk and took out her mobile. She typed a quick message to Jacobo suggesting they meet for a drink, and then looked at the scribbled notes she'd made during her interview with the Andersons. Something wasn't right there. Yes they were both very distressed about their missing daughter, but she was sure she could sense a feeling of guilt. And why had the older son left home? Did he know something? She'd play the recording back later and see if there was anything she'd missed.

'By the way, that wayward husband,' said Nacho. 'I've got the phone number for his work, if you want to ring him, now.'

'Good. Hand it over,' said JD. 'I might as well get that out of the way.'

Ten minutes later, she snapped her mobile shut and said, 'Well, that's confirmed it. He's done a runner.'

'Really? Why are you so sure?' asked Linda, her eyes glinting with interest. She thrived on gossip, which was very handy in their line of work.

'He handed in his notice six weeks ago. Told them he was moving to Madrid. I asked if he was depressed or worried about anything and the receptionist laughed. Literally, she nearly had hysterics. When she'd calmed down enough to continue, she told me how another of their employees had also handed in her notice; apparently they've gone off together.'

'And he never even told his wife he was leaving?' asked a shocked Nacho.

'It happens, boy,' said JD, sounding a bit like a maiden aunt. At times her computer assistant's innocence was touching.

'So do you want me to contact his wife?' asked Linda.

'Please.' Her assistant was good at the sympathetic touch. 'And don't forget to give her our bill.'

She took out her mobile and dialled Captain Rodriguez's office.

After a few rings, a deep voice answered. '*Digame.*'

'*Buenos días*, Federico.'

'Jacaranda, *cómo estás?*'

'I'm fine, but I need your help, Federico?'

'Always you ring me when you want my help. What is it, this time, *cariño?*'

'Can I come and see you? Not at the station; it's a delicate matter.'

'Of course, but not today, I'm afraid. Tomorrow at midday?'

They agreed to meet in a bar on the outskirts of the city at one o'clock. She was not worried that anyone would see them together—Captain Rodriguez had been divorced for many years—but she didn't want anyone else within the Guardia Civil knowing that she was looking into Julie's murder, not yet anyway.

JD hurriedly locked up and set off through the narrow back streets. As usual, she was running late, but despite that chose a route which took her past the place where poor Julie's body was found. As she crossed the road by the Bishop's Palace and walked through the crowd of tourists gathering outside the cathedral, she began to wonder about the person who had placed the girl's body on the lap of the Virgin Mary. He had to be a man—it was unlikely that a woman would have the strength to carry even someone as slight as Julie through the city streets—and a Catholic. Someone repenting for his sins, perhaps? And whoever he was, how on earth did he get in there? She stopped and looked up at the enormous double doors; they stood at least six metres high and were made of heavy oak panels. He would have needed help from one of the Brotherhood, maybe a *costalero*. It was very puzzling. Surely the police would have examined all the evidence and spoken to the *costaleros*. But there were over two hundred of them in this particular *Cofradía*, and hundreds more members of that Brotherhood. Besides which, the city had been awash with tourists and *penitentes*, all eager to participate in, or just watch the processions. What was one dead girl amidst all this religious passion? Any evidence would have been destroyed or compromised.

JD could see Jacobo already sitting outside the bar, next to the statue of Ben Gabirol, one of Málaga's famous poets. Jacobo was a good friend, and she was very fond of him. When she'd first arrived in Spain, they had gone out a few times, but soon realised they were better as friends than lovers. At the time, JD hadn't recovered from losing her husband—truth be told, she still hadn't and continued to blame herself for his death—and Jacobo had just been divorced. They were attracted to each other by loneliness as much as anything else.

She raised her arm and waved at her friend, then in her haste almost toppled one of the numerous living statues that worked the city streets, getting rich from the tips of tourists. Feeling guilty, she dropped two euros in his pot. He wasn't worth more; he was the worst one she'd ever seen.

'JD,' Jacobo said, standing up and embracing her. He smelled of soap and cigarettes, and his beard tickled her cheek. 'Lovely to see you. *Cómo estás*?'

'Very well, Jacobo. You're looking good. Been working out again?' she asked with a grin.

'I have to do something to keep the kilos at bay,' he said, patting his stomach. Jacobo was a bon viveur, and his job gave him the opportunity to indulge himself.

JD smiled at him.

'Have a glass of this excellent Rioja,' he said, pouring some into a second glass and handed it to her.

'Just what I need. I've had a difficult day.'

'Is this about the murdered girl?'

'Yes and no, the parents of her missing friend came to see me this morning. They want us to find her. I don't know what to do. You know the police have closed the case?'

Jacobo nodded.

'So, if they can't find anything after all these months, what chance have I? I don't want to raise the parents' hopes only to disappoint them.'

'Well tell them that.'

'But you should have seen them, Jacobo. They are heartbroken and the wife seems to be wasting away with grief. I feel I ought to do something to help.'

'You've always been a soft touch, JD. So what can I do for you?'

'Well, I vaguely remember you did a television show a couple of years ago, about modern slavery. I wondered if you still had a copy of it. I'd like to watch it again.'

'Yes, it'll be in the archives somewhere. So you think the girls could have been kidnapped and sold to slavers?'

'It's a possibility. I don't think we can stick with the theory that they ran away, not now that Julie has turned up dead.'

'I'll send it through to you tomorrow, although I'm not sure it will be much help in your case; it's a general look at slavery, so it includes working for slave wages in the Far East as well as domestic slavery. But you're welcome to watch it.'

'Thanks. It'll give me an idea of what sort of people think it's okay to own slaves in the twenty-first century.'

Jacobo sipped his wine. 'You could have asked me for the programme over the phone,' he said, smiling at her. 'Why come here?'

She laughed. 'Because you always cheer me up. And because I haven't seen you in a while.'

'That's two good reasons, I suppose. Hungry?'

'Starving.'

'Good. Shall we go to Emilio's?'

'Yes, I could just eat a plate of his seafood pasta. And then you can tell me what you've heard on the grapevine about the investigation into the dead girl, and why she was found inside the *Cofradía* building.'

Sophie is Still Missing

CHAPTER 4

JD was up early the next morning. Jacobo had promised to transfer the video straight to her office computer, and she wanted to watch it before the others arrived. She hurried down the main shopping street, struggling with her open umbrella as a stiff breeze from the sea tried to wrestle it out of her hands. Calle Larios looked strangely deserted, its expensive shops closed and shuttered, the road cleaning machine spraying the already wet pavement, and only a handful of sleepy workers waiting to get their first caffeine shot of the day. She was no exception and dashed into an open café, her umbrella dripping a trail of water behind her.

'*Un café soló,*' she said. 'And a double to take away.' The smell of the freshly brewed coffee was delicious; she was feeling more awake already. It had been a late night. After dinner she had gone back to Jacobo's flat and they'd continued drinking and talking until nearly two in the morning, when, after promising to ring him when she had anything to report, she had called a taxi and reluctantly dragged herself away.

'Sugar?' the waiter asked.

She shook her head and drank the strong black coffee eagerly. That second bottle of wine had been a mistake; she was going to regret it all day.

'Did you have a good night?' asked the waiter.

She grimaced. 'Does it show?'

'No more than usual,' he said with a grin.

JD was a regular customer and knew him well.

Sophie is Still Missing

'Here, I've made you a *bocadillo*. That will help settle your stomach.' He placed a wrapped roll next to her double expresso, and leant on the counter ready for a chat.

'Thanks, but I've got to dash. This is not the day to go into work with a hangover.'

'You got a new case?' he asked, his eyes lighting up.

'I have. I'll tell you all about it, later.' Although she liked the young barista, JD had no intention of telling Mario anything. If she did so, half of Málaga would soon know all about it.

By the time she reached her office, the rain had become a steady downpour that looked set to last the whole day. She put the ham roll on Nacho's desk, took a swig from her second coffee of the morning and switched on her computer.

As she waited for the file to open, she thought about what Jacobo had told her. It was amazing just how widespread slavery was in the twenty-first century. Mostly they were either illegal agricultural workers from Eastern Europe or sex-slaves, but there was also a big market for domestic slaves. According to Jacobo, these were usually young females who'd been kidnapped at an early age and were made to lead the most awful lives, often beaten, never allowed out of the house, never paid and subject to both physical and sexual abuse. A lot of them were from the Philippines, but sometimes the buyers had a preference for western girls. A number of questions were forming in her head; she hoped the video would help to answer them.

At nine o'clock Linda arrived, bringing the blustery morning with her. 'What a foul day. Might as well still be in Manchester,' she complained, pulling off her wet mac and letting it drip across the floor. 'Don't worry, I'll clean it up.'

'I didn't say anything,' said JD, watching Linda get the mop out of the broom cupboard. 'And don't complain about the rain; the farmers need it. It's been a long, dry summer.'

'Summer seems a long time ago.' She stared at her boss and added, 'You look awful. An all-nighter, was it?'

'Thanks. It was all in the line of duty.'

'So you spoke to Jacobo?'

'Yes. I've got a copy of his documentary on slavery, but there wasn't much that could help us.'

The door burst open again, letting in more wind and rain.

'What a morning,' said Nacho, almost spilling his styrofoam cup of coffee as he struggled to close the door.

'Mind your feet,' said Linda.

'*Buenos días*, to you too,' Nacho replied, putting down his coffee. 'Thanks for the *bocadillo*, JD.'

'Now we're all here, let's see what we've found out.' She picked up her case folder and led the way into their tiny meeting room and sat down, waiting for Linda to put away the mop and collect her notes, and for her computer assistant to organise himself.

'So,' said Nacho, 'Was it worth it?'

'If you mean last night, I'm not so sure,' JD replied. 'You can look at it yourself later if you want, but it's probably not worth your while. He covers sex-slaves and agricultural workers in Europe, and domestic slaves in the Philippines and the Middle East. Not sure where Julie fits in there.'

'Well, we can rule out the first two,' said Linda.

'Are you sure? Do we know if she was sexually assaulted yet?' asked Nacho.

'I'm seeing Captain Rodriguez this morning, and I hope he'll tell me what they found in the autopsy.'

Linda and Nacho exchanged smiles, but said nothing. That was the problem of working in an investigation agency, nothing was private.

'Well, I think it's more likely she was a domestic slave. The papers said she was undernourished and badly cared for; that doesn't sound like a child prostitute to me.'

'That's a bit flimsy, Linda. Anything could have happened to her.'

'Don't you remember that case, about five or six years ago, a young woman jumped off a balcony in Marbella and broke her leg. It turned out she was being kept against her will by the family. The newspapers said she was a domestic slave. Her owners were Saudis. I think. Or was it Russians?'

'But if Julie was working in someone's house, surely she would have been seen eventually, by a neighbour or a visitor to the house. If not before, then when they heard about her death, someone would have made a connection,' said Nacho.

'You would think so, but as far as I'm aware, nobody has come forward to say they have seen Julie or Sophie, since the day they disappeared. What about you two? Have you come up with anything?' asked JD. She was beginning to feel desperate. Perhaps she should tell Beverley that they couldn't help her.

'I've been looking through the newspaper articles the father brought in. There wasn't a lot of coverage of the murder. Certainly not as much as you'd expect,' said Linda. 'Maybe because it happened during Holy Week.'

'*Dios mío*, I know everything's shut during that week, but surely the death of a young girl warrants making an exception?' said Nacho; he was not a great fan of religious processions. 'I suppose the Guardia Civil were too busy with their own *Cofradía* to investigate fully, and the papers are filled with photos of the processions.'

'I'll be able to answer that better when I've seen the Captain. As for the journalists, you should know by now that they report what sells most newspapers, and Holy Week is very big in Málaga. So did you find anything that could be useful, Linda?'

'Not really, I looked in the press archives online and there was loads of stuff there about modern slavery and lots of dreadful articles about child trafficking. There's one article from June 2017, where a couple in Cartama were arrested for selling their daughters as sex slaves.'

'That's the year the girls disappeared.'

'Exactly. And in the same month, a fourteen- year old girl was sold by her parents for €5,000 and a van.'

'A van?' gasped Nacho. 'Who on earth would do that? What sort of parents are they, for God's sake?'

'They're not isolated cases, either. There are quite a lot of articles on child slavery. One claims that there are over a million child slaves sold every year, and some of them are sold over and over again, each time making a profit for the people involved.'

'I don't doubt it, Linda, but it doesn't really help us find Sophie,' said JD, beginning to feel irritated by the lack of progress. Their task was beginning to look more and more impossible. Perhaps she should tell Beverley that she couldn't help them find their daughter.

'Maybe not, but it shows that there are plenty of people out there willing to make money from a child's misery,' snapped Linda. 'And it's well organised. Maybe your police chums can help us with that? After all, some of these kids disappeared from our own doorstep, Marbella, Fuengirola, Torremolinos; what did the police find out about them?'

'They uncovered a Mafia run human trafficking ring operating in the Costa del Sol, in 2015,' added Nacho.

'Okay. Okay. You've convinced me. There's a possibility that Julie and Sophie were kidnapped; I'll grant you that. But do you honestly think we have the resources to take on the Mafia, Russian or otherwise?'

'When we have more information, we pass it on to the Guardia Civil,' said Linda.

JD could see that this case was upsetting her assistant, who had two teenage daughters herself and dreaded that something like that would ever happen to one of them.

'I take your point, Linda. Now did you find out anything specific to our case?'

Linda gave a characteristic shrug of her bony shoulders and said, 'Well, I did find something. In one of the English papers there was an interview with a close friend of the girls. She told the reporters that Sophie and Julie were planning to meet a boy whom they'd seen before. She said he wasn't a boyfriend exactly, just someone they liked.'

'Any name?'

'No, but they said he was English.'

'What about the friend's name? Did the police interview her?'

'She's called Sharon. And yes they did interview her and all the other kids in their school year, but found nothing.'

'I think we should make a list of questions for the parents. We need to speak to them again. What about you Nacho? Anything come up on social media? Facebook?'

Nacho grimaced. 'Teenagers don't like Facebook, JD. Not cool. But there are masses of other sites. I'm going through them now. Both girls were on Instagram and Tik Tok. I'm checking their history now, then I'll look at the others.'

'So nothing to report, yet?'

Sophie is Still Missing

He shook his head. 'Well I have found one interesting thing; that car accident you've got me looking into, it happened two nights before Julie's body was found. And guess where the accident took place.'

'Where?'

'Near the hospital. The car was heading for the motorway.'

'So?'

'It was at four in the morning, and the car was coming from the centre of Málaga.'

'So you're suggesting it could have been the person who'd dumped her body?'

'Why not? He's unlikely to have taken her into the centre of Málaga during the day.'

'But how did he get into the *Cofradía*? Someone had to have access to the keys. Okay, Nacho, put what we have up on the board, and Linda and I'll go and visit the school.' She looked at her watch, 'By the time we get there, the kids will be having their break.' Her appointment with Captain Rodriguez wasn't until one; there would be plenty of time to do both. 'Tonight we'll go over everything and see if we're making any progress.'

'Hey, Linda, what did you say that girl's name was? The friend,' asked Nacho.

'Sharon. Why?'

'She's just posted something on Julie's Instagram page. Her name's Sharon Brown.'

CHAPTER 5

Thanks to Linda ringing ahead to arrange for them to speak to the students, no sooner had they arrived at the school, when the doors opened and a stream of secondary children flocked out into the school yard.

'I think that's her,' said Linda. 'It's hard to tell when she's wearing her school uniform.'

Nacho had printed out a photo of Sharon from her Instagram page, a pouty-lipped version of the girl, with thick make-up and a low-cut dress. The teenager coming through the doors, flanked by two other students, looked younger and more vulnerable.

They waited until the girls were closer and then she said, 'Excuse me girls, can we speak to you for a minute.'

'If you're Mormons, we're not interested,' said the smaller one on the left.

'Nor Jehovah's Witnesses,' said Sharon with a laugh.

JD smiled. 'We're neither of those. I'm a private investigator and I'd like to ask you a few questions.' She flashed her PI card in front of them and guided them away from the crowd of sandwich-eating, coke-drinking teenagers congregating on the small patio. 'Sharon is it?' she asked.

'Yes. How do you know my name?' The girl suddenly looked anxious.

'From the newspaper,' said Linda.

'So what is it? Is this about Julie, because I told the police I didn't know nothing.'

'Yes, it is about Julie. You told the police that you were her friend. Did you know Sophie too?'

'Why do you want to know about Sophie?' asked the small dark girl, pulling out a ham sandwich and taking a large bite. 'My mum said the police have given up looking for her. My mum reckons she's dead as well.'

'We don't know that but we do know that Sophie is still missing and we want to find her. Her mother has employed me to search for her.' JD turned her eyes on Sharon again. 'So, was she your friend too?' she repeated.

'In a way. I knew both of them but those two stuck together most of the time.'

'Julie and Sophie?'

'Yes. We'd hang out with them sometimes but they weren't what you'd call our close friends. I'd been to Sophie's house a couple of times, for her birthday and that.'

'But you posted on your Instagram page that you're devastated about Julie's death and you're never going to get over it. That she was the best friend you'd ever had.'

'Well yes.'

'So, is that true? Was she your best friend?'

'I liked her. She was cool. But she was always with Sophie.'

'We've put up a memorial to her,' said the little dark girl. 'Do you want to see it?'

'Yes please,' said Linda.

They followed them to a corner of the school yard where the students had laid flowers in front of a hardboard panel displaying a school photo of Julie. The panel was covered with sympathy cards and a bank of candles had been arranged in front of it; it reminded JD of the religious shrines that dotted the countryside. One of the younger pupils was struggling to light one of the candles.

Sophie is Still Missing

'Here, let me help you,' said Linda, taking out her lighter and lighting it. 'So who are all these cards from?'

'Her friends,' said the girl.

'She had a lot of friends by the look of it,' said Linda, smiling. She turned to Sharon and asked, 'Did either of them have boyfriends?'

'I told the police. They were hoping to meet up with a boy that night, but I don't think he was a boyfriend, just some bloke they fancied.'

'What about boys in the school? Classmates?'

'Nooo,' said the other girl, who'd kept quiet until then. 'They didn't like the boys in school. Not cool enough for them. They liked them older and with money.'

'And your name is?' JD asked, as gently as she could. She didn't want to frighten them by behaving like a policeman, although old instincts were hard to suppress.

'Meg. And that's Lilley. We knew them, but like Sharon said, we never hung out with them. We tend to stick together, just us three.' She smiled at her friends.

'Can you think of anything you could tell us that would help us to find Sophie? Anything at all?'

'Well, it wasn't the first time they'd seen that boy.'

'Really. Do you know where they first met him? Was it at the cinema?'

'Naw. It was in a bar. Don't know which one but there are plenty of bars close to the cinema. They bumped into him one day a few months before they disappeared. I remember 'cos it was Julie's birthday and she boasted that she was sixteen so he bought them both Cosmopolitans. But she wasn't. She was only fourteen, like us.'

'But you didn't tell that to the police?'

'No why would I? Julie would only have got into trouble with her parents. They were very strict. They wouldn't even let her drink a shandy.'

JD stared at them. She'd never understand the teenage mind. 'So did she have any photos of this guy? If it was her birthday she must have taken a selfie with him?'

'Yes. I think she put some on Tik Tok,' said Lilley, but I don't remember what he looked like.

'I saw a photo of him,' said Sharon, rather sheepishly. 'He was older than her, about twenty, I'd guess. He looked Spanish. At any rate he had black hair and his skin was quite dark.'

'That's very helpful, Sharon,' said Linda. 'Can you remember what he was wearing? Anything unusual?'

'A tee-shirt and jeans, I think. He was quite handsome. Good pecs. Oh yes, and he had a ponytail.'

'Any tattoos?'

'I think he had one on his arm, but I don't remember what it was.'

'One more thing, Sharon, you told the police that you thought she was seeing an English boy. Is that someone else?'

Sharon blushed. 'No, there was only one boy she talked about.'

'Are you sure?'

'Well, I thought he was English at first, because she said something about him supporting Manchester City, then I saw the photo and he looked more Spanish.'

'So there could have been two boys?'

'Dunno. Maybe. There was only one on the photo she showed me. He looked Spanish.'

'Okay. That's been a great help, girls. Thanks. It looks like you have to go into class now, but if you think of anything else that could be of use to our investigation, please give me a call.' JD handed them each a business card with her number on it.

'Okay, boomer,' said Meg, pocketing her card and grinning at them. She and the others sauntered towards their classroom.

'Cheeky little beggar,' said JD.

'That's teenagers for you. At least we learnt a bit more about Julie and Sophie,' said Linda.

'Yes, if we can believe what Sharon told us. She was either lying or confused about the boy they were meeting.' JD looked at her watch and added, 'Before you go back to the office you can drop me off; I'll go and talk to the Captain. Ask Nacho to see if he can find anything about that mystery guy on Julie's social media pages.'

'Okay Boss.'

As always, JD felt a tingle running up her spine when she saw him; he was sitting at the bar, sipping his usual café solo. He wasn't a particularly handsome man, but there was something about him that she found very attractive. Not over tall, he was broad and muscular, with thick black hair that grew tight to his head. When he smiled, as he did now when she approached him, his teeth gleamed white against his dark beard. He was a man who gave off an aura of confidence and strength, something she found irresistible.

'Here you are, *cariño*. I've ordered you a very cold manzanilla,' Captain Rodriguez said, never taking his eyes from hers.

'Lovely. Just what I need after talking to a crowd of teenage girls,' she replied. 'How are you?'

'As always, overworked and underpaid,' he said, leaning across and kissing her, not in the usual Spanish way on both cheeks, but full on the lips. 'Now tell me what you've been up to.'

'You remember the case, about a year ago, where two teenage girls went missing?' she said, getting straight to the point. She knew he hated prevarication, although she would have been happy to sit there all afternoon with him, drinking cold sherry.

'From Torremolinos? Yes, I do. One turned up dead in Málaga, a few months ago. During Holy Week, wasn't it?'

'Well, the parents of the other girl have been to see me; they want me to find their daughter.'

'And they think you can do that, when the police, with all their contacts and manpower have failed? It's a year since her disappearance. If there was anything to be found, we would have found it.'

'Don't put on your Guardia Civil face. You know as well as I do, that there's always a chance that something will turn up; things get missed. Besides which, you're always complaining that the police are undermanned; it's quite possible that something got overlooked.'

'Of course, but we had dozens of men looking for the girls and they found nothing. They combed the countryside with dogs searching for traces of them; we even had the helicopters out. We interviewed their friends and family, and did door-to-door searches. Nobody had anything to tell us. There was not a shred of evidence that they had been kidnapped. In the end the conclusion was that they'd run off together, either with a couple of boys or on their own, and would eventually turn up. Honestly Jacaranda, you wouldn't believe the number of teenage girls who take off for a few days just in order to piss off their parents.'

'But they didn't turn up, did they? At least Sophie didn't. Poor Julie is in the morgue.'

'She isn't actually; her body was released last week to her family. They took her back to the UK to bury her.'

She groaned; so the only evidence, if there was any that is, was gone. JD bit her tongue; there was no point antagonising him.

'What do you want to know, Jacaranda? Or have you only come to berate me for the failings of the Guardia Civil?'

'I want to know what the pathologist's report said. Can you get me a copy?'

'Jacaranda, Jacaranda. How am I supposed to do that without anyone knowing about it. I didn't even work on the case.'

'Please Federico. Her body is the only evidence there is at the moment. If we are ever going to find Sophie alive, then we have to know what happened to them. Where has Julie been all this time? Were the girls together? Was she sexually assaulted? There are so many unanswered questions, but the most important one is, where is Sophie now?'

'Maybe they weren't together.' He finished his coffee and called the waiter across to them. 'A glass of cold manzanilla,' he said. 'And another one for the señora.' He took JD's hand in his and stroked it gently. 'You should walk away from this case, Jacaranda. You are going to find yourself out of your depth, I promise you. Please, for my sake, if not for your own, don't get involved.'

'I hope you're going to explain what you mean by that.'

'Why can't you just trust me when I say it's too dangerous for you to start snooping about? Why do you always have to have explanations?' He ran his hands through his thick hair in frustration.

'Snooping about? What do you think I am, a bloody dog? If you want me to stop investigating, you're going to have to give me a better reason than that.'

The barman placed two frosted glasses on the bar and poured the ice cold sherry into them. He then passed them a small dish of olives.

'Listen *cariño*, this isn't just about one dead girl found in the arms of the Virgin Mary—although the press were able to make a big thing out of that. Children get abducted every day. Hundreds of them. You've read the papers; it's big business. Modern slavery, whether it involves adults or children, is world wide, not just here on the Costa del Sol.'

'I know that.'

'And we're trying to stop it, but it's like trying to empty a river with a bucket; no matter how much water you take out, the river just keeps running by.'

'Then you must cut off the source.'

'Exactly. And that's what we're trying to do.'

'You keep saying we. Who do you mean?'

'The CNP division of Interpol.'

'But that's the National Police, not the Guardia Civil. So how are you involved?'

'If we have a case such as your two missing girls, and we have reason to believe they've been kidnapped and sold, then we pass it over to the CNP. I act as the co-ordinator.'

'Is that what you think has happened to them? They were sold as slaves?' He was confirming the horrifying thought that had been running through her head for days. 'You were lying to me just now, about them running away.'

'Not really. It sometimes starts like that. A nice-looking young man befriends them and they think they're going on an adventure, but by the time they find out what's really happening, it's too late. The truth is we don't know what happened to them. They just vanished.'

'But Julie's body was found here, in Málaga. How do you explain that? Unless you know of any local slave auctions; perhaps there's one in Torremolinos. We could pop down there and see what the going rate is for a young, white, female slave.'

'Don't be stupid, Jacaranda. All this is done on-line. It's a world-wide, multi-million operation. These aren't just local yobs running it; they have Mafia connections, and worse.'

Worse? Good God, what had happened to those two young girls? She thought of Sharon and her two friends; they acted big but they were still children underneath it all. If Julie and Sophie had been abducted by people traffickers they must have been terrified.

'So you think it could just be a coincidence that she ended up back where she'd been abducted?'

'I don't think anything, Jacaranda. I'm not on the case. But I have to admit that it's a bit strange.'

'So will you help me? Please.' She smiled up at him.

He took her hand again and lifted it to his lips. 'You know I will. I'll do anything for you, *cariño*.'

'The forensic report?'

'Yes, okay. I can tell you one thing now about Julie; there was evidence of regular sexual activity, but no signs of sexual assault.'

'So statutory rape?'

'Yes, and regular, according to the pathologist. It also looked as though she'd had an abortion.'

'Dios mío. That poor girl. You have to help me find who did this to her.'

'I will, *cariño*. I will.'

CHAPTER 6

At five o'clock JD returned to the office. Nacho was already working at his computer and Linda was brewing some tea. Despite all the years she'd lived in Spain, Linda still liked a cup of English tea in the afternoon. JD recalled how she'd first met her, in the tea shop in Calle Larios. She had dived in there one afternoon, having a sudden craving for something sweet and preferably with a chocolate topping—it was the only place in the city where the cakes were nearly as good as she'd eaten in London. The café was packed with tourists, and Linda was sitting outside at a table on her own, drinking tea and finishing off a chocolate eclair. She'd invited JD to join her and they had an instant rapport. It was strange how things worked out. All that day JD had been interviewing people to be her new assistant and now there she was drinking tea with a woman who had just lost her job as secretary to a criminal lawyer. Despite the fact that Linda had smoked three cigarettes while they sat there—a vice that she detested—JD offered her the job on a month's trial. She'd never regretted it.

'*Buenos tardes*, JD. Got some news for you,' Nacho said, swivelling round to face her. 'Stopped raining, I see.'

'Yes, at last,' said JD. 'It's good news, I hope.'

'Mmmn. Good and bad.'

'Well let me get myself organised and then we'll go through everything together, in the meeting room.'

'The cupboard, you mean,' said Linda, handing her a cup of tea. 'I've got some results, as well, but don't know how useful they are.'

Nacho had prepared the evidence board ready for their meeting, so all JD had to do was take her rather slim file of evidence and sit down in front of it.

'There's not much up there,' said Linda.

'Well at least there's something. Let's see what we've got.'

Nacho stood up, a perspex ruler in his hand. JD liked her team to share this particular task; she said it helped everyone to get a clearer picture of what was happening. During her years in the Met, the evidence reviews were always led by the senior detective, and she had sometimes thought it might have been better if one of the more junior ones had led them occasionally. But then they had teams of ten or twenty, so it wasn't so practical.

'Okay guys. Here's what we know so far. The two girls went to the cinema hoping to see a boy they knew,' said Nacho, waving his ruler at them.

'More a young man, than a boy, I'd say.'

'A young man, then. We have a description of him.' Nacho paused to let Linda fill in the details.

'Dark hair, looked Spanish, dark skin, been working-out, possible tattoo on his arm. And there's maybe a second man, possibly English, Manchester City fan, with long black ponytail.'

JD watched Nacho hurriedly add the information to the board.

'So first thing, we need to find these men,' said JD. 'What did you come up with on-line, Nacho?'

'Well Julie was all over social media; she had accounts on Tik Tok, Snapchat and Instagram. Sophie less so. I've found her

Instagram account but nothing has been posted since the day they both disappeared, apart from that single post from Sharon. And according to their phone records, their mobiles haven't been used.'

'How did you get hold of their telephone records?'

'I have ways. I got their mobile numbers off the Instagram accounts and hey presto.'

'Is it legal?' asked JD.

'Probably not.'

'Well, don't tell me about it, then. What about Julie? When was her last posting on Instagram?'

'The same. Neither girl posted on social media after they disappeared.'

'So it's pretty certain they didn't leave of their own accord. No teenage girl would go anywhere without her mobile or tablet.'

'But if you could find their accounts, then so could the police,' said Linda. 'So we'll find nothing new there. They'll have already looked at them.'

'Not necessarily so. Something is not right here; the police wound up the investigation far too soon. Keep looking, Nacho. Are there any accounts where Julie could have posted something she didn't want anyone to see? Something she wanted to keep private?'

'There are. I'll see what I can find.'

'And print out all the Instagram snaps that they posted in the three months before they disappeared. I want to see if any men appear on them that match the descriptions we have.'

'Can't I just download them onto your computer, JD? It will easier for both of us and if you find anything you want, I can print it out later.'

'Okay, if that's simpler. Now, what about this good news you've got for me?'

'Well, I have the name of the investigating officer?'

'Okay. Who was he?'

'He was Lieutenant Jose Maria Alvároz.'

'A lieutenant? Not a captain?' asked Linda, in surprise.

'And the bad news?' JD had to get that out of the way.

'He's dead.'

'What? How old was this lieutenant?'

'He was forty-five. Killed in a car accident, three weeks ago.'

'I don't believe it. Did you find out how it happened?' asked JD.

'No, just what it said in el Diario Costa del Sol. He was walking home and was knocked down by a hit and run driver as he was crossing the Avenida de la Alameda. Car went through a red light. The lieutenant had been celebrating a birthday in the centre with some work colleagues.'

'I can't believe this,' said JD. It was too much of a coincidence.

'I told you it was bad news.'

'Okay. Well I'll have to see what Tim can tell me. There must be more. Didn't they catch anyone on CCTV?'

'Apparently not. As I said, it gave very few details. There was more about his grieving widow and three children.'

'So, what happened to the case?'

Nacho shrugged. 'Maybe your friend the Captain can tell you.'

'Okay, let's leave that for the moment. Linda, what have you discovered, if anything?' She was beginning to feel as though they were banging their heads against a brick wall. 'What about the newspaper cuttings the father gave us?'

Sophie is Still Missing

'Not a lot. There was an interview with one of the teachers at the school, a Miss Hardy. I thought I'd go and see her tomorrow. I've got an appointment at lunchtime.'

'Good.'

'What about you, JD? Did the Captain tell you anything, apart from how lovely you're looking today?'

JD ignored her assistant's comment and said, 'Actually he was very helpful. But he warned me off the case; said it was dangerous.'

'He doesn't know you as well as he thinks,' said Nacho with a smile.

'Why?' asked Linda.

'Well, if you'd both let up on the silly remarks, I'll tell you. It seems that the case hasn't been closed, just moved to another department. It's now under the jurisdiction of the Cuerpo Nacional de Policia, in conjunction with Interpol.'

'*Dios mío*,' said Nacho. 'Why is that?'

'People trafficking, or so they think.'

'I told you so,' said Linda triumphantly. 'It had to be something like that. So what do we say to the parents?'

'Nothing. For now, we continue with our investigation. Just try not to draw too much attention to us, okay?'

'What about the forensic report?'

'Tomorrow. But in the meantime, Capitán Rodriguez has confirmed that Julie had been sexually active, recently. Not assaulted, however.'

'So no evidence of rape?' asked Nacho.

'Well, as she was only fourteen when she disappeared, then yes, it was statutory rape. But no evidence of her having been forced recently, although there were multiple bruises on her body. We'll just have to wait until we get the full autopsy report before we can work out what happened to her. There's one other thing; she'd had an abortion.'

'Poor kid. So what do we do, next?' asked Nacho.

'I think we should speak to Julie's parents,' said Linda. 'Ask them about Julie and any possible boyfriends.'

'Yes, you do that, but don't mention the abortion, for now. I'm going to interview the Andersons again. See what Julie's mother has to say about them while you're there, Linda.' She gathered her papers together, and added, 'Okay, anything else? Any questions?'

'No, Boss.'

'Only a few hundred,' said Linda under her breath.

'Right. Anyone fancy a drink this evening?' asked JD. 'Usual place?'

'Have to be a quick one,' said Linda. 'I promised Phil I'd cook dinner tonight.'

'You, Nacho?'

He shook his untidy mop of curly hair vigorously, 'Sorry, I've got a rehearsal.' Nacho played the guitar in a flamenco group. JD had never heard them, but Jacobo said they were very good. He was planning to ask them to appear in his new video about Málaga and its music.

'Okay, just us girls, then.' She checked her watch; it was six-thirty. Tim would still be at work. 'Give me five minutes, Linda. I want to ring Tim, first.'

Tim was a reporter at the English off-shoot of one of the main newspapers in the area, La Voz de Málaga. Surely he could tell her something about the policeman's death.

'JD? This is a nice surprise. What can I do for you?'

The enthusiasm in Tim's voice made her cringe, but she needed his help. 'Hi Tim. What do you know about a hit-and-run case, about three weeks ago? An off-duty policeman.'

'Straight to the point as always, JD. Well, off the top of my head, not a lot. I take it you want me to look into it for you?'

'Please Tim. Did you know he was the investigating officer in the Julie Bennett case?'

'The Virgin Princess?'

'The very one.' Should she tell him that they knew Julie wasn't a virgin? No, why spoil his little joke. 'Don't you think it's strange that he should be killed while on that case?'

'You think he'd found something?' Tim asked, his voice cracking with excitement.

'That's what we need to find out. Can you make some discreet enquiries? Look through the back copies or something?'

'Of course. I'll turn up something for you, don't you worry.'

'Discreet, mind, I don't want the police thinking we're treading on their toes.'

'Why would they mind? They've closed the case, haven't they?'

'Yes.'

There must have been some hesitation in her voice, because instantly Tim said, 'Is there something you're not telling me, JD? Do you think the policeman was killed deliberately?'

'I don't know, Tim. That's why I'm talking to you. You have lots of contacts in Málaga and in the Guardia Civil. If anyone can find out, it's you.'

'True. Look I've got to go now, but I'll ring you in a couple of days and let you know what I find.'

'See if anyone identified the car.'

'Okay. I'll ring you.' He hesitated. 'No, it would be better if I came to your office; I may need to show you things.'

'Fine. That's fine, just ring first, in case I'm out.'

'Okay, bye JD. See you soon.'

Sophie is Still Missing

She could hear the triumph in his voice. She'd better make sure all the team were there when he arrived.

'Well?' asked Linda, picking up her handbag.

'He'll get back to us.'

'I don't know why you're always so sniffy with him; he's a nice looking lad and he's besotted with you.'

'That's probably the reason. Come on, I'm dying for a drink.'

It was late by the time JD left the bar. Linda had long gone, but JD had got chatting to a few of the regulars, and then Jacobo had come in and so she'd had a glass of wine with him before she decided that she would go back to the office and pick up the case file. She lived in a small flat, just near the bus station, and tomorrow morning, it would be easier for her to go straight to the Anderson's house from there. She could catch the metro to Torremolinos.

It was a beautiful night; the sky was filled with stars. She could never look up at the night sky without remembering her father; he'd been an astronomer and died when she was only thirteen. He'd told her once, when she was little, that she was made up of all the elements from an exploding star; iron, hydrogen, oxygen and carbon had created her and when she died all would go back to the earth. They were all children of the stars, he'd said, and she believed him. It had made much more sense to her than what she'd been taught in her Religion class at school.

When Andrew, her husband, had died, she hadn't wanted to go on living, but gradually she had pulled her life together so that now, when she looked up at the firmament, she knew he was there, among the stars.

She turned towards the narrow lane that led to the office. Although it was after eleven o'clock, there were still plenty of people walking down Calle Larios, arm in arm. For a moment, she felt a pang of longing for someone of her own, someone who would be waiting for her to go home to them.

'*Buenos noches*, Jaydee,' called the man from the corner café.

'*Buenos noches*, Antonio.' She called, as she entered the gloomy passageway. The agency was at the end, between a shop that sold religious artefacts and a shoe repairers. She fumbled in her bag for the keys and was about to unlock the door, when it swung open and a dark figure burst out, pushing her to the ground and haring towards the cathedral.

'Hey. What the hell?' she shouted, picking herself up. 'Stop. Stop.' She was about to run after him, but he'd already vanished into the maze of dark alleyways; she knew she'd never find him, so she went into the office and switched on the lights. What a mess. Drawers had been pulled out and papers scattered everywhere.

'Are you all right, Jaydee?' asked Antonio, putting his head around the door. 'I heard you shouting.'

'I've had a burglar.'

'I can see. Shall I call the police?'

'No, it's not worth it. I think I arrived before he could do much damage.'

'Has he stolen anything? What about the computer?' He pointed to Nacho's desk, where a loose cable dangled over the edge.

'No, Nacho always takes it home with him. At least I hope he did tonight.' She rubbed her arm; it hurt.

'Are you sure you're all right?'

'Yes, thank you, Antonio. I'm fine. Just angry at the mess he's made.'

The café owner looked concerned, so she added. 'You go. I'll be okay. I'll just collect some papers and then I'm off home too.'

'I will wait and walk with you.'

She could see there was nothing she could do to deter him, so picked up her folder from her desk and was about to leave when she noticed that her computer was on standby. She never left it on standby, never. She clicked one of the keys and stared at the screen in astonishment. She recognised the photograph that came up; it was of her and her husband, taken the week before he'd been killed. They'd gone to Hastings for the weekend, to visit Andrew's aunt; the old lady had taken the photo. Where on earth had it come from? She never kept personal items on her work computer, and as far as she knew the only copy of it had been in Andy's wallet. Sudden fear gripped her chest so tightly, she could hardly breathe.

CHAPTER 7

Linda decided to visit Julie's mum first thing, before going to the school, although she didn't hold out much hope of learning anything new; she'd watched Fiona Bennett being interviewed on the television a few days after Julie's body had been found and the woman was a wreck. Linda hoped that by talking to Fiona she wasn't going to upset her again.

The Bennetts lived in a comfortable, detached house on the outskirts of Torremolinos. All the curtains were drawn but there was a small blue car parked in the driveway. From habit, Linda pulled out her phone and took a photo of the number plate and another of the house. She knew the area quite well; it would have been easy for Julie to walk into town from home and get a bus to the Plaza shopping centre.

When she pressed the bell, the door opened a crack. 'Who is it?' asked a woman's voice.

'Fiona Bennett?'

'Yes. Who are you?'

'My name is Linda Prewitt, I work for a detective agency. Mr and Mrs Anderson have asked us to look into the disappearance of their daughter.'

'Waste of time,' she said, attempting to shut the door, but Linda had already wedged her foot in it.

'I just have a couple of questions for you, Mrs Bennett. I promise I won't take up much of your time.'

Sophie is Still Missing

'My time? You can take up as much of it as you want,' she said, opening the door. 'But it won't do you any good. Sophie's dead, just like my poor Julie. There's nothing anyone can do to bring them back.'

Linda followed her into the sitting room; there were newspapers and magazines scattered all over the place, dirty plates stacked on the coffee table and an almost empty bottle of wine propped against the sofa.

'Mind your feet,' said Fiona. 'I think I dropped a glass last night.'

Linda caught the glint of broken glass in the fireplace. It looked as though it had been thrown there in anger.

'Sit down here,' she added, pushing the pile of old magazines to one side. 'Sorry, it's a mess. Haven't felt much like doing anything these last few months.'

'Do you live alone?' asked Linda.

'I do now. When he heard Julie was dead, he buggered off.'

'Your husband?'

'Yes. Can't say I blame him. I brought this on us. I should have kept a closer eye on Julie. It's all my fault.' She pulled a box of tissues towards her, took one and blew her nose. 'So, Linda, what do you want to know?'

'I just wanted to ask you about the day the girls went missing. Did you have any idea that they might be meeting someone? A boy perhaps?'

Fiona looked at Linda for a while, and then said, sadly, 'No. I didn't. I didn't know much about Julie's life at all, not these last few years. She spent all her time with Sophie, and sometimes with that other girl, Sharon. But she never said anything about boys. Mind you, she was always on her bloody phone. If it wasn't the phone, it was her tablet. Tap, tap, tapping away for hours. I don't know what they had to say to each other.'

'I know what you mean, my daughters are just the same. They can spend all day with their friends and as soon as they get home, they have to message them.'

Fiona smiled. 'Can I get you a cup of tea, Linda?'

'That would be lovely. Thank you.' She followed her into a kitchen even more untidy than the sitting room.

It was obviously an expensive house, but it seemed that Fiona had no heart to look after it.

'Don't you have any other children?' Linda asked.

'A son. He went with his dad. He said he couldn't bear to see me wasting my life. I don't blame him. I mean, how could he bring his friends home to this?' She waved her arms, nearly knocking over a vase of dead flowers.

'That's sad. How old is he?'

'He's eighteen now. He took Julie's disappearance very hard. He made me promise to keep her bedroom door closed, because he couldn't bear to walk past it. It was the best thing for him to do, go with his father.'

'So where are they now?'

'In England. They're living with my mother-in-law. That's good, because my husband works away a lot.'

'Does he write to you, or phone you?'

'My son? No. He doesn't want anything to do with me. I can't blame him. Look at me; I'm such a mess. I'm an embarrassment to him.'

'What makes you think it's all your fault,' asked Linda as gently as she could.

Fiona was clearly not in a good place, and she didn't want to make her feel worse.

Sophie is Still Missing

'Because I was too wrapped up in my own affairs to pay enough attention to what my only daughter, my beautiful young daughter, was doing. And then it was too late. She was gone.'

'But that's not your fault.'

'Isn't it? I didn't even know where my daughter was supposed to be sleeping that night. I didn't even miss her until lunchtime the next day. What sort of a mother is that? And all because of him.'

'What do you mean? Who? Your husband?'

It looked as though the tea was never going to be made, as Fiona had now sat down on a kitchen stool and had her head in her hands.

'Fiona?'

The woman lifted her head and looked at Linda. 'Well, you might as well know. I wasn't at home that night. I was in a hotel with Jim Anderson.'

Linda stared at her in surprise. 'Sophie's father?'

'Yes, we'd been having an affair for about three months. My husband works on the rigs and he's away a lot. It was one of those things; it just happened. I can't even remember how it started. I'd known Jim for years, since the kids were little. Then one day it moved from friendship to…' she hesitated. 'I can't say love. It wasn't love; it was lust. Boredom. You see I can't even find a good excuse for my behaviour; that's the sort of person I am. But I do know that if I'd been at home, I'd have realised that the girls were missing.' She dropped her voice and said, 'You see I knew they were supposed to sleep here that night.'

'But you told the Andersons that you thought they were sleeping at their house.'

'Yes. I was embarrassed. I didn't want Bev to know that I wasn't at home. She might have been suspicious. Jim told her he had to go to Madrid to the Motor Show. He goes every year, so it wasn't anything out of the ordinary.'

'Didn't the police check up on him?'

'Not really. They asked him a few questions, so he showed them the catalogue he had—one of his workers brought it back for him. That seemed to be good enough; they took his word for it. I think they were so convinced that the girls had run away they didn't bother to look further.'

'So you weren't here at all that night?'

Fiona shook her head.

'And you didn't get home until the next day?'

'That's right. It wasn't as though I thought Julie was on her own; she was with Sophie. I'd left them alone before and they were fine. After all they weren't kids; they were both fourteen. They were quite capable of looking after themselves,' she said, defensively.

'Obviously not,' said Linda.

'I told you. It was all my fault. I know it. I should have been here.'

'So you lied to the police?'

'I suppose so.'

'Did Mrs Anderson know about your affair with her husband?'

'Bev? No, I don't think so. We were very careful.'

'What about Julie and Sophie?'

'No. Why would they?'

'Are you sure?'

'They never said anything.'

'And your husband?'

'Definitely not; he'd never have been able to keep it to himself. He'd have been straight round to see Jim and probably thumped him.'

Sophie is Still Missing

'Is it possible that Julie ran away? Maybe to punish you for cheating on her dad? Did she take any clothes with her, for instance?'

'No, Julie wasn't like that. I'm sure she didn't know about us, anyway; I was very careful. Jim never came here; we always went to a hotel. And no, she didn't take any clothes, not even her little knapsack, the pink one with unicorns on it. She usually took that everywhere.'

'What about her mobile phone?'

'No, that's what's so strange. She was never parted from that, either.' She looked as though she was going to cry again. Instead she said, 'Do you want to see her bedroom? The police searched it at the time, and then they returned after they found her body and searched it again.'

'Yes, I'd like that.'

Linda followed the crying woman up a lavish staircase and into a bedroom overlooking the swimming pool. The room was decorated in pink and white, and it looked as though the girl had only just left it. Unlike the rest of the house, this room was meticulously cared for, with Julie's dolls arranged on the bed, staring expectantly at the door, as though waiting for her return. There were posters of pop groups on the walls and even fresh flowers on the dressing table. It wasn't unlike Linda's younger daughter's room, only a lot pinker.

'All her things are here,' her mother said, moving a photo of Sophie and Julie a fraction to the left.

'So nothing was missing?'

'No, nothing. Oh, some lipstick that she'd bought the week before. Her dad didn't like her wearing lipstick, but I said she could at weekends. All the girls do these days.' She opened a musical box which began playing an excerpt from Swan Lake. 'Julie used to like ballet when she was younger, so we bought this for her when she was ten. She always kept her jewellery in it.' She took a gold crucifix from inside it and held it up for Linda to see. 'A young policeman returned this when they came to tell me that they had closed the case. They said it was with the body when they found her.'

'It's lovely,' said Linda, taking it from her and holding it up to the light. It was made from 24 carat gold, delicately carved and very heavy; it was clearly very expensive. 'Are you Catholic?'

'Us? No. I don't know why she had it. I'd never seen it before and she wasn't wearing it when she went to Sophie's. Someone must have given it to her. Or maybe it was Sophie's, they were always wearing each other's clothes. You could ask her mum.'

'But who would give her an expensive present like that?'

Fiona shook her head. 'I've no idea. To be honest, I can't really see Julie wearing something like that. It's far too heavy for her, anyway. More a man's thing.'

'Do you mind if I take a photo of it?' asked Linda.

'Do you think her killer gave it to her?' asked Fiona, looking dazed. 'Why would he do that?'

'It might have nothing to do with her death, but my boss is very particular so I have to document everything that could be of interest.'

CHAPTER 8

Nacho stared at the scattered files. 'What a mess. How did this happen?' he asked as he took off his battered leather jacket and sat down.

'Someone wants to know what we're doing,' said JD.

'You think so? Someone broke in to see what we know about the case?'

'What else could it be?'

Nacho shrugged. 'I thought you were going to see the Anderson's this morning,' he said.

'I am, just wanted to pick up some files first.' She rummaged through the mound of folders strewn across the floor and extracted the ones she needed. 'Thank goodness, I was praying your laptop hadn't been stolen,' she said, as she looked up to see Nacho carefully removing his computer from his bag.

'You know I never leave it here. Never know when I might need it. So these burglars, what did they take?'

'Nothing as far as I can make out. But my computer was on, which was strange. I don't think they had time to download anything. One thing was a bit weird, though; my screen saver had changed. Maybe you can have a look at it later to check.'

'Sure. I'll do it while you're out.'

'It hardly seemed worth their while,' JD added. She was still puzzled by what had happened. 'And, by the way, it was just one person. A man I think, by the width of his shoulders, and the way he shoved me against the wall.'

'What did the police say?'

'I haven't rung them. I don't want them asking questions about why someone would be searching our office. Remember we're trying to keep a low profile as far as the police are concerned.'

'Did he go into the meeting room?' Nacho suddenly asked, getting up and throwing open the door.

'No, he didn't have time. Luckily I interrupted him.'

'So what were you doing here?'

'I came back to pick up my file for this morning.'

'The one you forgot to take with you?' asked Nacho with a grin.

'I didn't forget it, clever clogs; I just took the wrong one. Anyway, now that you're here I want you to clear up this mess and ring a locksmith to come and change the locks. I don't know how our burglar got in, but I don't want to make it easy for him to do it again. And make sure they're stronger than the old ones.'

'Okay Boss. So what are your plans for the day?'

'Going to see the Andersons, first. You might ring them for me please and say I'm on my way.'

'*A tus ordenes mi capitán,*' he said, giving her a mock salute.

'Less of the tomfoolery. Just get on with it. I'll be back by lunchtime and then we can go over what we've got. Maybe Linda's had some luck talking to Julie's mum.'

'Okay Boss.'

The Andersons were in the kitchen; Beverley looked as though she'd already been drinking and Jim was walking up and down, like a caged animal.

'Good morning. I'm sorry I'm late, there was a hiccup at work,' JD said, sitting down on one of the kitchen stools.

'We've sold the house,' said Jim. 'I really need to get to the solicitors, so I hope this won't take long.'

'Congratulations. That was quick. I didn't even realise you had it on the market.

'Well Bev and I agreed that there was no point in keeping a big place like this for just the three of us.'

JD looked across at Beverley, to see what she thought about it, but his wife was staring at the floor. She'd been crying again.

'So where will you move to?'

'I don't know yet, probably just rent something for now,' he said.

'What if she comes back and we're not here?' said Beverley, suddenly.

Her husband glared at her. 'Look, we've been over all that. It's been more than a year since Sophie disappeared. The company is on its knees; I can't afford to have so much money tied up in a big house. I need the cash.' He turned to JD. 'So what is it you want to talk to us about this time?'

'I just wondered if you had remembered anything about the day your daughter disappeared?'

'We've told you everything.'

'So where were you both that evening?'

'Jim was at the Motor Show in Madrid, and I was here,' said Beverley. 'Why do you want to know?'

'I was wondering why it was so important for Ricky to take the girls to the cinema. Couldn't one of you have gone with them, if you didn't like them going on their own? Or Julie's mum could have taken them?'

'She was always too busy,' snapped Beverley. 'Anyway they didn't want me to go with them.'

'Do you get on well with Julie's parents?'

'All right, I suppose,' said Beverley.

Sophie is Still Missing

JD could swear that Mr Anderson had started to look embarrassed. Was there something they weren't telling her?

'So you didn't socialise much with them?'

'He was away from home a lot of the time. He works for an oil company, Shell, I think,' said Jim.

'And as I said, she's always too busy for the likes of us,' said Beverley.

'Did Sophie have any friends on social media?'

'You're asking us? How would we know? She'd go into hysterics if we so much as touched her iPad. She never told us about any friends,' said her father.

'I expect she did,' added Beverley, 'because she was never off it. Ricky might know more.'

'Is Ricky at home? Could I have a chat with him? You're right, sometimes siblings know far more than parents.'

'The police have already questioned him,' said Jim. 'But you're welcome to try again; I just want this finished, one way or another.'

'He's in his room. I'll get him,' said Beverley.'

'It's okay. I'll go up. Probably easier to speak to him on his own,' said JD.

'Very well, you're the detective,' said Jim. 'It's the second door on the left.'

She couldn't miss it; it was covered with stickers: Keep Out, Private, Ricky's Den, Men Only. She knocked sharply.

'What do you want?' said an irritable voice. 'I'm trying to sleep.'

'Hi, Ricky. It's Jacaranda Dunne. I'd just like to ask you a few questions.'

There was silence for a moment and then the door opened and the disheveled figure of a teenage boy emerged.

'Hi. All right if we have a quick chat?' she asked.

'Spose so.' He stepped back into the darkened room.

'Can I sit down?'

He grunted what she took to be a yes, and pulled open the curtains.

JD removed a pile of clothes from a chair and sat down, motioning for him to do the same.

Ricky sat on the floor and pulled his knees up to his chin.

'Do you know who I am, Ricky?'

'Yeah. You're that private eye. I've heard them talking about you. It was Mum's idea to hire you; Dad said it was a waste of money. But that's just like him, always worried about what things cost.'

'Well, I thought I'd ask you a couple of questions, while I was here. You don't mind, do you?' She smiled her most winning smile at him, but he seemed unimpressed. 'I believe you normally accompanied your sister and her friend when they went to the cinema?'

He grunted.

'And was that usual?'

'What do you mean?'

'Well is it the sort of thing brothers do? Do your friends take their sisters to the cinema?'

Ricky laughed. 'Naw.'

'But you didn't mind doing it?' The boy looked uncomfortable; she could tell straight away that he was lying. 'Your mates didn't think it was strange? Did they make fun of you?'

'Naw. They wouldn't dare.'

'Please tell me the truth, Ricky. I need to know what happened that day if we're going to have any chance of finding Sophie.'

'You'll never find her; she's dead. Look, I told the police I went to see my mates. That's all there is to it.' Ricky looked as though he was about to cry; he wasn't as tough as he pretended to be. After all he was only seventeen.

'But was that planned, going to see your mates? I thought you changed your mind at the last minute? Ricky, did you ever go to the cinema with the girls, or were they using you as an excuse to get out without any parents?'

He brushed his hand across his eyes and said, 'Mum will kill me, if I tell you.'

'No, she won't. She just wants to find your sister. Come on Ricky; it's important. We know that Julie is dead but there's still a good chance we can find Sophie. But you have to tell us everything. At the moment it's as though the girls vanished into thin air.'

For a while he sat, hugging his knees and staring at the floor. 'We'd been doing it for months,' he said, at last. 'It was Julie's idea. She was angry with her mum about something, and said it wasn't fair when her dad was away all the time working to earn money for them. She said her mother wouldn't bother checking up on her; that she didn't care what Julie did. If they said that they were going to the cinema with me, nobody would know otherwise.'

Do you know what she meant by that?'

'Naw.'

'So that evening, it was the same?'

'Yeah. I didn't mind because it meant that Mum didn't keep asking me where I was going.'

'But you did mind. You told your mother that you didn't want to go with them. I think you said that you were going to the leisure centre with your mates. Isn't that right?'

Sophie is Still Missing

'Yeah, well I might have said something like that. They were taking me for granted. Sophie was always like that, never wanted to share anything.'

JD waited for him to explain.

'I just wanted to borrow her iPad for a few hours, but she made such a fuss about it. So I told her she owed me, but she still wouldn't let me use it.'

'Is that when you decided to remind them what you were doing for them?'

'Yes. You should have seen Sophie's face. She was furious.' He laughed, then said, 'I really wish I hadn't been so mean to her now.'

'I doubt if it would have made any difference. Did you know they were meeting some boys?'

'They never said so, but I wouldn't have been surprised. Julie was boy-mad.'

'Did she or Sophie ever go out with any of your friends?'

'Naw. They didn't like them. Not cool enough for Julie; she liked older boys.'

'I don't suppose Sophie ever mentioned anyone she liked?' JD was fishing at straws by now. Ricky didn't really have anything to add to what they had already deduced.

'You're joking. Naw, she'd never tell me that. We didn't really have much to do with each other. Not like when we were kids. We played together all the time then.' He looked sad. 'I miss her.'

'I'm sure you do. Well thank you Ricky, you've been a great help.'

'I hope you find her. Mum's going crazy with worry.'

'We'll do our best.'

They'd need to do more than that to find Sophie before she ended up in the morgue too.

CHAPTER 9

JD pushed her short, sandy hair back from her face and began to remove her make-up. She had decided to run a bath and soak in it for an hour; her back was still sore from where the intruder had pushed her over the night before. She could just make out a dark bruise forming below her shoulder blade.

She sighed; she'd be forty soon and what did she have to show for it? No husband, no children, a rented flat and no car; not that she'd drive it if she had one. She opened a bottle of the Sauvignon Blanc that she'd bought on the internet and poured herself a glass. She and Andrew had always talked about having a family, but they'd never got round to it, always too busy with their jobs. Well it was too late now. That was probably for the best. She drank a little wine and then leant over the bath to feel the temperature of the water.

JD had met Andrew when she was working for the Met; it had been a whirlwind romance. She'd been loaned to the drug squad on a six-month secondment, and they'd partnered her up with one of their inspectors, a young man who'd been fast-tracked to Detective Inspector by the time he was thirty. She had been all prepared to resent this university graduate who had made it to the top without going through the ranks, but instead she'd fallen in love with him. How she got through that secondment without a major catastrophe was a miracle; they were besotted with each other. Nothing else mattered. At last they decided the best thing to do was to get married before their superintendent found out about them. They'd been married for six years—six wonderful, happy years—before it all came to a sudden end.

She thought of her sisters, both married and with five children and three dogs between them, living their perfect lives; all that was missing were the country cottages with roses around the door. No, she didn't feel jealous of them. She loved her sisters and enjoyed being an aunty to their offspring. It was probably better than having children of her own, she told herself unconvincingly, all the fun and none of the responsibility.

JD balanced the wine on the edge of the bath and was just about to get undressed, when the doorbell rang. 'Bloody hell. Who's that?' she muttered. She padded down the hall and peered through the spy hole. It was her mother.

'Mama, what are you doing here?'

'Just open the door and let me in,' Rosa McNab ordered.

JD unbolted the door and stood back to let her mother billow into the room, followed by two miniature schnauzers and Paco, her current boyfriend.

'I had to see you as soon as I heard,' her mother continued, talking as she always did to JD, in Spanish.

'Heard what Mama? What's so important that you couldn't just phone?'

'He's been released. *El monstro*. I had to come over to make sure you were all right,' she said, waving her arms around in agitation. In moments of anxiety, Rosa's Spanish blood surfaced and everything became much more dramatic. 'You are all right, aren't you, *cariño*?' she asked, enveloping JD in an enormous hug.

'I was, until you arrived, Mama.'

Sophie is Still Missing

JD had inherited her father's Scottish genes, his sandy blonde hair, fair skin and blue eyes, his phlegmatic manner. She was not as prone to hysteria as Rosa.

'Pour me a glass of that, *cariño*, whatever it is,' her mother said, throwing herself onto the sofa, whereupon the two dogs leapt up beside her. '*Dios mío*. I knew something like this would happen. I just knew it.'

'For you Paco?'

'*Si, JD, gracias*. Some white wine would be delightful.'

JD poured out two more glasses of wine. 'Here. Just a minute, I've got to turn off the bath. I won't be long. And get the dogs off the sofa, please Mama.'

She felt her stomach turn over. What had happened? Her mother wouldn't come all the way into Málaga at this time of night, unless it was urgent. She bounded up to the bathroom, turned off the water and retrieved the wine, then rejoined her mother in the lounge.

'Okay, so what's this all about?' she asked, sitting opposite her.

'Don't get so agitated, *cariño*. You should learn to unwind more.'

Her mother had removed her coat and put her feet up on the footstool. The dogs were either side of her. She looked every bit the grand lady she was. The Most Excellent Lady, Rosa Maria de la Luz, Marquesa de Calderón del Bosque. What a mouthful. No wonder her mother, who was a very down to earth woman, actually preferred to be called plain Rosa MacNab.

JD sat down beside her, skilfully removing one of the dogs without her mother realising. 'I would Mama, but people keep barging in when I'm trying to relax.'

'You need to hear this, Jacaranda. He's been released,' said Rosa. 'You must be careful. I think you should move in with us for a while.'

'Are you talking about Steed?' JD asked, hardly able to say his name. The thought of that man being here in Málaga terrified her. 'Are you sure? He wasn't supposed to get out for another five years, at the earliest.'

'Well he's out. And you remember what he shouted across the court room when they found him guilty?'

How could she forget it? It had been her testimony that had been the deciding factor in his conviction. Steed had turned and looked at her with such hatred and screamed, 'I'm going to get you, bitch, if it's the last thing I do.'

The judge had added another six months for contempt of court, and he'd been ushered out to begin his fourteen-year sentence in a high security prison. Then the next week JD's husband had been killed. Unlawful killing, the coroner had said. Shot in a mugging that went wrong. And yet nobody linked the two things. Only her. She knew Steed was behind it. How the hell had he managed to get early release? And now he was coming to get her.

For a split second she thought of the break-in and the photo on her computer. Could that have anything to do with Steed? No, there was no way he could have done that.

'How do you know he's been released?' she asked, hoping it was all some dreadful mistake, some rumour that her mother had heard.

'The Assistant Commissioner rang me.'

'The Assistant Commissioner of the Metropolitan Police? Why on earth would he do that?'

'Oh, Jacaranda, you must know he's a great friend of the Duke of Arradondo; he's had a summer place out here for years.'

JD shrugged. She had given up trying to follow all her mother's influential connections.

'I really think you should pack a bag and come with us,' Rosa said. 'You really shouldn't be on your own.'

'And what about my job? I'm in the middle of the biggest case we've ever had. I can't just leave. Anyway I've had enough of running away. I gave up my job at the Met because of that bastard. I'm not changing my life again for him.'

She sounded braver than she felt. She had come across Thomas Steed when she was investigating the death of a fifteen-year old boy who'd died from a heroine overdose. Normally the case would have been handed over to the drug squad straight away, but as JD had experience with the narcotics division, and insisted that she had a good lead on who was behind it, they let her get on with it.

Steed had been running drugs from Amsterdam and grooming the teenagers in her area as pushers; the fifteen-year old hadn't been the first youngster to die from an overdose. She'd promised the boy's mother she would find the culprit and bring him to justice and that's just what she did, but at a cost to herself and her family. Once she'd gathered enough evidence to get Steed convicted, the Drugs Squad stepped in and broke up the Amsterdam connection. It had been a good result all round and everyone was pleased. Nevertheless, even as she watched him being led away to start his sentence, JD was left with the distinct feeling that it wasn't over for her. And then Andrew had been shot. If that was a warning, then it had worked. She'd been looking over her shoulder ever since.

Sophie is Still Missing

'Oh, *cariño*, you have to be careful. You're too vulnerable in that job of yours. Look, just this week your name was plastered all over the paper. Anybody could have seen it and told him where you are.'

'What are you talking about?'

'The local newspaper. It comes out daily, and there you were, photograph and all. Not the best one, I might add, but you could tell it was you. You know the one, Diario something.'

'El Diario Costa del Sol,' said Paco.

JD swore under her breath. So much for keeping the investigation quiet. Now she'd have the police coming round to see what she was up to. 'Do you have a copy?'

'There's one in the car; I'll get it for you,' said Paco. 'I only bought it for the golfing news. The rest is a load of rubbish; I think they make half of it up.'

'Are you sure you won't come with us?' asked her mother, yet again, as she gathered together her coat, handbag and dogs.

'No, Mama, but if it will make you feel better, I'll tell my friend in the Guardia Civil about it, and get him to put a check on the airport.'

Her mother hugged her. 'Take care, *cariño*, and ring me if there's a problem. You know I have lots of contacts if you need someone to pull a few strings.'

'I will Mama.' Her mother knew everyone who was anyone in Andalusia. Since she'd returned to Spain after JD's father had died, she'd embraced her place in the lower ranks of nobility with gusto. The rebellious, socialist minded young woman who'd moved to England and married a commoner, had returned to her roots. Or so it seemed to JD.

'Here you are. I'm afraid the dogs have pulled it about a bit, but you'll be able to read it,' said Paco.

'Is it today's?' she asked.

Sophie is Still Missing

'No, I think it's a couple of days old,' he said, peering at the newspaper. 'Yes, the day before yesterday.'

'Thanks.'

'I haven't seen you at the golf club, lately, JD,' he added. Paco was captain this year, and very proud of it.

'No, I haven't had time. I've been too busy at work.'

'There's a mixed foursome competition at Paraíso Park on Saturday, and I need a partner,' he added.

'That's very tempting. I'll see what I can do.' Her mother's boyfriend was a likeable man, and a very good golfer. Not only did he belong to the same golf course as her, on the outskirts of Málaga, but he'd lately joined a very exclusive golf club in Marbella—she'd bet money on it that it was her mother's influence that had got him in there. Nevertheless, she should take him up on his offer; she'd never had the opportunity to play Paraíso Park before. It was a members' course, and other golfers could only play it strictly by invitation. Also, she'd had no exercise lately, not even her morning run along the Paseo Maritimo, and it was beginning to show; her brain was getting stale and she was sure she'd put on a kilo or two. She would have to do something about it.

'That's great. Ring me if you can make it.'

'I will. Thanks, Paco.'

As soon as they'd gone, JD poured herself some more wine, spread the crumpled newspaper on the kitchen table and began to read it. Yes, it was made abundantly clear that Jacaranda Dunne was working as a private investigator in Málaga, and had been asked by Mr and Mrs Anderson to look into the disappearance of their daughter. Apart from that, the reporter had obviously not been able to find out much about their investigation; there was some nonsense about the girls going to meet their boyfriends and an interview with Sophie's grandmother which, considering she was eighty-five and lived in Kent, revealed nothing. She sighed with relief. There was little that the police could complain about. However, if what Federico had told her was true, and if by any chance, the Mafia bosses behind the child trafficking ring were to read this rather insignificant little newspaper, they too would know that JD was investigating the case. She laughed. That was hardly likely. But what about Steed? Her mother was right; someone might read it and make the connection with DS Jacaranda Dunne of the Metropolitan Police. It wouldn't hurt to talk to Federico and tell him that Steed had been released. She looked at her watch. No it wasn't too late to ring him.

By the time Federico arrived, JD had taken a quick and cold bath, dressed, applied some make-up and was looking less fraught than she felt.

'Well Jacaranda, this is a very pleasant surprise,' he said as he stepped into her flat. 'And there was me thinking you only wanted me for the information I could give you.'

'No, you're much more to me than that,' she said, almost throwing herself into his open arms. She felt safe with him. Perhaps she should reconsider his proposal that they move in together, if it was still open that was. When she had told him, a few months ago, that she wasn't ready for a new relationship, she had seen the hurt in his eyes.

'I'm glad to hear it.' He held out a bottle of Ribero de Duero and a blue folder. 'Look, I bring gifts,' he said.

'The autopsy report? Excellent. Shall we look at it now?'

He gave her a look that said, 'Are you kidding me?' and put it on the table as far away from them as possible.

'Not now. I'll pour the wine, first.' He followed her into the kitchen and began to uncork the bottle. 'I see you've already had some guests,' he said, looking at the unwashed glasses in the sink.

'Just Mama and Paco. They brought me this.' She pushed the newspaper towards him. 'Someone has told the press that I'm investigating the case.'

'So how is the Duchess?' he asked, picking up the newspaper.

'How many times have I got to tell you, she's a marquesa, *una marquesa*. And she's fine, just worried about me, as usual.'

'Naturally, you're her heir. She doesn't want anything to happen to you.'

For a minute, JD felt irritated with him; he just couldn't resist reminding her of the differences in their social background. She wished she'd never told him about her mother. Although, knowing Federico, he would probably have found out anyway. Not much escaped the Captain.

He began to read the newspaper. 'That's not so bad; the police were bound to find out sometime. They're not stupid, you know.'

'But now that the murderer knows I'm working for Sophie's mother, he'll be a lot more careful. I was hoping he would become careless when he heard that the case was closed.'

'It is closed and I still haven't found out why. It's not as though they can hide it away as a suicide, or an accidental death, or even natural causes. Whoever placed Julie's body on the Virgin's throne wanted to tell us something. He, or she, couldn't have chosen a more conspicuous place to leave her.'

'I agree. But why? What was their message?'

He shook his head. 'Could just have been guilt. Or maybe he didn't realise she'd be found so soon.'

'A foreigner, maybe, or someone who didn't understand about Holy Week.'

'Or the opposite, someone who knew that the *trono* would be taken out that day and wanted everyone to see her lying there.' He handed her a glass of wine. 'Anything to eat?'

'Just some cheese.' JD was an erratic shopper; her fridge was either filled to overflowing or empty.

'That'll do. So is that why you invited me over, to talk about Julie Bennett?'

'No, actually it wasn't. I shouldn't have rung you; it seems silly now.'

'Jacaranda?'

'Okay. The reason my mother was here was because she had heard something that worried her.' She paused. 'You remember when I told you that I'd left the Met because my husband was killed?'

He nodded.

'Well I didn't tell you the whole story.' She began to relate what had happened years before and how she was convinced that Andrew's death had been because of her. 'Afterwards I just wanted to get as far away as possible from London. I took out a PI licence and opened a small agency in Oxford. It was easy work: lost dogs, cheating husbands, the occasional stalker, and although I wasn't earning a fortune, I could make sufficient to live on. It was enough for me; after all I had Andrew's pension as well. Then I heard that Steed had been moved from the high security prison to a category B prison in Bedford, which isn't that far from Oxford, so Mama suggested I move out to Málaga to be nearer to her.'

'That's strange. A convicted drug trafficker. Why would they do that?'

'I don't know. He'd only been in there two years. Nobody gave me a satisfactory explanation when I queried it. But it did seem weird. Besides the drug trafficking, the evidence linked him to the deaths of at least six teenagers, but we couldn't make those charges stick.'

'He sounds a nasty character. So what has upset the Duchess now?'

'He's been released.'

'Really? How long did you say his sentence was?'

'Fourteen years, the maximum. And he got an extra six months for pissing off the judge.'

'And now he's free?'

'Yes, and I'm frightened he'll come looking for me.' She wondered if she should tell him about the photo of her and Andy, but decided against it; she didn't want him to think she was becoming paranoid.

'Jacaranda, it could just have been a dreadful coincidence that your husband was shot at the same time; it might have nothing to do with Steed's conviction at all.'

'It felt like it, at the time.'

'What do you want me to do?'

'I don't know. I said it was silly of me to ring you.' She took the newspaper from him. 'Is there an online edition of this?'

'Bound to be. All the papers have online editions; it's how they make their money. Why?'

'I'm worried that Steed will have seen this article. Then he'd know where I was.'

'That's highly unlikely. I can't see him trawling through the Spanish newspapers looking for information about you. Does he even know you're living in Spain now?'

'No, but he might consider it a possibility. I have a Spanish mother after all; that's hardly a secret.'

'The Marquesa. No it's hard to keep that secret.'

She glowered at him. She didn't want people to know about her mother's title, and even less that she'd inherit it one day.

'Look, if you give me more information about this man, I can make sure his details are on our police computer, and then he'll find it hard to get into the country without us knowing.'

'No, I'm over reacting. He'll be on probation, so he won't be allowed to leave the UK, and I'm pretty sure he'll be wearing an electronic tag.'

Federico laughed. 'If he's the hardened criminal you make him out to be, then neither of those things will deter him. Getting a false passport and removing the tag will be child's play to him. We need to get his photograph and fingerprints.'

'I can arrange that,' said JD, feeling a little relieved. He made it seem easy. She inched her way along the sofa so that she could lean against his shoulder. 'So, are you going to tell me what's in the autopsy report?'

'Not tonight.'

'You're not leaving, are you?' she asked, as he stood up.

'Not until after breakfast, my little princess,' he said, smiling at her as he pulled her up and into his arms. 'You can read the report at work.'

CHAPTER 10

The autopsy was quite detailed. JD, Linda and Nacho sat in the meeting room and went through it together.

'So what does it tell us about the killer?' asked JD.

'He had a conscience,' said Nacho.

'Or he knew her, was fond of her maybe,' said Linda. 'That's why he washed her body.'

'That doesn't fit. She was undernourished, her feet were cut and bruised and her hands were calloused; there were rope marks on her wrists. She hadn't been treated kindly, so why wash her body? That shows affection.'

They looked at her blankly.

'So, what does that tell us?' asked JD.

'The man who brought her to the *Cofradía* wasn't the man who killed her. So who was he, then?'

'Someone who worked with the killer, perhaps?'

'It says that her fingernails were torn and broken, as though she'd tried to claw her way out of something.'

'A wooden fence, or a door, or maybe a chest. Good God, you don't think she was in a chest?'

'I don't know what to think. Let's not get carried away with too much speculation. What does the evidence say?' said JD.

'That she was trying to get away from someone or something,' said Nacho. 'She had escaped.'

'Exactly. She had escaped and then she got caught. This was retribution for running away.'

'It could have been an accident,' said Linda. 'Didn't you say she had multiple fractures to her back and legs? Maybe she fell off a building when she was running away, or a bridge. That would explain the head injury as well.'

'It says a blow to the head was the cause of death, but the pathologist hasn't confirmed if the injuries to her back and legs were the result of a fall or being beaten,' said Nacho.

'I don't like the way this is shaping up,' said JD. 'Julie was locked up somewhere, she escaped, tearing her fingernails in the process. They chased her and she fell, breaking her legs, but she wasn't dead, so the killer finished her off with a blow to the head, using a blunt instrument. That doesn't sound like the sort of person who would then wash her body and place it at the feet of the Virgin Mary, and sprinkle pink carnations over it. Someone else had to be involved.'

'Maybe he didn't mean to kill her,' said Nacho. 'Maybe it was an accident.'

'But he couldn't leave her alive, you mean?'

'Yes. He had no alternative.'

'No, you've been watching too many American movies,' said JD. 'It's possible someone else found the body and didn't want to go to the police, so took it to the *Cofradía*.'

'I think we're going round in circles,' said Linda. 'Remember, as far as we know the girls were together. Julie escaped, but where from? It can't be that far away from where her body was found. No-one would be driving around with a dead girl in their car for any longer than was necessary.'

'Yes, and if they were still together—and that's not certain by any means—then it means that Sophie isn't too far away, either.'

'If she's still alive.'

'What I can't understand is why he left her body there in the first place. Málaga is a port; there are miles and miles of beaches. It would be the easiest thing in the world to drop her body in the sea, and far less risky.'

'Perhaps he panicked, and that was all he could think of,' said Nacho.

JD laughed. 'Okay, put yourself in his shoes. You have a dead girl's body to dispose of, so what do you do? Breaking into the *Cofradía* a few days before the start of Holy Week doesn't seem like the first thing that would spring to my mind. Nor is it the most sensible thing to do.'

'He wanted her to be found.'

'Yes, I agree, but more than that, he had to be familiar with the interior of the *Cofradía*. He'd been there before.'

'You think he's one of the Brothers?' asked Linda.

'It's a thought. Nacho, find out how the Brothers gain access to the *Cofradía*. Do they have keys? And talk to that old man, Jorge. Try to find out who might have had reason to go in there a few days before the procession.'

'The pathologist's report says that she'd been dead two or three days,' said Linda.

'Yes, so see who were the last people to have been in there before they found the body, Nacho.'

'What else does the report say?'

'Just what we already knew, that there were signs of regular sexual activity, but not forced.'

'That doesn't mean it was consensual,' said Linda. 'If the girls were held captive, they wouldn't have much say in it.'

JD shuddered. The picture they were forming was not very nice. Julie had obviously suffered, both physically and sexually, and probably mentally as well. And Sophie was still missing. They had to find her before it was too late.

'Anything else to add?' she asked. 'Linda?'

'Well I have actually. You may be surprised to know that our grieving Mrs Bennett has been having an affair with Mr Anderson. And that's where they were the night the girls disappeared.'

'Really? I'm amazed. So Jim Anderson was lying about his whereabouts on the night the girls disappeared. I think we need to look more closely at our Mr Anderson, don't you? Nacho, it's time you updated the board.'

'Okay Boss. Will this do?' He drew a line linking the two names and placed a big heart on it.

'Okay, cupid. That's not exactly what I meant, and remember to leave some space; you don't know what other secrets we're going to unearth. What else have the parents been lying about?' She turned back to Linda. 'Do you know if the affair is still going on?'

'I think so, but, to be honest I didn't ask her outright. What about the Andersons? Did they say anything? Does Beverley know about her husband cheating on her?'

'Not sure, but something's not right between her and Jim; maybe she does know and that's why she was so bitchy about Fiona the first time we spoke to her. It all makes more sense now you've told me about the affair. Do you think the police knew about it? I wonder if it came out when they were questioning them?' She looked down at her notepad. 'By the way, Mr Anderson has got a buyer for their house, and Beverley is not happy about it. I think he's planning to go back to the UK and take Ricky with him. She won't like that.'

'Or maybe he and Fiona are going to set up home together. She said straight out that her husband walked out as soon as he heard about Julie's death,' said Linda.

Sophie is Still Missing

Nacho had been busily scribbling on the board. Now he turned to JD and said, 'That's all very interesting, but all it tells us is that the Andersons and the Bennetts were not in happy marriages. I can't see how it helps us to find who took Julie and Sophie. Surely you don't think they're involved in the girls' abduction.'

'Mr Anderson lied to the police about being at the Motor Show on the night the girls disappeared. Now he's sold his house and is talking about going back to the UK. That makes him a suspect in my book.'

'But Fiona says he was with her.'

'Can you believe her? Maybe he asked her to give him an alibi.'

'No, I don't buy that,' said Linda. 'You haven't seen Fiona. She's a complete mess and wracked with guilt about what she's done. Anyway why would Jim abduct his own daughter? And where did he keep her and Julie all this time? No, just because he's lied to us, doesn't make him the murderer.'

'See if the police found out he was lying about where he was that night.'

'I don't think they did. According to Fiona, they weren't that bothered; they accepted his alibi about the Motor Show at face value.'

'Didn't you find anything else, JD?' asked Nacho.

'I did, actually. I had a long chat to young Ricky; all that nonsense about him going to the cinema with them was a cover so that the girls could go off on their own. It looks as though they'd been lying to their parents about who they were with for at least a month before they disappeared.'

'That could be helpful,' said Nacho. 'It gives us a wider window to look for them. We need to see that CCTV footage. The police might not have looked at the older stuff.'

'If they have it. How long do you suppose these security companies keep the videos?'

'It will depend on the company. It's worth a try.'

'You like shopping, Linda. How would you like to visit the Plaza centre and see what you can find out. Try to persuade the security guys to let you look at their CCTV for the day the girls went missing and the previous three Saturdays, just in case the police missed anything. See if they will let you bring copies of them away.'

'If they still have them.'

'Well, if they haven't then we'll have to see if we can get them from the police.' JD smiled, thinking of Federico. 'What about the school teacher, Miss Hardy? Did she have anything to say about the girls?'

'She said they were just normal teenagers, didn't always do their homework, giggled a lot in class but other than that they were no trouble. She wasn't aware of any boyfriends. In fact it was much the same story; the girls spent most of their time together. They didn't have a lot of other friends,' said Linda.

'This isn't adding up. Everyone says they were just normal girls, no boyfriends, never in any trouble. Either they had more freedom than their parents are letting on or people are lying.'

'Well, we know that Julie's parents weren't around much,' said Nacho.

'Neither was Mr Anderson. I bet both girls knew about the affair between Jim and Fiona. That would make them rebellious. All that stuff about not going out on their own, while their parents were cheating on them, would make them angry,' said Linda.

'Is there any way we can find out if they knew?' asked JD.

'They might have posted something on social media about it,' suggested Linda.

Sophie is Still Missing

'True. Have you found any more information on the girls' social media accounts, Nacho?'

'Not yet. Still going through them.'

'Well, get on with it, then. What's taking so long? I'm certain there will be something there that will tell us more about the girls' state of mind, and the kidnappers.'

While Linda set off for the Plaza centre, JD decided to get in touch with an old friend from her days in the Metropolitan Police. She waited until Nacho had popped out to get some coffee, and rang the Specialist Crime division of the Metropolitan Police. When someone answered, she said, 'Serious and Organised Crime Division please.'

'Who did you want to speak to?'

'Inspector Bill Tennant. It's an old colleague of his, Jacaranda Dunne.'

'Hold the line, please.'

She could hear the chatter and bustle of a busy office, and then Bill came on the line, 'JD. Well this is a nice surprise.'

'Is it, Bill? Is it such a surprise? You do know he's been released?'

'Yes, I'm sorry about that. I was going to ring you, but I didn't want to worry you unnecessarily. He can't do anything to you in Spain. You're quite safe there.'

'But why? How? Even with parole, he shouldn't be out for a couple more years. And it's always been on the cards that an early parole would be turned down. So, what's going on?'

'I don't know, JD. I'm as mystified as you are. All I can tell you is that he's been a model prisoner; according to the governor he's been doing an IT course with the Open University. I'm sorry, I don't know what else to say.'

'Open University? So he has access to a computer and the internet?'

'Yes. Most prisoners do these days. But it's strictly monitored.'

She felt sick. So Steed could have seen the article about her. All he'd have to do was type in her name and up it would come.

'Can you send me his photo and fingerprints, and any other identification you have. If he does decide to have a week in sunny Spain, I want to be ready for him.'

'He doesn't know you're living in Spain. How could he? He won't have a clue about where you are, if he even remembers you.'

'Remembers me? You've got to be joking. He murdered my husband. Have you forgotten that? He threatened me in court in front of witnesses. Now you tell me he's been doing a computer course. The model prisoner? You can't really believe that. He's the man who turned in his own father to the Drug Squad and watched him die in prison. He's evil, and worse than that he's cunning and calculating. Don't tell me I haven't got anything to worry about.'

'There's no proof that he was connected with Andy's death. Remember he was in custody when Andy was killed.'

'So you're like all the rest now, Bill, are you? Well, I'm not being paranoid and I'm not hysterical. It's too much of a coincidence that my husband gets mugged and shot a couple of days after I give testimony in court. I thought it was you who said there was no such thing as coincidences in police work?'

'All right. I'll find you as much as I can, fingerprints, DNA, the lot, but I'm sure you don't need to worry. We'll put a tail on him for a few weeks at least. I promise you he won't be able to blow his nose without us knowing.'

Sophie is Still Missing

'It's not his health I'm worried about; it's mine. Thanks anyway, Bill, I appreciate it. Don't tell anyone I phoned, will you.' She could see Nacho coming along the alleyway, with two coffees and an interesting bag with the cake shop logo on it.

'I won't. Take care of yourself, JD. And don't worry.'

That was easy for him to say. She knew what a vindictive man Thomas Steed was.

CHAPTER 11

The Plaza shopping precinct was crowded with shoppers; Linda headed for the escalator and straight up to the cinema complex. Some elderly people were queuing to buy their tickets for 'La La Land' otherwise it was fairly quiet. It was a long time since Linda had been to the cinema; they had gone there a lot when the children were younger, but now her daughters preferred the company of their friends to Mum and Dad. She didn't mind; in fact she enjoyed watching films on Netflix in the comfort of her own home, feet up on the sofa and a glass of wine in her hand.

'Excuse me, where can I find the manager?' she asked the young lad serving popcorn and fizzy drinks to an overweight couple, who should have known better.

'I'll buzz him for you,' he said, handing over a huge box of popcorn to his customers.

Almost immediately the manager appeared from within the dark corridors of the multiplex. 'Can I help you?' he asked.

'I hope so,' said Linda, handing him her card. 'I'd like to have a look at your security footage for August 2017.'

He stared at the card, and then said in an awed voice, 'You're a private investigator?' It was as though she'd just jumped down from the screen and walked into his life.

'I am. Do you think it's possible to let me have a look at the CCTV? It's very important.'

'When did you say?'

'August last year.'

Sophie is Still Missing

'Last year?'

'Yes.' This was hard work.

'Sorry, we only keep the CCTV for two months. That would have been wiped ages ago.'

'You're absolutely sure?'

'Sorry. What are you looking for?'

'I hoped to find something to help with our investigation.'

He stared at her.

'The two girls who went missing.'

'I remember them. Tragic it was. So they never found them, then. They were here that week. Not the day they disappeared, though. I remember thinking that when I saw their photos in the paper. Nice looking girls. Bit heavy with the make-up, but then aren't they all these days. I've got daughters; they all want to look like super models.'

'Well, thank you for your help.'

'Why don't you try the big store opposite? I know they've got CCTV, but whether they'd still have it from back then, is anybody's guess.'

She looked to where he was pointing at a large electrical appliance store; the CCTV cameras were clearly visible and there were a number of them.

'I will. Thanks.' She paused. 'By the way, did you notice if the girls were with anyone the last time you saw them?'

'No. They were always on their own. Good luck.'

It didn't take long for Linda to locate one of the shop assistants hovering amidst the rows of televisions, hoovers, refrigerators and every other type of electrical appliance, and ask to speak to the security manager.

'You wanted to speak to me?' asked a man of roughly her own age, wearing a dark blue suit. A badge in his lapel said 'Tomás Moreno, Manager.'

'I need your help, Señor Moreno,' Linda said, getting straight to the point. She handed him her card, and continued, 'Do you remember the two girls who disappeared last year?'

He nodded.

'Well is it possible that you still have the CCTV footage for that period?'

He looked at her in amazement, then his face broke into a wide smile. 'I do indeed. I've been waiting for someone to come and ask for it. Come with me,' he said, leading her into his office.

Linda could hardly believe her luck. This man had kept the CCTV film for over a year.

'We normally dispose of it after six weeks, but I couldn't bring myself to get rid of it. I watch a lot of old crime movies, you know—it's my hobby—and I can never help thinking that if they had had CCTV then, how easy it would have been to solve the crimes. I'd been following the case in the newspapers and I knew they hadn't found the girls, so instead of wiping the footage, I thought why not keep it, just in case. It doesn't take up much room. And who knows, maybe it would become one of those cold cases.' He unlocked a small safe and took out a USB stick. 'Here you are. You're lucky; I was about to get rid of it after I heard they'd found one of the girls. Pity that. Poor girl, what was she sixteen?'

'Thank you so much, this could be very useful.'

'So you're a private investigator. Very interesting job I expect,' he said, beaming at her. 'Your Spanish is very good; I expect that helps with the job.'

'It does. The work can be interesting but a lot of my time is just going through files and photographs, or CCTV footage if we can find it,' she said, holding up the USB stick. 'My boss is going to be so pleased with this.'

Sophie is Still Missing

'They do a crime film night once a week, over there,' he said, indicating the Plaza cinema complex. 'It's very popular, especially with the older people. They have old Humphrey Bogart films, Cary Grant, mostly American but some English crime films too. Maybe you'd like to come along one evening?'

Linda stared at him. 'Well, it sounds interesting, but I get enough of solving crimes during the day; it's not my idea of how to spend a relaxing evening.' And before he could suggest an alternative, she added, 'Anyway my husband hates crime movies, especially the old ones.'

'Ah well. You don't know what you're missing.' He smiled at her, sadly. 'Good luck with your investigation.'

Linda had excelled herself. Not only had the security manager of a large store opposite the cinema, kept the CCTV video from the date of the girls' disappearance, but also for the six weeks previously.

'It wasn't usual; normally the files are cleared after six weeks,' said Linda, with a wide smile on her face, as she explained how, because of his love of crime films, the security manager had kept it, convinced that one day someone would ask for it. When he heard the investigation into Julie's death had been closed, he was considering getting rid of it. Then I turned up.'

'Superwoman Linda to the rescue,' said Nacho.

'That was lucky. Right, you and I can go through them, while Nacho keeps looking through the girls' Facebook pages,' said JD.

'I told you, they won't be on Facebook,' he said. They both ignored him.

'I think he was impressed that I worked for a detective agency,' said Linda, rummaging through her bag for the USB drive. 'He even invited me to the cinema. Apparently there's a season of old crime movies on next month, and I mean old, Agatha Christie and Alfred Hitchcock, even some Cary Grant films.'

'Did you say you'd go?' asked Nacho, looking a bit puzzled that anyone could be interested in such out of date films.

'No, I showed him this,' she said, flashing her wedding ring under Nacho's nose. 'He looked quite disappointed.' She inserted the small flash drive into her computer and instantly the security company's logo appeared on the screen.

JD pulled up a chair and sat down beside her. 'Let's start with the day the girls went missing.'

They had been trawling through scenes of people wandering past the cinema, going in and coming out, heading for the nearby bars, standing, sitting, arguing, kissing, for what seemed like hours, but there was not a sign of either of the girls. 'Where are we up to now?' asked JD.

'That last one was three Saturdays before they disappeared,' said Linda. 'I don't know about you, but I'm going cross-eyed looking at the screen. I need a break.'

'What you need is to run it through some face recognition software,' said Nacho. 'That might quicken things up.'

'But we don't have any,' said JD, irritably. She was getting a headache.

'We do actually, or rather I do. I bought the app a few weeks ago. I've been dying to try it out.'

'Well, here's your chance. Linda will show you where we've got up to, and then it's down to you.'

'No promises, mind. As I said, I haven't tried it out properly yet. I'll need photographs of the two girls.'

Linda handed him the case file. 'Here. take your pick.'

Sophie is Still Missing

The door buzzer rang. Through the opaque glass window, JD could see the tall, thin figure of a man. The buzzer went again. 'It's Tim,' she said. 'Close the meeting room door, Nacho, and don't tell him anything about the case. Just be vague if he asks you anything.'

'I thought he was a friend?' said Nacho.

'He is, sort of, but he's a journalist; you can never trust a journalist, not one hundred percent.' Again the buzzer rang. 'Okay, Tim. I can see you,' she called unlocking the door.

'JD, what's going on? Why are you locking yourselves in?'

'We're not, we're locking other people out,' she said with a big smile. 'How are you, Tim? Got anything for me?'

'JD, you are so exasperating. Yes I have, as a matter of fact. It's about the car you were interested in; the one that killed the policeman.' He placed a grainy looking black and white photo on her desk. 'This was the best I could get, it's not great but you can see part of the number plate, and it matches this car that was caught speeding near the hospital, six months ago.' He laid the second photograph beside it. This was clearer and had obviously been taken by a speed camera. 'You can see the date and time on it. 4 a.m. I'm pretty sure it's the same car that killed the policeman.'

'How on earth did you get those?' she asked, rather impressed with Tim's work.

He tapped his nose and smiled. 'I have plenty of sources, you know JD.'

'That's why I came to you,' she said.

'Look at the number plates,' Tim added. 'They don't look Spanish. They seem to be Russian, but it's not a plate I recognise, so maybe an Eastern European country.'

'Okay. So did you find anything more about the policeman's death?' She steered him away from her assistants and pulled out a chair for him next to her desk. 'Did it seem suspicious to you? You've got a nose for these things, I know.'

'To be honest, I haven't found out a lot more, but there were a couple of things. The police think the driver had been drinking, which is why he didn't stop—that usually turns out to be the reason. Also, they say it ought to be a murder charge because the pathologist put in his report that Lieutenant Alvároz wasn't killed by the impact; he died from his injuries. If the driver had stopped and called an ambulance then he might have lived.'

'Really. So why didn't the Guardia Civil make that known at the time? Was it released to the press?'

'No, that's what's so interesting. If a policeman gets killed it's usually all over the news. And especially if he died because the driver of the car didn't stop. Then that is big news. There was nothing about him dying from his injuries on the television nor in the papers, only that he was killed in a hit and run accident. His colleagues are furious, but they've been told to leave it alone. Why is that? Do you think there's some sort of cover-up?'

'You tell me. You're the journalist.'

'Well, I'm going to look into this further. There could be a big story here,' he said, his eyes gleaming.

JD's mobile began to ring. 'Sorry, I've got to take this,' she said with a smile. 'Thanks so much for the photos.' She opened the door and waited for him to leave.

'Okay. No problem. Sure you haven't got time for a coffee?'

'No, sorry. Another time.'

As soon as she shut the door again, she opened her mobile and saw it was a number she didn't recognise. 'Can I help you?' she said.

'Hello. Is that the detective agency?'

'Yes, how can I help?'

'My name's Norah Catchpole. It's about the missing girls.'

'Do you have information for us, Norah?'

'I think I saw them. I'd been to the cinema; I often go to the Plaza in the afternoon. I live alone, you see, and it's something to do. Well, I was just coming out when I saw these youngsters; they were fooling about, as teenagers do, and then one of the boys stumbled backwards and spilled his drink all over me. Luckily it wasn't hot; it was one of those energy drink things, sticky, sweet stuff, and it went all over my dress and my handbag. I was annoyed, although I could see it was an accident, and the girl was very kind and tried to mop it up with a tissue. So that's why I remember them.'

'What makes you so sure it was the missing girls?'

'I saw them in the paper, just yesterday. Are you the private detective? It said you were investigating their disappearance.'

'Yes, I am. My name's Jacaranda Dunne. Look, Norah, can I send someone along to talk to you?'

'Oh, I don't know about that. My neighbour says I shouldn't get involved, but she was so sweet to me, that young girl, I felt I should ring you.'

JD had the feeling that Norah was going to hang up. She pressed the record button on her phone and said, 'I'm so glad you did, Norah. This information could be very helpful to us. Can you tell me what time it was when you saw them?'

'Yes, that's easy. I'd just come out of the cinema and the film ended at four so it was roughly ten past four.'

'And it was the day they disappeared, Saturday 12th August?'

'Oh no, I never go to the Plaza on a Saturday; it's far too busy. It was the day before, the Friday.'

JD felt her excitement turn to disappointment. 'Oh I see. But these youngsters, how many were there?'

'Four or five, I can't remember now. I know there were two girls, the two who were in the paper. And there were at least two boys, older than the girls, in their twenties maybe. And I think there was someone else, but I'm not sure. Sorry it was a long time ago, but I thought I should phone.'

'Yes, of course. You've been very helpful. I don't suppose you remember what the boys looked like?'

'One was definitely English, and very rude, because I heard him say, "You should watch where you're going, you silly old bag." I don't know about the other one, darker skinned I think. Sorry.'

'You do realise that the police have been calling for witnesses for months. Why didn't you come forward before?'

'My friend told me some girls had disappeared, but I didn't know it was them. I flew back to the UK the next day, on the 13th, and I've only just got back. I live in Salisbury, you see. I often spend the summers here, but last year Britain was having such glorious weather that I decided to stay there longer. I'm sorry; I would have told someone if I'd known. I hope those poor girls are all right.'

'Well, one of them has been found dead,' said JD, keen to impress the woman with the seriousness of the crime, 'and the other is still missing.'

'Oh, my goodness. That's awful. I do hope you find her.'

'I hope so, too. If we do find the boys who were with them that day, would you be able to come here to identify them from some photos?' she asked.

There was a long hesitation.

'It would be all right. It would be just a few photos and nobody would know you were here.'

'Yes, all right. I could do that. When do you want me to come?'

'Maybe in a few days. I'll phone you; I have your number. Now can you remember anything else about them, especially the men?'

'The bald one had a tattoo. A woman's head, I think. Horrible things those tattoos. I really don't know why they bother. Disfiguring yourself with all that pain and the risk of infection, I can't see what it's all for.'

'Body art, lots of people like it,' said JD, thinking of the small tattoo she had on her left shoulder. It was of half a heart and Andy had had the other half tattooed on his right shoulder. 'Well, thank you again, Norah. I'm very pleased you called us.'

'What was that all about? asked Linda.

'A witness. We have a witness at last. Listen, I'll play back our conversation.' JD placed her iPhone on the table and pressed play.

'She doesn't sound very reliable. And it wasn't even a Saturday when she saw them,' said Nacho.

'But that shows we were looking at the wrong CCTV footage. To save time, we went through all the Saturday recordings. Now we should look at Friday's,' said Linda.

'I wonder who the third person is, and if he is involved in their disappearance,' said JD. 'God, this case is worse than doing a jigsaw.'

'I didn't know you liked jigsaws,' said Nacho.

'I don't.'

'Right Linda, let's run the CCTV through the face recognition program. Maybe we'll get lucky.'

'I'm going out. I won't be long,' said JD. She felt she needed to clear her head. The questions were mounting up but not the answers. She turned right and headed for the port; a blast of fresh sea air was what she needed to sharpen her mind. It was as she'd said, just like a jigsaw, a bloody hard one; they had more pieces of the puzzle now but how did they all fit together?

She went over the autopsy report in her head; there were multiple fractures to Julie's legs and back, as well as the head trauma that was the cause of death. Was it possible that she had been hit by a car? Had that been the cause of death? Had it been an accident by someone who hadn't meant to cause her harm but was too frightened to go to the police? A person whose remorse was so strong that he carried her into the *Cofradía* and left her there?

She began to feel excited and quickened her pace, cutting through the park and across the main road and into the port. Summer was over and just as the torrid heat that they'd been labouring under for the last two months had suddenly diminished, so had the crowds of tourists and holiday makers drifted off home. She blinked, momentarily dazzled by the sun glinting on the water. The port was quiet, just a few dog walkers and the occasional cyclist making their way along the promenade. A strong smell of cooking drifted across from one of quayside restaurants, and a pang of hunger reminded her that she had missed breakfast. She needed to eat.

As she walked towards her favourite restaurant, she considered the information Tim had given them. A car driving at speed could easily have caused Julie's injuries. It was beginning to look possible that the speeding car that had been caught on camera outside the hospital could have killed her. And was it the same car that ran down Lieutenant Alvároz a few weeks ago? If so, whose car was it? Something wasn't right here. Surely the CCTV of the policeman's accident had shown more than that grainy image of the number plate. She needed to see the whole video. She'd ring Federico; he'd know how to get access to it. Perhaps he'd meet her for lunch.

CHAPTER 12

Sophie stepped out into the yard and squatted down by the dog. His name was Ludo. Igor, the chef, had told her that he was called after a famous boxer in Russia because he was always getting into scraps with other dogs. She rubbed Ludo's ears; one had a big tear in it. He was a Russian spaniel and didn't look much different to the old spaniel her grandfather used to have. Despite his name, he didn't seem much of a fighter to her; he was quite a softie. He and Igor were the only two friends she had now that Julie had escaped.

'Sophie, Sophie. Where is that girl?' The housekeeper was calling for her. Wearily Sophie dragged herself up and headed back into the sumptuous house which was the family's summer residence. Once upon a time she would have been overawed by such a display of extravagant wealth, but now she just saw it as the mountain she had to climb every morning. The housekeeper was a stickler for cleanliness and expected Sophie to clean the house thoroughly, on a daily basis. It had been hard enough before when there were two of them, but now it was impossible to meet her captor's high standards and she often suffered for it. Her shoulders still stung from where the housekeeper had lashed at her the night before, just because she hadn't swept behind the corner cabinet.

A small dog snapped at her heels; it was Goya, a Russkiy Toy that Madame idolised and Sophie detested. 'Get away, you little rat,' she hissed at her.

Sophie is Still Missing

At that moment the housekeeper came into the kitchen. 'Why are you standing there, stupid child? You should be upstairs by now.' She turned to Madame's husband who had followed her in and now stood watching Sophie, 'She's less than useless, that one. A complete waste of money. I thought the other girl was bad enough, but this one is hopeless. All she does is mope about and cry. I've told her if she doesn't make more of an effort, she'll be sorry.'

'She's missing her friend,' Madame's husband replied, smiling at Sophie.

She looked away, avoiding his eyes. Julie had been his favourite and he used to come into their sleeping area—it was too small to call a bedroom— when his wife was asleep and take Julie out into the garden with him. Julie would never tell Sophie what happened, but she knew it wasn't anything good because afterwards she would lie in her bed sobbing until it was time to get up. Then one day Julie wasn't there. The housekeeper said she had collapsed while she was hanging out the washing and that they'd taken her to the hospital. The next day she was back and when Sophie asked her what had happened she didn't answer, just burst into tears. Sophie had never seen Julie so upset before; even when Kevin and his friends, who'd been so kind and promised them so many nice things, had suddenly turned on them and thrown them in the back of the van as though they were sacks of rubbish, she had been angry and frightened but not as distraught as when she came back from the hospital. It had to have been something really bad because Madame's husband said that Julie didn't have to do any cleaning for two days, and Madame didn't argue with him, although she looked very angry. Julie had lain in her bed and cried, and even though Sophie had tried to comfort her, she wouldn't tell her what was wrong.

Sophie is Still Missing

Sophie trudged upstairs with the hoover and began cleaning the rugs in the bedrooms; the little dog slept upstairs and her hairs were everywhere. It was impossible to remove them all but Madame would be furious if she spotted a single one. Sophie hated these rugs; they were old fashioned and boring and she had to hoover them on both sides. The housekeeper said they were expensive and came from Persia. She didn't understand why they didn't have Russian rugs, like they did in Moscow? She and Julie had been taken to Moscow after they had been sold at the auction. They hadn't realised it was an auction. Kevin had told them it was the audition. How could they have been stupid enough to believe him? She had hated it in Moscow: they had been so cold and miserable in that flat, and they couldn't understand anything any of the other servants said. The only nice thing had been teaching Madame's daughters.

'Haven't you finished yet?' shouted the housekeeper. 'Just because the children aren't here, doesn't mean you have nothing to do.'

Not long after Sophie and Julie arrived in Moscow, Madame's husband decided that as their maids were from England—that was what they called them when they weren't angry with them— they could teach their daughters how to speak English. Madame had liked the idea. For once she had smiled at him. But now the girls had been sent to boarding school in Sussex, so there was no need for English lessons and Sophie's life had become harder.

Madame was an unhappy woman, and she had taken her unhappiness out on Julie. Sophie was sure she knew what her husband was doing to her friend, so why didn't she stop him? She remembered how her own parents had quarrelled when Dad had an affair with a woman from the garage; her mother had threatened him with divorce so he'd stopped seeing her. Now he was doing the same thing with Julie's mum. It was Julie who'd told her about their affair. At first Sophie couldn't believe it, and then she wanted to tell her mother, but Julie stopped her. She said if her mother found out then she'd stop Sophie from being friends with her; she might even go back to England and take Sophie with her. Neither of them wanted that to happen. They couldn't bear to be separated; if anything that awful news had made them cling to each other even more. And then Julie had disappeared. She still couldn't understand why her friend would run away and leave her behind. It was so cruel. Now she had nobody.

Thinking of her mum was like someone turning a knife in her heart; she missed her so much. Was she ever going to see her again, or her brothers? Had they given up hope of ever finding her? They probably thought she was dead. A tear trickled down her cheek. She couldn't bear to think that.

But most of all, she missed Julie. If only she could find out if her friend was all right. Why did nobody ever speak about her? Sometimes it was as if she'd never existed.

'Igor wants you in the kitchen,' said the housekeeper. 'What are you crying about now? I've told you before, it's time you got used to your new life. It's not going to change, you know. And wipe your eyes before you go down there. Madame is with him, planning the menu, and you'll only get into more trouble if she sees you've been crying.'

She had to escape. Julie had managed it, so why not her? It had happened when Julie was out in the garden with Madame's husband. Sophie had heard someone shouting and crept out of their tiny cupboard, to see what was happening. She saw Mr Lebedev come in through the kitchen door, clutching his head; blood was dripping onto his pyjamas and he was calling for

Sophie is Still Missing

Jaime, his chauffeur. Then Madame came downstairs and Sophie had darted back into the cupboard and pulled the door shut.

She'd lain there until daybreak, unable to sleep and too frightened to move. At last the door opened and the housekeeper had said, 'Get up, child. You've got the work of two to do today.' Sophie remembered how angry she looked. What had happened? And where was Julie now?

CHAPTER 13

JD sat sipping her coffee and watching people disembark from the Trasmediterránea ferry; they had just arrived in Málaga from Melilla, on the coast of north Africa. It was simple to smuggle things, and people, in and out of the country. Travellers arrived from that Spanish outpost daily, and although the Guardia Civil were always alert to the smugglers and illegal immigrants, they couldn't catch them all. Is that what had happened to Julie and Sophie? Had they been taken aboard the Trasmediterránea, with the promise of seeing a new country and having a little excitement? Had they expected to be going home again afterwards? A Moroccan man accompanied by two women in full burqa dress disembarked. How easy it would have been to dress the girls in burqas and smuggle them out of Spain; nobody would have recognised them. Nobody would have even given them a second glance. The more she thought about what could have happened to the two girls, the more depressed she became. All they had to go on was Julie's dead body; if it wasn't for that they wouldn't have a clue where to start.

'*Buenas tardes, cariño*. Sorry I couldn't get here in time to join you for lunch. So, why so sad?' asked Federico, sitting down opposite her. He waved at the waiter. '*Un café exprés.*'

'Just thinking about the case.'

'And?'

'She could be anywhere.'

'Sophie?'

'Yes. It's impossible. We're never going to find her.'

'Nothing's impossible, Jacaranda. Anyway, I thought you said you were progressing well. Did you find any CCTV of them?'

'The guys are going through it now. We might get lucky. A woman telephoned today to say she remembers seeing the girls with a couple of men.'

'So, not all doom and gloom, as you British say.' He smiled at her and took her hand. 'How is Nacho, by the way?'

'He's fine. A great worker.'

'I hope you're not getting him to do anything illegal.'

'Of course not,' she said, pulling her hand away.

'Because, as far as I'm concerned, he's still on probation. I don't want you to jeopardise his chances. It will mean prison for him next time he does any illegal hacking. You do understand that?'

'Of course, I understand. Don't worry. He's just my computer assistant.'

' Okay. Anyway, why did you want to see me?'

'Do I have to have a reason?' she said, beginning to feel more positive. Federico always had that affect on her.

He tilted his head to one side and waited.

'All right. I want you to get me the CCTV for Lieutenant Jose Maria Alvároz's accident,' she said with a smile. She placed the photo which Tim had given her on the table.

'Where did you get that?'

'Tim got it for me. But as you can see it's a pretty poor image. He also got me this; it's a photo of a speeding car on the night that Julie was killed. It looks like the same car to me.'

The Captain picked up the speed trap image and stared at it.

'Is it possible that the same car killed the investigating officer and Julie?' she asked.

'It's possible, but almost six months apart? Is that likely?' He stared at the photo then added, 'Still, that's an interesting number plate. Leave it with me and I'll see what I can do.'

'I have something else for you, too. A photograph of Steed, his fingerprints and also his DNA.'

'Is that legal?'

'Probably not. That's why I've put them on a USB stick.' She opened her bag and took it out and gave it to him. 'I didn't want to compromise you by sending it to your computer.'

'Very thoughtful of you. Not worried that I'll get kicked out of the force for interfering in a case that has nothing to do with me?' he said, taking it from her.

She smiled sweetly at him.

'Don't worry, Jacaranda, I'll make sure he doesn't manage to get through customs. With the help of your mate at the Met, he shouldn't be able to leave the UK, but, as you know, it is still possible. If someone wants something badly enough, they can usually find a way to make it happen. That's why I want us to be ready this end. Between us, we should be able to keep you safe.'

'Thanks, Federico. I don't know what I'd do without you.'

'Get some other soft-hearted mug to do your dirty work, I expect.' He drank back his coffee in one gulp and leaning over to kiss her, whispered in her ear, 'I will be collecting payment, tonight, *cariño*. Eight o'clock. *Hasta luego*.'

JD watched him walk back towards the car park. Did he believe her when she said Nacho was keeping out of trouble? It was Federico who had introduced her to her computer assistant, and for that she would be forever grateful. He was a brilliant young man when it came to computers but that's what had got him into trouble. When he was nineteen he'd broken into the university computer for a dare. He'd never done anything with the information that he'd found, but the police were brought in.

Sophie is Still Missing

In the end the dean had dropped the charges against him, saying expulsion was punishment enough. Federico had been involved in the case and decided to keep an eye on the boy. He'd approached JD and asked her to employ him; he said Nacho needed a job that would stretch his abilities and keep him out of trouble. She'd never regretted it, but she couldn't guarantee that everything Nacho did for the agency was strictly legal, nor illegal for that matter. The truth was that she preferred not to know.

Federico was such a good friend to her; more than that in fact. What was the current expression? They were friends with benefits. She knew Federico wasn't happy with that arrangement; he wanted them to have a more permanent relationship but although she loved him dearly, she wasn't ready for that. Until she had found out who had killed Andy, she couldn't settle with anyone else. There was unfinished business to be dealt with first. And Steed's release had reminded her of that, more than ever.

She would have like to have sat there watching the ships come and go in the harbour and soaking up the afternoon sunshine, but she needed to see what Nacho and Linda had come up with on the CCTV. She hurried through the park, only stopping briefly to toss some bread to the ducks, and was soon passing the cathedral; the homeless man who regularly sat on the cathedral steps, gave her a cheery wave.

'*Buenas tardes*, JD,' he called.

She dropped a couple of euros in his cap and said, 'Anything new, Carlos?' It was surprising what Carlos could come up with; he had helped her solve more than one case before.

He shook his head. 'So where are you off to, in such a hurry?' he said.

'Work. Where else?'

'Not meeting that boyfriend of yours then?'

'You haven't been here for a few days,' she said, ignoring the comment. Why was everyone so interested in her love life?

'No, I like a change from time to time. Been sitting outside the *alcazaba* all week, but the tourists aren't so generous there. Churches are best. Pricks people's conscience to see me sitting there.'

The *alcazaba*, Málaga's Moorish fortress, was opposite the *Cofradía*. 'Do you often sit there?' she asked.

'Now and again. Why? Thinking of joining me? Is business that bad?' He cackled.

'I don't suppose you were using that patch back in March, just before Holy Week?'

'March? I don't even know what month it is now. How do you expect me to remember something from half a year ago?'

'Just an idea. Must get on.'

'Me too,' he said, smiling and treating her to the sight of his black and broken teeth.

She laughed, and skirting around the tourists queueing to climb the cathedral's tower, she headed straight for the office.

Linda was sitting at her desk, reading a newspaper.

'At last. I was about to call you. Have you seen the local rag? It's saying that Beverley was with a boyfriend the night Sophie disappeared,' said Linda.

'A boyfriend? Really? Some marriage that is; they were both at it, then?' said JD, picking up the newspaper.

'Sounds like it. Do you want me to go over there and speak to her?'

'What a load of crap. Beats me how they can get away with slandering someone like that,' JD said, tossing the paper onto her desk. 'Yes, go over and see how Beverley is taking it. The poor woman has enough on her plate without this as well. And get the boyfriend's name.' Her assistant picked up her bag and her car keys and headed for the door. 'Just a minute, Linda. Did you find anything on the CCTV?'

'Yes, we did actually. Nacho will tell you all about it; he's out getting himself a sandwich and a coffee. His face recognition software worked a treat, but my head is spinning after hours of staring at the screen. I have to get out of here or I'll go mad.'

'Fine. Off you go. We'll go over everything this evening.'

JD sat down and opened the paper again. The lurid headline made her cringe. What had poor Beverley felt when she saw it? Now all her family would know what she'd done. JD couldn't find it in her heart to condemn the poor woman; she knew what it was to be lonely.

She read the article carefully, hoping there might be something the reporter had found out that could be useful to them, but it was as she'd thought, all supposition and innuendo. Beverley had obviously spent the evening in the Marriott Hotel with someone—the receptionist had identified her from an old photograph—but the reporter either didn't know who she was with, or he was keeping it quiet.

'Hi, JD. You're back. I'd have got you a coffee if I'd known,' said Nacho, sitting down at his computer and skilfully making room for the large polystyrene cup and baguette that he carried.

'Why do you always insist on eating your lunch at your desk? Why don't you eat in a bar, like the rest of the population of Málaga?' she asked.

'Don't have time. My boss works me too hard,' he said, taking an enormous bite out of a tuna and tomato baguette.

'Talking of which, Linda says you've found something.'

Nacho brushed the crumbs off the keyboard and opened up his computer. 'We have indeed. I think we have the guy with the ponytail. A chap called Kevin Butler. I've traced him on Instagram, but there's not much personal information on him. Mostly pictures of Manchester City FC, or semi-naked girls on the beach in Fuengirola.'

JD pulled her chair up alongside him and said, 'Okay. Show me what else you've got. Anything linking him to the girls?'

'Well, it was on the Friday. The day before they disappeared. Watch this.' He began to play the video. 'See, the girls had been to the cinema to see "My Little Pony" but not on the Saturday, like they said. They must have bunked off school for the afternoon. That's why their parents never missed them.'

'Crafty little things. They decided to see it the day before so they could talk about it if their parents asked them.'

'Exactly. So they never went to the Plaza at all on Saturday, which is why we couldn't find them on the CCTV. The police were looking in the wrong place. No wonder there were no witnesses.'

'There he is. The one with the ponytail. Kevin. Can you freeze it? Zoom in?' said JD. 'He looks English and I can see his tee-shirt, Manchester City. Can you print out a copy of it?'

'Already done, Boss. And better still, I've got one of him standing next to Julie. Just in case the police think we're making it up.'

'Good job, Nacho.'

'Team effort, JD.'

'What about the other men? Any photos of them?'

'Yes, but there isn't a clear shot of their faces. It's as though they knew the camera was there.'

'Interesting. What does that suggest to you?'

'That they are more experienced at that sort of thing than the ponytail guy?'

'Exactly. I would guess that he was the bait, to get the girls interested.'

'So he might not even have known what the other men had in mind?'

'It's possible, but I doubt it. Can you enlarge that image there? I think we might be able to see his face reflected in the plate glass window.'

'I'll give it a try.' Nacho fiddled about with the editing tools and eventually said, 'How about that?' A grainy but clear image of a man in his thirties appeared on the screen. 'What do you think, Moroccan?'

'Could be. Print it out, would you.' Was this the point where she handed everything over to the Guardia Civil? But what would they do with it? File it away with the rest of the evidence? No it was too soon; they needed to get more information before they could go to the police. 'We'll hang on to this for now, Nacho. No point showing our hand until we have the winning cards.'

CHAPTER 14

Beverley poured herself a large glass of Sauvignon Blanc. She looked at the bottle; it was nearly empty. Had she really drunk almost a whole bottle already? Well why not? She needed it; her nerves were shattered. She took a cigarette from the packet; her hands shook as she tried to light it. 'Damn,' she cried, 'Can I do nothing right?' At last she succeeded and throwing the lighter down, inhaled deeply, breathing in the bitter smoke. Then, slightly calmed by the fresh intake of nicotine, she picked up her glass and sat by the window; this had become her usual place these days. From here she could see the garden and the entrance to the house; she would know the minute Sophie returned.

She couldn't stop thinking about her daughter; she would toss and turn all night long, imagining where Sophie was and what was happening to her. Then when she couldn't stand it any longer, she would get up and swallow a couple of sleeping pills and lie down again, with her head on the tear-soaked pillow.

Beverley wasn't a bad mother—nobody could say that—but she knew she could have given Sophie more attention. It had been easy when she was little; Beverley had taken her to school every morning and picked her up in the afternoon. Sometimes they would walk around the shops before going home, just the two of them. They had spent more time together as a family in those days, going to the beach or the cinema, meeting up with friends who had children the same age so they could all play together, but as she grew older, Sophie didn't want to do things with her mother; she wanted to be with her friends. Beverley understood that, but she had missed her daughter's company. After all, who else did she have? Jim was always working, and the boys were off playing football or messing about with their mates; there was no way they wanted to spend time with their mother. Kids grew up so quickly these days; they were young adults before you knew it. It wasn't fair. One minute you were the most important person in their lives and the next they could hardly find time to talk to you, and if they did, it was usually to ask about clean socks or what was for dinner. She began to feel sorry for herself. It wasn't as if Jim had made it any easier; she hardly saw him, except at work, and even then he was always going to meetings he couldn't explain.

'Mum. You in?' It was Ricky.

Hurriedly she stubbed out her cigarette and opened the window.

'You okay, Mum?'

Beverley wiped her eyes and smiled at him; Ricky had been very sweet to her lately. Strange how Sophie's disappearance had brought them closer together. 'Yes, I'm fine.'

'You don't look it.' He picked up the newspaper and flapped it about, trying to remove the cigarette smoke. 'Dad'll moan like hell when he sees you've been smoking indoors.'

'He won't know. He's not due back until late. Some committee meeting or other, the Lions, I think. Are you hungry?'

'Not really. I had a burger down at the leisure centre.' He laid the paper down on the table and stared at it. 'Have you read this, Mum?'

'Oh, take no notice. It's all a loud of rubbish,' she said, trying to snatch the newspaper away from him.

Sophie is Still Missing

'Is this why you're upset?' He read aloud, 'MISSING GIRL REVELATION. Mother of missing girl, Sophie Anderson was with her lover while her daughter was snatched. Sources close to the family reveal that Beverley Anderson was in the Marriot Hotel with her lover on the night her daughter disappeared.' He stared at her. 'Is that true Mum?'

Beverley began to cry.

'Mum?'

'Yes, it's true, Ricky. I'm so sorry.'

'Mum, how could you? Does Dad know?'

'Not yet. Look, Ricky, it was nothing. Really. It meant nothing. I was fed up with your father always being out on business and I wanted a bit of fun myself. That night he was in Madrid at the Motor Show and I was angry with him because I'd wanted to go with him. I fancied a day out in Madrid, doing a bit of shopping, having a nice lunch. Anything for a change from the old routine, but when I suggested we could make a weekend of it, like the old days, he came up with some pathetic excuse. He always had an excuse for doing things without me.'

'So how did you meet this bloke?'

'Mark? He'd been hanging around me for ages, trying to get me to go for a drink with him. So I thought, why not?'

'You're not seeing him now?'

'No, Ricky. I told you, it was nothing. One night. And how do you think it makes me feel now, knowing that I was in that hotel while Sophie was being kidnapped?'

'They shouldn't be allowed to print such things,' he said, continuing to read. 'How can they say those awful things about Sophie and you; they don't know you. Where are they getting it all from?'

'Don't get angry, Ricky. It doesn't matter.'

Sophie is Still Missing

'Of course it matters, Mum. They can't print such things. How did they know you were at the hotel anyway?'

'I don't know. Someone probably recognised me.'

'But what about all this other stuff? It's all lies. They're saying horrid things about Sophie hanging about in bars with loads of boys? That's not true. Who told them that?'

'I know. It's rubbish. It just says sources close to the family. It was probably your Dad's cousin.'

'Uncle Bob? But we haven't heard from him in years; Sophie must have been nine the last time he visited us. What does he know about our family?'

'I know. He was always jealous of us living in Spain, but never had the gumption to do anything about moving here himself.' She remembered how Bob had made a pass at her once, and been distinctly annoyed because she'd brushed him off.

'I never liked him much.'

She took the newspaper from him. What was the reporter trying to suggest; that it was her fault that Sophie had been kidnapped? Well, she didn't need any pimple faced journalist telling her she should feel guilty; she was doing that already. She wiped her eyes again. Could things get any worse? She bitterly regretted her actions but there was no escaping the consequences. Now she'd have nobody, no friends, no family; everyone would hate her. 'Don't hate me, Ricky. Please don't leave me. I'm not a bad person. I just made a mistake.'

Her son put his arms around her and hugged her. 'I don't hate you, Mum and I'm not going to leave you. Don't worry; we'll find Sophie. You see, we'll find her.'

Poor kid, he shouldn't have to think about her problems, not at a time like this. She could see he was angry, but was it with the reporter for writing the article or with her?

Sophie is Still Missing

'Are you sure you don't want anything to eat, Ricky?' she asked.

'Okay, what have you got?'

As Ricky tucked into a plate of egg, bacon and chips, Beverley went into the garden to have another cigarette. How had that reporter found out that she and Mark were in the Marriot that evening? It didn't mention him by name, so did they really know anything at all? Was it all some bluff to see what her reaction would be?

She had never intended to cheat on Jim, and she was sure that if he had been around more, she would never have agreed to seeing Mark that night. It had been a spur of the moment decision, fuelled by anger at her husband. Mark owned the garage which serviced their hire cars, so she'd had a lot of contact with him. He was funny, handsome and more than anything else, he made her feel alive. It had been a good evening, and for the first time in a long while, Beverley had felt she was still attractive to a man. She had to admit to herself that she probably would have carried on seeing him if things hadn't changed.

Now it had all turned sour. She'd never forgive herself for being with him when she should have been at home. Suppose Sophie had tried to phone the house. Beverley poured the remains of the wine in her glass. Suppose she'd needed their help. Beverley had let them all down by her actions that night. Now what would Jim say when he read the article? She could hardly deny it, but would he be as forgiving as her son?

She drank the last of the wine.

'Okay, Ricky?' she asked, going back into the kitchen and taking a fresh bottle of wine from the fridge. She wouldn't drink it all, just one more glass. She needed it.

Sophie is Still Missing

CHAPTER 15

Jorge Perez still hadn't got over the bitter disappointment he'd felt when the police had announced that it was impossible for them to take part in the Holy Week processions. He'd tried to explain how important it was, that it was something they had been preparing for all year, but the lieutenant remained firm. In the end they had sent for the president and their local parish priest, and after some discussion with the Guardia Civil, the Christ figure was allowed to take part in the processions, because it and its throne had been housed in a separate part of the *Cofradía*, but their beloved Virgin had to remain where she was, behind the blue and white police cordons. He knew it was selfish to think only of himself and not that poor child who had ended her life so tragically, but it pained him to realise that now he would never have another chance. He had been a member of the Brotherhood of the Virgin of Remorse for sixty-five years, since he'd taken the place of his grandfather at the age of fifteen. His family had been members of the Brotherhood for as long as he could remember, and it had been an honour to walk beside his father and his uncles that day. Their traditions went back five hundred years and were an important part of their religion and their identity. Although nowadays—even he had to face the truth of it—most of the people who flocked to the city during Holy Week were tourists who came for the spectacle rather than for any religious reasons. The penitents who accompanied the procession, with their heads covered and their feet bare, were fewer each year.

His knees creaked as he stood up and genuflected before the altar. Since he'd found the dead girl, he had come here most days to pray for her soul, and for forgiveness from the Virgin Mother; he should never have allowed her statue to be violated in that way. It was his duty to have kept a closer watch over her. He sighed. There was no-one at home he could talk to about it; he'd been a bachelor all his life. Only God would listen to him.

'Señor Perez, I'm sorry to disturb you. The secretary at the *Cofradía* said I might find you here,' said a young man with an untidy mop of black hair. He looked like a student in his baggy jeans and old blue trainers.

'Buenos días,' Jorge said, trying to work out who he was, and if he'd met him before.

'*Buenos días*, my name is Ignacio Moreno de Avila. I work for a detective agency which is looking into the death of Julie Bennett and the disappearance of her friend Sophie Anderson.'

Jorge looked at him blankly.

'Julie was the girl you found lying across the lap of the Virgin,' Nacho explained.

'Oh, yes. Poor child. I thought that case was closed.'

'The police have stopped investigating, that's true, but we have been asked to try to find the missing girl.'

'I see. I didn't realise there was another girl. Missing? Her friend, you say? Oh yes, I think I remember reading something about it.'

'Yes. I wonder if I might ask you a few questions?'

'Yes, of course, but I doubt if I can help you. I don't know anything about the other girl, and all I know about the dead girl is that she is dead.' He sat down in the pew.

Sophie is Still Missing

'It's not so much about the girls as about why Julie was placed where she was. Do you have any idea why anyone would want to put a dead girl on the throne next to the Virgin? Does it have any symbolic significance, do you know?'

Jorge shook his head. He was as baffled as they were.

'Well does it make sense to you that someone would kill a young girl then take her to the *Cofradía*?'

Jorge looked at the young man who'd sat down beside him. He had pondered over the same thing ever since the day he found her. 'So she was definitely murdered?'

'It's looking like it, I'm afraid.'

'Well, I don't think that whoever placed her there was the person who killed her,' he said. 'Unless it was an accident. Then maybe.' He remembered the gold crucifix he'd seen caught in her hair. He should have told them that he recognised it. But how could he? The scandal would be devastating for the *Cofradía*; it would never recover from it.

'The police seemed to have ruled that out. After all she'd been missing for nine months and then she turns up dead. They have declared it a suspicious death.'

'Well, in that case, I doubt it was the same person.'

'Why do you say that?'

'It doesn't make sense. A total stranger murders a young girl and then brings her to the *Cofradía*. No, it had to be someone else, not the murderer.'

'What makes you think it was a total stranger?' asked Nacho.

'Well it couldn't have been anyone connected to the Brotherhood.'

'What else can you tell me?' asked Nacho. 'Why do you think a total stranger would choose this *Cofradía*? Did the girl have any connection to the Brotherhood? What have the other Brothers said about it?'

Sophie is Still Missing

'Nobody has any idea why she was there. Nobody knew her and they were all very shocked by the incident. However I can tell you one thing I am certain of, and that's that it wasn't one of the Brotherhood.' he repeated. 'Nobody would do that a few days before we were about to move the Virgin. Nobody. Holy Week is very important to us all; no-one would want to desecrate it in this way.'

'So, if it wasn't one of the Brotherhood, then how did that person get in? Aren't the doors locked?'

'Of course they're locked. There are a lot of very valuable things inside the *Cofradía*, a great number of gold and silver objects that have been collected over the years. And there's an alarm system. You can't be too careful, these days.'

'So who has a key, or could get access to a key?' asked Nacho.

Jorge was becoming a bit impatient with this young man; he was behaving like a policeman, asking him all these questions. 'There aren't any keys; we have an electronic code system,' he said. 'It's changed every month. I hope you're not suggesting I am responsible?'

'No, of course not. I just want to know how easy it would be for someone to let himself, or someone else, into the throne room of the Virgin?'

'Well there are a number of people who know the code, the president of the *Cofradía*, the secretary, the head of the maintenance team, quite a few in fact. But nobody is supposed to tell anyone else what it is. We operate on trust in the Brotherhood.'

'What about the alarm system? Did anyone have the code for that?'

'It's the same as the entry code. The security company send it to us every month.'

'So the security company know the entry code as well?'

'Of course. You're not suggesting that they're involved?'

The young man shrugged his shoulders and said, 'So anyone having that code can open the doors and shut off the alarm system?'

'That's right. But, as I said, it's changed every month,' Jorge was now getting annoyed with the man's persistent questioning.'

'Well someone passed on the code. Can you get me a list of all the names and phone numbers of those who knew it?' asked Nacho.

'I will have to speak to the president. I'm not authorised to do that.'

'That'll be fine. Perhaps you could ask him to email it to me,' said Nacho, handing him his card.

Jorge took the card and placed it in the inside pocket of his jacket. 'Is that all?'

'I wondered if you could tell me if anyone else was in the *Cofradía* in the week before you found Julie? Anyone who normally wouldn't be there?'

'That was six months ago,' Jorge protested. 'How do you expect me to remember?' But, if he was honest, he remembered everything about that week; he'd gone over it time and time again in his head. He doubted that he'd ever forget.

'Is there usually a lot of coming and going before Holy Week? You mentioned the maintenance manager, were there a lot of extra people working on the throne? Repairs, for example?'

'No, all that work had been finished weeks before.' He paused. 'Well there was someone, a press photographer. It wasn't unusual for the press to be hanging about in Holy Week, but this young man wanted some photos of both thrones while they were still on their trestles. Normally they like to take the photos as the men are carrying them out; that's much more interesting.'

'Can you describe him?'

'No, sorry. I was busy sorting out the Virgin's crown; someone had dropped it and there was a small dent in it.' Jorge had been furious with the Brother responsible.

'Surely you can tell me something about this photographer?'

'Not really. As I said, I had more important things to do.'

Nacho waited.

'Very well. He was youngish, thin, quite tall; I remember that because he didn't want to borrow any steps to look more closely at the thrones. He said he could see perfectly well without them.'

'What about his face?'

'No. I don't remember his face. He was wearing a cap. I thought it was very disrespectful to keep his cap on in front of the Virgin Mary, and I told him so.'

'Anything else, a tattoo, or something about his clothing?'

'Well, now that you mention it, there was something that caught my attention; it was a hot afternoon and he carried his jacket over his shoulder. I glimpsed what looked like a tattoo on his arm, but I have no idea what it was. Sorry. I wasn't wearing my glasses at the time.'

'Okay, that's really helpful. Do you remember which newspaper he worked for?'

'Again, no. In fact, I don't think he said which paper he worked for, just flashed a press badge at me and sauntered in. I let him get on with it.'

'Could he have seen anyone punching in the code, while he was there?'

'I doubt it. The doors were already open.'

'And did you let him out after he'd finished?'

'Well, no, I didn't actually. I'd moved into the other room; I told you I was very busy. I never saw him leave.'

'Just a couple more things, Señor Perez, do you have a list of all the members of the *Cofradía*?'

'You're talking of a lot of names, young man. We have almost five hundred members. Again, I would have to speak to the president about that.'

'Of course. Are they all Spanish?'

'What a strange question. Membership is strictly controlled; it's not like joining a golf club you know. It is inherited. I, for example, became a member of the Brotherhood on the death of my grandfather. Some families can trace their membership back to the seventeenth century, you know.'

'So that's the only way you can join, by family connection?'

'We make some exceptions, of course. There are a lot of powerful people in Málaga, and occasionally someone with no prior attachment to the Brotherhood is allowed to join. But that isn't often.'

'Rich enough, you mean?'

Jorge scowled at him.

'Can you remember the last time that happened?' Nacho asked.

'No, I can't, young man. Now I think I have answered enough of your questions for one day. I will speak to the president and try to get the names you want, but I don't think they will do you any good.'

The young man stood up. 'Thank you, Señor Perez. I am very grateful for your help. One last thing.' He handed him two photographs. 'I don't suppose you can recognise either of these men? Could one of them have been the photographer?'

Jorge took his glasses from his jacket pocket and looked at them. 'No. I've never seen them before. Who are they?'

Sophie is Still Missing

'Well, thank you again for your time, Señor Perez.'

Jorge waited until he heard the heavy doors of the church swing closed, and knelt down to resume his prayers. His heart felt heavy. He fingered his crucifix lovingly. Not all the Brothers wore them; it was an honour reserved for those who'd done something special. He had recognised an identical one on Julie's body, and instantly knew where it had come from. Maybe he should have told the young man about it. But what if it had nothing to do with her death? He would be exposing the Brotherhood to unnecessary suspicion. He groaned. What on earth should he do? He knew he should have told the police; he was withholding evidence, but how could he betray his comrades? No, best he said nothing.

CHAPTER 16

Linda was feeling frustrated; it was over a month and they didn't seem to be any closer to tracing the men who were with Julie and Sophie the day before they disappeared. Surely someone had seen them hanging around. Perhaps she should go back over the ground she'd already covered; maybe somebody would have remembered something by now. She pulled out her notebook and looked through her notes. The obvious thing was to visit the school again.

'JD, I think I'll pay another call on that teacher,' she said.

Her boss looked up from her computer and said, 'Miss Hardy? Is it worth it? She didn't have much to tell you last time. What's changed?'

'I think we have. I can ask her more pointed questions this time and I can show her the photo of Kevin, our ponytail boy.'

'Well, it's worth a try. It's not as though we're getting very far at the moment. Ring her first. They get a bit funny about strange people turning up without an appointment.'

'And they don't get much stranger than Linda,' Nacho muttered.

'I heard that,' said Linda.

JD ignored their banter and said, 'Why don't you chase up Jorge for that list of names, Nacho.'

'I'll call round there again this afternoon. By the way, I might have found something on Julie's social media page,' he replied.

'Great. What is it?'

'Not sure. Give me another hour and I might have something for you.'

'I'm off then,' said Linda. 'I'll ring from the car.'

'Okay. Call in on Mrs Bennett as well while you're in Torremolinos, to see how she is.'

'Will do.'

It was a pleasant drive to Torremolinos along the coast road, and as she drove she went over in her mind what they knew about the girls; a picture of them was becoming clearer. They had been seeing some boys, or men, for about a month before they disappeared, and at first it appeared to be casual, going to the cinema, meeting the boys afterwards in a bar, but then something changed. They knew they were going somewhere special that Saturday night. They'd planned for it. But what had the youth with the ponytail promised them? It had to be something that had made it worth lying to their parents.

Linda thought of her own teenage daughters, what would tempt them to deceive her and Phil? A party? Meeting a pop star? It would have to be something exciting for them to risk her wrath. But then, both Julie and Sophie knew their parents wouldn't miss them; they were too busy with their own lives. That had to be a factor in their decision. She smiled to herself. Phil called her Mrs Eagle-Eye; it made the girls laugh, but they knew their mother didn't miss much.

Her timing was perfect as she drove into the school carpark; the children were just coming out for their mid-morning break. She watched them for a minute as they milled around the playground and separated into their own little groups. How vulnerable they looked. Youngsters on the verge of adulthood, expressing their individuality in a dozen small ways; the girls with forbidden nose-rings that would be removed again the minute they re-entered the classroom, eye-shadow and lipstick, pink or green streaks in their hair, and the boys—much more conservative—with the latest fashion in haircuts, football scarves and little else to distinguish them from their uniformed classmates. She smiled to herself, thinking of Laura and Jane; her daughters loved to rebel but they still liked to keep in step with their friends. Nonconformity wasn't really their thing.

She parked her car and headed straight for the staffroom. The door was open and one of the teachers was just coming out.

'Excuse me, I'm looking for Miss Hardy,' Linda explained.

'Susie,' he called over his shoulder. 'There's a woman to see you.'

The teacher put down her coffee cup and came to door, 'Oh, hello,' she said, looking a little bewildered, 'You're from the detective agency, aren't you?'

'Yes, it's Linda Prewitt.'

'Did we have an appointment?'

'No. I'm sorry to just drop by like this, but I wondered if you could spare me a few minutes? I won't keep you long.'

The teacher looked at her watch. 'Well, I'm on my break at the moment, so yes, if it doesn't take too long. Come with me; it's far too noisy in here to talk.'

A heated discussion about salaries had just broken out between two of her colleagues.

As they walked back towards the carpark, she asked, 'So what's it about? I told you all I know, last time. There was nothing exceptional about the two girls who went missing; they were normal teenagers. A bit scatty at times, but they were nice girls.'

'I wondered if you had seen either of these men hanging about outside the school?' Linda asked. She handed her the two photos.

Sophie is Still Missing

Miss Hardy stared at the photos. 'Yes, I've seen that man before, but he wasn't with Julie and Sophie. He was standing over there, on the other side of the road, talking to some of the Sixth Form boys. I went across to see what he wanted, but by the time I got there, he'd gone. I recognise him because of the ponytail. It's not exactly the latest fashion at the moment.'

'How long ago was it?'

'It was last year, just before the school holidays, it must have been about the middle of June.'

'Do you think I could speak to the 6th Formers that he was talking to?'

'They don't know anything; I asked them at the time. They said they'd never seen him before.'

'Did you believe them? They might have said that to avoid getting into trouble.'

'Possibly. What could I do? They weren't doing anything wrong. I asked if he was trying to sell them drugs, but they denied it.'

'They might tell me something if I explain why I'm here.'

'They might. Wait here a minute and I'll check with the headmaster.' She headed back into the school and left Linda, leaning against the side of her car.

She felt pleased with herself; here was another connection between Mr Ponytail and the girls. But why was he hanging about outside their school? She pulled out her notebook and wrote down what she'd been told. In itself it didn't amount to much, but she felt it was still worth talking to the Sixth-Formers.

After about ten minutes, the teacher reappeared, followed by two boys. 'The Head has agreed to you speaking to them, but I must be with you,' she said. 'These are the only two who are still in the school; the others left last year. I've explained to them who you are and why you're here.'

'Thank you.' Linda turned to the boys who looked rather surly, probably irritated that their break had been disturbed. 'I won't take long. Were either of you friends with Julie Bennett and Sophie Anderson?'

Both boys shook their heads.

'But you know who they are?'

'Of course we do,' said one of the boys.

'So you won't object to helping me to find out how they disappeared?'

'Nah. Are you really a detective?' the other boy asked.

'I am. And I want to ask you if you can remember speaking to this man?' She handed the photo of Ponytail to them.

'That's Kevin,' said the first boy, straight away. 'He plays pool with us sometimes.'

'Do you remember why he was outside the school, that day? According to Miss Hardy, it was just before the end of the summer term last year, a couple of months before Julie and Sophie went missing.'

'No reason, really. He just wanted to chat.'

'He kept asking if we had any girlfriends,' added the other boy. 'I said no.'

'That's right, he wanted to know if we fancied any of the girls in our year. One of the older boys told him that he used to have a girlfriend, but she'd dumped him.'

'That was when he invited us to play pool in this club he went to. He said we could bring girls if we wanted.'

'Which club? Do you know its name?'

'The Crooked Cat. It's in Fuengirola.'

'Did you go?' asked Linda.

'Yes, but it was really expensive.'

'Did you take any girls with you?'

'I think one of the older boys did, but I didn't.'

'Most of the girls in our school are too stuck up to go out with us,' said his friend.

'What about this man, did you see him at the club?' She gave him the photo of the Moroccan.

'No.' He passed it to the other boy.

'Yes, I think so. He was with some other men, but they didn't come over to our table.'

'Is that him? The one who sent us some beers?' asked the first one, looking sideways at the teacher.

'I'll pretend I didn't hear that, Alex,' said Miss Hardy.

'So he was a friend of Kevin?' asked Linda.

'Yes, they seemed to get on together,' said Alex.

The bell to signal the end of their break began to ring. 'They have to go to class now,' said Miss Hardy. 'I hope they've been a help with your enquiries.'

'Are you really a private detective?' asked Alex, obviously having doubts as to her authenticity.

'I am. I have an identity card to prove it.' She took her ID from her pocket and showed it to them.

They looked from the card to Linda in disbelief. Whatever their vision of a private detective was, it wasn't a six-foot tall, middle-aged woman. They both shrugged, as though dismissing her from their thoughts, and headed into the school.

She looked at her watch; there was still time to visit Fiona.

At first Linda thought the house was empty, then she saw the curtains twitch and a few minutes later, Fiona opened the door. She was still in her nightdress and had a cardigan over her shoulders. She looked as though she hadn't slept in weeks.

'Hi, Fiona. It's Linda, from the detective agency,' she said, as Fiona blinked at her in bewilderment. 'Can I come in?'

Fiona stepped back and held the door open. 'He's not coming back,' she said.

'Who's not coming back? Your husband?'

'No. Well, yes, him too. Jim has dumped me. Gone back to his wife, even after she cheated on him.' She began to cry.

'Let's make you a cup of tea,' said Linda, taking her gently by the arm and leading her into the kitchen. 'Then you can tell me all about it.'

The kitchen looked as though a dozen hungry teenagers had been rampaging through it looking for food. There were opened packets of cereals, their contents spilling onto the breakfast bar, the sink was full of dirty plates and glasses and a small group of flies were dining on the remains of a ham sandwich. She removed two empty cans, one of baked beans and the other of tuna, from one of the kitchen stools and made Fiona sit down, while she filled the kettle.

'Has nobody been round to help you?' she asked.

'No, my friends won't speak to me now they know about Jim. Kindness itself they were at first, after Julie disappeared, now they treat me as though I'm the one to blame for her death. It's so unfair.'

Linda plugged in the kettle and began to search for the tea caddy. It was in the fridge. She refrained from asking Fiona what it was doing there when she saw the number of empty wine bottles stacked by the kitchen door. 'Have you eaten anything today?' she asked.

'No, I don't think so. I don't have much appetite at the moment.'

'Well, let me see if I can tempt you with something.' Linda opened the fridge again, but all that looked edible were some eggs. 'How about an omelette?'

'If you want. But I'm not hungry.'

Linda ignored her, and began to prepare the omelette. 'So what happened? I thought you and Jim were pretty solid.'

'So did I. Then he came round a few days ago, Sunday I think, and said it wasn't right that he was messing about with me, when he should be looking for his daughter. Messing about? Can you believe that? I thought he loved me.'

'Does he have some new information about her whereabouts?'

'He says that your boss is confident she'll find her, and he doesn't want Sophie to come back and find that he's gone off with her best friend's mum. So he took all his things and left.'

'Did you know he's sold the house?'

Fiona stared at her; obviously he had said nothing about it.

'He says they're going back to the UK.'

'What? The lying bastard, trying to put all the blame on me. Make me the guilty one.' Her tears were wiped away and now she was angry.

Linda hoped she wasn't going to start throwing things. 'Here you are, drink this. There's nothing like a good cup of tea for calming the nerves,' she said, putting the tea on the breakfast bar in front of Fiona. Personally she preferred a gin and tonic, but she didn't think it was a good idea in this situation.

She flipped the omelette onto the only clean plate she could find and sat down beside Fiona. 'So what are you going to do?'

'What can I do? My husband wants to divorce me, and I haven't heard from my son in ages. I'll have to sell this house; it's in our joint names. Then I suppose I'll try to get another job.'

'I'm really sorry. You've had a terrible time this last year.'

Fiona wiped her eyes, and said, 'So, are you making any progress?'

'Yes, but not as quickly as we'd like.'

'Was that necklace any help to you?'

'Necklace?'

'The crucifix the police gave me. It wasn't hers; I'm certain of that. She'd never wear anything like that; she hated anything to do with religion. I checked with everyone who could have given it to her. Beverley said she didn't know anything about it, and neither did Julie's dad or her brother. And her teacher said she never saw her wearing it at school; they're not allowed to wear jewellery, but that wouldn't have stopped Julie, if she'd liked it.'

Linda had forgotten all about the crucifix. How could she have overlooked something like that, a vital piece of evidence? JD would not be pleased. 'Can I see it again, please?' she asked.

'Of course. I won't be a minute.'

'I'll come with you, if I may. I'd like to take another look at Julie's bedroom.'

As before, Julie's bedroom was immaculate, with everything in its place.

'I expect the police searched her room?' she said.

'Yes, but only after they found her body. They didn't bother before, well only to see if her mobile was here.'

'And it wasn't?'

'No. I told you at the time. She never went anywhere without it.' Strains of Swan Lake began to play as Fiona opened the jewellery box and took out the crucifix. She snapped it shut. 'I can't bear to listen to that music anymore,' she said. 'It breaks my heart. I just can't come to terms with the fact that Julie's dead. It was hard enough when she was missing, but at least we had hope then. Now I have nothing.' A silent tear fell on the lid of the music box. 'Here, you can take it with you, if you like. I don't want it.'

Linda took the crucifix gently by its chain and dropped it into one of the plastic bags she always carried when she was working. 'Thanks. Did Julie have any photos of her friends?'

'A few. The police took them when she disappeared, but I've got them back now. I don't know what I did with them. They're here somewhere. They're just those daft photos they do in the photo booths.'

'Like passport photos?'

'Yes. She and Sophie were always taking them. All silly ones, pulling faces and messing about. I think they're in here.' She pulled out a box with an assortment of odds and ends: old birthday cards, bits of ribbon, novelty key rings and a number of Photo Booth snaps, all date stamped. 'Yes. That's them. I can't see that they'd be much use; she hasn't got her face straight in any of them.'

Linda spread them out on the bed. Fiona was right; they were all of the girls larking about. 'Who's this?' she asked, pointing to a grimacing lad on the last strip of photos. He had his arms around both girls and they looked to be having fun.

'I don't know. The police asked that too. Probably some boy they met in the shopping centre; I've never seen him before.'

Linda looked at the date; it was 31st July, two weeks before Julie and Sophie disappeared. 'May I take this with me?' she asked.

'Yes. I don't want it.'

'It could be useful,' said Linda, trying to be optimistic. She followed Fiona down to the kitchen. 'I ought to be going now; my boss wants us to have a review of the case this afternoon.'

Fiona didn't answer.

Sophie is Still Missing

'I'll keep you informed how it's going.'

She nodded.

'Take care of yourself, and let me know if you need anything. You have my number.' Linda was reluctant to leave her; she looked so lost and unhappy.

As she made her way back to the car she couldn't help wondering how Fiona would ever get back to living a normal life; the death of a child was not something that was easy to recover from.

CHAPTER 17

Ivan marched into the living room and threw the paper down on the breakfast table in front of his wife. 'Annika, have you seen that? Some damned private investigator has been snooping around and is trying to get the case re-opened.'

'It's probably nothing. They'll make a show of doing something and then it'll all go quiet again,' his wife said, buttering her rye bread. 'What have they said?' She picked up the paper. 'So she wants them to look for Julie's killer.'

'Not just that, to look into the disappearance of both girls.'

'I thought you'd spoken to that friend of yours? The one you're supporting in his election campaign.'

'Enrique de Valdes? Yes, I had, but it seems he doesn't have as much influence as I thought he had.'

'Well speak to him again. Tell him they'd be wasting public money; if they couldn't find anything a year ago, they won't find anything now,' said Annika, tossing the paper away in disgust and eating her bread.

'But now the press are saying that the police aren't doing what they're paid to do, that they gave up too soon and this private detective is doing their job for them.'

'Well remind Valdes that he's just as involved in this as anyone. Get him to do something. That's what you paid him for, isn't it, Ivan?'

'I'll speak to him.'

'I wish you'd never bought those damn girls. They've been more trouble than they were worth.'

Sophie is Still Missing

'How was I to know that they'd been abducted and the police would be looking for them?'

'It's never happened before,' said Annika.

'You're right; Sergio has always been so reliable before, but what's done is done. Now we have to think of what to do with the other one, before she gets ideas into her head about running away too.'

'We won't be able to fly her out of here now; there's been too much publicity. Even your diplomatic connections aren't going to help.'

'Don't worry. I've thought it all out; we'll take her in the yacht. Getting her aboard will be easy and then we'll sail down to Tangier and get the flight from there,' Ivan said.

'When? I've got plans for the rest of the month; I can't just cancel everything,' she said.

Sophie could see that Madame was getting angry, and when she was angry she generally took it out on her staff, so she picked up her bucket as quietly as she could and crept back towards the kitchen.

Madame wouldn't beat her in front of the cook; Igor always defended Sophie, and Madame never said anything to him because she couldn't risk losing the best chef in the area. That's what she called him. Russian chefs were not easy to find in Marbella, and he was a particularly good one, according to the housekeeper. Madame valued the reputation she had for giving extravagant dinner parties, so she tolerated what she called his little foibles, but Sophie had often heard her swearing about him in Russian when she went back upstairs.

As Sophie carefully closed the door behind her she heard Madame's husband say, 'All right, but it will have to be soon. I've been thinking for a while that it's time we left the Costa del

Sophie is Still Missing

Sol. I might even sell this place. What would you say to a house in Florida? Or Turkey, maybe?'

Sophie couldn't contain the gasp of horror that escaped her. Florida? She would never be able to escape from there. Never. Even Turkey was too far away from Spain.

That night Sophie couldn't sleep, so she got up and crept down to the kitchen. Ludo was outside in the garden, his nose pressed against the glass door. Carefully she slid back the bolts and unlocked the door. As soon as it was open the dog shot in and dived under the table.

'We'll both be in trouble if Madame comes down,' she whispered to him, scratching him behind the ears. He looked up at her with his big brown eyes. 'You miss the girls, don't you, Ludo. Never mind they will be back from school soon.'

Both of Madame's daughters loved Ludo and played with him constantly when they were at home. When they had first gone off to boarding school, poor Ludo had lain by the front door for weeks waiting for them to come back.

She stood at the open door, breathing in the scented night air, heavy with the smell of jasmine and Dama de la Noche. The swimming pool lights flickered yellow across the surface of the turquoise pool. The water looked so inviting, but she'd never been allowed to use the pool, not once, not even when the girls were at home. One day they had begged their mother to let Julie and Sophie swim with them, but their mother had been furious. She had made it quite clear to them that it was inappropriate for them to socialise with the maids, under any circumstances.

Tonight Sophie's attention was not so much on the swimming pool but beyond it, where the manicured lawns stretched down to the high wall that surrounded the garden. The wall was over three metres high and had shards of broken glass along the top of it; the housekeeper had boasted that it was very effective at keeping out intruders. It also made it difficult for anyone, like Sophie, to escape. So how had Julie managed it? It had been as much a surprise to Sophie as to anyone else when she heard that Julie had run away. She and her friend had often talked about escaping together, but it had seemed impossible. And yet she'd done it. Julie had managed to get away from this awful place. Someone must have left the gate open, that was the only explanation she could think of. Or perhaps she had just been lucky and Jaime had been driving in at that moment and she'd taken the opportunity to run out. That would be just like Julie; she wasn't afraid of anything. If only she could be that brave and get away before Madame's husband insisted they move to Florida.

She sighed. There was something that had been bothering her ever since Julie had escaped. Why hadn't anyone come to rescue her? Surely Julie would have told her mum and dad where Sophie was? So why hadn't the police come for her? Julie would never have left Sophie behind unless she planned to send help; she was her best friend. Both Sophie and Julie knew where this house was; they had often discussed it and it wasn't very far from their own homes. Of course Madame didn't know that; she didn't know that Julie and Sophie had lived in Torremolinos. She didn't know where they were from and didn't care either. As far as she was concerned they were two homeless girls who were sold to them in Moscow. What would she think if Sophie told her that her parents lived only a few miles away? Madame had unwittingly brought them home. She smiled to herself.

When Julie and Sophie had arrived here from Moscow, they'd been sedated, so at first, they weren't sure where they were, although it was soon obvious they were somewhere in

Spain. But then they began to realise that the area looked familiar, and one day Sophie heard Igor boasting about how he was going to open a restaurant when he had enough money, and it would be near here, on the coast in Marbella. Of course he didn't say that in front of Madame; she'd have been furious. In some ways it had been comforting to know that her parents and her two brothers were just down the road in Torremolinos, and then on other days it made her want to scream with rage, to be so near to them and yet so far.

She shivered; the wind was getting stronger, and the garden lamps lit up the swaying palm trees. She pulled the back door shut and relocked it just as the kitchen door opened and in walked Madame's husband.

'Sophie, what are you doing down here?' he asked, smiling at her. He was wearing green silk pyjamas and his feet were bare. She could smell his aftershave, heavy and cloying.

She pulled her robe around her and said, 'I was thirsty.'

'Me too. Here let me pour you a glass of milk.'

She watched as he poured her the milk and then took a bottle of vodka from the freezer and poured some into a glass.

'Would you like some in your milk?' he asked, staring at her.

She desperately wanted to leave and run back to her room, but she was frightened he'd follow her, so she shook her head and said, 'The milk is fine, thank you.'

'So Sophie, I suppose you miss your friend Julie?'

She nodded. Fear was making her tongue-tied.

'She was a delightful child. I admit, I miss her too.' He pulled a chair close to him. 'Sit down, my dear, while you drink your milk. It's nice to be able to talk to you. I don't see much of you, you know; you're always scurrying about doing things. I expect my wife keeps you very busy.'

Sophie is Still Missing

Sophie's stomach was churning; she had to get away, even if it meant going back into her cramped room. 'I think I can hear Madame,' she said. 'I'd better go to bed. I have a lot to do, tomorrow.' She could see he looked annoyed, but she ignored him and drank down the milk as quickly as she could, then hurried out of the kitchen before he could stop her.

Sophie is Still Missing

CHAPTER 18

It was already getting dark in the office and JD was tired; she would have liked to have gone home and got into a relaxing bath, but they needed to review the case. At last she felt they were getting somewhere. She switched on the lights and was letting down the blinds when she saw a movement opposite. A man was standing in the doorway of an abandoned building. There was something suspicious about the way he stood completely still, as though he didn't want to be seen. Was he watching her? She finished pulling down the blinds and went outside to see who it was. There was nobody there. Either she'd been imagining it or he knew she'd seen him. She looked down the alleyways; she could see no-one except a group of young girls looking in the window of a dress shop.

'Hi, JD. What's up?' asked Nacho, coming from the direction of the Bishop's Palace.

'Did you pass anyone in the alley?' she asked. 'A man?'

'Not that I recall. There was a couple, tourists, I think. They stopped for a coffee at Mario's, just as I was leaving. Why?'

'I think someone was watching the agency, but when I went out he'd gone.'

'Do you think it was the person who broke in before? Did you recognise him?'

'No. It was too dark. Anyway I never got a good look at the intruder; it could have been anyone wearing a black hoody. Don't worry; it was probably my imagination.'

'Linda here?' asked Nacho.

'Not yet. Why don't you update the board, while we wait for her.'

JD had been puzzling all day over why Julie had been found inside the Cofradía; it didn't make sense. It was risky to take her there, even if it was the middle of the night. So why take that risk? She sat watching Nacho adding comments to the board; he'd been to speak to Jorge that morning, so he might have some more information on it.

'Good evening all,' said a breezy Linda, taking off her coat and sitting down beside JD.

'You're looking pleased with yourself,' said JD.

'Yes I am, I suppose. Been to the school, saw Fiona and had a few hours with my lovely husband. So, all in all, a successful day.'

'Okay, let's get started. Linda, what did Miss Hardy have to tell you?'

'She didn't add anything to what she'd already told us, until I showed her the photo of Ponytail, or Kevin as I should call him now. She saw him chatting to some of the older boys at the end of last term, just outside the school gate. I spoke to two boys who knew him; he took them to the Crooked Cat in Fuengirola to play pool.'

'Nacho found him on Instagram,' said JD. 'So Kevin was hanging around with the Sixth Formers at the girls' school?'

'Yes, but the boys weren't keen on the club; apparently it was too expensive for them.'

'Did they recognise our Moroccan?'

'Yes, they saw him at the club. One of the boys said he seemed very friendly with Kevin.'

'That's interesting. So what do we know about this place?' asked JD.

'Well, I googled it and it sounds a bit of a dive to me,' said Linda. 'Members only. I expect Kevin signed them in.'

'We need to check it out. Better if you go Nacho? You'll draw less attention than Linda or me.'

'Okay, but how will I get in if I'm not a member?'

'Take your guitar with you and say you're looking for a gig for your band. You'll think of something,' said JD. 'You'll probably fit in very well. But don't let them know you're looking for anyone.'

'Okay Boss.'

'Anything else from the school, Linda?'

'No.'

'Doesn't Ricky go to the same school as his sister? He must be in the Sixth Form by now?' asked Nacho. 'Maybe it's worth speaking to him again.'

'Yes, good idea. How did you get on with Jorge?'

'Well, he didn't recognise Kevin or the Moroccan. I pressed him about how easy it was to get a key to the *Cofradía*, but it seems you don't need one; they have an entry code system.'

'So we just have to work out who could have got hold of the entry code,' said Linda.

'He's going to send me a list of those who have the code; it's updated every month and emailed to them.'

'Not very secure then.'

'No. Anyone could intercept an email, or look at someone's computer.'

'If it's changed every month, I bet people write it down,' said Linda.

'Or put it on their mobile.'

'So what are you saying? It's easier to find out the code than steal a key?' said JD.

'Yes,' Linda and Nacho said in unison.

'So who was able to access it? Did you ask Jorge if there was anyone there he didn't know, any strangers hanging about?'

'He said that a few days before they discovered Julie's body, there was a press photographer in the *Cofradía*.'

'The press are everywhere during Holy Week,' said Linda. 'That's not unusual.'

'Yes, but this one wanted to go inside to take photos of the thrones on their trestles. According to Jorge, that is a bit unusual.'

'So we ought to check it out. Which paper did he work for?'

'He didn't tell him. Also the man was left alone for a while, because Jorge had to do something. And he didn't see him leave.'

'I don't suppose they have any CCTV?' asked JD.

Nacho shook his head. 'No, despite the fact that he says there are some valuable things in there. And by the way, nothing was missing, so there was no robbery.'

'How many newspapers are there in Málaga?'

Nacho shrugged. 'About ten?'

'Ring round them all and speak to their photographers.'

'But that's dozens,' Nacho said. 'Is it worth it? Why would a newspaper photographer want to murder Julie?'

'Did he have a press badge?'

'He showed some sort of identification to Jorge, but I don't think Jorge looked at it carefully.'

'So, the photographer might have been lying. I know this has to have some connection to the Brotherhood,' said JD. 'But what?'

'Jorge vigorously denies that any of the Brothers would be involved. He says everyone knows each other; it really is a brotherhood. You can only get in there by stepping into dead men's shoes.'

'No other way?' asked Linda.

'Well, he was a bit cagey about it, but it sounds to me that if you are powerful enough and/or rich enough you can join.'

'That's always the way,' said JD. 'So do we know who these elite members are?'

'He's getting me a list of them. But he wasn't very happy.' Nacho scribbled 'Press photographer' and 'Brothers' on the wall.

'Fiona gave me this,' said Linda, putting the crucifix on the table. 'She said the police gave it to her; they thought it was Julie's.' She took it out of the bag and held it up so they could see it. 'Fiona said it wasn't Julie's; she'd never seen it before, and Beverley knew nothing about it either.'

'Was it on her body when they found her?' asked Nacho. 'It didn't say anything about it in the report.'

'You're right. That's strange, don't you think?' said JD.

'Maybe it got missed off the list of her personal effects.'

'Why didn't Fiona mention it the first time you spoke to her, Linda?'

Her assistant looked embarrassed. 'Actually JD, she did. I took a photo of it with my phone, but forgot to tell you. Sorry.'

'Bloody hell, Linda. This could be the only bit of solid evidence we've found, and you forgot.' She turned away from her and snapped, 'What is it, Nacho? What are you thinking? Come on. Don't keep us in suspense.'

Nacho was staring at the crucifix. 'I've seen one like that before, JD. Jorge was wearing an identical one.'

'So it looks as though we may have something at last. And someone didn't want anyone to know about it,' said JD. 'Other than Linda, that is.'

'Do we think the killer put it on her?' asked Linda, ignoring the jibe.

Sophie is Still Missing

'That's what we need to find out. Get over to the *Cofradía*, right away, Nacho and see what you can find out about these crucifixes. Who has them? Is it standard issue to the Brothers? Or do only certain people have them? That list of members is more important than ever, now. I have a feeling that the key to this case lies in the Brotherhood of the Virgin of Remorse.'

'Don't you want to know what I found on Julie's social media page?' Nacho asked.

Both JD and Linda looked up.

'You've found something?' said Linda. 'What?'

'And spare us the technical details,' added JD.

Nacho frowned at them. 'You two don't understand how much work goes into breaking into some of these web sites. Facebook is easy but Kik is designed to keep people out.'

'Okay, we understand,' said JD. 'Just get on with it.'

'Well, as I said before, there was nothing on the usual sites, nothing of any interest, but it seems that Julie opened a page on Kik. It's a site where they can text for free but it doesn't show up on their phone messaging service. Kids like it because their parents can't trace what they're texting. In itself it's not that different from the other messaging systems but Kik has two apps, Match and Chat, and Flirt. These can be dangerous for teenagers, because the paedos can contact them anonymously. They can pretend to be someone else and lie about their age, and it's hard to trace them.'

'So you think Julie contacted her killer on Kik, or one of its apps?' asked Linda.

'I don't know if she contacted her killer, but she definitely contacted Kevin. Here, this is what I found.' He handed them each a printed sheet. 'She arranged to meet him and his friend—sadly she doesn't mention his name—on the Saturday afternoon.

Look, she asks whether she should bring a change of clothes and he says, not necessary.'

'Everything will be provided,' JD continued. 'So they knew they weren't just going out for the evening.'

'And, she asks about money,' said Linda. 'The stupid girl, where did she think they were taking her?'

'When was that?' asked JD.

'Two days before she disappeared. There was another message on the Friday and then Kevin tells her to stop using all her social media accounts in case her parents see them. After that, nothing.'

'We should give this to the police. It definitely links Kevin to her disappearance,' said Linda.

'But it doesn't mention Sophie. Does that mean she wasn't with Julie? Did something happen to her?' asked JD. 'You need to keep looking, Nacho. We need to find out if Sophie is still alive.'

'I still think we should tell the police. We can't hang on to this information. Kevin might be able to help them find her,' said Linda.

'Once a case is closed, they are reluctant to re-open it; it means they have to spend more money,' said JD. 'Anyway Interpol are handling the abduction now and they aren't going to listen to us.'

'That's another thing,' said Nacho. 'Kevin is back in England, according to his Tik Tok page. He posted this evening. Look.' He swivelled his computer round so that they could see, and brought up a photo of Kevin standing outside Etihad Stadium, holding up a blue and white scarf in one hand and an entrance ticket in the other.

'Is it a recent photo?'

'I'm pretty sure it is. I checked and there was a home match last Saturday.'

'Can you download that page?'

'Yes.'

'Good, I'll send it to my old mate, Bill, and see what he can do to help.'

'I still think we should leave it to the police, JD. This is getting serious now.'

'One girl dead and the other missing, it's always been serious, Linda. We'll do it my way for now. If that doesn't work then I'll take everything we've got down to the Guardia Civil.'

'And if Sophie's body turns up in the meantime?'

JD knew Linda was beginning to identify with the case. She had two teenage girls of her own; it could so easily be them.

'Right, this is what we know. The girls were lured away by Kevin, and then abducted by some other men, whom we've yet to identify. They'd been missing for seven months, when suddenly Julie's body turns up in Málaga. We can't be sure why they wanted to abduct those girls, but I think we can safely guess it was to sell them, or turn them into prostitutes. Girls of that age can be worth a lot of money in the right marketplace. So why on earth did someone leave her body in the *Cofradía*, where it was bound to be found? There's something we're missing here.'

'It's not the same man,' said Nacho. 'We should be looking at two different crimes, the abduction and the murder.'

Linda stared at him. 'You're right. Of course. It's obvious that the people who abducted her would never have shown her that kind of respect, putting her body right next to the Virgin Mary and sprinkling her with pink carnations,' she said.

'Okay. So let's focus on the murder for the moment. What do we know about this man—I think we can safely assume for now that it's a man?' asked JD.

'He's Catholic.' Nacho began scribbling on the board again.

'He's got connections to the Brotherhood.'

'He drives a black car, or dark colour anyway.'

'Do we know the make? I think we should look more closely at the hit and run.'

'I'll check it out tomorrow,' said Nacho. 'It's not a make I recognise, but then I'm not great on cars.'

'It's probably foreign. Have we heard back on the number plates?' asked Linda.

'Not yet. Anything else?' asked JD.

Both her assistants shook their heads.

'Okay, I'll check that out with Tim, tomorrow.' If Nacho was right, and the car was coming from the centre when the speed camera caught it, then there should be more CCTV somewhere along the route. 'Nacho, how long would it take you to print out the quickest route between the centre and the spot where the car was caught speeding?'

'No time at all. I can do it for you as soon as we've finished. But it will be a hell of a lot of CCTV to go through, and that's if they still have it.'

'Yes, but we only need to look at one lot, as long as it's on the route.' She closed her laptop and said, 'Right, the plan for tomorrow guys, is this. I'll visit Jorge about the crucifix, so that you, Nacho, can concentrate on looking for traces of Sophie on social media. There has to be something. This would be too tempting for the girls; they'd be dying to tell someone where they were. And I'll speak to Tim again.'

'What about me?' asked Linda. 'What do you want me to do?'

'I'd like you to go and see Ricky again, before his father spirits the family off to England. Find out if he knew that the girls were seeing Kevin. Then, in the evening, I want you to take Nacho to the Crooked Cat; he can't go there on his bike. Keep an eye out for anyone that could be of interest, but don't go inside; I think you'd be too conspicuous. Take the surveillance camera.'

'Okay. I suppose by conspicuous, you mean old?'

JD smiled, 'You said it.'

'And you'll do something about Kevin?' Linda asked.

'I will. I promise. Just let's wait a couple more days before we contact anyone about him.'

'And the crucifix?' she asked, dangling it by its chain. 'You'll need that.'

'Yes. I'm interested to hear what Jorge has to say about it. Odd that he hasn't mentioned it. He saw the girl. Didn't he think it was a strange coincidence that she wore the same crucifix?' JD took it from her assistant, slipped it over her head and tucked it inside her tee-shirt. 'If this belonged to her killer, then it's possible this was what our intruder was looking for when he ransacked the office.'

CHAPTER 19

Beverley poured herself a glass of Sauvignon and sat down. Jim was out as usual; she tried not to think about where he might be. When he went to work that morning he said he would be home for lunch; that had been eight hours ago.

'Mum, I'm going round to Shaun's for a bit,' Ricky said, grabbing his coat and heading for the door.

'Don't you want any supper?' she asked his retreating back.

'I'll have something there.' The door slammed and he was gone.

She desperately wanted a cigarette, but she'd promised Jim that she'd try to stop smoking; it was harder than he realised. Her husband had never smoked; he just couldn't understand the awful craving for nicotine that clawed at her insides.

The house was very quiet; even the cat had slipped out through the cat flap to begin his nightly prowl around the garden. How different it had been when they first moved to Spain; Sophie had been eight then. She had been such a delight. After having two boys Beverley had been so excited to have a daughter, someone to share girly things with. And Sophie had been a real girly girl; she played with her dolls for hours, pushing them around the garden in an old pram, organising them into rows and pretending it was a classroom. Beverley had often wondered what Sophie's teacher would have thought if she could have heard her daughter bossing the dolls about in a high pitched voice, which was presumably supposed to sound like hers. Jim had said that she was stereotyping their daughter by buying her so many pink clothes, but it wasn't her intention. That's what Sophie wanted; she didn't like denim, or blue or any other colour for that matter, except pink. Then, by the time she was thirteen, she'd grown out of it and gone to the other extreme, jeans with holes in the knees, tight black sweaters, shiny black boots, and the battle began over when she'd be old enough to have a tattoo. But she never threw out her dolls. They still sat in her room; Beverley had arranged them on her bed and they sat there, their sightless eyes staring at the door, waiting for Sophie to come home.

She wiped a tear from her cheek and switched on the television. At this time of night there was usually a good drama to watch; tonight it was a new series, called 'What's Happened to Alfie?'.

She felt she shouldn't be watching it; it would be too close to home, but she was compelled to switch it on. As usual, it started innocuously enough with a young couple on holiday in Denmark but then suddenly their small son had disappeared. That's how it was. One minute they're there and then they're not. You watched it on the screen and it was entertainment, but when it actually happened…. Her mind froze as she desperately tried to remember the last time she saw Sophie, the last words they said to each other, where they were, what she had been doing at the time. She wanted to recall it all in its minute details but she couldn't. It slipped away from her like smoke through her fingers.

She tried to concentrate on the drama. The father was distraught. She usually liked the actor who played his part, but he was too dramatic, too hysterical in this role. Jim hadn't been like that. Not at first, anyway. They had both been numb, unable to comprehend what was happening. The mother was more realistic; she looked as though all the life had been sucked out of her. That was just how Beverley had felt. That was how she still felt. She understood why people said they wanted to die when something like that happened to them. It wasn't an exaggeration; it wasn't hyperbole—it was true. Life suddenly seemed very insignificant. What was the point in going on when the person you loved had disappeared? It would have been bad enough if Sophie had died, but she knew she would have got over it in time. This however, this was something different. Not to know where she was, whether she was alive or dead, happy or sad, all the time wondering if she was frightened; this was so hard to bear. To be constantly asking yourself if she was suffering. Had her daughter given up hope? Was she all alone now? Or had they killed her as well as her friend?

She poured herself some more wine and resisted the temptation to light a cigarette. The detective had appeared on the scene now. He was supposed to find the child by some mixture of instinct, experience and the detection of vital clues. By the end of the series she fully expected the boy to be back at home with his parents, thanks to the efforts of this wonderful detective. That was what she'd hoped would happen when she'd spoken to Jacaranda Dunne, but so far their private investigator had found nothing new. There was still no sign of Sophie; things were just the same. It wasn't the detective's fault; it had been too long. Nobody was going to bring Sophie back to them now. She was dead, or somewhere where they'd never be able to find her. A wave of anger suddenly swept over Beverley and she hurled her glass of wine at the television with all the force she could manage. The glass shattered into a hundred pieces and fell onto the white rug; the wine ran down the screen. She stared at it and all she could think was, thank goodness it wasn't red wine. Then she burst into tears.

Sophie is Still Missing

She was picking up the pieces of glass when Jim arrived home. She saw him look at the television, go into the kitchen and pick up a cloth then begin to wipe up the wine.

'Having a bad day?' he asked, squatting down beside her and picking up some glass.

She swallowed back her tears and said, 'Sorry. I just lost it for a moment.'

'So you decided to take it out on the telly? Can't have been a very good programme.'

She smiled. 'I should never have started watching it. It was some silly drama about a missing boy.'

'Big mistake, Bev. Come on, let's find something to eat, if that son of ours has left anything in the fridge, that is. It's like a swarm of locusts have been in there whenever he gets home from school.' He stood up and pulled her to her feet.

'You're late,' she said. 'Where have you been?'

'Just tying up some loose ends.' He went into the kitchen and opened the fridge. 'Lasagne. That's good. Shall I pop it in the oven?'

'Please.' She paused. 'Jim have you any idea where Sophie's iPad is?'

'I didn't know she had one,' he said, pulling the foil cover off the lasagne and putting it in the oven. '150 degrees?'

She nodded. 'Yes. I bought her one for her birthday. Just before she disappeared.'

'Maybe she took it with her?'

'But in that case why didn't she take her charger and her phone? Doesn't make sense that it's the only thing missing.'

'Are you sure it's not in her room?'

'I've looked everywhere.'

'Maybe she hid it. You know she was becoming a bit secretive.'

She looked at him. Although she didn't like to admit it, he was right; Sophie had been much more secretive, not wanting to tell them where she was going or who with, and now they knew she'd lied to them about going to the cinema with her brother. So maybe her iPad was still here.

'Where could she have hidden it?' she asked him. 'She knew I went in her room to tidy up; she'd never hide it in there.'

'So not in there, then. And not in our room. What about Zak's bedroom?'

Of course, she'd barely touched her older son's room since he went back to England; she'd hoovered it and changed the bed, just in case he came back, but otherwise it was as he'd left it.

'Come on, I'll help you look for it, while we're waiting for the lasagne to cook,' Jim said, taking her arm.

Beverley felt uncomfortable searching Zak's room—her son hated anyone to touch his things—but then he wasn't here and this was an emergency, she told herself. She checked the chest of drawers while Jim went through the wardrobe.

They searched in silence for a bit, then Jim said, 'No, there's nothing here. What about Ricky?'

'Yes, he was always asking her if he could use it. But if he's got it, why hasn't he said anything?'

'Where is he?'

'At Shaun's.'

'I'll ring him,' said Jim, while Beverley sat on the bed looking around her older son's room and wishing he was there with them. The house was so empty these days.

After a few minutes, her husband put his mobile in his pocket and said, 'Well that son of ours has a lot to answer for.

Sophie is Still Missing

He's had her tablet all this time. He said he only wanted to borrow it for a while but then he was too embarrassed to give it back.'

'So where is it?'

'He left it at Shaun's house. He's bringing it round now.'

'How could he be so stupid? He knew the detective was asking about it.'

Well we might as well have some supper while we wait for him,' said Jim, heading back to the kitchen.

Beverley went to wash her face and tidy her hair. She was angry with Ricky but she was also excited. Maybe there would be something on the iPad that would explain where Sophie had gone; maybe this was the breakthrough they'd been waiting for.

When she went into the kitchen, Jim was sitting at the table with the newspaper open in front of him.

He looked up at her. 'Why?' was all he said, looking shocked and unhappy. 'Why, Beverley?'

'I think you know why, Jim. You and Fiona, that's why. Did you think I didn't know about you two? At least I didn't choose your best friend to mess around with.'

'That's all over, now. I've told her I couldn't carry on deceiving you like that. I told her you needed me.'

'Would it have made any difference to your decision if you'd known I was seeing someone?' she asked.

'No. This family is falling apart, and I don't want that to happen. Sophie's disappearance has affected us all, but we have to stick together, for the boys' sake. We can't abandon them.' He picked up the newspaper and threw it in the rubbish bin.

She looked at her husband. 'It wasn't serious,' she said. 'It was a one night stand. I was lonely. You were always out and I knew you were with her. Then you said you were going to the Motor Show and I knew it was a lie. So when he invited me to go for a drink, I agreed. I was flattered. That's all there was to it. And I wanted to get back at you.'

'Revenge?'

'Mostly.'

'Is it over?' he asked.

'Yes. It was one time and I immediately regretted it. Don't you want to know who he was?'

'Not really. It's better like this.' He held out his arms. 'Come here. I'm so sorry, Beverley. I really am. We'll get through this, you see. We'll go back to England with Ricky and we'll be a family again.'

She began to pull away from him.

'I know it won't be like before, and we won't forget Sophie, but we have to come to terms with it.'

'I can't, Jim. I just can't leave until I know what has happened to her.'

'I understand. Really I do. We'll leave it a few more months; the sale's not due to be completed until January. We can think about it then. Okay?'

'Okay.' He was feeling guilty; she could see that, but nevertheless he was right. They had to try to hold the family together, for when Sophie came home.

After they'd finished the lasagne, she slipped outside for a cigarette to calm her nerves, while Jim cleared away. He was a strange man. His wife's infidelity was splashed all over the local paper and he was washing the dishes. He definitely had something on his conscience; maybe his affair with Fiona had been more serious than she'd thought. Maybe he'd been planning on leaving her and the boys.

'Ricky's here,' he called.

Her rather dishevelled and embarrassed son came into the kitchen and handed them to iPad. 'I'm so sorry Mum. I was going to tell you. Honestly. I just didn't know how to.'

'Is it charged up?' asked his father.

'Yes.'

'Give it to me. I'll deal with you later. Do you want to look at it, Bev, or shall I?' he asked.

'We'll do it , together,' she said, stubbing out her cigarette and coming inside. Her stomach was churning with excitement.

'There could be nothing on it,' Jim said. 'Nothing to say where she is. Don't get your hopes up, Bev.'

At first it seemed as though he was right; there were dozens of messages to Julie but none of them made much sense to them. Then, at last, there was one that grabbed their attention. It was from Julie. Bev's eyes filled with tears as she thought of the dead girl, joking and sending messages to her friend. 'You read it,' she said. 'I can't.'

'Okay.' Jim began to read Julie's post. 'Guess what. It's on. Meet them in the usual place on Saturday. K says not to bring anything with us. They'll buy us everything we need. She's put a load of those funny emoji things after the message.'

'So they ran away? I can't believe that Sophie would do that to us.' Beverley was horrified. Her daughter had planned this. She hadn't been kidnapped. She'd run away. How could she do that to them? If she'd been in pain before, it was now much worse. What had she done to her daughter that would make her run away?

'You don't know that, Bev. Yes, they planned something, but I don't think they meant to stay away all this time. Something must have gone wrong.'

'So who is K? And what was Julie talking about? And why tell them not to take anything? It's all so strange.'

Sophie is Still Missing

'I think they were tricked into it by promises of new clothes, or whatever. They may not have intended to be away for long but whoever they were meeting didn't want them to return or to be traced, hence no mobiles.'

'So you think they were abducted?' She stared at the smiling face of her daughter gazing up at her from the iPad. 'What a silly girl. My beautiful, beautiful, silly girl.'

'Let's see if she took any photos.' Jim clicked onto iPhotos and started scrolling through them. There were dozens of snaps of their neighbour's dog, and even more of their own cat. There were photos of her friends at school, of Ricky and his mates, and some young men whom they didn't recognise. He zoomed in on one of the photos and asked her, 'Who are they? Are they friends of Ricky?' He went to the stairs and called, 'Ricky. Come down here a minute.'

'Yes, what is it?'

'Do you know any of these boys?' He handed him the iPad.

'No. That detective woman asked me about him,' he pointed to the boy with a ponytail, 'but I don't recognise any of them.'

'They're not from your school?'

'No, definitely not.'

'What about where was it taken?'

Ricky shook his head.

'Do you think that could be the place Julie mentions in her text? The usual place?' Beverley asked, excitement in her voice.

'Well, it looks like a bar, but not one I recognise from around here. What does it say on the sign?' He zoomed in even further, and although the image was out of focus the shape of an arched cat was clearly visible. 'I think we need to give the iPad to JD,' he said. 'I'll take it to her in the morning.'

'Why wait? Let's ring her now.'

'Okay, but neither of us are in a fit state to drive; we've both been drinking.'

She handed him JD's business card and while he rang the detective and explained how they'd found Sophie's iPad, she continued looking through the photographs. It was painful to look at them: Sophie on the beach, Sophie and Julie, lying on her bed pulling silly faces, posing and pouting at the camera, having fun. The photos were bitter-sweet and it broke her heart to remember how funny and full of life her daughter had been. Where was she now? Please God, she wasn't lying dead in some dark, cold place.

'She's sending someone round to pick it up,' Jim said. 'Nacho, he's called. He'll be able to find out if there's anything else hidden on the iPad, but I told her I doubted it. Sophie was no computer expert. She said he would check her browsing history; it could tell us what she was thinking about during those days before she went missing.'

'Did you tell her about the bar?'

'Yes, she was very interested in that. Said it sounded like somewhere she knew.'

'Oh, Jim. Perhaps we're going to find her after all.' For the first time in a long while she felt hopeful.

CHAPTER 20

Something woke her. Sweat was trickling down her neck. Then the nightmare came back to her in a flash; she was there, running and running, yet not moving. She could feel her heart hammering in her chest. She wanted to cry out, to scream for help but no sound came. She just had to get away from him but she seemed to be going nowhere. She couldn't escape. There was nowhere to go. The end of the harbour wall lay in front of her. Beyond it, nothing but a wide expanse of grey sea.

Suddenly it was over. JD opened her eyes and sat up. The street light cast a pale luminescence around her room. Steed. She was letting him get into her head. She couldn't allow that. She switched on the bedside light and got up and went into the kitchen. A half empty bottle of Rioja was on the table. She poured a little into a glass and took it back to bed. Her digital clock showed 05.00. She'd drink the wine and try to get back to sleep.

For a while she tossed and turned, trying not to think about her adversary. But it was impossible. She needed a diversion. She began to go over what they'd found out about the girls' disappearance. They were moving forward but time was running out for Sophie. She knew it. JD was convinced that Sophie was still alive, but for how long?

Maybe the girl's iPad would give them some more clues. Nacho had texted her to say he'd picked it up but hadn't said anything else. She'd wanted to ring him last night and ask him what was on it, but forced herself to wait until the morning; just because she didn't have a life outside work, it didn't mean her staff couldn't have one, either.

Sleep refused to come, so in the end she got out of bed and put on her running clothes. It was ages since she'd gone for a run in the early morning; it was time she started again.

The streets were deserted, so she turned left out of the apartment block and ran towards the sea, past the bus station and through the main entrance to the port. The promenade that bordered the harbour was deserted except for a few runners like herself, and a couple of dog walkers. She soon slipped into an easy rhythm and, feeling a burst of energy, lengthened her stride. She was heading east and the sun was just creeping over the horizon. For a moment she forgot about the case, and Steed, and Federico, even the unpaid bills; all she was aware of was the pounding of her feet on the ground and the cool morning air on her face. She arrived at the end of the harbour wall and doubled over, gasping for breath. The sun was fully visible now, an enormous orange ball of fire gleaming across the sea. She could see the fishing boats on the horizon; they would soon be coming in with their nightly catch. She took some deep breaths and turned back towards the city.

Nacho was already at his desk, the iPad in front of him. JD handed him his coffee and pulled her chair up next to his.

'Did you ever find out if someone had been tampering with my computer?' she asked, pulling the plastic top off her coffee cup.

'From the break-in? Yes, I did. Sorry, I forgot to tell you; so much else going on.'

'That's okay. What did you find?'

Sophie is Still Missing

'Well someone had definitely opened your computer that night. They downloaded that photograph at ten forty-five. But I couldn't find anything else unusual. Are you sure you didn't do it yourself?'

'No, I didn't. I'm not going crazy, you know.' She could feel her heart racing. 'At ten forty-five I was still in the bar. I didn't leave until eleven. I remember checking my watch to see if I'd missed the last bus. And I had. So how did someone gain access to my computer anyway?'

'Pretty simple, I'd say,' said Nacho pointing to the yellow stickers she had all over her desk.

'*Joder*. My password.'

'You should find a better way of remembering it, Boss.'

She was puzzled. Who on earth had it been? Did this have anything to do with Steed? The awful feeling of panic she had during her nightmare came back to her with its full force. It was ridiculous. She had to do something to stop this fixation on Steed. After all he was in England. He wouldn't be able to enter Spain without someone knowing.

'Are you all right, Boss?'

'Yes. Fine. Sorry, I was miles away. Well? Found anything useful?'

'Not sure, but I think we may have proof that the girls were at the Crooked Cat and that they had met both Kevin and the Moroccan. Look at these photos.' He turned the iPad so she could see better. 'There. That's the pub sign outside the Crooked Cat. And there's Julie with the two of them. They'd been texting each other about their plans. I've printed a copy out for you.' He handed it to her. 'It was definitely no accident that they went off with them that Saturday; it had been planned from the start.'

'Anything in the browsing history?'

'Just bits and pieces. Mostly she was reading about film stars and football players, oh and make-up. She seemed very interested in that. But one thing was interesting; she googled this posh hotel in Tangier, five star with a swimming pool, jacuzzis, the lot. Do you think they had promised to take them there?'

'It's possible, but they'd need their passports to go to Morocco. Do we know if they had passports? Has anyone mentioned them?'

'Yes, Sophie didn't take hers with her and Julie didn't have a valid one. Anyway I'm sure the police would have checked customs as part of their enquiry. Of course, they may have had fake ones.'

'Here's something,' said Nacho. 'There are some earlier text messages between Sophie and Julie. It seems they knew about Fiona and Jim having an affair.'

'Is that Sophie's iPad? What does the message say?' asked Linda, who'd just arrived. She hung her jacket over the back of her chair and sat down.

'Sophie texts Julie first.' Nacho began to read from the screen. 'Worried about my poor Mum. She doesn't deserve this. Then Julie replies: She probably knew all about it. They all deserve to suffer, but I agree, it's not your mum's fault. Nor my dad's. But he doesn't care about me anyway. He's never around. He didn't even remember my birthday last year.'

'What does Sophie say to that?'

'Well, we won't be gone for all that long. When we get our new phones we can ring them and tell them we're all right.'

'Don't be silly. They won't even miss us.'

'My mum will, said Sophie.'

'Definitely some resentment there on Julie's part,' said Linda. 'Maybe it's not the first time her mother has cheated on her father. Not much of a life being married to someone on the rigs; they're never at home.'

The agency phone rang.

'JD Detective Agency,' said Linda, in her best telephone voice. 'Oh Beverley, how are you?'

'Not great.'

'I understand, but finding the iPad was a good move; we now have proof that Sophie and Julie knew those men.'

'So, you can arrest them?'

'We can look into it.'

'But you said you knew the place where they were. That bar.'

'Yes, we're going to check it out. It's a good lead. I'm positive something will come of it.'

'But you'll tell the police, won't you?'

'When we're sure we have enough proof, yes of course we will. Look, I have to go now, Beverley, I'm in a meeting. I'll ring you as soon as I have some news.'

'Is she all right?' asked Nacho.

'She sounded very disappointed. I think she thought that the iPad would reveal their kidnappers,' said Linda.

'I'll send photos of the girls and the two men to the hotel in Tangier to see if they recognise them,' said Nacho.

'Good. Let's hope they do. I'm going to ring Tim and see if he can tell us anything more about the car,' said JD.

She pulled out the case file and stared at it. There were a lot of leads but they weren't getting them very far at the moment. Maybe Tim had something for them. She punched in his number and waited.

'Good morning, JD. You're bright and early.'

'Any more news on the car, Tim?' she asked, putting him on speaker so she could open up her computer.

Sophie is Still Missing

'Straight to the point, as always,' he said. 'Actually yes, I do have some news for you. Your car is Russian, and a pretty nice one, too. It's a Pobeda M20. Expensive, and must be fairly new because that's the most recent model.'

JD quickly typed it into Google. 'I've never heard of it, but I'll take your word for it.' The image of a sleek black car came on her screen. He was right; it did look expensive. 'So we can confirm that the car's Russian, but what about the driver? Did it have Russian number plates?'

'Can't tell you anything about the driver, but what I can tell you is that the car belongs to the Russian embassy. I thought those green plates looked familiar; it's a consular car.'

'So a consular officer from the Russian embassy in Madrid, was in Málaga and killed a policeman in a hit and run accident? Is that what you're saying?'

'Not necessarily from Madrid. There's an Honorary Consulate of Russia in Málaga.'

'Really.'

'And, you're assuming it was an accident, JD.'

'I'm not assuming anything, Tim. I'm just gathering facts.'

'How's the investigation going, anyway?'

'We're making progress,' she said cagily. 'I don't suppose it was your paper that sent a photographer to take some photos at the *Cofradía* where Julie's body was found?'

'Yes, but the police wouldn't let anyone in.'

'No, I mean before she was killed. A man, claiming he was a photographer for some local newspaper, said he wanted photographs of the Virgin and the Christ before they were taken out.'

'What, on the trestles? That sounds odd. We've got plenty of stock photos for that kind of thing. What we usually want are photos of the procession; they are much more interesting. So, you think he was an imposter? Maybe the man who killed Julie?'

His imagination was running away with him; if she wasn't careful he'd have it all over the front page. She cringed as she imagined the headline: Fake photographer is the Virgin Princess killer. 'I don't think anything at the moment, Tim. As I said, I'm just checking things out.'

'Well, I'll ask, but I would doubt it.'

'Thanks. I appreciate it. Ring me if you have something. Bye.' She hung up before he could ask her anything else.

Nacho had transferred the Instagram photographs to her computer, so she began to go through them one by one hoping to see anything that would help them identify the mystery boy in the photo booth with Julie and Sophie.

'You do realise that he might have nothing to do with them.' said Linda, who was looking over her shoulder. 'Kids do things like that. He might have thought it was a great laugh to get in on their photo, and then just walked away.'

'I know. That's why I'm seeing if he turns up anywhere else.' JD swiped across to yet another photo of the girls pouting at the camera. 'So far, it seems to be just the two of them. No wait a minute, here's some of them on the beach. Bingo. There he is. I'll send it to your phone. You can show it to Ricky when you speak to him. He may know him. He looks about his age.'

'Okay JD. I thought I'd try to catch Ricky in his break.'

'And see if our mystery guy turns up anywhere else on Sophie's iPad, Nacho. We need to know if he was friend or someone stalking them.'

'Okay Boss. What did Tim say?'

'He's identified the car; it belongs to the Russian Embassy.'

'As we thought. So now we need to know who it was allocated to.'

Sophie is Still Missing

'Tim wasn't able to find out anything else, but Federico might. I'll call him later, when I've seen Jorge. Give me his home address, Nacho; I'd like to talk to him away from the *Cofradía*, and preferably not in a church. Maybe he'll be more open with me. I hope he doesn't live outside the city,' she added.

'No, he has a flat in Miraflores; it's easy to get to. I'll WhatsApp you the address. There're plenty of buses out that way.'

Her phone rang; it was Paco, her mother's boyfriend. Damn. She'd promised to get in touch with him and had forgotten all about it. '*Buenos días*, Paco. I was about to ring you.'

'*Buenos días*, JD. How are you fixed for Saturday? I have to put our names on the list today if you want to play.'

JD was about to make an excuse about being too busy with the investigation, then changed her mind. It might do her good to get away from the case for a few hours and relax, and besides which she was dying to see if Paraíso Park was as good as everyone said it was. Although they were making progress with the case, she was beginning to feel that she couldn't see the wood for the trees. There were so many pieces to this puzzle and so far she couldn't see the overall picture. 'Yes, put my name down. I'd love to play. I might not be on my game, though; I haven't played for a couple of months.'

'*Fantastico*. I will send you the teeing-off time when I have it. *Hasta pronto*.'

'*Adios, Paco*.'

'Another boyfriend?' asked Linda.

'My mother's actually. Not that it's any of your business. And weren't you going to the school?'

'Yes, Boss. I'm going now.'

Sophie is Still Missing

JD could hear Nacho asking about the photographer, then he put down the phone with a deep sigh. 'Only another ten to go,' he said.

'Well, there's no need to phone La Voz de Málaga; Tim is making enquiries but he's pretty sure they didn't send anyone.'

'Okay, only nine then.'

'What about the hotel in Tangier?'

'Nothing yet.'

'Well keep trying. We need to know where the girls were taken. Right, I'm going to visit Jorge. You keep the fort, Nacho, until I get back.'

CHAPTER 21

Linda was beginning to feel like a regular at the school; some of the younger children even waved at her as she walked across the playground looking for Ricky. However, the headmistress wasn't happy that she wanted to ask him more questions, and rather reluctantly agreed that Linda could speak to him again.

'Hi Ricky. How's it going?'

The boy grunted some sort of reply.

'I just wanted to ask you a couple more things.'

'I'm going to England next week,' he said.

'So it's a good job I'm here today then, isn't it,' said Linda. 'Are you pleased about going back?'

Ricky shrugged.

'Okay, tell me, do you know this boy?' She passed him the two photos of mystery boy.

'Darren.'

His answer came so quickly that Linda was taken aback. 'Is he a friend of yours?' she asked.

'Naw. He's in the 5th Form.'

'So he's the same age as Sophie?'

'Yeah.'

'Were they in the same class?'

'Yeah.'

'So where is Darren now?' she asked.

Ricky turned his head and nodded towards a group of boys kicking a football around the playground. 'Can I go now?' he asked.

'In a minute. Do you recognise this man?' She handed him a photo of Kevin.

'Naw. Who is he?'

'His name is Kevin. Have you heard of him?'

He looked at the photograph again. 'That's the guy who was on Sophie's iPad.'

'Yes, that's right. And you don't know him?'

'I said so, didn't I?'

'What about the Crooked Cat?'

Ricky looked bewildered. He shook his head. 'What's that, the Crooked Cat?'

'It's a club. One more question, did you know that your sister was seeing Kevin and his friends?'

At this news, Ricky looked genuinely surprised. 'What?' He looked at the photo again, studying the image. 'Naw, she wouldn't go out with anyone like that.'

'Like what?'

'She was shy around boys. Some of my mates fancied her, but she wouldn't even talk to them. Naw, she wouldn't have anything to do with someone like Kevin,' he repeated.

'What about Julie?'

'Yeah, well Julie liked older boys, so maybe.'

'But a photo of him was on Sophie's iPad.'

'So what? Doesn't mean she'd go out with him. I told you, Sophie wasn't like that. Julie probably sent it to her.'

'Like what?'

'Going out with older blokes.'

'Julie and your sister were meeting them in the shopping arcade when they were supposed to be at the cinema. You knew they were meeting some boys.'

'I guessed they were but they never said.'

'So you didn't know about Kevin.'

'No. Do you think he killed Julie?' Ricky continued to stare at the photograph.

'At the moment we don't know, but we do want to know as much as we can about him.' It looked as though their break was coming to an end, so Linda said, 'Thanks for your help, Ricky. I hope it all goes well for you in England.'

She headed for the footballers and called out, 'Can I speak to you, Darren?'

A sweaty young man was struggling into his school jacket as he walked towards her. 'I'm Darren. What do you want?'

'Hi. My name's Linda Prewitt. I'm a private investigator. I just wanted to ask you a couple of questions.'

'What about?'

'These girls.' She showed Darren the photos of him with Sophie and Julie. 'Are they friends of yours?'

'They used to be. Have you found Sophie yet?' he asked.

'Not yet I'm afraid, that's why I'm asking everyone who knew her if they can help.'

'I'll help if I can, but it's ages since those photos were taken; we'd stopped hanging out together. To be honest they began behaving a bit weird just before they disappeared. Never said where they were going and didn't hang out with anyone in our class. Sometimes they didn't turn up for classes at all, which was strange, because Sophie had never been absent before.'

'Was Julie your girlfriend?'

'No. We were just mates, and not even close mates. Julie wasn't interested in anyone at school, only Sophie.'

'When they didn't turn up for school, did you ask them why?'

'Yes, but they told me to mind my own business.'

'What about these two men? Did you ever see them?'

Sophie is Still Missing

'I saw them once with Julie and Sophie; Julie wanted me to go with them to a club, but I said no.'

'Why was that?'

'I didn't like the look of the blokes. They frightened me.'

'But you didn't mind the girls going with them?'

'They seemed to be great friends; I didn't think they were going to hurt them.'

'I don't suppose you know their names?'

He shook his head. 'No. I didn't want anything to do with them. My dad would have slaughtered me if he thought I was going to a club.'

It was obvious Linda wasn't going to get anything useful from him; all he'd done was confirm what she already knew. 'Thanks for your help, Darren. If you think of anything else, please give me a ring.' She handed him her card and watched as he charged across the playground to catch up his friends.

She walked back to her car, wondering if they were ever going to make a breakthrough with the case. She wished JD would listen to reason and take what they'd found to the police; they were starting to get out of their depth. Missing jewellery and lost dogs were one thing but Sophie's life might be in danger; they had to move quickly. She hoped JD and Nacho were having more success with the Brotherhood.

The school yard was quiet now with everyone back in class, so she decided to make a couple of phone calls as she walked back to her car.

'Hi Beverley, it's Linda. I just thought I'd ring and see how you are. Sorry I couldn't chat earlier.'

'That's nice of you to phone, Linda. Much the same. I'm sorting out some things before we move.'

'So it's definitely happening?'

'Yes. The people who've bought our house want to move in at the end of the year. Not sure how I'm going to cope; there's such a lot of stuff to organise.'

'I was wondering if you could give me Zak's telephone number? I want to see if he can recognise some photos.'

'Yes, of course, but I doubt if he'll speak to you. He's very upset about his sister's disappearance.'

'Can you send it to me on WhatsApp?'

'Okay. I don't suppose you have any more news yet?'

'No, but we are progressing with the enquiry,' said Linda, trotting out their standard reply. 'I hope we have something to tell you before you leave for England.'

'So do I. Between you and me, Linda, I don't know if I can do it. Jim wants to go to the UK next week to look for a house. What if Sophie comes back and we've gone; she'll think we didn't care about her.'

'You mustn't be like that, Beverley. I know you miss Sophie but you have the rest of your family to consider too. She'll understand.'

'I can't do it. I just can't.'

It sounded as though she'd started to cry.

'Don't upset yourself. After all, you just told me they don't want to move in until the end of the year; you've plenty of time to decide. You don't have to go next week. Let Jim and Ricky go without you.'

'Yes, you're right. I'll send you Zak's number now. Thanks for calling.'

She sounded exhausted. Poor woman, the strain of not knowing what had happened to her daughter was getting to her.

Linda wound down the windows and lit a cigarette. She was supposed to be trying to quit, but somehow she couldn't get through the day without at least a couple of cigarettes. She'd tried vaping, but didn't enjoy it. Phil had encouraged her to use nicotine patches but they weren't that much help, so she had become a closet smoker, sneaking out to have one in the alleyway when she was at work and sitting alone in the garden when at home. Phil didn't complain but she knew he was angry with her for not making more of an effort. It was all right for him; he'd never been a smoker. He really didn't understand. He was calm and placid by nature. She, on the other hand, needed something to sooth her nerves.

Her phone pinged. It was Zak's number. Well she might as well try ringing him now. It was worth a video call; she didn't want to leave any loose ends.

'Hello?' A tousled headed young man answered the phone; he looked just like his father.

'Zak? This is Linda Prewitt. I'm a private investigator. I just wanted to ask you a couple of questions about your sister.'

'Bloody hell. A private eye?'

'Yes, your mother has asked us to try to find Sophie.'

'She's mad, fucking mad. Sophie's dead. You see, one day she'll turn up just like Julie. Mum's just grasping at straws.'

'Maybe, but while there's the slightest chance of finding her, don't you think it's worth trying?'

'It's her money, so I suppose she can throw it away if she wants. What do you want to know?'

'I'm going to send you a couple of photos. Can you tell me if you've seen the people in them before.' She forwarded the photo of Kevin with the Moroccan man. 'We think Julie and Sophie saw these men on the day they disappeared. Do you recognise them?'

'Yes, I've seen them both. You think they have something to do with my sister's disappearance?'

'It's possible. Where did you see them?'

'They were always hanging around the school. There was another guy with them sometimes, an older man. I thought they were selling drugs.'

'Were they?'

'One of the boys in my class bought some weed from the Moroccan guy. I think he called him Ali. Don't know the other one's name.'

'Can you describe this other man? Was he Moroccan too?'

'No. I think he was Spanish.'

'What was he like?'

'I'm not sure. Bald, short and had a moustache. Quite old.'

'How old? As old as me?'

'No, not quite.'

'Did you ever see any of them with your sister?'

'No. I'd have dragged her home if I had. So do you think she's still alive?' he asked, a little less aggressive now.

'It's possible. What we need to find out is who took her and why.'

Beverley was right; he was very upset about his sister's disappearance. She could see that for herself.

'You'll let me know if you find anything,' he said, wiping his eyes with the back of his hand.

'I will. I promise. You have my number now, so you can ring me if you want to tell me anything.'

'Okay.' He rang off.

CHAPTER 22

Jorge lived in a small apartment overlooking a children's play area; he looked particularly annoyed to see her. 'What is it now?' he asked, when she explained why she was there. 'I've told your young man everything I can remember about that unfortunate child.'

'This is just a quick enquiry; I won't keep you long,' said JD, putting on her most winning smile. She took the crucifix from her neck and showed to it him. 'What can you tell me about this? Julie was wearing it when she was found. Did one of the Brothers put it there?'

The man hesitated. He looked embarrassed, and said, 'I'm sorry, I should have mentioned it to you before.'

'So you do recognise it?'

He pulled his own crucifix out from under his shirt and showed her. 'I wouldn't say she was wearing it; it was caught in her hair. These crucifixes are worn by some of the Brothers. Not all, just those who have done some particular service for the *Cofradía*.'

'Such as?'

'Well, in my case, it was to commemorate my fiftieth year as a *costalero*. I was very proud to receive it.'

'And in other cases? What else do the Brothers have to do to be presented with one?'

'It can be anything. Service to the community, service to the church, it isn't set out in a list, you know. The General Council meet once a year, just before Holy Week, and they decide who will be awarded them.'

'Are many given out each year?'

'Again, it is not something that is prescribed. Some years hardly any are presented to the Brothers, and another time it could be quite a lot. It depends on what had been happening during the previous year. The Brotherhood is not just about Holy Week, you know; there is plenty to do all through the year.'

'What about donations?' she asked. 'Do people get rewarded for giving money to the *Cofradia*?'

Jorge scowled at her. 'If you're suggesting that this honour can be bought, then no.'

'But?'

'We do have some very wealthy people in the *Cofradia*. Sometimes they can be extremely generous and the General Council likes to acknowledge that,' he said. 'Now, is that all?'

'Whose crucifix is this?' JD asked, holding it up again, before putting it around her neck once more

'I have no idea.'

'Did someone lose it?'

'Well if they did, I think they would have told everybody. It's made of solid gold and each one has a mark on it to show the year it was presented to them.' He turned his own crucifix over and showed her a tiny dragon.

'So you can trace who this belongs to?' JD asked in surprise. 'Didn't you tell that to the police?'

'They didn't ask. I assumed they weren't interested.'

'The police believed it belonged to Julie; they returned it to her mother.'

'Well, I'm sorry. I didn't think it was important.'

JD squinted at the crucifix around her neck; it had a tiny image of a dog on the reverse side. 'So, in which year was this presented?'

'A dog? I don't remember. I would have to look it up.'

He was being particularly uncooperative. She was going to have to up her game.

'By the way, you promised my assistant some lists of names?'

'Yes, he wanted all the members' names; I told him I would need permission to do that.'

'And have you spoken to the president yet?'

'Well, he's a busy man,' Jorge said, looking embarrassed.

'I tell you what. Why don't I sit here while you ring him? Or if you like I can speak to him directly?'

'There's no need. I'll ring him later.'

'Or, of course I can always call the Guardia Civil and tell them I have found a crucial piece of evidence that you have been concealing.'

Jorge looked at her in disbelief. 'There's no need for that,' he stammered. 'I will send you the names this afternoon, and the year of the crucifix.'

'This morning,' JD said, firmly. 'And I believe you promised a list of all the entry code holders?'

He nodded.

'Well that too, and now I want you to do something else for me. When you find out the year this crucifix was presented, I want you to send me a list of all the recipients that year.' She tucked the crucifix safely inside her blouse and added, 'With phone numbers. Thank you for your help, Señor Perez.'

'There's really no need to contact the police,' muttered Jorge. 'No need at all.'

There was no sign of Linda when JD arrived back at the office, but Nacho was busy going through the two girls' social media accounts.

'Hey JD, you must have a way with old men; the lists have arrived already,' he said.

'Good. I'm glad he saw sense. Print them out and pass them to me, will you.'

'Already on your desk. That photographer doesn't seem to exist; none of the local papers knew anything about him.'

'But that doesn't mean he had anything to do with our crime scene; he could just have been a tourist who wanted to get some pictures,' said JD.

'But if he was involved, who was he and what was he doing in there?'

'Well if we stick to our theory, it isn't Kevin or any of his cronies; I agree with you, I don't think they had anything to do with Julie's death,' said JD, starting to scan the first of the lists.

'Do you want me to help you?' asked Nacho. 'I need a break from all these silly teenage girls' comments.'

'Yes. As the car was Russian then let's look first of all for some Russian names. Jorge did say that there were a few foreign Brothers in the *Cofradía*, and some rich ones too. Highlight any you think might be interesting.'

'Ok, JD.'

'You look through the list of Brothers who knew the entry codes and I'll start with those who have crucifixes.'

Her mobile rang. '*Digame*,' she said, recognising the voice straight away. '*Buenas tardes*, Señora Reina. I'm glad you rang. No, I'm sorry we haven't been able to find your missing bracelet; my assistant has been to all the places you said you might have lost it, but there was no sign of it. I'm afraid that if it was found then whoever found it decided to keep it. I'm sorry but there's not much more we can do. Of course. Yes, I'll put the bill in the post.'

'Was that the batty bracelet woman?' asked Nacho. 'She's always losing something.'

'It was. Don't be rude about her; at least she pays her bills.'

The list of men who had been awarded one of the crucifixes in 2012, the year that corresponded to the dog symbol, was short and contained no foreign names. 'Well it looks like we're going to have to speak to all these men,' JD said. 'One of them must be missing a crucifix. How are you getting on?'

'No foreign names and certainly no Russian ones amongst the key code holders. Do you want me to cross check with your list?'

'Yes, good idea. Meanwhile I'll start on the complete list of Brothers. There might be something there.'

They worked in silence for a few minutes and then Nacho said, 'There are a couple of names that appear on both lists: Ramon Garcia Moreno and Juan Fernandez Romero.'

'Okay, we'll start with them. Find out all you can about those two men,' said JD, feeling a thrill of excitement. They were getting somewhere at last.

She opened her computer and again the photo of her and Andy came up as her screen saver; she could swear she hadn't put it on her computer. So who had? Or was it one of those weird things that sometimes happened when the computer programs made decisions for you? As she looked at it, she felt the usual tug at her heart; they'd been so happy.

'I think I'll go and get us some coffee. I need a bit of fresh air,' she said.

'Good idea. And some donuts while you're at it,' he said, moving over to her desk. 'Nice photograph. Boyfriend?'

'No. He was my husband. He died.'

'Oh, sorry to hear that.' If Nacho was surprised, he hid it well.

She should have told him and Linda before, but somehow she couldn't bring herself to do it. Well, now that Steed had been released they ought to know; she was going to need the backing of her team.

She grabbed her coat and headed for Antonio's cafe. She had to clear her head. Whoever had put that photo on her computer was very clever; they knew just how much it would upset her. Just one week after it was taken and her husband was dead. She had witnessed it all. That was the worst of it, to have seen what was happening and been unable to do anything to help him. She'd rushed down from her fourth floor office and out into the street but he was already dead. She didn't even have time to tell him she loved him. She'd sat on the cold pavement cradling his body in her arms, watching the blood soaking through his shirt and dripping onto the ground, unable to believe what had happened. Later, when the investigating officer asked her, she'd been incapable of identifying the killer, except to say that it was a man wearing a black hoodie. He had walked straight up to Andy and shot him. She hadn't seen any more; by then she was running down the stairs. It had all happened so quickly. The conclusion the investigators came to was that it was a random mugging; the man had taken Andy's wallet and his credit cards, and his life. There had been no other witnesses. It could have been anyone, but she knew it was someone Steed had sent. She had sensed it from that first moment. Only Steed would arrange a mugging outside the Metropolitan Police Headquarters, in full view of everyone. That was his message: 'I can get you, no matter where you are.'

CHAPTER 23

Linda had arranged to collect Nacho from home at nine o'clock. He lived with his mother and two older sisters in an apartment in el Limonar, a residential area to the east of the city centre. Nacho's father, he'd told them once in a rare moment of introspection, lived in the Canary Islands with his girlfriend.

When she pulled into his road, Nacho was waiting on the pavement for her, and hopped in the car as soon as she stopped. 'Put your guitar on the back seat,' she said. 'I must say, you certainly look the part.'

Nacho's hair had been gelled so that it stood away from his head, and he was wearing sunglasses, even though it was already dark. His black jeans were skintight and he wore a black tee-shirt and a white jacket.

'Is that how you dress for the band?' she asked.

'Yes, when we're on stage. I don't bother if it's just a rehearsal.'

'So you're ready for this?'

'Of course, I've done the rounds of the clubs looking for gigs before. How did you get on with Ricky?'

'Fine. Nothing new though. Our mystery guy is a boy in the school. He was a friend of the girls, but he didn't have much to tell me. Just backed up what we already knew, that they were behaving a bit oddly before they disappeared.'

'It's looking like this was planned; they didn't just snatch the girls with no warning,' he said.

'No, they were grooming them for a few weeks so that when it was time, they went willingly,' said Linda. 'Lambs to the slaughter.'

'Anything else?'

'I spoke to Zak, but he didn't have much to add; he just admitted that he recognised both the Moroccan and Kevin by sight. He said the Moroccan was dealing in weed,' said Linda. 'Oh, yes, and there was another man with them, short, bald and old. And by old I mean about forty.'

'Well that's something.'

'Yes. How did JD get on with Jorge Perez?' asked Linda.

'Okay. I think we're getting somewhere. The lists have arrived; I think JD must have put the fear of God in him,' Nacho said with a laugh.

'And?' she asked, flicking the indicator and slipping into the motorway traffic with ease.

'We checked the names of the entry code holders and those who had a crucifix that matched Julie's but there were no foreign names, and definitely no Russian ones. We'll go through the list of Brothers on Monday.'

'That will be fun.' Linda pulled out a cigarette. 'Do you mind?' she asked Nacho.

'Will it make any difference if I say yes?'

She laughed and lit the cigarette. 'Sorry, I need this,' she said, lowering the window.

'I'll tell Phil.'

She ignored his threat and asked instead, 'Tell me about the band. What have you been doing lately?'

That was enough encouragement for Nacho to expand on his favourite subject, and for the rest of the journey he entertained her with snatches of their latest songs.

Just before ten o'clock they pulled up outside the Crooked Cat. Unlike many clubs and bars, it wasn't on the main seafront promenade, but tucked down a narrow side road. It was a dingy looking place, with a neon sign of a cat arching its back. 'What a dive. I hope you'll be all right.'

'Of course I will.'

'I won't come in,' said Linda. 'JD made it quite clear that I would look out of place, so you're on your own, buddy. I'll wait down there, near the junction. If there's a problem just ring me.'

'I'll be fine. See you later.'

After about an hour, Linda saw Nacho walking nonchalantly along the street, his guitar over his shoulder. As he approached the car she spotted a man come out from the club and look up and down the road. She put the car into gear and drove off, turning left and stopping out of sight. Within a few minutes, Nacho came into view. He strolled over to the car and got in.

'Drive,' he said.

'Was he watching you?' Linda asked, driving away with one eye on the rear-view mirror.

'It's quite likely. I did ask the barman a lot of questions.'

'So, how did it go?' she asked, once they were back on the motorway and she could relax.

'They offered me a gig for this Saturday and, if we're a success, the following Friday as well. I just have to confirm with the guys.'

'What? They've hired you to play there?'

'Don't sound so surprised. We're quite good really. The money's not great, but it'll cover our expenses with a bit over.'

'But how does he know what you sound like?' Linda was almost lost for words; Nacho wasn't supposed to get himself a job. 'Did you do an audition?'

'No, of course not. I took along a CD we'd taped. He liked it. So he said he'd give us a trial; they always have a music night at the weekend.'

'But what did you find out? Did you see the Moroccan?'

'I did. He works there, I think; at any rate he's very pally with the owner. His name is Ali Harrak.'

'How did you find that out?'

'I asked the barista. Don't worry nobody else heard me.'

'So, what can you tell me about the place?' Linda asked.

'Something dodgy is going on there, without a doubt. But whether it's people smuggling, I can't say. I did ask about the customers, and the barista said they were mostly teenagers; he said they liked to order Mojitos and Cosmopolitans.'

'How can teenagers afford drinks like that?'

'Beats me.' He began singing quietly, beating out the rhythm on the dashboard. 'There was a small group of kids there; two boys playing pool and drinking San Miguels and three young girls sipping cocktails.'

'Were they together?'

'Yes, I think so, although the boys didn't pay much attention to the girls. Then an older guy came in and sat down next to them; he bought them more cocktails although one of the girls said she didn't want any more to drink. Do you think Julie and Sophie came here?'

'I think it's a possibility. How old were the girls?'

'*Dios mío*, how would I know? Sixteen maybe. They wore a lot of make-up. They could have been younger.'

'Do you have a girlfriend, Nacho?'

'Me? No. No time.'

Not for the first time, Linda wondered if Nacho was gay. He was a good looking young man yet never seemed to be interested in girls.

'You're in a good mood,' she said, as he continued to hum to himself.

'Yes, well I'm excited about the gig,' he replied. 'Don't worry, I'll find out more on Saturday.'

'I think we should tell the police,' Linda said. If these men were people smugglers, things could get nasty for Nacho if they found out he worked for a private investigator.

'Tell them what? That a Moroccan man was seen hanging about with Julie and Sophie? That's not proof that he did anything to them. We need more than that before we involve the Guardia.'

'You sound just like JD. Don't either of you realise that this could be dangerous? And especially for you, Nacho.'

'Linda, did you know that the boss had been married?'

She stared at him. 'JD? Married? No, I didn't. Are you sure?'

'Yes. She asked me to find out how a photo of her and her husband turned up on her screen saver. She thought it might have happened during the break-in.'

'That sounds weird. And did it?'

'It's certainly possible. That particular photo was uploaded the same day as the break-in.'

'What did she say?'

'Nothing. But she did look a bit worried.'

'So where's her husband now? Did they divorce?'

'He's dead. And before you ask, no, I don't know what happened to him.'

'Why would anyone break into our agency and upload a photo of JD and her dead husband onto her computer? It sounds very strange.'

'It is strange, but I expect she'll tell us when she's ready.'

CHAPTER 24

Saturday was a perfect day for golf; the sun was shining, there was no wind and it wasn't too hot. Now that JD had agreed to play with Paco she was looking forward to being out in the fresh air, with nothing more than a small white ball to worry about. Before she was married, she'd played regularly—it was a sport she'd taken up as a young girl, encouraged by her father, a very keen golfer. She'd always been very competitive and had soon got her handicap down to single figures. So when she found out that her colleagues in the Met were organising a golf tournament, she immediately put her name down for it. What happened next shouldn't have come as a surprise; she'd met plenty of chauvinistic golfers before. Her boss had immediately called her into his office and asked her to withdraw; the men didn't want a woman playing in their tournament, he'd said. It was a serious event, not something for a woman to take part in. It would only cause bad feeling. JD had been furious, refused to remove her name from the list and threatened to go to the police commissioner if they insisted. So when she went up to collect her prize—because she'd been by far the best golfer there that day—she told them what she thought of their golf society. It hadn't affected her career, but some of her colleagues had taken a while to get used to her self-assured manner. For a long time she was referred to as that aggressive blonde, but never to her face.

Sophie is Still Missing

Things had changed since then and, at least in Spain, women had equal status on the golf course. Her mother's boyfriend was a likeable man, and a good golfer; she was sure they would have an enjoyable afternoon.

They were playing at one of the more prestigious golf courses on the Costa de Sol. She drove into the car park and parked by a group of large fir trees. She couldn't help noticing how out of place her old Mini Cooper looked amidst the members' BMWs, Mercedes, Bentleys, and there was even a bright red Ferrari. The whole place reeked of money, and probably ill-gotten money at that, her policeman's brain told her.

She unloaded her golf clubs from the boot of her car and went to where Paco was chatting to a tall, sharp-faced woman wearing designer golf clothes.

'JD, you found it all right,' he said, in English, and kissed her on both cheeks. 'May I introduce you to Annika; she and Enrique are our opponents today.'

JD extended her hand and was met with a cold, limp handshake and an even colder smile. Her heart sank; this wasn't promising. Although JD was very competitive, she liked to have a pleasant round in sociable company. She hoped Annika's partner would be more agreeable.

'Enrique?' she asked Paco, while Annika went off to organise her clubs. 'Is he a friend of yours?'

'Enrique de Valdes. No, not really; he's not my sort. You must have heard of him; he's one of the candidates for mayor of Marbella.'

'No, I don't think so. I try to keep out of politics; I come across enough criminals as it is.'

'You are very, what's the word?'

'Cynical?'

'Yes, that's it. And funny.'

'I hope he's more pleasant than his partner. What is she, Polish?'

'Russian. Her husband is a retired diplomat. They divide their time between Moscow and Marbella. You'll like him; he's very charming. All the ladies like Ivan.'

'Maybe that's why she's so unfriendly. Is she like that to all the women, or is it just towards me?'

'I can't say I've noticed, JD. I'm here to play golf. Come along, I'll show you the changing rooms and then we can spend a few minutes practising on the putting green. You'll find the greens very fast here. Many a game has been won, and lost, on the greens, as you well know.'

Both she and Paco had played well, but not well enough to win; their 35 points didn't even warrant a mention.

'Sorry we didn't do better,' said Paco. 'If only that putt had gone in on the 16th.'

'If only,' she echoed with a smile.

Annika had thawed a little during the game, but was still not very talkative; this didn't bother JD because she preferred to concentrate on her game. However it was now time for the prize giving and a few drinks; she hoped Annika would be better company over a gin and tonic.

Now that the golf was over, JD couldn't prevent her thoughts from returning to her current investigation. How strange that yesterday they were looking for Russian names on the list of Brothers and today she was playing with a Russian golfer. But as Paco had pointed out on many occasions, there were a lot of Russian residents in Marbella, rich ones too. But were there many diplomats? How curious that Annika's husband was a retired diplomat.

Sophie is Still Missing

'Ah, here is my husband, at last,' said Annika, scowling across the room at a handsome man in his sixties.

'Darling, did you have a good game?' he asked, leaning over and kissing his wife. And without waiting for a reply, turned to JD and bowed. 'Ivan Lebedev, at your service, señorita. I hope you enjoyed your game.'

'I did. The course is beautiful, if somewhat challenging. You're very lucky to be a member of such a lovely golf club.'

'Indeed I am. I take it we have no winners here,' he said with a smile. 'Still that's no reason not to celebrate. Waiter, champagne for our guests. So you liked our lovely course, señorita. Jack Nicklaus designed it, you know. It's said to be the best golf course in Spain.'

Paco, who'd been talking to some of his cronies, came back to join them. 'Good, you've introduced yourselves,' he said.

'Actually, no,' said JD.

'Ah, well. Ivan, this is Rosa's daughter, Jacaranda.'

Ivan leapt to his feet, and made another ridiculous little bow. '*Encantado* Jacaranda.'

JD could feel her dislike growing for this rather smarmy individual.

'So what do you do with yourself, when you're not playing golf?' he asked.

She could see Paco was about to say something, so she beamed at Ivan and said, 'I work in the Hacienda in Málaga.'

'Really, a tax inspector?'

'No, just a lowly clerk.' If there was one thing she'd learned over the years, it was that nobody liked talking to anyone from the department of revenue and taxes. They certainly never encouraged you to talk about your job. She caught Paco's eye and smiled sweetly; there would be some explaining to do, later. 'And you? What do you do for a living?' she asked Ivan. She could see that this question embarrassed Paco, but he said nothing.

'A good question. What do you think, Darling?' he asked his wife.

'I think you play golf all day and poker all night,' she snapped.

'My wife is not keen on my hobbies, but then I am retired, so I have to fill my days somehow, don't I?' He looked to JD for sympathy. 'Ah, here's the champagne. Excellent. Just in time.'

The waiter poured them each a glass and left the bottle in a cooler beside them. A man in a dark red jacket was standing on a small dais, tapping the microphone.

'Oh God, now it's the dreary prize giving,' said Annika, emptying her glass and signalling for the waiter to refill it almost immediately.

It was the usual litany of complements and words of appreciation for members and staff alike, followed by a short prize giving, and while it was going on JD took the opportunity to observe her companions. Annika had changed her golf clothes for a silk suit of the most exquisite shade of blue, which clung to her slender figure in the most flattering way; around her neck she wore a sapphire necklace, with matching earrings. The necklace alone must have cost roughly the same as JD earned in a year. Annika was a beautiful woman, and obviously had the money to make the most of her looks, but a certain hardness in her face made it devoid of any charm. Ivan, on the other hand was working overtime at being agreeable, flashing his smile at everyone who walked past. They made a handsome couple but there was something she didn't like about either of them; they both gave off an air of superiority as though there was no-one there that they considered their equal.

'So you know my mother?' she asked Ivan.

'The lovely Rosa, Marquesa de Calderón del Bosque? Yes, I have met her several times at golf club dinners. A charming lady.'

Before she could ask any more, the fourth member of their game, Enrique de Valdes, pulled up a chair next to JD and poured himself some champagne.

'Sorry about that,' he said 'Had to speak to one of the Board.'

'I wondered where you'd got to,' said Ivan. 'I thought maybe you were avoiding me.'

Enrique looked flustered for a moment, then said, 'Of course not. Why would I do that? Has your wife been telling tales about me again?' He laughed and looked at JD to make sure she understood it was all taken in good part. 'I don't suppose we won anything, did we?'

JD smiled and said, 'Hardly. The winners had 45 points. We were both a long way behind.'

'How's your election campaign going?' asked Paco. 'Not long now, is it?'

'December. Still plenty of time for me to rustle up some more support.' He turned to JD and said, 'I hope I can count on your vote, Jacaranda?'

'Well, I live in Málaga, so I'm afraid not.'

'Ah well.'

'Valdes. We need to speak,' said Ivan, brusquely.

'What now? I've only just sat down. Let me at least enjoy this delicious champagne.'

'Now. It's important.'

'Oh, very well. Excuse me, Jacaranda. Annika. Paco.'

What, JD wondered, could be so important that Ivan had to drag a very reluctant Enrique away like that?

'Excuse me,' said Annika and stood up. 'I have a headache. I think I have had too much sun.' She held out her hand for JD to take.

'Thank you for the game,' JD said, shaking the limp hand. 'I hope you soon feel better.'

She watched Annika follow her husband out onto the terrace.

'Well she was a bundle of laughs,' she said to Paco.

'She's not an easy woman to get to know,' he admitted. 'Here, let's finish off the champagne before we go. You probably need it after an afternoon with her.'

'Do you know them very well?' she asked, accepting a glass from him.

'No, hardly at all. And Valdes hasn't been a member for long, a couple of years maybe.'

'I don't mean to be rude, Paco, but how did you manage to get membership of this place? It seems very exclusive. They say members of the royal family play here, and lots of politicians. Was it through my mother?'

'Well, as you ask, yes she did put in a word for me. I have to admit that I find the annual membership fee a bit steep, but it's worth it. Did you enjoy the course?'

'I did, very much. You're very lucky to be a member.'

'Well, you'd have no trouble getting membership, JD.'

'I know, but it wouldn't be worth it; I'd never find the time to play,' she said, omitting to tell him that she wouldn't be able to afford it anyway. 'What about Ivan, he's retired?'

'Yes.'

'He doesn't have any business connections these days?'

'Not that I know about. But they're not here all the year; they spend a lot of time in Moscow. I think it's Annika who always wants to come to their house in Marbella.'

'I wonder what all that was about between Enrique and Ivan. Do they have some sort of business connection?'

'JD, you're not at work now. And, by the way, what was all that about working for the Hacienda? I thought Ivan was going to have a heart attack when you said that.'

JD laughed. 'It seemed to be a good way to stop him asking questions. The less people who know I'm a detective, the better.'

'I suppose you're right. But, I ask you, the Hacienda! Couldn't you have thought of something better than the tax office.'

CHAPTER 25

Monday morning, JD and Nacho began to go through the complete list of members of the Brotherhood of the Virgin of Remorse; there were about eight hundred names on it, although many were no longer active members.

'Okay, JD, what are we looking for?' asked Nacho.

'Much the same as before. Anything unusual, foreign names, or anything sounding Russian. We'll know it when we see it.'

They worked in silence for a while, methodically moving down the list, which was in alphabetical order. 'Jorge was right when he said membership was a family thing; I've twenty-five men here with the first surname as Gomez, and ten of those are Gomez Muñoz. Brothers I suppose,' she said.

'It's a common name,' Nacho replied. 'All Spanish so far.'

'Me too.'

'Hang on. This is interesting; I'm sure this guy is on the list of entry code holders.'

'What's his name?' asked JD, picking up the list.

'Pablo Ruiz Requena.'

She skimmed down the list. 'Yes, you're right. Now why does that name sound familiar?' She picked up the list she'd checked the night before. 'And he also owns one of those crucifixes. I wonder what he did to deserve it.'

'We could ask him,' said Nacho.

'Later. Let's see if we have any more matches between the Brothers with crucifixes and those that know the entry codes.'

Sophie is Still Missing

They put aside the main list and ran through the two shorter ones.

'Felipe Duran Garcia,' Nacho read out.

'Yes, I have him as well.'

By the time they had cross checked all the names of those with crucifies and those who knew the entry codes, they had three names: Pablo Ruiz Requena, Jaime Ortega Moreno and Felipe Duran Garcia. 'So our man could be one of these three,' said JD.

'Yes, but what's their link to the Russian car?' asked Nacho. 'We need to go back to the main list. So far we haven't found any foreign names at all.'

'You're right.' JD handed him the original list, and they continued to go through the names, one by one. Suddenly she stopped. 'Well, I never.'

'What is it?' asked Nacho.

'This one here. I met him on Saturday. What a coincidence.'

'Enrique de Valdes. Who is he?'

'A pretty awful golfer, for one, but he's also a candidate in the upcoming elections for mayor of Marbella.'

'Really, but how does that help us?'

'I'm not sure, but he was very pally with a Russian couple who were there.'

'I don't remember him on any of the other lists, so it can't have been him,' said Nacho, but making a large red mark next to his name anyway.

'Bit of a coincidence though.'

'Yes, and you don't believe in coincidences, do you Boss?'

She smiled and shook her head. 'Come on, let's see who else is on this list.'

'What's the surname of your mother's boyfriend, JD?' asked Nacho after a while.

'Paco? Sastre, not sure about the second one.'

'There's a Francisco Sastre Tellez, could that be him?'

'Yes, that sounds right. Are you telling me he's a member of the Brotherhood? Well, I don't know what to say; Paco has never mentioned anything about that. It must be someone else.'

'Would your mother know?'

'She might do. But why did neither of them say anything? I didn't discuss the case with them, but they knew we were investigating Sophie's disappearance. And they must have known her body was found in the *Cofradía*. Why didn't he tell me he was connected to the Brotherhood?' JD was stunned; she'd spent all afternoon with Paco and he'd never said anything about it. Was he deliberately hiding something from her?

'I've got something else, JD. Does this sound Russian enough for you? Ivan Lebedev. Joined in 2014, occupation Consular Officer at the Russian Embassy in Madrid, now retired.'

'Bloody hell.'

'What is it?'

'I played golf with his wife.'

'Don't worry, I don't think that will make you an accessory,' said Nacho laughing. 'Well, I think we're beginning to get somewhere at last.'

'I want you to find out as much as you can about those three men: when they joined the Brotherhood, where they were the night Julie was killed and whether they have any connection with our Russian friend and Señor de Valdes.'

'Okay JD. What are you going to do?'

'I'm going to talk to Federico. We have to find out if Ivan Lebedev was driving that car. But first I'm going to ring Paco.'

Sophie is Still Missing

'Sorry I'm late,' said Linda, arriving with two large coffees, one of which she handed to Nacho. 'Had to take Jane to the doctor.'

'Thanks, Linda. I was just thinking of going out for one,' said Nacho.

'Is she okay?' asked JD, putting on her coat.

'Yes, she'll be fine. Has Nacho told you about our trip to The Crooked Cat?'

'Not yet. We've been busy going through the lists Jorge sent us. We'll talk when I get back. Nacho will bring you up to date.' JD grabbed her bag and was out of the door before Linda could comment.

'Where's she off to, in such a hurry?' JD heard Linda ask, as the door swung shut.

She wasn't in the mood for any witty comments about her and Federico.

Once she was away from the office she rang Paco.

'Buenos días, JD,' he said. 'What can I do for you?'

'You never told me you were a member of the Brotherhood of the Virgin of Remorse.'

'You never asked. Why, what's the problem?'

'But you realise that's where Julie Bennett's body was found?'

'Yes, but I never gave it much thought. I haven't had anything to do with the Brotherhood for years; I inherited my membership from my father. I was never interested in any of that stuff, but it was important to my mother, so I accepted it, for her sake. In fact, now that she's dead, I was thinking of resigning, so someone else could take my place. Why are you so agitated? Is it a problem?'

'Did my mother know?'

'I don't think so. Why would she? I never talk about it. In fact I never even think about it. What's this all about, JD?'

'I just find it strange that last Saturday we played with one of the Brothers and the wife of another one. I can't help thinking it's not just a coincidence that we were all there together.'

'I can't help it if we get partnered with Valdes and Annika. You know how it works; it's a draw.'

'You told me they weren't friends of yours,' JD said. She was sure Paco was hiding something.

'They're not. Look what is this?'

'How did they both get membership of the *Cofradía*? I know it's not easy.'

'Okay, I introduced them to some people I know, old friends of my father, and they proposed them. You can't just have one sponsor; if you have no family ties to the *Cofradía*, you need at least two people to vouch for you.'

'And you could do that, could you? Vouch for them?'

'Yes.'

'Lebedev and Valdes?'

'Yes, both of them. Satisfied?'

'Who else proposed them?'

'Look JD, that's enough. I'm not going to tell you any more. The Brotherhood likes to keep these things secret. You'll have to take it up with the President.'

She was tempted to tell him about the Russian car that was seen the night Julie died, but now she wasn't sure she could trust him. 'I might just do that,' she said.

'I've got to go, now. I'm due on the first tee in ten minutes,' Paco said. He sounded angry.

She rang off without saying any more, then walked quickly back to the office. Nacho was still busily going through the lists.

Sophie is Still Missing

'Nacho. See if you can find out when Valdes and Lebedev joined and who sponsored them for the Brotherhood. I have a feeling it's the same man.'

'Okay JD. I take it, your conversation with Paco didn't go well?'

'I hate it when people keep secrets from me,' she said.

'Well, if people didn't have secrets, we'd be out of a job,' said Linda, with a cheery smile. 'Off to see the Captain?'

JD ignored her and walked out for the second time that morning.

She wandered down Calle Larios and sat down on a bench next to some granite statues that were part of a temporary exhibition. This case was getting more and more complicated; she needed some time to think. The pieces were coming together but so far not falling into place. She was convinced that there was a real Russian connection behind it all, but how exactly? She knew the Russian mafia had a presence on the Costa del Sol—only the previous year eleven Russians had been arrested for money laundering, including the owner of Marbella Football Club—but what did that have to do with the disappearance of two teenage girls? Perhaps Federico could help; she rang his number.

'Can we meet?' she asked as soon as he answered.

'*Buenos días* to you too, Jacaranda.'

'Sorry. I've got such a lot on my mind. I really need to talk to you.'

'All right. Twenty minutes.'

'The usual place?'

'Of course.'

Sophie is Still Missing

Jacaranda had almost finished her coffee by the time Federico arrived. For once he wasn't smiling. In fact he looked quite annoyed about something.

'*Buenos tardes, cariño,*' she said, standing so she could reach up and kiss him.

He pulled away slightly, so her lips only brushed his cheek.

'Is something wrong?'

'You tell me.' He sat down and signalled for the waiter to bring him his usual coffee. 'I suppose there must be something wrong for you to ring me.'

'What do you mean by that?' she asked. What on earth was the matter with him?

'Come on, Jacaranda. When was the last time you rang just because you wanted to see me?'

'I always want to see you, Federico. You know that.'

'What I know is that you are using me to help you solve your case.'

JD felt the blood rush to her face. It was true; she was using him but she thought he didn't mind. 'I thought you liked helping with my cases?'

'I did, until I realised that you were putting my job in jeopardy and your own as well. You have to realise, JD, that you don't have the strength of the Metropolitan Police Force behind you any more. You are just an Englishwoman living in Spain and playing at being detective.'

His words stung, but before JD could retaliate, the waiter arrived with Federico's coffee. 'Anything else, caballero?' he asked.

'Yes, a large brandy,' said Federico.

JD stretched out her hand and placed it on top of his. 'What is it, *cariño*? Why so angry?'

Sophie is Still Missing

Federico didn't answer but neither did he remove his hand, so she continued, 'You're right. It's been selfish of me to keep expecting you to help with my investigation. I'm sorry.'

'But?' he asked. 'Come on Jacaranda, now that you're here you'd better tell me what it is that you want.'

'I just wanted to tell you what we've found out. That's all.'

He looked at her, his head tilted to one side; she hadn't convinced him, but she might as well go on.

'That speeding car, the one we caught on CCTV, we're pretty sure it was the car that killed the lieutenant and most likely the one that took Julie to the *Cofradía*.'

'So?'

'The car belongs to the Russian Embassy, consular department,' said JD, explaining how they'd got better CCTV footage and identified the number plates.

'What the hell are you getting into, Jacaranda? A diplomatic car? You'll never be able to pin anything on the driver.' He took the brandy from the waiter and tipped half of it into his coffee.

'We just need to locate the car and get forensics to go over it.'

'What do you hope to find? If this car was involved in either of those deaths, two things will have happened to it. It will have been destroyed, either burnt or dumped in the reservoir, or it will have been so thoroughly cleaned that forensics won't find anything. You're wasting your time.'

'But that's not all,' JD said, trying to stay calm. 'I played golf on Saturday, and I met two very interesting men.' She explained about Señor Valdes and Ivan Lebedev. 'And Lebedev used to be in the consular department of the Russian Embassy in Madrid. Bit of a coincidence, don't you think?'

'And you don't believe in coincidences,' Federico said, finishing his coffee and calling for another.

'I don't.'

'Where was this golf course?'

'Marbella.'

'And do you know how many wealthy Russians have homes in Marbella?'

'No, but I expect you're going to tell me,' she snapped.

He was being decidedly unhelpful today. It wasn't like him.

'Around 20,000 in Marbella and the surrounding area. The Russians are the third largest group of foreigners, after you British and the Norwegians. So, you see, it is not surprising that you found yourself playing with the wife of a retired Russian Consul.'

'I didn't say he was retired.'

'Well, what else could he be, if he's playing golf in Marbella?'

'Do you know something you're not telling me, Federico?' she asked.

'I think this case is getting beyond you, Jacaranda. There are some nasty characters amongst those Russians. You just don't want to get mixed up with them.'

'Have you been told to warn me off? Is that it? Or have they threatened that you'll lose your pension if you can't get me under control? Is that why you're behaving like a grade one shit head?' As soon as the words were out, she regretted them. But it was too late.

Federico swallowed the remaining brandy and stood up. 'One day your stubbornness will be your downfall. These people are out of your league, Jacaranda. They are dangerous. You really don't know who you're dealing with.'

'I think I do, someone capable of kidnapping two teenage girls and murdering one of them. And, in case you've forgotten, the other girl is still missing.'

Sophie is Still Missing

But Federico wasn't listening; he was already walking inside to pay the bill.

CHAPTER 26

JD headed straight back to the office. It had been a waste of time talking to Federico. Not only had he been in a bad mood, but she was convinced that someone had been putting pressure on him. Someone wanted her to stop investigating the case.

'Back so soon,' said her assistant.

'Don't start, Linda; I'm not in the mood.' JD tossed her coat over the chair and picked up the case file. 'Right, let's go over all that we know so far.'

The three of them squashed into the meeting room, and Nacho asked, 'Did the Captain give you the forensic report on the car?'

'Not yet, but we have to find out who was driving it. How far have you got with those three men, Nacho?'

'Nowhere.'

'Would you like to hear about our night at the Crooked Cat, instead?' Linda asked.

'Yes, how did you get on, Nacho?'

'They've booked me for this Saturday,' he said with a big grin. 'They liked me.'

'Dios mío. You did realise that it was just a disguise; you weren't actually supposed to start working there. I don't want your mother giving me a hard time, Nacho.'

'She'll never know. Anyway, it seemed to fool them.'

'Did you find anything to help with the case?'

Sophie is Still Missing

'Yes, the Moroccan guy was there; apparently he's at the club most nights according to the barman. He's called Ali Harrak, and he's from Tangier.'

'Did you see anything suspicious?'

'Not really, most of the clientele were teenagers. A few boys were playing pool and there were about half a dozen girls, all under age and drinking expensive cocktails. There was an older guy chatting to two of them and buying them drinks. Later, another guy came in and got into a deep conversation with Ali.'

'What was he like?'

'Spanish, bald and covered in tattoos. I couldn't hear what they were talking about, but they kept looking across at the girls.'

'So this could be where Julie and Sophie went that night,' said JD.

'What, you think the men got them drunk and then abducted them?' asked Linda.

'It's possible. You might learn more on Saturday, Nacho.'

'You're not letting him go back?' asked Linda, horrified. 'What if something happens to him?'

'I can look after myself, Linda. And anyway, it will look suspicious if I don't go back.'

'How many of you are there in your band?' JD asked.

'Leila, she's a flamenco dancer, José is another guitarist and Manuel is a singer.'

'So you won't be on your own.'

'Why don't we just tell the police that they're dealing drugs from the club, and probably involved in people smuggling?' asked Linda, who was clearly unhappy at the thought of Nacho returning to the Crooked Cat. 'Let them deal with it.'

'Because we don't have any proof and so far we still have no idea what has happened to Sophie. If we can find her, then she'll be a witness and we can hand it all over to the police. In the meantime, I want us to concentrate on the car and who was driving it.'

'If Julie was killed in an accident, it's possible that the car was damaged. Do you want me to check the local garages? People wouldn't forget a car like that,' said Nacho.

'Yes, that's a good idea. And while we're at it, let's check out the A&E records for that night, in case the driver was injured.'

'That might be difficult,' said Nacho. 'Hacking into a Social Security database isn't easy.'

'I know a couple of nurses in A&E in the Hospital Regional de Málaga. They might remember,' said Linda.

'No, I doubt it; after all it was six months ago. Have you ever been there at night? It's chaos. No, you do the garages, Linda, and Nacho can try out his hacking skills. We need to find the driver of that car.'

'You know it's illegal, JD?' said Nacho.

'Well make sure you don't get caught.' She knew Federico would be furious if he found out what she'd asked Nacho to do, but right then she couldn't care less. 'If this was the car that killed the policeman and then crashed into Señor Ramirez's car, then it had to have sustained some damage. It must have been repaired somewhere. We just have to find out where.'

It was odd how the Pobeda M20 kept cropping out. It was possibly the car that had transported Julie's dead body, maybe even run her over. Then six months later it had been involved in both a hit and run where the lieutenant investigating Julie's death had been killed and, later, possibly an accident with Señor Ramirez's son. If they could find the car, and better still, its driver, she was sure it would help solve the investigation.

Linda was exhausted. She'd already visited six garages and telephoned ten others. No-one remembered repairing a Pobeda M20. In fact she'd had to spell it for most of them, because they'd never even heard of the make.

'I thought all Russian cars were made by Skoda,' one of them said.

But was it really likely that someone involved in a hit and run accident would take the car to be repaired in the same city as the accident? She didn't think they would be stupid enough to do that. But if the driver was hurt, then that would be different; he would want to get help as soon as possible. But even that was unlikely; how injured would he be? She knew it was important to find the driver of the car, but it looked as though both these lines of enquiry were going nowhere. She decided to go back to the office and go through the pile of old newspapers that Jim Anderson had given her at the start of the enquiry. Maybe there was something there that they'd missed. After all, now they had a clearer idea of what they were looking for.

'Hi Linda, finished already?' Nacho asked.

'No. It's a waste of time. I don't think the driver would take it to a local garage if he'd just run someone over. Do you?'

'No, but if it's the same car that was in the accident with Señor Ramirez, then that's possible. Remember he said it had unusual number plates. What if it is the same one? It's worth finding out if anyone's repaired a Pobeda M20 recently.'

'Well I haven't had any luck so far. But I've got another idea. What about you? Any luck with hacking into the Social Security database?'

He shook his head. 'It's a lot more secure than I thought. It could take me months.'

'We don't have months,' said JD, looking up from the list of names she was laboriously going through.

Sophie is Still Missing

They all worked in silence for a bit then suddenly Linda let out a shriek of delight. 'Guess what I've found,' she cried. 'Do you know who was in the Hospital Costa del Sol Emergency room on the night Julie was killed?'

JD and Nacho stared at her.

'Ivan the Terrible.'

'What? Ivan Lebedev?'

'Yes. He was getting a head wound stitched. Apparently he'd been mugged while walking along the promenade. Look it says quite clearly, ex-Consul Ivan Lebedev was attacked and injured at 10pm on Saturday night, while walking by the beach with his dog,' Linda read.

'But that's too early. According to the pathologist Julie didn't die until some time between 10pm and midnight. He can't be our killer,' said Nacho.

'Are you sure?' asked Linda.

'Positive. Even if the timing is out by a bit, it still wouldn't give Ivan time to kill Julie and take her body over to Málaga. Besides which, it says he stayed in the hospital until the next morning,' said Nacho, handing the paper back to her. 'He has a cast-iron alibi. Look there's a photo of his wife collecting him from the hospital.'

'But don't you think it's strange that he suffered a head wound on the night that Julie died?' said JD.

'It might have nothing to do with it,' said Nacho. 'Maybe he was mugged.'

'Rubbish. People like him don't go anywhere without some sort of bodyguard. No, something happened that night, that ended up with Julie running away and getting hit by a car.'

'Maybe she clonked him over the head and escaped,' said Linda.

Sophie is Still Missing

'Mmn. That's one theory. And not such a bad one. We know she'd been held prisoner by the marks on her wrists.'

'But they were old scars,' said Nacho.

'True, but that doesn't mean she wasn't still a prisoner. I think you're right, Linda. I think she escaped, perhaps after attacking our Russian, and ran away.'

'Yes, and someone chased her and ran her over, either accidentally, or on purpose,' added Nacho.

'But who?'

'The driver of the car.'

'You said something interesting, JD, that people like him would have a bodyguard. Maybe it was his bodyguard who ran her over,' said Linda.

'Or his chauffeur,' said Nacho, picking up the old newspaper again. 'Look at this.' A man in a chauffeur's uniform was holding the car door open for Ivan. 'It's not a very good photograph but it's something to work on.'

'Linda, see if you can get the original from the newspaper. Pay them if you have to,' said JD. 'Now we're getting somewhere. Let's get back to those lists of members, Nacho. The answer has got to be in there, somewhere.'

CHAPTER 27

Annika was worried about Ivan and Sophie. She'd seen him watching the girl and she knew that look in his eyes. The older he became, the more he seemed to like young girls; he hadn't been able to leave that other one alone. He thought she didn't know what he was up to, but nothing remained secret in this house for long; she had heard the servants talking about it and felt humiliated. It was bad enough when he'd had affairs with girls in the Embassy, but to have a fling with a housemaid in his own home; that was unbearable. She'd never forgive him for that. And to make her pregnant. What was he thinking of? If their friends heard about it, her reputation would be ruined. Everyone would be talking about it. They would be ostracised. She couldn't bear that; her social circle and her golf were the only things that had kept her going since the girls went away to boarding school.

Fortunately the stupid girl had managed to escape, so in the end, Annika hadn't had to confront her husband with an ultimatum. How Julie had wound up dead in Málaga of all places, was a mystery to Annika. She must have a hitched a lift from a stranger; it was much too far to walk. At first she'd been worried about the police coming round to the house, but Ivan had reassured her that there was nothing to link the girl back to them, and besides which, he told her, he knew someone influential in the police force who would make sure of that. Then, once she heard that they'd closed the case, she knew she could relax.

But now things had changed. Ivan was turning his sights to Sophie. She couldn't believe it. Julie was a lively young girl, pretty in a common sort of way, and she could imagine some men being attracted to her. But Sophie? She was a plain little mouse. What on earth did he see in her? Well she wasn't going to let it happen again. Did he take her for a complete fool? She would get rid of the girl before it could go any further. And as for moving to Florida, that was never going to happen. She wasn't going to give up everything for a slip of a girl. She knew someone in Ronda who would buy her. She'd tell Ivan that Sophie had run away. After all, if one of them could do it, then why not the other.

She picked up her mobile and looked for the number. 'Greta. It's Annika. Yes, I'm fine. Look, you remember telling me that you needed some help in that great big house of yours? Well I've found just the person for you.'

'What nationality is she?' asked Greta.

'English. Is that a problem? I only want a thousand euros for her. It's a bargain.'

'I'm not sure, Annika. Have you seen the papers? There's a lot of talk about those two English girls that went missing last year. It's not one of them, by any chance?' she laughed.

'How can you say that, even in joke?'

'Sorry. It's just that I don't want the police nosing around here. Gregorio wouldn't like it.'

'That case is closed. The police aren't interested anymore. I just need to get rid of her.' Annika hesitated. Greta was an old friend from their Moscow days. 'It's Ivan. He's becoming a bit too friendly with her and I want her out of the way. You'll like her. She's a quiet girl and a hard worker.'

'Oh, I understand. Ivan has always had roving hands, as I remember.'

Sophie is Still Missing

Annika bit her lip. She felt like ringing off, but Greta was her best hope of getting rid of Sophie.

'She's a good worker, you say?'

'Excellent.'

'Look, I'll talk to Gregorio about it, and get back to you.'

'Don't leave it too long. I'm sure I can sell her to someone else; it's just that I remembered you telling me you were desperate for someone.'

'I am. I'll talk to Gregorio tonight.'

Annika smiled to herself as she switched off her phone. Greta was just holding out to get her to bring down the price. Well, if the truth was told, she had no idea what to charge for Sophie; she had said the first number that came into her head. Ivan always dealt with that sort of thing. She would tell him when she needed help in the house and he provided it; she neither wanted to know how much it cost nor where it came from.

Sophie had been cleaning the brass ornaments in the hallway when Madame was on the telephone; she had heard every word. Her name hadn't been mentioned, but she knew it was her that Madame was talking about. She vaguely remembered a woman called Greta; she was a friend of Madame's and had been to the house a couple of times. What she didn't know was where she lived. If it was Torremolinos then she would be nearer to her parents and maybe would have a chance to escape, but it could be somewhere further away, up in the hills somewhere. She couldn't risk it; she was going to have to be brave and try to escape at the first opportunity.

Ivan was getting impatient; he'd been waiting in the restaurant for almost half an hour. Where on earth was Enrique? He pulled out his mobile and was about to ring him again, when he saw his colleague's stocky frame almost blocking the doorway.

'At last,' he said. 'I was thinking of leaving.'

'Relax, Ivan. You're in Spain now. Nobody arrives on time.' Enrique pulled out a chair and sat down opposite to Ivan. 'I'll say one thing for you Ivan, you certainly know the best restaurants in town.' He looked around him appreciatively. 'Now what is it that's so urgent that you'd call me away in the middle of an election campaign?'

'If that nosey investigator isn't stopped, you can say goodbye to your election campaign. You'll be spending all your money on lawyers.'

'What on earth are you talking about?'

'The woman investigating Julie's murder.'

'Murder? You told me it was an accident.'

'Same thing. You'd be in trouble either way, for trying to cover it up.'

'Now, hang on, Ivan. I said I'd do you a favour, not that I'd become a co-conspirator in a child's murder.' He pushed his chair back and started to get up.

'Relax. She won't find anything. Not if you do as I say.' He waved the waiter away. 'Five minutes.'

'What do you want me to do now? I'm in enough trouble as it is with the Commissioner.'

'Just tell the Commissioner it's time he revoked that woman's licence. We don't want her snooping about. I suppose you do realise that it was her you were playing golf with last weekend?'

'What? Paco's partner? Jacaranda something?' asked Enrique in astonishment.

'That's her.'

'But you said she worked for the Hacienda.'

'Exactly. It didn't sound right, so I had her checked out, and her name is Jacaranda Dunne and she's a private detective. Now why was Paco playing golf with a PI? He said she was the Marquesa's daughter, but she didn't bear any resemblance to the exotic Rosa. Why would he do that, especially when he knew you and Annika were his partners? That seems very strange to me. We need to stop this woman from looking into our business. Or we'll both suffer.'

'I'll see what I can do, but friendship only goes so far, you know, Ivan.'

'I do, Enrique. But you should have realised that once you start on something, you can't give up half way through. I've been very generous to you and your campaign. Don't forget it.'

'But I never agreed to all this violence. And the policeman…' his voice faltered. 'That wasn't meant to happen. It was only supposed to be an accident that would keep him out of work for a few weeks. If he hadn't been so pig-headed we wouldn't have had to do anything.'

'So he brought it on himself?' Ivan asked, smirking at him.

'I didn't say that.' Enrique looked as though he was going to burst into tears.

'I know. Don't upset yourself. Just have one more word with the Commissioner and then it will all go away.' He waved for the waiter to come over. 'We're ready to order now.'

CHAPTER 28

JD decided to speak to Jacobo. She knew the bar where he always ate breakfast; it wasn't far from the agency. It was a while since she'd seen him, and it would be nice to catch up. Just as she'd expected, he was sitting at a table outside, his newspaper open in front of him, alongside a cup of sweet black coffee and half a baguette filled with bacon and tomato.

'*Buenos días*, Jacobo,' she said, sitting down opposite him.

'JD. This is a surprise. Have you eaten?'

She shook her head, so he raised his arm and beckoned the waiter across.

'Café solo,' she said.

'Nothing to eat?' he asked.

'I'm not hungry.'

'So what's up? Is it the case?'

'Yes. It's becoming a lot more difficult than I expected,' she admitted. 'There seem to be some influential people involved and nobody is talking.'

'What about your friend, the Captain? Can't he help?'

'No, he keeps warning me off. Says I'm treading on dangerous ground. I thought you might be able to help.'

'I will if I can. What is it you need?'

'Can you go through the archives and see if you can find any TV footage on Enrique de Valdes?'

'The politician? Isn't he standing for mayor of Marbella in the next election?'

'Yes. But I think he's involved somehow.'

If Jacobo was surprised, he didn't say so, just asked, 'Is that all?'

'No. Have you ever come across a man called Ivan Lebedev? He's a retired Russian diplomat, from the consular office in Madrid, and a member of the Brotherhood of the Virgin of Remorse.'

'You think he's involved in the kidnapping of the two girls?'

'Yes, maybe not directly, but I'm sure he's connected with it somehow. That's what I need to find out.'

'So, what am I looking for, exactly?'

'I don't know, any interviews with either of them, or any connections to the police.'

'Why the police, in particular?'

'There has to be a reason why the investigation was shut down, and why I'm being told that I'm getting out of my depth. Somebody doesn't want me to find out who's behind this, and I don't know if it's because they're involved with people trafficking or have been unwitting participants in it,' JD replied.

'And there's murder, as well. I always thought it was a bit fishy, the investigating officer being run over like that and nobody responsible. Something must have been on the CCTV footage.'

JD hesitated, then said, 'Well there was actually. We found it. It was a Russian car, one of those posh ones, with diplomatic plates.'

'Really.' Jacobo raised his eyebrows in surprise. 'Now I understand. Although I'm still not sure of Valdes's connection.'

JD explained the links they had found between the two men. 'But, you see, at the moment it's not enough. I can't take it to the police until I have more evidence.'

'Well, JD, you certainly know how to liven up a man's morning. I'll do what I can. It may take a couple of days.'

'Thanks, Jacobo. I owe you.' JD drank her coffee and added, 'Sorry, I've got to dash. See you one evening perhaps, for a drink.'

'Sounds good. I'll ring you when I have something.'

'Adios.'

JD decided to visit her mother rather than phone her. She took the metro from the bus station and it dropped her off in the centre of Torremolinos; from there it was a short walk to her mother's apartment. She had to find out exactly what Rosa knew about Paco and the *Cofradía.*

Her mother's apartment was large and luxurious, and overlooked the beach; she'd lived there for almost twenty years, ever since her husband had died. It was still early when JD arrived and rang the bell; she was sure her mother, who'd never been an early riser, would still be having breakfast.

'Jacaranda. Goodness me. Is something wrong, child? What are you doing here at this time of day?'

'No, Mama. I was in the area and thought I'd call in and have a coffee with you,' said JD, slipping easily into her second language.

Her mother smiled at her and said, 'That's a nice thought, Jacaranda, but you don't fool me. What is it that you want?'

JD followed her into the kitchen. A half-eaten piece of toast lay on the table. 'I wouldn't mind something to eat,' she said, anticipating her mother's next question.

'Of course, toast and marmalade?'

'Lovely.'

Even after so many years in Spain, her mother always had to have English marmalade for breakfast. She'd developed a taste for it during her years living in Edinburgh.

'So how are you?'

'As well as can be expected,' her mother said, pouring her a cup of coffee.

'Is Paco at home?'

'No, he's playing golf. That's all he does these days, since he retired. He said you had a good game together last weekend.'

'We did. He seems to know a lot of the members.'

'Does he, *cariño*? I wouldn't know. I've only been there a couple of times. Golf club dinners must be the most boring events in the world. All everybody ever talks about is how they played, and what they scored.'

'Did you know he was a member of the *Cofradía* where Julie's body was found, Mama?' She could tell from her mother's face, that this was a surprise.

'No, I didn't. I didn't think Paco was interested in that sort of thing. Why? Is it important?'

'I just think it's strange. He knew I was investigating the girls' disappearance and he knew that Julie was found in a building belonging to an organisation of which he was a member. I'm surprised that he never mentioned it, not even to you.'

'Why would he? He didn't have anything to do with the girl's death. I hope you're not saying that he did.' Her mother was adopting her defensive stance. If JD wasn't careful it would descend into a row, which would mean she would be asked to leave, followed by weeks of silence on her mother's part.

'Of course not. I just wondered if you knew about it.'

'All Paco talks about is golf.'

'Do you know anything about his past? His family, for example?'

'Not much. He never knew his father; his mother brought him up. No brothers nor sisters as far as I know. There's not much to tell. I think he worked in Melilla for a bit, as some sort of engineer. To be honest, I wasn't all that interested and he was reluctant to talk about it.'

'Did he ever say how he became a member of the *Cofradía*? I thought it was supposed to be through family connections?'

'You'll have to ask him.'

'I did, he said it was inherited from his father.'

'Well there you are then. Why are you asking me?'

'You just said he didn't know his father.'

Her mother scowled at her. 'What is it, Jacaranda? Do you suspect Paco of being involved in that murder? I'm telling you now, you couldn't be more wrong. Paco wouldn't hurt anyone. If you must know, his father died when he was a baby.'

'I'm sorry to hear that. Do you know anything else about him?'

'Nothing that would interest you.'

JD ate the toast, then said, 'Well I'd better get going, Mama.' She looked at her watch. 'The next train is in fifteen minutes. I should just make it.'

'You came on the metro? Oh, Jacaranda, when are you going to get rid of this phobia of yours. How can you be a private investigator if you don't drive? Surely you need to get out and about to meet people?'

'I manage, Mama. Linda has a car.'

'Huh. One car between the three of you. Look if it's a question of money, I'll help you buy one.'

'No, it's nothing to do with money. I just prefer not to drive. What's so strange about that? Anyway, I must go; they'll be wondering where I've got to. If you think of anything else that could be helpful, please let me know. That young girl is still missing; I'm worried she will end up like her friend.'

'All right. I will. Do you really have to go so soon? You've only just got here.'

'There's a lot to do; I can't leave it all to Linda and Nacho. I'll come over one evening, if you like.'

'That would be nice, Jacaranda.' Her mother appeared to have mellowed. 'Do you want me to ask Paco anything in particular?'

'No, I can see it was nothing. I'm sorry if I upset you.'

'You didn't upset me.' Her mother's hackles were up again. It was time she went.

'Adios, Mama,' she said, kissing her mother on the cheeks.

'*Adios, cariño.*'

JD still wasn't convinced that Paco was who he said he was. Maybe she was being paranoid, but it wouldn't hurt to add his name to the list. After all, her mother didn't seem to know anything about him; she'd only been going out with him for just over a year. Even if he wasn't directly involved with their case, he might be up to something else. It seemed too much of a coincidence that he knew both Valdes and Lebedev.

Besides which, it wouldn't be the first time her mother had got involved with someone who wasn't what they seemed to be; a lot of people thought her mother was rich. They didn't realise that having a title didn't necessarily mean you had a lot of money.

Sophie is Still Missing

CHAPTER 29

Before she could get to the office, Nacho had phoned to say that Federico had dropped off the forensic report on the car, and wanted to speak to her, urgently. He would be in their usual bar. That in itself was strange, because he always rang her mobile, never came to the agency. Did this mean he was still angry with her? Her stomach felt weak as she considered the possibility that they might break up. She had become very fond of Federico, in fact, if pushed she would have to admit that she was in love with him. And she had believed that he was in love with her. What had gone wrong? Her mother was always telling her that she put up barriers which scared men away. Was that true? Was that what she'd done with Federico? So it was with trepidation she made her way to their usual meeting place. She couldn't stop thinking about his coldness the last time they'd met; what had she done to cause it? Or had he met someone else and didn't know how to tell her? Well, she'd know soon enough, because she could see him sitting at the usual table, staring at the harbour. She felt her chest tightening as she looked at him; she wasn't sure how she'd feel if they broke up. It wasn't something she wanted to contemplate.

'*Buenos días*, Federico,' she said, feeling a little awkward. 'What did you want to tell me?'

'Did you get the forensic report?' he asked. 'I dropped it off with Nacho on my way here.'

'Thanks. I haven't been into the office yet; I've been out all morning. Thanks anyway.'

'Who else would take such a risk for you?' He called the waiter across. 'Coffee?' he asked JD.

'Yes. Café solo,' she told the waiter. 'So what's this all about?'

'I've been told to tell you, by my Lieutenant Colonel, that you are overstepping the mark.'

'The Lieutenant Colonel says what?'

'That they will revoke your licence if you don't stop meddling in police business.'

She stared at him. 'Can they do that?'

'I don't know. I'm just the messenger here, but I know they can make life very difficult for you, and me by association.'

'That's not fair. I'm trying to help. If they'd done their job properly in the first place maybe Sophie wouldn't still be missing. Is that why you were in such a bad mood the last time we met?'

'Partly.'

'And the other part?'

'You just don't realise how dangerous these people can be, Jacaranda. It's just a game to you, but you are putting your life and those of others at risk.'

'How can you even suggest that, Federico? It's certainly not a game when two girls are abducted and the police fail to find them, and then one of them turns up dead in the Cofradía in the centre of Málaga, and the next thing that happens is that the case is closed. It may be a game for the Guardia Civil, but it certainly isn't for me.'

'I knew you wouldn't listen to reason.'

'I will always listen to reason, but this isn't reason. This is a cover-up and I mean to find out who's behind it.' She stood up. 'If you won't help me, then I will do it alone.'

'Jacaranda. Jacaranda,' he called, but she was already walking away.

Revoke her licence. Let them try.

As she walked past the cathedral she began to calm down a little, but a niggling doubt was running around in her head. Was Federico really concerned for her safety, or did he too want her to stop investigating? She must be getting close to something if important men like the Lieutenant Colonel wanted to warn her off. She didn't even know who he was, so who was bending his ear?

'JD. JD.' She stopped; it was Carlos, sitting in his usual place on the cathedral steps.

'I have something for you,' he whispered as she bent down to put a couple of coins in his bowl. 'Buy me a beer and I'll tell you.'

'It'd better be good, Carlos. I'm very busy today,' she said, following him across the square and sitting down at one of the empty tables. The bar was busy with tourists; she could see them staring at her and Carlos. They must have looked a pretty odd couple.

'It's about that dead girl. I heard something,' he said in a stage whisper, and leant closer to her.

'Keep your voice down,' she said. Then added for the benefit of the waiter, 'Two beers and some tapas, *por favor*.' She wondered how long it was since Carlos had had a bath; the smell emanating from him was mind numbing. 'So, tell me, what did you hear?'

'Someone high up in the Policia Nacional was paid to shut it down. I heard them moaning about it.'

'Who? Whom did you hear?' He was spinning this out; she wished he'd get to the point but she knew better than to antagonise him.

'*Dos grises*,' he replied, using their old nickname.

'The Guardia Civil?' she asked in surprise.

The waiter delivered the beers and immediately Carlos drank his down without taking a breath and then nodded at his empty glass.

'Drink the other,' she said. 'I'm not thirsty. Are you telling me that two Civil Guard officers were complaining that someone in the National Police was paid to close the investigation?'

'That's right.' He wiped his mouth with his sleeve and let out a gentle burp. 'Said it was a crying shame that a young girl could be murdered and nobody did anything about it.'

'Do you know anything else about this CNP officer? His name? Where he was stationed? Was he from Málaga?'

Carlos shook his head. 'I think he was from Madrid. Yes, that's right. They didn't like that either, someone coming down from Madrid to close it all down. Not his business, they said, to close down their case.'

'Did the Guardia officers know you were listening to their conversation?' she asked.

'No. You know me; I'm invisible.'

'Did you know them?'

'I've seen them about.'

'Their names?'

He shook his head. 'I don't ask people their names,' he said. His glass was empty again.

'I've got to go,' JD said, putting a twenty euro note on the table and getting up. 'Here, buy yourself something to eat. And thanks for the information.'

'Any time JD.' He flashed his blackened teeth and another wave of halitosis drifted up at her.

She was quite fond of old Carlos, but generally preferred to keep her distance; living rough didn't lead to the best of hygiene. But right now she was more concerned with what he'd told her. And if there was any truth in it. Closing down the investigation into the suspicious death of a young girl was not normal; she'd thought that from the outset. But a senior officer in the National Police coming to Málaga from Madrid to close the case? What was that all about? Did he even have the right to do that?

She turned the corner into the alley that led to the agency, just in time to see Linda coming out of the office.

'Linda, hang on a minute,' she shouted.

'Hi, JD. I'm just off to collect the photos from the newspaper office. In fact I've ordered copies of Ivan and his wife as well. I thought they might be useful.'

'Good idea. Hey Linda, you've got lots of contacts. Who do you know in the Guardia Civil? Any female officers?'

'Yes, a couple. Why?'

'I've heard that there's been some disquiet amongst them about the case being closed; apparently the order came from someone in the National Police. Can you find out anything about it?'

'That doesn't make sense. Nobody in the Civil Guard takes orders from the National Police. I bet it was Carlos who told you that.' Linda shook her head, and added, 'No, I very much doubt it's true, but I will ask around. There are so many odd things in this case, I suppose it's worth investigating.'

'Yes, do that, please. I think we're getting close to finding things that some powerful people don't want us to uncover. I've just been talking to the Captain and he said we're to drop the case or they will revoke my licence. How's that for justice?'

Linda stared at her in surprise; her big blue eyes even wider than usual. 'He said that? To you? And he's still alive?' She laughed. 'Well, it was one way of telling us we're on the right track.'

'Just what I thought,' said JD. 'Is Nacho in?'

'He is at his computer, as always.'

'Good. See you later, then.'

She walked into the agency, thinking to herself how lucky she was with her team. Linda, in particular, had many useful contacts which she'd made through the law firm where she'd previously worked, and now it seemed that they included members of the Guardia Civil.

CHAPTER 30

Just as Linda had said, Nacho was at his computer, three empty coffee cups lined up on his desk.

'Busy?' she asked.

'Where have you been, JD? And why aren't you answering your mobile? I've been ringing you.'

JD looked at her phone; there were three missed calls. 'What's so urgent?'

'I've found out who sponsored them,' Nacho said, with a big grin.

'Really?'

'Yes, well one was your friend Paco, and the other was a long-standing member of the *Cofradia* and an officer in the National Police, Comisario Sanchez.'

'Well done, Nacho. That's good news. Is he on the list of those who've been awarded one of those crucifixes?'

'No. But he's been a member for a long time, since he was a boy. All his family seem to be *cofrades*, well the men at least.'

'So, how did he know these two men? And did he know Paco?'

'He must have done if they both sponsored Valdes and Lebedev. And that's another thing, Paco lied to you.'

'Yes, I know. My mother says that he never knew his father; he died when he was a baby.'

'He's only been a member for four years.'

'So he didn't inherit his membership of the *Cofradia*?'

'No, he was sponsored. And guess who one of his sponsors was.'

JD looked at him.

Nacho was enjoying this. 'Comisario Sanchez. They're members of the same golf club.'

She groaned. Was this what it was all about? Doing favours for members of the golf club? Surely it was something more sinister than that.

'What is it, JD?' asked Nacho.

'It doesn't sound like a motive for murder, does it? Just a few stupid men, wanting to be members of the same Brotherhood. We'll need more than that.' She felt deflated.

'I'm not saying they are all involved in the murder, but they might be implicated in the cover-up. I mean why would Paco lie about something like that? Who cares if he was sponsored for the stupid *Cofradía*, or inherited his place? It doesn't make sense.'

Nacho was right; she shouldn't dismiss it out of hand. 'All right, put it up on the board with the rest of the puzzle. Have you found out anything about the three men who knew the entry codes and had crucifixes?'

'Felipe, Jaime and Pablo? Yes, they're all long-term members of the *Cofradía*. Just as Jorge said, it's a father to son thing.'

'Did you find out where they were on the night that Julie died?'

'Yes, Felipe and Pablo were at the *Cofradía*, carrying the other throne, the one with the Christ figure. They were out until gone midnight.'

'And the other one?'

'Jaime. Apparently he'd hurt his back and couldn't take part in the procession. I don't know where he was. But I've discovered something that's very interesting. Jaime is a taxi driver; but before that he used to work for the Russian Embassy car pool, in Madrid. Then he moved back to Málaga about five years ago and bought his own taxi.'

'So that's how he could have met Lebedev?'

'It's possible. Bit of a coincidence, isn't it? And he's got no alibi.'

'We need to check it out. Let's concentrate on Jaime. When Linda gets back I want you to take the photo of the car's driver and see if anyone recognises him. Confirm that it really is Jaime driving that car. Start with Jorge; he seems to know everybody there. See if he has a photo of Jaime. If he was presented with one of those crucifixes they probably took a photo of the presentation. Oh, and find out all you can about him. Is he married, kids, girlfriend, boyfriend? Everything you can. Ah, here she is now. Linda, do you have the photographs?'

'I do. What's the rush?'

'We think we may have found the driver of the car.'

'So he might be our killer?'

'It's looking likely. While Nacho is doing that, can you ring your friend in the Guardia Civil and check on Carlos's story. And if it's true, then we need to know the name of the man who shut down the investigation.'

When Nacho had packed up his things and left to find Jorge, and Linda was on the telephone to the Guardia Civil, JD studied the evidence board. At long last things were beginning to hang together. It was now very evident that they were investigating two different crimes, three if she included the dead policeman. She moved the pieces of evidence around the board until the picture became clearer. There was nothing to suggest that Ivan or Valdes had anything to do with the kidnapping, or that Kevin and Ali were involved in Julie's murder; that had happened more than six months after the girls had vanished, and Kevin at least was back in the UK by then. The questions that still had to be answered were, where had Julie been for those six months and where was Sophie now? She drew a large question mark on the board, half way between the two sets of evidence. What were they missing? She needed to look further into the lives of Ivan and his wife.

'JD. Carlos was right. May God forgive me for ever doubting him, the dirty old vagabond. I spoke to my contact in the Guardia Civil and she confirms that all her colleagues are furious that it's been swept under the table. The official reasons for closing it down were lack of evidence and that too much time had already passed.'

'What about the dead policeman?'

'Oh, they're even more angry about that. It's been filed away as an unlawful death due to a traffic accident. Again the official line is that there was no way of identifying the driver of the car.'

'Did they even try?' asked JD.

'She says not.'

'Who is this woman, anyway?'

'Lola? Her daughter went to primary school with Jane. We used to chat while we waited for them to come out.'

'Did she tell you the name of the National Police officer who closed down the investigation?'

'No, but she's going to make some discreet enquiries and get back to me. She says nobody can understand why the CNP were involved anyway.'

'Let me know as soon as you hear from her.'

'Okay, Boss. I see you've been rearranging Nacho's board.'

'Yes. Come and look at it, Linda. What are we missing?'

'Besides Sophie, you mean?'

'Yes. I have a feeling we've been so bogged down with all these clues, that we've lost sight of something.'

'Well, we've never discovered why the girls were taken in the first place. We thought it was a white slave ring, but then Julie turned up dead, back in the place where she was kidnapped. If they were going to sell the girls into slavery they would hardly do it here. So where did they take them? And why?'

'You're right. We need to find out where Julie's been. If she'd been kidnapped to sell into prostitution, how does that link up with Valdes and Lebedev? We haven't found anything to link either of them to prostitution rings.'

'Maybe they have nothing to do with it at all. Or maybe they are just part of the clientele and don't want their wives to know,' suggested Linda.

'I'm convinced they're involved somehow. I just don't know how. You could be right about them being clientele of a high class brothel, but did Julie look as though she'd escaped from somewhere like that? Remember, she was undernourished and dressed in rags when they found her, hardly a high-class prostitute.'

'We're assuming that the two girls remained together, but we've no evidence for that. Even if we find Julie's killer, it doesn't mean we will find Sophie,' said Linda. 'Oh, by the way, I came across this last night. Phil's got a thing about buying a boat. I don't know how on earth he thinks we can afford one; the boats in here cost more than our house.' She handed JD a copy of 'Yachting in the Mediterranean.' 'Look at page twenty-five.'

JD opened it. There was a photograph of an enormous yacht, and sitting on board, smiling for the cameras, were Ivan Lebedev, his wife Annika, Enrique de Valdes and another glamorous woman who, according to the article, was Valdes' wife. It was part of an interview about the advantages of having a mooring in the exclusive Puerto Banus.

'So where does a retired consular officer get the money to afford a yacht like that?' she asked.

'Don't ask me, but Phil was green with envy.'

Linda's phone began to ring. JD winced; it had the most annoying jingling tune.

'It's Lola,' her assistant said. 'I'd better get it.'

JD continued to puzzle over the board while Linda chatted to the officer from the Guardia Civil.

'Well?' she asked, when Linda returned.

'Yes, she's got his name. It was Capitán Luis Malveno but, according to the rumour mill, it was our friend Comisario Sanchez who put the pressure on him to do it. He had visited the station just days before the case was closed.'

'So what was a Commissioner of the National Police doing at the Guardia Civil Cuartel? Is that usual?'

'Arranging a game of golf?' said Linda.

'Malveno, you said. That sounds familiar. Just a minute.' JD went to Nacho's desk and picked up the list of members of the *Cofradía*. 'Just as I thought. He's another bloody member.'

'What, of the Brotherhood?'

JD nodded. There were far too many connections now for it to be a mere coincidence. These men had deliberately tried to cover up Julie's murder. They had closed ranks to protect someone. But who? And more importantly, did any of them know where Sophie was now?

'What are we going to do?' asked Linda. 'Even if we go to the police, they won't take any notice of us. They'll stick to their story that there's not enough evidence to warrant reopening the case. And what about your licence? We don't want to provoke them.'

'I don't know, Linda. I think we just have to carry on and build up as much evidence as possible. Let's see what Nacho has to say when he gets back. If we can identify the driver of the car then we'd have something to take to the police.'

'Why don't you talk to the Captain, again?'

'I might have to, Linda.'

CHAPTER 31

Jorge was not pleased to see Nacho again. 'What is it you want this time?' he snapped, as Nacho followed him inside the offices of the *Cofradía*. 'I haven't got anything else to tell you.'

'I just need two minutes of your time, and then I'll be gone,' said Nacho, taking the photographs from his bag. 'I wondered if you recognised this man?'

Jorge took the photo and peered at it. 'It could be anyone. Don't you have anything clearer?' He took off his glasses and polished them, then picked up the photograph again. 'Ah yes, I can't be certain, but he does look familiar.'

'Do you know a man called Jaime Ortega Moreno? He and his family have been members of the *Cofradía* for years.'

'Yes, I recognise the name. I knew his father and uncle very well; we joined in the same year. Why do you want to know? Is this supposed to be him?' He peered at the photo again. 'Well I suppose it's possible. I remember his father told me once that his son was a driver for someone important. Paid him very well.'

'Jaime Ortega owned one of those crucifixes you told us about. When they're presented to the Brothers, do you take photographs?'

'Usually. I suppose you want to see if I have one of Jaime?'

'That would be very helpful,' said Nacho.

'Which year would that be?'

'It said 2012 on your list.'

'Ah, yes, the year of the dog.' He walked over to a big metal cabinet and unlocked it. It appeared to have folders going back to the beginning of the twentieth century, many dusty and dog-eared. 'If there is a photograph of the presentation, it will be in here.'

'No digital copy?' asked Nacho.

Jorge gave him a look of disgust. 'Of course not. Our camera wasn't digital then. Maybe one of the newspaper offices will have digital copies if you particularly need them.' He thumbed through the album and held it out for Nacho to see. 'You're in luck. 2012. Yes, that's Jaime there, at the back on the right. But I can't see him being involved in that poor girl's death. He's a very pious man, and as you saw, he's been a member of the *Cofradía* for years.'

Nacho took the album. It wasn't a brilliant photograph but it was a lot clearer than the one they had, and there was a definite likeness. If he could get a digital copy he could run his face recognition software and compare the two images.

'Excellent,' he said with a smile. 'Do you mind if I borrow it for a few days? I'll take good care of it.'

'Very well, but we will need it back. I think you'd better sign for it.' The old man pulled out a small notebook, and indicated where he had to sign. 'Shall we say one week?'

Nacho felt he was back in his old school library. 'A week is great. Thank you.'

As he walked back towards the agency, he decided to make a detour and go to the offices of La Voz de Málaga. The presentation had been in 2012; they were bound to have a digital copy of the photograph.

He arrived back at the agency, a big smile on his face and carrying three coffees and a bag of croissants.

'Good news,' he said, distributing his purchases to his companions. 'Pretty sure he's our guy. I'm just going to run the face recognition software and confirm it.'

'You're a star, Nacho,' said Linda. 'How soon will you know?'

'Oh, it won't take long because it only has to scan two faces, not searching through thousands of images.'

'Well, we'll leave you to it.'

JD considered going straight to *cuartel* of the Guardia Civil, and asking for Federico, but she knew that would antagonise him ever further, so she rang him instead.

'*Buenos días*, Jacaranda. More questions?' he said.

'I wondered if we could have lunch today, Federico? I have a lot to tell you.'

'Jacaranda, I told you before, I can't get involved in your case. I'm sorry.'

'For what? That you can't get involved in the case, or that you can't have lunch with me?'

'You know very well what I mean. Yes, I'll meet you for lunch, on one condition. No talking about missing girls.'

'Agreed. The usual place? In half an hour?'

'Fine. I have to go; I've got some things to finish first.'

She could feel her heart racing at the thought of seeing him again; she really didn't want them to split up. She grabbed her coat, and said to Nacho, 'I'm going to talk to the Captain. I want to see what he knows about the National Police's interference in a Guardia Civil investigation. I'll be back after lunch. Ring me as soon as you can confirm that Jaime was the man driving the car.'

'Okay Boss.'

With any luck, by the time she had screwed up the courage to ask Federico for his help, Nacho would have phoned her with confirmation.

She arrived before him, and sat there with a glass of Rioja in front of her, wondering if he would come or not. At last she saw his familiar outline walking along the promenade and her heart gave a skip. At that moment her mobile rang.

'Nacho?'

'It's him. Jaime is the driver of the car.'

'That's good news. See if you can find out where he's working now. You said he was a taxi driver. Is it here in Málaga?'

'Okay Boss.'

'Anything else?'

'Nothing interesting. He's been married since he was twenty-one, his wife is a nurse and he has three teenage daughters. He goes to Mass every Sunday and he doesn't have a criminal record. Nothing sinister there. Oh, and his mother died in March.'

She smiled to herself. Nacho was nothing if not thorough. 'Speak to you later,' she said, turning her mobile to silence and slipping it into her handbag.

Federico had stopped and was talking to a man who looked like a policeman, but wasn't wearing a uniform. They were both very serious. Then abruptly the man turned and walked off.

'Jacaranda, how are you, *cariño*?' Federico asked, bending down and kissing her on both cheeks.

'Well, thank you. Who was that?' she asked, nodding towards the man, who was heading towards the underground parking.

Sophie is Still Missing

'Nobody important, although he thinks he is. Let's order; I'm starving.'

JD didn't press it; she was going to wait until Federico had eaten, drunk a couple of glasses of his favourite Rioja and then tell him what they'd found out.

It had been lovely, sitting there in the winter sunshine, chatting about nothing in particular and watching the boats in the port, just relaxed and happy in each other's company, but all the time, at the back of her mind, was the worry of how he would react when she told him about the case. When he asked the waiter to bring them coffee, she knew she had to say something before it was too late.

'Federico.'

He looked at her and cocked his head to one side, 'At last. I wondered when you'd get round to it.'

'To what?'

'Whatever this delightful lunch is all about.'

'I just wanted to tell you that we've had a breakthrough. We know who the man is that was driving the hit and run car.'

The smile was gone from Federico's face. He was paying attention to her now.

'It's a taxi driver called Jaime Ortega Moreno.'

'Are you sure it's him? If I remember rightly the CCTV photo was very grainy.'

'Yes, we're sure. And what's more, he used to work in Madrid, as a chauffeur at the Russian Embassy.'

Federico's eyebrows went up. 'Interesting. What else have you and your busy little team discovered?'

JD went through all that they knew about the members of the *Cofradía*, the golf club and Comisario Sanchez.

Sophie is Still Missing

At the mention of the CNP, Federico asked, 'How did you find out about Sanchez?'

'It's common knowledge amongst the rank and file of the Guardia Civil. I thought you'd know that.'

'I did. I just didn't realise that so many people were talking about it.' He looked annoyed.

'But how was it possible? That's what I can't understand. I can see why he did it, favours for his mates. It happens everywhere. But interfering in another police force's investigation, I wouldn't have thought that was possible.'

'Anything's possible if you know the right people,' Federico said, bitterly. He poured out the remains of the wine. 'So what do you want me to do?'

'Well, it's murder, or at the least manslaughter. We think this man was involved in Julie's murder, in some way. I'm convinced it was him who placed her body in the *Cofradía*; he had the entry code and his crucifix was found at the scene.'

'But why would he do that? Why didn't he just toss her body in the port?'

'I think he was filled with remorse, either for what he'd done, or because he couldn't bring himself to go to the police.'

'There's a lot of supposition there, Jacaranda.'

'But enough for the Guardia Civil to investigate?'

He didn't reply, so she continued. 'I also think he deliberately ran down the police lieutenant who was investigating Julie's murder, probably because he'd found something incriminating. Maybe he was told to do that.'

'So you don't think he was working alone?'

'Well, the thing is, Federico, where have the girls been since August last year? They couldn't have been with Jaime; he has a family.'

Sophie is Still Missing

She thought about what Nacho had told her about Jaime Ortega's family. He was a religious man who had daughters himself; maybe he placed her in the *Cofradía* because he was trying to make his peace with God. Or his recently dead mother.

'I still think you need more. If he wasn't working alone, who was the other person? And why wasn't he driving his taxi that night? How did he get his hands on a Pobeda M20?' said Federico. 'We could search his house, but if he does have an accomplice that might scare him away. Remember the priority is to find Sophie.'

'So you think the girls were together?' JD asked.

'It's a possibility we can't ignore. Get me some more evidence and I'll take it to my boss.'

'Is that a promise?'

'Yes, it's a promise. I can see it's the only way to get some peace. But be careful, Jacaranda; if these people killed an investigating officer, they can kill again.'

Sophie is Still Missing

CHAPTER 32

JD was just finishing breakfast in her usual bar, when the phone rang; it was Tim.

'Hi, JD. I've got some news that might interest you,' he said. 'That car you were asking about, well it's turned up.'

'Really?' she said, excitement making her voice rise. 'Where?'

'You're not going to like it. It's in the mountains of Málaga. Someone must have driven it up there into the forest and set light to it. It was lucky that the whole area didn't go up.'

'But they could still identify it?' she asked.

'Yes, a man walking his dog alerted the fire brigade straight away, and they had the fire out before it could spread into the forest. One of the number plates was still intact.'

'And you're sure it's the same car?'

'Definitely. I went up to see it myself.'

'That's good news. What about the inside? Maybe forensics can find something there,' she said.

'Most of it was burnt out but it's a possibility. That's what I said to the officer at the scene, but the police don't seem very interested. Just a stolen car as far as they're concerned. If you want to have it checked out, you'll need to hurry. I expect they'll be taking it away to the scrap yard any day. That's why I thought I'd give you the heads up.'

'That's good of you, Tim. You've been a great help.'

'Oh, and something else, that photographer chap. He was one of ours after all, a trainee. He just thought it would be fun to get inside and take some photos; he didn't realise that we already had dozens of photos of virgins on their thrones. Thought he was getting something different. Sorry, bit of a wasted line of enquiry for you.'

'It happens. Thanks for letting me know.'

'So what about that drink, JD?'

'Maybe when the investigation is over; I'm just up to my eyes in it at the moment.'

'You still seeing that Guardia Civil chap?'

'Federico?'

'Yes, that one.'

'As a matter of fact, I am.' She was tempted to tell him to mind his own business, but she reminded herself that he was a valuable source of information, although he wasn't that indispensable that she would agree to sleep with him. 'Maybe we could go for a drink one evening and you could bring your girlfriend along? We could make a foursome.'

There was a short silence at the other end of the line and then he said, 'I'll let you know if I hear anything more about the car, JD.'

'Thanks, Tim. Much appreciated,' she said, smiling to herself.

JD was studying the evidence board when Linda and Nacho arrived. They had barely removed their coats when she said, 'Come in here. It's time we went over what we've got. Things are starting to move and I don't want us to miss anything important.'

'And good morning to you, Boss,' said Linda, picking up a pad and pen and joining her in the meeting room.

'What's happened, JD?' asked Nacho, looking around. 'No coffee?'

'No, I had breakfast in the bar this morning. Sorry. You'll have to wait until we've finished,' said JD.

'Well if I drift off, it'll be your fault. You know I don't function until I've had at least three cups of coffee.'

'I don't think you'll do that when you hear what I have to say. First of all the car has turned up. As we expected someone had tried to destroy the evidence but they weren't very successful; one of the number plates was legible. So Linda I want you to get over there right away and see what you can find out. Speak to your contacts and find out what they're going to do with the car. I'll ring Federico. We have to move quickly on this before it's scrapped.'

'What do you want me to do, Boss?' asked Nacho.

'We need to know why Jaime wasn't driving his taxi at the time. Why was he driving an embassy registered car? Had he stolen it or had someone given it to him? And let's see if we can get precise dates for when Ivan arrived at the Russian Embassy in Madrid, and when he retired.'

'Okay JD.'

'Boss,' Linda said hesitantly. 'I think we should try to keep a low profile on this. At the moment everyone thinks that the case is closed and that even though we're working on it, nobody believes that the police will re-open the investigation. If Ivan and Jaime were involved in Julie's death we don't want them doing a disappearing act because they think we're on to them.'

'You have a point, Linda. What do you suggest?'

'Well until we have collected enough evidence for the police to take us seriously, I think we should be careful whom we talk to.'

'Such as? Are you talking about the captain?' JD was instantly on the defensive.

'You did say he was warning you off.'

'Yes, but he wouldn't do anything to jeopardise our investigation. He's not like that.'

Linda smiled at her, 'If you say so. How much have you told him?'

'Only what I want him to know.' Linda had a good point. Maybe JD had been too free with her information. 'But you've reminded me of something. I should make sure that Tim doesn't mention anything about the burnt out car being connected to the hit and run case.'

'You're probably too late. Even if he doesn't report it, there are other journalists who will find it very interesting that the car has embassy plates. Let's hope it doesn't spook Jaime, before we can find Sophie.'

'You know we're backing a lot on one assumption, for which, I might add, we haven't a shred of proof,' said Nacho.

'And that is?' asked JD.

'That Sophie and Julie were together. We know they were together when they were abducted, but until we know what happened next, we can't be sure where Sophie is. Which is more important, finding Julie's killer or finding Sophie alive?'

'Point taken, Nacho. I think you'd better go and get yourself some coffee and start looking for why Jaime was driving that car in the first place. I'm convinced that Jaime is the link to solving both cases. He's a man with a conscience; he's religious and he's a family man. I don't think he wanted to be involved in these murders; that's why he took Julie to the *Cofradía* and sprinkled her body with pink carnations. If we can prove he was involved, then maybe he'll help us to find Sophie.'

'Have we found out why pink carnations?' asked Linda. 'Why not red, or white?'

'They stand for remembrance of the deceased,' said Nacho unexpectedly.

Both women looked at him. 'How do you know that?' asked Linda.

'My mother told me. She always takes pink carnations to the church when there's a funeral.'

'So what does that tell us?' asked JD. 'Was it a sign of his conscience troubling him?'

'It could just be that there were some lying around in the *Cofradía*,' said Linda.

'Ring Jorge and ask him if he knows where they came from.'

'Okay, Boss.'

Nacho's first stop was at the bar around the corner; they served the finest coffee in Málaga, and had been doing so for almost a hundred years. He ordered a large *café solo* to take away, and a *café exprés* which he drank standing at the bar. Instantly he felt better. His mother was always complaining that he drank too much coffee, and that it wasn't good for him, but he needed that caffeine boost, especially when he was working.

'Feeling better?' the girl behind the counter asked him. He was a regular there. 'You're late today. I thought you'd taken the day off.'

'No, my boss wanted to go over some things first thing. We've a lot on, so I'd better get back.'

'The investigation going well? Are you any nearer to catching the bastard who killed that poor girl?' she asked, wiping down the bar with a wet cloth.

'Mmmn. Got to go. See you tomorrow.' He was sure he hadn't told the girl anything about the investigation, but yet she knew they were looking into it. It was that bloody newspaper article; he'd hoped that people would have forgotten about it by now.

Sophie is Still Missing

The office was deserted when he got back, so he went straight to his computer and began to look for details of Jaime's taxi. It was straightforward. He was part of a pool of independent taxi drivers who worked the airport routes. He found an address and telephone number for the rank and the number of Jaime's cab. Now all he had to do was get to the airport. He sighed. Well, it would have to be his bike; it would only take him about half an hour. That was okay; it would give him time to work out what on earth he was going to say when he got there.

The airport was quiet and only a handful of taxis were parked outside the concourse, their drivers lounging about, chatting and smoking. He approached them, a little apprehensively, and asked, 'Anyone seen Jaime Ortega?'

'Jaime? Don't think he's working today,' said a small man in his forties. 'In fact I haven't seen him for a few days.'

'Oh, that's a shame. My sister is a friend of his daughter and I wanted to give him something for her. When will he be here?'

'No idea, mate. He comes and goes,' said an older man, with a thick beard.

'Oh, I thought he'd be here every day,' said Nacho. 'She said he worked here, at the airport.'

'He does, but he has other jobs as well. You know, private jobs. Off the books so to speak,' said the first man.

'What he means, is that Jaime has another job. He sometimes has to drive this rich foreign bloke about in a great black limousine. It's not regular, but when he rings him Jaime drops everything and off he goes. I reckon he must pay him very well.'

'Is there a rota or anything? Could I find out when he's due in next?'

Sophie is Still Missing

'You could speak to Ana. Here's the number,' the bearded guy handed him a business card with AIRPORT TAXIS printed on it.

'Thanks. That's very helpful.' Nacho pocketed the card and cycled off. He didn't need to ask who the rich guy was; it was pretty obvious it was Ivan.

As soon as he got back to the agency, he dialled the number on the card. 'Buenos días, Ana. This is Antonio Casados from the Guardia Civil. I want to make an enquiry about one of your taxi drivers,' he said. 'I believe you have a Jaime Ortega Moreno working for you.' He waited while she consulted her computer.

'Yes, he's been working with us for about five years. Why, is there anything wrong?'

'No, no. Can you tell me if he was working on the night of 22nd March?'

There was a pause and then she said, 'No, he wasn't working that night. He had a couple of weeks off for Holy Week; he's a *costalero*.'

'And the night of 8th September?'

After a moment she said 'No, he wasn't working then, either.'

'Thank you, I won't take up any more of your time, Ana. *Buenos días*.'

Nacho rang off. That was easy. Maybe she got lots of calls from the Guardia Civil. At last it was making sense; Jaime was still working for Ivan, on a temporary basis. He picked up the marker pen and went to the evidence board. Now it looked like they had a real suspect. He paused, staring at the photo of Ivan coming out of the hospital on the morning that Julie's body was found. His wife was there, and another man. Bodyguard, chauffeur or taxi driver? It looked like all three. It was Jaime.

Sophie is Still Missing

But he wasn't holding open the door of the Pobeda M20. It was a typical airport taxi, his taxi.

CHAPTER 33

JD made her way to the recording studio to meet Jacobo. It was a beautiful morning, with a bright blue sky and a fresh breeze coming in from the sea, so she decided to walk through the park rather than take the bus. A flock of screeching parakeets flew past her and landed in a large eucalyptus tree. She could make out their nests, high in the branches. Every year there seemed to be more and more of these brightly coloured birds. Some thought them a nuisance but she didn't mind their noise; they were exotic. She breathed in the scent of the late flowering jasmine, and let her mind wander back over the case and what they had actually achieved.

Although they had discovered a lot about the girls' abduction, and the two deaths, they had very little in terms of concrete evidence. If she had been working for the police she could have brought in her suspects by now and questioned them formally, but it seemed like she had a double mountain to climb, not only to solve the case but also convince the police to listen to her.

Her mobile rang. It was Linda. 'Hi, any news?'

'Yes. I spoke to Jorge. He says they always used white carnations for the Virgin Mary, symbolising pure love and innocence. It had been a surprise for him to see the pink ones, but he will ask the woman who normally does the flowers, and ring me back.'

'Anything else?'

'No, I'm just going to see Lola, to ask about the car.'

'Okay. Don't you think it's a bit strange that he got rid of the car now, six months after Julie died? Why didn't they dispose of it right away?'

'Too confident that nobody would know it was them?' suggested Linda.

'Maybe. Or maybe they knew the investigation would be closed down and didn't want to draw attention to the fact that an embassy car had gone missing.'

'It shows we're on the right track,' said Linda. 'They're panicking. Where are you, by the way? What's with the heavy breathing?'

'I'm on my way to Jacobo's studio.'

'Walking?'

'Yes, why?'

'You must be mad. See you later then.'

By the time she arrived at the recording studio, JD was beginning to agree with Linda. She definitely needed to get fitter. She would enrol on a self-defence course; she'd done many of them in the past but her skills were definitely rusty these days. If Steed was back in the picture, she needed to be in good shape.

'Hi JD,' said Jacobo, opening the door and ushering her into his office. 'You're looking hot and bothered. Can I get you anything?'

'Some water would be good.'

'Did you walk?'

'It seemed a good idea at the time.'

He handed her a bottle of water and said, 'I've found something, but I'm not sure if it's what you're looking for. It's from 2013.' He pulled down the blind and switched on his computer. 'Lebedev, your Russian guy was involved in a building development called Lago de la Sirena. It looked good, and plenty of people were interested in buying the properties. It had a golf course, fishing and boating lakes, and thirty luxurious houses. It was going to be a very exclusive estate.'

'And?'

'This is an investigative documentary about the construction that was going on at that time in Marbella, much of which has since been declared illegal by the government. It's by one of our best investigative journalists, José Garcia. Sadly, he's no longer with us. He stepped on the toes of too many important people.'

'What he's dead?'

'No, of course not. He works for a Madrid paper now.' Jacobo laughed. 'I think the job is getting to you, JD.'

'Maybe it is. So what was Valdes' connection with the new development?'

'He was on the planning committee, and according to José Garcia, received enormous backhanders from all the developers, but Lebedev in particular.'

The virtual tour of the new development showed luxurious detached houses with gardens and swimming pools. Some properties even had their own jetties on the edge of the lake. It looked very exclusive. Their business logo was of a glamorous mermaid, sitting by a lake.

'So what happened? What went wrong?' she asked.

'The site was in a designated natural park, and building was prohibited—a bit like your Green Belt in England—but Valdes gave them planning permission. There were a lot of protests from local people, but the construction still went ahead. Then suddenly, six months into the project, it was stopped; the Junta de Andalucia stepped in and shut everything down. The company went bankrupt and people lost a lot of money. Not Valdes of course, nor your friend Lebedev. There was talk of money laundering, corruption, and taking bribes but nothing could be proved.'

Now it made sense. That was the connection between the two men; they relied on each other's silence.

'Has that been of any use?' he asked.

'Yes, it explains a lot. Thanks Jacobo.'

He switched off the computer. 'The rest is about other illegal construction sites,' he explained.

'So is Lago de la Sirena still unfinished?'

Jacobo laughed, 'No. They pulled it all down and have built one hundred and fifty terraced houses on it.'

'But?'

'I know. They stop one illegal development and then another one goes up. They'd have been better staying with the first one; this new one is a complete eyesore.'

When JD got back to the office, Linda was working at her desk.

'Jorge phoned. The woman who does the flowers told him that the florist had sent them by mistake and wouldn't give them a refund, so she'd kept them,' she said. 'She was going to take them home after the thrones had been taken out, but then someone used them to scatter over the Virgin.'

'So nothing very significant there, then.'

'Doesn't sound like it. How did you get on?'

'Well, Valdes and Lebedev have history.'

As Linda updated the evidence board, JD explained what Jacobo had found out about their two suspects.

'So that explains why Valdes is so friendly with Lebedev. It's not just about golf and the Brotherhood, there's big money there too.'

'Exactly. Any luck with Lola?' asked JD.

'Yes. The Captain must have spoken to someone because they collected the car and forensics are going over it as we speak.'

'Have they found anything?'

'Give them a chance JD; they've only had it a couple of hours. Lola's going to ring me as soon as she knows anything.'

'I've got the CCTV on the car,' said Nacho. JD looked at him blankly. 'Remember, you wanted to know if we could catch him on route from the centre to where he was caught speeding.'

'Oh, yes. So what did you find?'

'Have a look.' He turned his computer round so that she could see it. 'This is Calle Victoria, less than a kilometre from the Cofradía, and ten minutes before he went through the speed cameras.'

'So we have him at the scene of the crime. That's excellent work, Nacho.'

'We just need to find some evidence in the car and we'll have him nailed,' he said.

'One more thing, did you find out exactly when Lebedev started working at the Russian Embassy?' JD asked.

'I did. Not sure that it's of much use, but he joined the diplomatic service when he left university and was posted to Madrid in 1990, worked there for five years and then was sent to Paris, followed by Beirut. In 2010 he returned to Madrid, and was there until his retirement in 2013.'

'So property development was his new career?' said Linda.

'Looks like it, or money laundering,' said JD. 'But nobody would believe a retired diplomat was involved in money laundering.'

'Or kidnap and murder either?' added Nacho. 'Why don't we check out where these two guys live? You know, what sort of life style do they have?'

Sophie is Still Missing

'Might give us something, I suppose.'

'Well, we can't do it. We're busy tomorrow,' said Linda.

'It's Saturday, tomorrow.'

'I know. Nacho and I are going to the Crooked Cat.'

'I thought we said that was too dangerous, Nacho,' JD said, turning to look at him.

'Sorry Boss, I'm booked. I have to honour it. Anyway the other guys will expect me to turn up.'

'Don't worry JD. I'll look after him.'

'You'd better.'

CHAPTER 34

Linda glanced across at her husband; he had that look on his face that said he thought she was making a big mistake. 'I'm sorry, but I promised JD I'd go and keep an eye on him,' she said.

'He's a grown man, for heaven's sake. Not some kid.'

'He's only nineteen, not much older than Laura.'

'And if your boss is so worried about him, why doesn't she go and sit outside in the freezing cold to keep an eye on him?'

'Because I want to do it. It will look less suspicious if you and I are both there. I've booked a table for nine o'clock, by the window, so I can see what's happening.'

'Oh great. I'm really looking forward to it,' he said, with little enthusiasm.

'It's a nice restaurant. You've always said you wanted to go there. Argentinian steak.'

'I don't think so, Linda. I never even knew that place existed before you announced that we were going there tonight.'

'Maybe not that exact place, but you're always saying you'd like a nice juicy Argentinian steak. Now you can have one.' She moved over to the sofa and sat on his lap. 'We'll have a great time. You see,' she said, nibbling his ear.

'Get off. What are you trying to do? Break my legs?' But he couldn't resist smiling. 'All right, I suppose I've got no option. I'm not letting you go on a stake-out on your own. What time have we got to leave?'

Sophie is Still Missing

'Let's say quarter past eight. I'm not too sure about the parking round there at night.'

'Good. Just time to watch the football highlights before we leave.'

'I'll ring Nacho and remind him to take his mobile with him.'

'Linda.'

'Oh, all right, I know I'm fussing.'

She needed to relax, so she put her coat round her shoulders and went into the garden. Although the weather was still warm and sunny during the day, the evenings were definitely getting colder. She took a pack of cigarettes from her pocket and lit one. It was all right for Phil to say she shouldn't fuss, but she knew these men could be dangerous. If they discovered Nacho was spying on them, goodness knows what might happen. She had to be there in case he needed her. Although, to be honest, she had no idea what she expected to happen tonight, or what she could do to help. All she could do was be there if Nacho phoned. If the worse came to worst, she always had her pepper spray in her handbag.

The restaurant was small and decorated in an Argentinian style, with photos of the Andes on the walls and herds of grazing cattle and poncho clad cowboys. By the lilt of the owner's Spanish, he himself was from Argentina, and this was soon confirmed by his pride, not only in their excellent steak, but also for their fine wines. It was all surprisingly good, and soon Phil had forgotten his reluctance to go there.

'I wish you'd try some of this Malbec wine, Linda. It's excellent,' he said, swirling the wine around in his glass and holding it up to the light. She often wondered if he really knew what he was looking for when he did that, but he obviously enjoyed the ritual of examining and tasting the wine as much as the actual drinking of it.

'I'm driving tonight, remember,' she said. They always took turns in who should drive when they went out for dinner, but tonight she had insisted it would be her; if anything happened she didn't want her judgement to be impaired.

The view from their table was perfect. She could see the front entrance to the Crooked Cat quite clearly. Everything looked quiet at the moment; a few single men had gone in earlier followed by a crowd of youngsters—some of whom she was sure were too young to be there. She checked her watch; Nacho and his friends were due to start performing at nine-thirty. She and Phil had walked past the group's van on the way to the restaurant; it was conveniently parked just around the corner.

She smiled at the waiter as he placed an enormous piece of fillet steak in front of her. Thank goodness she'd only ordered a green salad to go with it; it would take her all night to get through so much food. Well there was no hurry; all she had to do now was enjoy her meal and wait.

They were drinking their coffee when he phoned.

'Nacho. Is everything all right?' she asked, signalling to Phil to ask for the bill.

'Not really. Ali is here with another man. They've been plying two young girls with drinks all evening, and now I think they're planning to move on. Can you watch out for them. The girls look wasted and I'm sure they're under age.'

'Okay. We're here, right opposite the entrance.'

'That's no good. I think they're heading for the back door. They've got a van parked out there.' He sounded very agitated.

Sophie is Still Missing

'Oh God.' Linda snapped her phone shut. 'Phil, we've got to go. That Moroccan guy is abducting two young girls. I need to stop them.'

'Hang on a minute. There's no way you're getting involved in this.'

'But we can't just let it happen. You phone the police and tell them you think two girls are being abducted, while I go and see what's going on. Tell them they are underage.'

Before her husband could do anything to stop her, Linda had grabbed her coat and was out the door, leaving a number of the customers staring at her in amazement. She had no idea where the back door to the Crooked Cat was, but decided it must be somewhere near where Nacho had parked his van; they wouldn't have wanted to lug all their heavy gear very far.

Sure enough, just past Nacho's van there was a narrow green door set into the wall, with the logo of the Crooked Cat embossed in red letters. Directly outside it, someone had parked a white camper van. She pulled out her mobile and took a photo of the van, then crossed the road and waited in the doorway of a dilapidated looking bar, where she was partly hidden by an ice cream kiosk that had been closed for the winter.

Linda didn't have long to wait. The green door swung open and Ali and another man came out, supporting two young girls who were finding it hard to keep upright.

'*Dios mío*,' she murmured to herself. Nacho had been right to say they were wasted; not only did the girls have difficulty walking, they looked as though they'd been drugged. The men must have spiked their drinks for them to be in that state; alcohol alone couldn't have done it. She switched her phone to video and began to film them. Where was Phil? And the police? If they didn't hurry up, the kidnappers would get away. She wondered if she should say something to the men. But what?

She had to delay them somehow. She balanced her phone against the wooden shutters of the kiosk and left its video camera running.

'Excuse me,' she said loudly, walking up to Ali. 'I'm completely lost. Can you direct me to the bus station please.' She spoke in English, clearly and slowly 'They told me it was this way, but I think I've been walking in circles.'

The bald man was leering at her. 'You're in wrong place, lady. The bus station not here. Other side of town. Where you going? You want a lift?' His English had a strong Spanish accent, and he had a tattoo of a woman's head on his arm. It was the man Norah Catchpole had seen.

'Up there, turn left, go to the end of the road and it's on your right,' Ali said, brusquely in perfect English. He glowered at the bald man, who was looking lasciviously at Linda.

'Thank you. Your friends look as though they've had a bit too much to drink,' she said as one of the girls bent over and was sick down the side of the van.

'They'll be all right in the morning,' said Ali and jumped into the driving seat.

The bald man said nothing. He shoved the girls into the van and slammed the door.

Before she knew it, they had driven off. So that was it. She wanted to scream with frustration.

'Linda, are you all right?' Phil asked, running towards her, his coat flapping. 'I rang the police; they'll be here in five minutes.'

'It's too late. They've gone. We've missed them.' She couldn't help thinking that those two girls would end up like Julie and Sophie, and two more families would be devastated.

'You got the number plate, didn't you?' her husband asked. He looked very relieved to see her.

'I did, and a video of the men pushing the girls into the van. That should convince the police to do something.' She crossed the road and recovered her phone from where she'd propped it up. She played it back. Perfect. She had clear pictures of the faces of both men and the girls, and her own backside. It was time she went on a diet, she told herself.

'Well, I can't see what else you could have done. It's not as though you have any right to go around arresting people. Even if you could.' He laughed. The thought of his wife taking on two kidnappers obviously amused him.

'I'm stronger than you think,' she said. 'Can you stay here and wait for the police while I go and see what Nacho is up to. Here take my phone and show them the video.'

'Okay, but don't be long. The Guardia Civil always make me nervous.'

The Crooked Cat was crowded, and it seemed that Nacho and his group were successfully entertaining them. She pulled up a stool and waited until they finished playing before going across and speaking to her colleague. 'Can you take a break?' she asked. 'The police are on their way.'

'What about the girls?'

'There was nothing I could do. They bundled them into the van and drove off before we could stop them. Do you have any idea where they're taking them?'

'The bald guy said something about Algeciras, and that they needed to get a move on. Tell me that you at least have the number of the van, Linda.'

'I do, and a video of the two men. I'm going back to Phil now, to see if the cavalry have arrived.'

She could see the barman staring at her. JD was right; she did look out of place in there.

Sophie is Still Missing

Phil was talking to two Guardia Civil officers who appeared to be very interested in what he had to say. One of them was watching Linda's video.

'You've done very well, *señora*,' he said. 'We've alerted the traffic police to stop and detain the van and its occupants. They won't have got far.'

'I think they're heading for Algeciras,' Linda said, greatly relieved that the responsibility was now theirs and not hers.

'What makes you think that?' asked his companion.

'The bald one said something about it; he said they should hurry.'

'The midnight ferry. That's where they're going, to Melilla.' The officer said, pulling out his mobile and issuing instructions.

Of course, they were taking the girls to Morocco; they wouldn't need passports to enter Melilla because it was a Spanish city. Then it would be easy to move them from there to Tangier. Should she tell them that they were investigating the disappearance of Sophie? No, maybe it was best not to complicate things. Anyway she had to ring JD and tell her to get in touch with the Captain.

'You can continue with your evening now,' said the first officer. 'We'll handle this from now on. But I'll have to keep your mobile phone, Mrs Prewitt.' He began to write her a receipt for her mobile. 'Just call into the *cuartel* in Fuengirola and collect it in a couple of days. And thank you for your help.'

'You will catch them, won't you,' she said.

'Of course. Don't worry.' They climbed back into the police car and drove off.

'Give me your phone, Phil. I need to ring JD.'

At first she thought her boss was never going to answer and then a sleepy voice said, 'Who is this?'

Sophie is Still Missing

'It's Linda. JD, you have to get in touch with the Captain. We have to stop Ali and his mate abducting two girls. They're on their way...'

'Hang on, Linda. Better if you tell him yourself.'

She smiled. So it was true. JD and the Captain were in a relationship.

'*Buenos noches*, Linda. Now can you tell me everything that's happened,' said the deep voice of the Captain.

CHAPTER 35

It was early Sunday morning when Federico returned from the *cuartel* of the Guardia Civil in Málaga; he had gone straight there after speaking to Linda. Now he sat drinking strong black coffee in front of a bleary-eyed JD, who was still trying to get her head around the fact that they'd found the men who'd kidnapped Sophie and Julie.

'So, the police caught them both?' she asked, barely able to believe it.

'Yes. But only just in time. They were about to board the ferry to Melilla. Those poor girls were so out of it they didn't even realise they were being kidnapped.'

'Where are they now?'

'They're being questioned by my men. Then their parents can take them home. You won't believe this, but they didn't even know that the girls were out; each couple thought their daughter was staying overnight with the other girl.'

'Same ruse as they used with Julie and Sophie,' said JD. 'What about Kevin?'

'We'll get the British police to pick him up. Interpol will speak to them. And I think you'd better hand over all the evidence you've collected so far. I'll have to give it to the CNP; it will help them with their wider investigation. And we're going to need it anyway, if we are to include the abduction of Julie Bennett and Sophie Anderson in the charges against them.'

'Do you know what they planned to do with the girls?'

Sophie is Still Missing

'They're not saying much at the moment, but I'll let you know if I find out anything that will help us to track down Sophie's whereabouts.'

'Thank goodness you were here last night. Otherwise we might have been looking at two more missing girls.'

'Happy to oblige,' he said, his eyes twinkling at her. 'Well I'd better get back to work. I'll ring you later.' He kissed her lightly on the cheek.

'Yes, it's time I had a shower and got to work, too. I'll send Nacho round with the case notes later.'

There was no sign of Nacho, nor Linda when JD arrived at the agency. Even though it was Sunday, she'd asked them to come in for a couple of hours; she wanted to hear for herself how things had gone the night before. They'd done well; she was lucky to have such conscientious staff. She unlocked the door and went straight across to the evidence board. Just as she was about to remove the photographs of Ali and Kevin, she stopped. It was too soon. She still didn't know for certain if there was any connection between those two men and Lebedev and Valdes. Everything was pointing to the Russian and/or his chauffeur being involved in Julie's death, but if that was the case, then how did they get to know her in the first place? And who was the father of her aborted child?

'Hard at it already, Boss?' asked Nacho, handing her a cup of coffee. 'Sorry I'm late. Had a long night.'

'A very successful one by the sound of it.'

'Linda and Phil took me back to their place after I'd finished at the club, and told me about what happened.'

'So you didn't see anything?'

'I was inside all the time, playing. I'd been keeping an eye on Ali all evening. He and the bald guy were already there when we arrived. They latched on to these two girls and kept buying them fancy, expensive cocktails.'

'Laced with something else, I bet.'

'Probably. The girls were a mess. I was sure that the two men were going to do something, so I rang Linda.'

'Good job you did. Much later and they'd have been out of the country. The Guardia Civil found fake passports in the van. The men were taking them to Melilla and then probably on to Tangier.'

'I expect that's what happened to Sophie and Julie. They must have been getting the photographs for their passports that time when the schoolboy put his head in the booth with Julie.'

'Without a doubt. What we need to know now is what the men planned to do with them once they got there.'

'What do you want me to work on today, Boss?'

'Finish your coffee and then take this evidence round to the Captain. You know where his office is, don't you?'

'Yes. Bit surprised he's working today.' Nacho sat on the edge of his desk, drinking his coffee and watching her as she went through the evidence file, carefully extracting only the documents that related to the abduction. 'Lucky that you were able to get hold of the Captain so quickly last night, JD,' he said.

She didn't reply, just handed him the papers and told him, 'Photocopy these before you take them to Captain Rodriguez. And make a copy of the interviews Linda had with the teacher and the people in the shopping precinct. Oh and give him the address of that hotel that Julie googled. Did they ever get back to us?'

'No. That seems a bit fishy to me.'

'Well that's why it's best if the police handle it from now on. Just in case they're involved.'

'What about the photographs and the CCTV?' asked Nacho.

'I suppose you'd better take them as well. And anything else that's directly linked to the kidnapping.'

'The stuff we've got on Kevin?'

'Yes, that too.' She sat back and pulled the lid off her coffee cup. 'God, I'm tired,' she said.

Nacho just smiled.

She knew exactly what he was thinking. Linda was bound to have told him that Federico was at her place last night.

'Anything else, Boss?'

'No, just take the stuff to the Captain and then you can go home. We'll go over it together on Monday.'

'Fine with me. I'll go back to bed,' he said and gathered up the evidence for the Guardia Civil and left.

There was still no sign of Linda, so JD decided to ring her; she was still in bed.

'Sorry, JD. Didn't get much sleep last night. Look, why don't you come round and have lunch with us today. Phil's cooking roast lamb; there's enough for another one.'

JD hesitated; she was keen to get on with the investigation. 'Yes, why not. That would be lovely.' Her headache hadn't lifted all morning; it would be good to relax for a few hours. And if she were lucky, Federico might pop round in the evening.

'Two o'clock?'

'Fine. I'll be there.' Linda's husband was a great cook. She hoped he'd made one of his famous desserts; she was rather partial to his lemon tart.

Apart from a text message to say that the investigations into Julie's death and Sophie's disappearance had been reopened and that he'd be in touch, JD heard nothing from Federico until

Sophie is Still Missing

Monday morning when he arrived at the agency carrying two bottles of an expensive cava and his laptop.

'Well done, everyone. We've arrested the two men who abducted Julie and Sophie, plus a number of their associates. Kevin has been apprehended and will be returned to Spain to stand trial, and we have passed on much of the evidence to Interpol. There's a strong chance that this particular people trafficking ring will be broken up,' he said, sitting at Linda's desk, the only one that wasn't littered with papers.

'What about the owner of the Crooked Cat?' asked Nacho.

'He's helping us with our enquiries. At the moment I don't know if he was involved, or had just turned a blind eye to their activities.'

'I hope it was the latter. I've got another gig booked there next Saturday. I don't want them shut down.'

JD frowned at him.

'I thought you might like to see what our search turned up,' the Captain said, opening his lap top and turning it so they could all see. 'This is what was on their web page.'

JD gasped. It was a video of some young girls. First they were parading about in bikinis on the beach, then there were some shots of them drinking in a bar and finally, walking along the road in their school uniforms; there were about twenty girls in total, all aged between twelve and fourteen. The kidnappers had obviously visited many of the international schools along the coast in order to film and groom these girls, as evidenced by the variety in the school uniforms.

'*Dios mío*. That's Sophie, and there's Julie. Look at them. They seem perfectly happy.'

'And isn't that Kevin?'

'Yes, the girls all think they're taking part in a modelling audition.'

Sophie is Still Missing

'So they still didn't know what was really happening?'

'No. Not at that point; it's just a bit of fun to them. The auction takes place next.' He clicked onto a second video. 'This is what they put up for the actual auction.'

The same girls appeared on the screen; this time it was like a beauty parade, each one holding up a card with a number on it. First they paraded in their school uniforms, then in summer dresses and lastly in their bikinis.

'The sad thing is that the silly girls don't have a clue what is happening to them. They don't realise they are being auctioned. They think it really is a beauty parade and could lead to an audition with a film director.'

'They look so confident,' said Linda. 'Where were the videos taken?'

'It looks like Marbella.'

'So they were going to sell them?' asked an incredulous Nacho.

'They did sell them. The question we're trying to answer now, is who bought them?'

'Won't they tell you?'

'It's all anonymous. The men running the auction never know who the buyers are. But our tech team are working on it to see if they can trace the money. That might give us something.'

'Don't they have any idea? What about their nationality?'

'No.'

"So how did they deliver the girls to them?' asked Nacho.

'They organised a pick-up place at a hotel in Tangier, and someone collected them. No names, no addresses.'

JD went into the evidence room and took down the photo of Jaime. 'See if any of them recognise this man,' she said, handing the photo to Federico.

'Who is it?'

'Someone we think may be connected with Julie's death.' She saw Nacho open his mouth to say something and glared at him. If Federico knew it was Ivan's chauffeur he might refuse to show it to them. 'See if he was the man who collected Julie or Sophie. Also ask them if they often sold two girls to the same person.' If the answer was negative, then she'd know for certain that Julie and Sophie had gone to different buyers.

'A suspect?'

'Not necessarily.'

'Okay, I'll see what they say.'

'That's awful,' said Linda, who hadn't said a word all this time, just stared at the video. 'They are so gullible at that age.'

'Indeed. Still, you did a great job to prevent this happening to any other young girls, and the parents of the two we rescued are extremely grateful for your intervention,' said Federico. 'You're a brave woman, Linda.'

JD saw Linda blush, and said, 'All right, are you going to pour out that cava or is it only for show?'

'Isn't it a bit early?' asked Nacho.

'What do you think Linda?'

'Absolutely not. Open it up.'

Once Federico had left, JD called Linda and Nacho into their meeting room. 'Thanks to your work on Saturday night, we have made a big step forward in the investigation, guys. However if we want to be paid, we have to find Sophie; it's her mum who hired us.' She pointed to Valdes and Lebedev. 'This is the only lead we have. We need to find out if either of these two men bought Julie or Sophie. It doesn't look as though the kidnappers are going to tell us much.'

'Maybe they're lying when they say they don't know who bought the girls.'

'I don't think so. It makes sense that people would want to keep their identities secret. But, as we know, it's hard to keep everything secret. There must be something that will lead us back to them.'

'The police have the resources to investigate further,' said Nacho. 'They can get into people's bank accounts and trace payments and deposits. I can try, but, as you know, it's illegal, and I don't want to upset the Captain.'

'But they won't bother,' said Linda. 'They are only reopening the investigation because we have forced them to. As far as they are concerned they have the kidnappers, and now they can say with certainty that they will never be able to trace Sophie's whereabouts. They don't care about two kidnapped girls.'

'More than two. There must have been twenty girls on that video. Where are they now and where did they all come from? Are you saying that the police won't try to trace them?'

'I hope they do. At least they should contact the families and let them know what they've found out. But that's not our job. Our job is to find Sophie,' said JD.

'And Julie's killer,' added Linda.

'What we need to do now, is dig up as much personal stuff about Ivan Lebedev as we can. Everything there is to know, where he lives, how long he's lived there, children, dogs, cats. Everything. We need to find a link between him and the kidnappers,' she said. 'Nacho, you get right onto it.'

'Okay JD.'

'Linda, I want you to find out where someone would go to get an abortion, because I'm pretty sure it wasn't done in a state hospital. And it wasn't a back street job either; according to the pathologist it was a professional termination. Somebody had to pay for it, but who?'

'But we don't know if she had it done in Spain.'

'No, we don't, but according to the autopsy report it was done not long before she died, so it's worth checking out.'

'So Lebedev's bank statements would be useful for that too?'

'They would, but I don't want you to end up with a criminal record, Nacho. As you said, Captain Rodriguez would not be happy, and I'm sure I'd be the one he'd blame. If we can find where the abortion was done, then I'll ask him if the police can check Lebedev's bank statements.'

'That's never going to happen,' said Linda. 'I will check out the clinics, but I think we should concentrate more on the chauffeur. Remember, it was once you started to mention Lebedev and Valdes that you were warned off. Someone is protecting them. Let's try to get to them through Jaime. After all, if he was driving that car, he has a lot to lose and not much to gain.'

JD looked at her assistant; Linda had made a good point. After all, she didn't want them to shut down their investigation or to lose her licence. º

'Okay, Linda. Find out what you can on all three men, but discreetly. In the meantime, I will go over all our evidence and see what we need to do next. I have a horrible feeling that once the arrest of the kidnappers hits the news, our suspects will be spooked and anything could happen.'

CHAPTER 36

Igor was baking some kind of Russian bread that Madame liked, and Sophie was peeling potatoes; it was one of the few jobs she was allowed to do in Chef's hallowed kitchen. As always, the television was switched on; it was fixed to the wall that backed onto the scullery and was visible from most places in the kitchen so that the housekeeper could watch her favourite soap operas, and Igor the football. At the moment it was tuned to Mijas TV, a local television station that they both enjoyed. Suddenly the usual bland chat show that they watched was interrupted by a news flash. The banner 'Kidnappers of Missing Girls Arrested' was splashed across the screen, and suddenly Sophie was looking at a photograph of herself and Julie. A reporter came into view explaining how they had been kidnapped back in August 2017 but only now had the police been able to identify the men responsible. She recognised their abductors immediately and felt sick when she remembered what they'd done to them, how frightened she'd been and how homesick. How the men, who had been so pleasant at first, had turned nasty when she and Julie said that they wanted to go home to their families.

Igor suddenly realised what was happening and moved across to switch the television off, but Sophie had taken the remote control and slipped it into her pocket before he could see it. What was the reporter saying? Something about one of the girls still being missing and the other found dead six months ago. Did they mean Julie? Was Julie dead? Surely not.

'Turn it off,' shouted Igor. 'Right now. We'll all be in trouble if Madame catches you watching it.'

Sophie shook her head. She had to hear what had happened.

'Where's the remote. Give it to me,' Igor shouted.

'No. I want to hear what she's saying,' Sophie cried. 'I want to know what's happened to Julie.'

Before she could stop her, the housekeeper marched in, saw what the commotion was about and pulled out the television cable.

'Get back to your work or it will be the worst for you,' she bellowed. The news seemed to have upset the housekeeper and Igor as much as it had Sophie.

'Is Julie dead?' asked Sophie, struggling to hold back her tears. No-one answered. 'Tell me. Is Julie dead? What has happened to her? Tell me.' Her voice was getting louder and louder. 'Tell me what happened to her. I have to know.' She began to scream, 'Tell me. Tell me or I'll ask Madame.'

'Okay, okay. Calm down. Yes, Julie is dead. She was run over, the night she ran away from here. It was an accident,' said Igor.

'Why didn't anyone tell me? All these months and I thought she was alive. I thought she was coming to rescue me,' Julie continued shouting, heedless of who heard her. 'Did he kill her? Did he? Did Mr Lebedev kill her? She was scared of him, you know. Terrified. What did he do? Did he murder her?'

'Of course not, child. You're talking rubbish. Come and sit down. I'll pour you some hot tea to calm your nerves,' said the housekeeper. She looked scared now. 'You mustn't say things like that. Not ever. Mr Lebedev would never hurt anyone. It was a road accident. Julie should never have run away. She was too headstrong.' She took a cup from the cupboard and poured Sophie some tea, adding two spoonfuls of sugar. 'Now drink this, and stop these wild speculations. They will cause nothing but trouble.'

'Lourdes, did you know that the girl had been murdered?' Igor suddenly asked the housekeeper.

'What are you on about? You just keep your mouth shut or we'll all be in trouble,' she snapped at him.

Suddenly Sophie realised that the housekeeper was as scared of Mr Lebedev as she was. They all were. Well, no matter how dangerous it was, she was going to have to get away from this house as soon as possible. She had no choice. Her life was in danger. The situation had changed; the police would be looking for her and if they found her in Mr Lebedev's house he would be arrested. He was never going to risk that. He would be forced to get rid of her, just as he'd got rid of Julie. She sipped the tea; it was very sweet. There was no time to be lost; she would escape tonight, when they were all in bed.

Annika switched off the television. How had this happened? Enrique had said they would never be able to trace the girls back to them, yet here they were in this mess. One girl dead, now the kidnappers arrested and a private investigator snooping around. It wouldn't take much for them to find a link between her and Ivan and the two girls. Thank goodness she had never allowed Julie and Sophie to leave the house; none of her neighbours would be able to recognise them. Only her own staff knew who they were, and they would never betray her; they were paid far too well for that. Suddenly she thought of Greta. Sophie couldn't go to work for Greta now. Thank goodness it had happened today and not next week; that would have been a disaster.

Sophie is Still Missing

She picked up her mobile and phoned her friend. 'Hi, Greta. It's Annika. Look I'm sorry, I've just had a terrible row with Ivan; he says Sophie has to stay here. I'm so sorry. If I hear of anyone else I'll give you a ring straight away.'

'That's all right. Have you seen the news?'

'No. What's happened?'

'Remember those girls who disappeared last year? They've caught the kidnappers. So Gregorio has told me that I'm not to employ anyone unless I'm absolutely sure where they've come from. So, I would have had to say no to your girl, anyway. Not that I'm suggesting anything is wrong with her. It's just Gregorio would have been furious with me.'

What was she insinuating? 'Quite right. Ivan always says the same. Look, I have to dash. See you at the club on Friday?'

'Of course.'

Sophie waited until dinner was over and she had washed up all the dishes and tidied the kitchen. The housekeeper had retired to her sitting room with her usual gin and tonic, and Igor was sitting out in the back yard, smoking a cigar and drinking brandy. Now was the time to speak to him. It was risky, but she could see that Igor was a kind man. One day he'd told her that he had children of his own, back in Saint Petersburg, but he only saw them once a year when he returned in the summer. He told her how much he missed them. Surely he would understand how her parents were feeling, how they must be missing her. She hesitated. She'd trusted someone before and they'd betrayed her.

Sophie remembered how she and Julie had stupidly believed Kevin and his friends when they said they'd help them become models. Kevin had been so nice to them, promising them new clothes and an audition with a famous modelling agency. He'd persuaded them that it was best not to take their old phones with them, and promised to buy them the latest iPhones. She looked down at the dirty, drab dress she wore now; so much for the new clothes. Madame didn't believe in spending money on her maids. Yes, it had been easy to trust Kevin; he had been fun to be with, and was so kind and understanding. He knew what it was like to have a broken home; he said that his parents had divorced when he was twelve. Julie had told him about her mum having an affair with Sophie's dad and he'd understood how let down they both felt. Then he'd said there was no point in feeling sorry for themselves, they should do what he did, become independent, make their own lives. They had to look to the future. That was when he mentioned the modelling agency. He'd said it was the perfect opportunity for them. He had a friend who was looking for girls just like them, pale-skinned, fair haired and beautiful. Sophie had blushed when he said that; nobody had called her beautiful before.

What an idiot she had been. Now she was trapped here, working all hours of the day for a Russian family, who treated her like a slave. Did Kevin really know that this was what would happen to her and Julie? Did he know that Julie was dead? Would he care? She still found it hard to believe that he would do this to them. But he was right about one thing, she had to make her own life. Well that was just what she was going to do. She wasn't going to stay here until she ended up dead, like Julie. If that meant putting her trust in Igor, she would do it. After all, who else was there?

She crept outside and sat on the step near him.

'You feeling better now, Sophie?' he asked, puffing a cloud of blue smoke into the air.

Sophie is Still Missing

'Yes, thank you. But I miss Julie, so much. She was my best friend.' She edged closer to him. 'I have to escape, Igor. Can you help me?'

He stared at her in astonishment. 'What are you saying?'

'He will kill me, Igor. I know he will. Just like he killed Julie.'

For a long while Igor said nothing, then he said, 'What makes you think Ivan killed Julie?'

'She wouldn't do what he wanted. She was very unhappy. And then she disappeared. What else could have happened to her?'

'He said it was an accident.'

'Please Igor. I must get back to my parents; they will be so worried about me. You could help me and nobody would know. All you have to do is open the gate for me to slip out. My parents don't live that far away from here.'

At this, Igor turned and stared at her. 'I thought you were from England,' he said.

She thought she saw fear in his eyes.

'I was once. But we moved to Torremolinos when I was ten. It's not far from here, is it?'

'A bit too far to walk.'

'I don't mind. I just have to get away before he decides to get rid of me.'

'It's very risky. And dangerous. You'd have to walk down an unlit road until you got to San Pedro, then head for the bus station. There might not even be a bus at this time of night.'

Sophie began to cry. 'I don't have any money for a bus, anyway' she sobbed. If Igor wouldn't help her then it was impossible.

Igor looked at his watch; it was almost midnight. 'Look. I sometimes go to a club in Marbella for a few drinks. I'll unlock my car. You climb in the boot and wait for me. I'll take you into the centre and give you some money for a taxi. Mr Lebedev and his wife are out tonight playing cards at their club; they don't usually get home until about one. So we need to go right away. But be very careful that Lourdes doesn't see you.'

'Oh, thank you, so much.' She couldn't believe it; he was actually helping her to escape and giving her money for a taxi. Her parents would be so surprised to see her.

'Stay here until you hear me unlock the car. And keep quiet. Lourdes has ears like a bat.'

Sophie sat there, looking at the moon, and shaking with excitement. This was her chance. Soon she'd be home, with Mum and Dad, and Ricky and Zak. She felt a tremendous wave of homesickness engulf her. She usually tried not to think about her family because it made her so sad, but tonight she couldn't help it. She'd be with them again very soon.

After a short while she heard Igor come out; he'd removed his chef's coat and replaced it with the blue jacket he always wore when he went to the market. Then she heard the car being unlocked and saw the back lights winking. That was her signal. She crept over to the car and climbed in the boot; it was roomy but smelled of rotten vegetables and fish. She curled up on some old newspapers and lay there waiting for him.

'Okay, Sophie?' he asked, smiling at her as he closed the boot. She waited in the dark, hoping they would leave soon, before anyone discovered she'd gone. Her stomach was tight with excitement. After what seemed forever, the car started and they were driving out of the driveway; she heard the heavy iron gates swing open then slam closed behind them. She was free. Free.

Sophie is Still Missing

CHAPTER 37

Linda was just on her way to work when her mobile rang.

'Hi. I'm sorry to bother you so early. It's Jim Anderson here. I thought you might like to know that Beverley is in hospital. She collapsed last night with the pains in her chest and I rang for an ambulance. They said she'd had a heart attack.'

'Oh dear, I'm very sorry to hear that, Jim. How is she?'

'They say she's stable but they may need to operate.'

'So she'll be in hospital for a while I suppose?'

'We'd planned to be move back to the UK before Christmas, but now I think that will have to be put on hold, at least until she's strong enough to travel.'

'Of course. Let me know if there's anything I can do for her. Is she allowed visitors?'

'Not at the moment. I think they're worried about the general state of her health, as well as the heart. You've seen how she's been neglecting herself since Sophie disappeared.'

'Yes, I know. Well here's some positive news for her, for both of you. They've arrested the men who abducted the girls.'

'What? Really? You've got them? That's great news,' he replied, his voice cracking with emotion.

'Yes, but don't get too excited. The men don't know where Sophie is. They sold both girls in an online auction. That's all we've got so far. But it's a start and now the police have reopened the investigation, so we should get some results soon.' Linda sounded more positive than she felt.

Sophie is Still Missing

'An online auction? Bloody hell. What on earth has happened to my lovely daughter? Where in God's name is she?'

She could hear the anguish in his voice. There was no denying it now, those black thoughts that haunted him at night were out in the open.

'I hope we will have something more positive to tell you very soon. The police have many more resources than us, I'm sure they'll find her.'

She heard him sob, and then say, 'Thanks Linda. I'll let Bev know. She's always been the positive one, never given up hope like me.'

'Tell her I'll call in and see her soon,' said Linda.

She heard him ring off. Poor man, he'd been so convinced that Sophie was dead. Now his hopes had been raised again. She prayed that they'd find the poor girl alive.

When she arrived at the agency, Nacho and JD were in deep conversation.

'Morning all. I've just had a call from Jim Anderson. Beverley's had a heart attack,' she said, then went on to relate what Jim had said, and how he'd reacted when she told him about the arrest of the two men.

'Poor woman. As though she hasn't got enough on her plate, without having a heart attack as well,' said JD.

'Probably why she had one,' added Nacho. 'All that stress.'

'Without a doubt.'

JD went into the meeting room, and Linda grabbed her notebook and followed her.

'Nacho was just about to tell me what he'd found out about our Russian friend,' her boss said.

'Yes, it wasn't as difficult as you would imagine. He's one of that wealthy group of Russians that have bought property on the

Sophie is Still Missing

Costa del Sol, so there's been plenty written about him. I suppose you'd call him one of the Marbella elite, and his wife is a bit of a socialite. She has soirées; would you believe that? I had to look it up,' Nacho admitted with a laugh. 'Yes, it's considered quite something if you get invited to one of Annika Lebedev's soirées. Although what you do there, other than drink expensive cava and eat exotic Russian food, I don't know.'

'Probably just an up market coffee morning,' Linda said.

'Anyway, the couple have two daughters, both away at boarding school in England. Annika and Ivan are currently living in the summer house, an enormous residence off the road from San Pedro to Ronda. They usually split their time between Marbella and Moscow, where they have a flat near Red Square. So they're pretty loaded I would say.'

'Anything else?' asked JD.

'Well you already know about the yacht. Oh, yes, they do have a very good Russian chef. They brought him with them from Moscow.'

'So what do you know about the daughters?'

'Went to school in Moscow until this September when they were sent to a boarding school in England,' said Nacho, reading from his notes.

'Do you know if they went to a boarding school in Moscow?'

'No, a girls' private day school. Why?'

'So, they came home each night. If, and it's only an if, the Lebedev's bought Julie and Sophie and took them to Moscow, then their daughters would have met them. Nacho, find the name and address of their school in England and see if either of them are on social media. Right away.'

'But it doesn't make sense. Why would a wealthy couple buy two young women? For sex? To work in the house? If you're that wealthy you don't need to have slaves,' said Linda, feeling unconvinced by the way JD's mind was working.

'It's only a hypothesis, Linda, but we have reached the point where we have to explore every avenue. Maybe they get a kick out of being able to buy someone and dominate them. Like you, I don't know what motivates people to own slaves.'

'Well they can treat them however they want, and no-one will ever know,' said Nacho. 'They don't have to pay them the minimum wage, and no social security contributions.'

Linda didn't say anything. She just couldn't understand how people could own slaves in the 21st century and get away with it.

'What about Valdes? What sort of lifestyle does he have?' asked JD.

'Well we know he has a big house, drives the latest Mercedes and seems to have enough money to belong to that exclusive golf club, but that's about all. Nothing out of the ordinary, except maybe some offshore investments.'

'So your regular rich guy?'

'Yes, but not in Ivan's league.'

'Linda, have you found out anything about Julie's abortion?'

'Nothing so far, JD. I've got a few more clinics to visit this morning though.'

'Well go carefully. If it wasn't through the proper channels they will be very cagey about telling you anything.'

'You don't have that photo of Annika, do you? The one on the yacht? I think it would be useful. She's not exactly someone you could easily forget, is she?'

'So you think she might have taken Julie for the abortion?'

'Well, let's suppose that Ivan made Julie pregnant, Annika wouldn't want anyone to know about it. She'd want to keep it secret. If it came out it would ruin her reputation.'

'You've got a point.' Her boss took the magazine out of the case file and handed it to her. 'But I doubt if she took her alone. What if Julie tried to escape? Someone else must have been with her.'

'Jaime?'

'Now, that is a possibility. And it would have looked suspicious if he'd taken Julie on his own. Okay, Linda, you keep on with your investigation, and take a photo of Jaime, as well.'

Linda was getting tired; she'd visited four abortion clinics that morning and so far, no-one had admitted to carrying out an abortion on anyone resembling Julie. She decided to try one more and then she'd go back to the office.

'Buenos días, I wonder if you can help me,' Linda said, showing her ID card to the receptionist. 'We're trying to trace the clinic where this young girl had an abortion.' She passed her the photograph of Julie.

'Isn't that the girl whose body was found in the city centre?' the receptionist asked. 'That was so sad. That's my church, you know. My family always make a point of following the Virgin of Remorse during Holy Week.'

'So you do recognise her?'

'Yes, but only from the papers. She didn't come here for her abortion; I'm sure of that. I'm the only receptionist and I'd remember.'

'But you have records?'

'Yes, but they're highly confidential. And anyway, young girls like that don't always give their real names. That's one reason they come to a private clinic, instead of going to their own doctor. But if it'd make you feel better, I'll look though the records and see if there has been a Julie… What's her surname?'

'Anderson.'

'Do you know when she would have had it?'

'February or March this year.' Linda waited while the receptionist searched the computer.

'No, nothing. It's like I said, without more information, it's hopeless.'

'Yes, I'm beginning to realise that.'

'Why is it important now? The poor child is dead.'

'When she disappeared she was with her friend. We still don't know what's happened to her, and we thought that whoever brought Julie here might be able to help us.'

'Well, I can tell you something, but don't tell anyone I told you,' she said, rather dramatically.

Linda nodded her agreement.

The receptionist lowered her voice and whispered, 'Not all gynaecologists are as scrupulous as ours. There is one clinic where anyone can get an abortion, no questions asked.' She tore a piece off her notepad, scribbled something on it and handed it to Linda.

'Thank you.' It was the address of a clinic, and the name and phone number of a Doctor Dominguez. 'You've been really helpful.'

'I hope you find her friend,' the woman called, as Linda hurried out.

Sophie is Still Missing

CHAPTER 38

It was difficult to judge, lying there in the dark, but Sophie guessed about half an hour had passed by the time she felt the car slow down and come to a halt. Instead of opening the car boot at once, as she had expected, Igor began talking to someone on his mobile phone. She strained to hear what he was saying, but all she could make out was that he was speaking in Russian. But to whom? At last he pulled the boot open and reached in to help her out.

'You okay?' he asked. 'A bit stiff? Sorry. It must have been bumpy in there.'

She nodded and stretched her legs. 'It was okay,' she said, looking around her in surprise. This wasn't the town centre. It was the marina in Puerto Banus; she recognised it at once. The place was deserted. There were boats and yachts of all shapes and sizes, but no people. Why on earth were they there?

'Igor, what are we doing here?' she asked. 'Where's the taxi rank?'

'Sorry, Sophie, I had to make a detour to collect something from Mr Lebedev's yacht. He rang me just now to tell me to pick it up because he needs it first thing tomorrow. As we're here, I thought you might like to see his yacht. It's very special.'

'I don't like boats; I'll wait here, if you don't mind. Or I could walk to the centre. It can't be far. I really don't want to be any bother to you, Igor.' She was beginning to feel uncomfortable. Something wasn't quite right. Mr Lebedev hadn't phoned him; she would have heard his mobile ring. It was Igor who made the call.

'You're no bother, Sophie. Come on, it's not far and you won't believe what it's like. I reckon it's one of the biggest yachts here. Worth a couple of million at least.' As he chatted, he gently led her down the moorings between the boats.

The Lebedevs' yacht was at the very end, and it was exactly as Igor had described. She had never seen any boat as big as this one before, nor as luxurious. It was like something out of a film.

'Careful how you go up the gangplank. You don't want to fall in; the water is cold at this time of night.' He followed her on deck and pulled out a large flashlight. 'Go through there; I think that's where he said it would be.'

'What do you have to pick up?' she asked. She was frightened; even though he was still smiling at her, Igor was behaving strangely. Why had he brought her all the way out here? Something wasn't right.

The chef took out a key and unlocked the cabin door. 'Go on in, Sophie. It's fantastic inside.'

Gingerly she stepped inside and looked around her. He was right; it was just like a film set. She heard the door close behind her and spun round just in time to see Igor produce a pair of steel handcuffs. What was happening? Before she could stop him, he had her arms behind her back and her wrists handcuffed together.

'Igor, what are you doing? I thought you were my friend. Stop. You're hurting me.' She began to cry. 'Why are you doing this, Igor? You're not going to kill me, are you?'

'I'm sorry, Sophie. It can't be helped. You're not a stupid girl; you realised this would happen sooner or later. Ivan can't allow you to escape; it would put all our lives at risk.'

'So you're going to kill me too?' she gasped.

Sophie is Still Missing

'Of course not. Ivan isn't a killer. I told you; Julie's death was an accident. It was as much her fault as anyone's. He just wants you somewhere safe until they are ready to leave. Don't worry it will only be for a few days and I'll come and bring you food every day. Now sit here on the sofa, so that you're comfortable.' He bent down and taped her ankles together. 'I'm really sorry about this, Sophie. You're a very sweet girl. I hope you understand.'

'No, I don't understand,' she started to shout, but her words were cut off as he pulled some tape across her mouth.

'I'll be back tomorrow morning, first thing. Try to sleep.'

She glared at him and tried to wriggle free, but Igor had known what he was doing and she lay there, like the boned turkey he had stuffed and tied up for Christmas lunch. Then he was gone and she was in the dark, with just the rays of the moon coming through the yacht's portholes. She was never going to be free. Tears trickled down her face but she was unable to wipe them away. Was this to be her life forever? Was there nobody in this world she could trust? Maybe she would be better off dead.

Igor was as good as his word and the sun was barely creeping through the porthole when she heard his footsteps on deck.

'Did you manage to sleep?' he asked, as he pulled the tape off her mouth.

'Help,' she screamed. 'Somebody, help me. Help.'

Instantly his hand was over her mouth. She struggled to pull away but he was too strong for her, so she sunk her teeth into his hand, as hard as she could.

Igor let out a roar of pain. 'You stupid child. What did you do that for? I'm just trying to help you. Now, unless you promise to be quiet and eat your breakfast, I will tape up your mouth again,' he said.

Sophie realised there was nothing she could do; she was too weak to get away from him.

'All right? If you scream again you'll go hungry. Understood,' he shouted.

This time she let him remove his hand, and sat there watching him as he took a bread roll from his pocket, broke off a piece and placed it in her mouth. It was dry and she thought it would choke her.

'Sorry, Sophie, but I can't risk removing your handcuffs. This won't be for long. A couple of days, that's all.' He unscrewed a bottle of water and raised it to her lips.

She wasn't hungry, but she was very thirsty. The water was wonderful, and she drank it down greedily. 'I need the toilet,' she said, when she'd finished.

He lifted her up into his arms and carried her to the bathroom. 'Okay, I'm going to remove the handcuffs for a few minutes but don't get any ideas of trying to get away. I really don't want to hurt you, Sophie, but I will if you force me to.'

The bathroom was roomy and luxurious but there was no way to escape; there was only one door and Igor was standing behind that, and the portholes were far too small to allow even her sparse frame to pass through them. She would have to wait until he took her back to Madame, or wherever they were going to, and try to get away then. Igor had said he wasn't planning to kill her. What was it he'd said about Julie? Her death had been an accident. They hadn't intended to kill anyone. So there was no need to kill her. She prayed that it was true.

Later, after Igor had left, she began to cry. It seemed hopeless. Was it true what he'd said, that it would only be for a couple of

Sophie is Still Missing

days? But then what? They must be travelling back to Moscow and taking her with them. The tears flowed faster. She would never see her family again. Never. This had been her one opportunity to escape and get home. Now that Igor knew her parents lived in Torremolinos, he would tell Madame and they would never bring her back to Marbella again. They might even sell her to someone else in Russia. She'd never see her parents again.

CHAPTER 39

Enrique de Valdes was worried. What on earth had Ivan got himself into?

'What's the matter *cariño*? You look dreadful,' asked his wife, pouring him his morning coffee. 'Is it the election?'

'Yes and no. It's Ivan. He's got himself mixed up with that case of the two missing girls from Torremolinos.' Enrique tried to have no secrets from his wife; he relied on her too much to hide anything from her.

'The girls that went missing last year?' she asked, replacing the coffee pot and looking at him in surprise. 'In what way?'

'That's what I don't know, but he put pressure on me to get the case closed.'

'You were behind that? You didn't say anything.' She looked annoyed.

'I was going to tell you but I knew you'd be angry.'

'Too right. It's one thing to have a crooked business partner, but quite another to cover up a serious crime. They say that girl was murdered.'

'Yes, but Ivan wouldn't murder anyone. He may be crooked but he's no killer. Anyway he claims it was an accident.'

'Well he would, wouldn't he,' she said, walking out of the kitchen and through the open door onto the patio.

Now she was really angry with him.

He finished his coffee and went to find her. 'You have to understand *cariño*, what else could I do? He knows too much about what happened to the money from the construction business. If he started talking to the press, it would kill any chance I have of being elected.'

'But all that was five years ago. The company went bankrupt; what more is there to say?' She looked at him. 'Unless there's something else you haven't told me?'

'No of course not. It's just it wouldn't look good would it, if people knew I had an account in the Cayman Islands, while others had lost their investments?'

'That's the way of the world, Enrique. Everybody wants to be rich; that's why they risk their money. They just don't always realise that they could lose it. All the buyers knew that the land was Parque Natural, but it didn't stop them from wanting to buy a house there.'

'I suppose you're right, but I didn't want the press to bring it all up again, not with the election so close.'

His wife went back into the kitchen and began loading the dishwasher. 'Well I think you should distance yourself from Ivan and his wife,' she added. 'No more playing golf with her, at least until the election is over.'

Enrique's mobile rang. '*Digame*,' He said rather curtly.

'Enrique, it's Albero. We need to talk.'

'But we're meeting this evening, What's so urgent?' he asked his campaign manager.

'Have you seen the papers this morning?'

'No, why?'

'Well go online and find the Voz de Málaga. Read the headlines on the front page. You were complaining about not getting enough coverage for your campaign, well you've got it now. Not sure it was what you were hoping for, though.'

'I'll ring you back.' What the hell had happened now? 'Maria, where is my iPad? I can't find it.'

'What's the matter? Was that Albero? What's happened?'

'I don't know. That's why I need my iPad.'

'Here, use mine.'

It only took a few moments for him to find the online newspaper and realise that his chances of becoming mayor had suddenly disappeared. He let out a groan and handed the iPad back to his wife.

'Secret bank account in the Cayman Islands. Enrique de Valdes, widely expected to win the upcoming election for mayor of Marbella, has some explaining to do,' she read. '*Dios mio*. Where did they get this from? And how did they find out about the money in the Cayman Islands? I thought that was private and confidential.'

'Nothing's private nor confidential to a journalist. What worries me is what else they've found out.'

'It doesn't look as though they have anything, *cariño*. It's all speculation. They just want to see how you'll react.'

'So what do you suggest I do?'

'Deny it. If they had any proof, the police would be knocking at the door. It'll blow over. You'll see.'

'You miss the point, Maria. Even if it does blow over, the damage is done.'

His phone rang again; it was Albero.

'*Si?*'

'You've read it?'

'I have. Nothing to worry about. It's all total rubbish.'

'Well, I'm sure that's true, but your backers have decided to pull out. They don't want their party to be associated with anyone who may be involved in criminal activities. I'm sorry, but you know how it is. Marbella has been there before. We've had our share of dirty mayors over the years, and this time they want their candidate to be squeaky clean. Sorry, old boy.'

'Can't you talk to them, Albero? Isn't that what you're paid to do, look after my interests?'

'It is, Enrique, but you haven't been honest with me. If you had, I'd have warned you of the dangers. There's nothing I can do. You're a liability now.'

'But the election is in two weeks. They can't pull out now. It's too late for them to find anyone else. They need me. You have to speak to them, Albero.' He was pleading with him now. 'They need me.'

'Actually, they don't. They already have someone lined up to take your place. Face up to it, Enrique, it's over.'

'Albero, wait. Let's meet and talk this through,' he said, but his ex-campaign manager had hung up.

'That bad?' his wife asked.

'They've ditched me. I'm a liability. That's what he said, a liability. I can't believe it. The money I've spent on this campaign and they didn't even want to discuss it with me.'

'So what will you do?'

'First of all I'm going to ring Ivan. It's his bloody fault that newspaper reporters have been poking about in our business anyway.'

At first he thought his friend wasn't going to answer. 'Ivan have you see the papers? My name is splashed all over the front page,' Enrique said.

'Good morning to you, Enrique. Yes, I have. Don't worry. That will soon quieten down. They don't have anything really, just hot air. Relax.'

'They've dumped me. They don't want me to run as mayor. I'm a liability.'

'So? You can wait for the next election. When's that? Four years time. Not so long.'

'That's if the Guardia Civil haven't found out by then that I asked Comisario Sanchez to get the case closed. How would that look? Mayoral candidate involved in suppressing evidence? My career is fucked. Ivan you have to promise me that this will go away.'

'Relax, Enrique. Just carry on as normal. If the press bother you, don't say anything. Within a few days it will be old news. People won't even remember why it was that you pulled out of the election. You could put about a rumour about personal reasons, your wife's health, a problem with your kids. In four years time that's what they'll remember, not your money in the Cayman Islands.'

'What about the police? What if they come round?'

'The same thing, say nothing. Remember, the more you say, the more they can twist your words and before you know it, it will be you who killed that girl. Just remain calm. And keep away from the police.'

'But what about the other girl? Where is she?'

'You don't need to worry about her. At the moment she is safely out of sight and very soon she'll be back in Moscow. I suggest you and your lovely wife go away for a short holiday, somewhere the press can't find you, until this all blows over.' He hung up.

'Well?' asked Enrique's wife.

'He says we should go away for a break.' He put his phone in his pocket. 'I've got a bad feeling about this, Maria. A very bad feeling.'

CHAPTER 40

Linda typed Doctor Dominguez's address into Google maps and realised that she could walk there; it was only fifteen minutes away, down a small alleyway off the Alameda de Colón.

It was easier to find than she'd imagined. A brass plate on the wall announced that the clinic of Doctor Ricardo Dominguez González, gynaecologist, was on the third floor. She rang the bell and a voice asked what she wanted.

'My name's Linda. I'd like to speak to someone please,' she said, not wanting to give away her reason for being there until she was inside.

'Third floor for reception,' said the anonymous voice.

Despite the old building's rather worn and battered exterior, the inside was all gleaming tiles, glass and chrome. The waiting room was decorated in pastel shades and a small aquarium of tropical fish sat in the middle of the room. Two unaccompanied girls were reading glossy magazines while they waited.

Linda walked up to the receptionist and asked, in a low voice, 'I wonder if you can help me?' She showed her ID card and said, 'Can you tell me if any of these people have visited this clinic? They may have had a young girl with them.'

She showed her a photograph of Ivan, but the girl shook her head. 'We're not supposed to give out any information about our patients,' she said.

'Of course. I quite understand that. I'm not interested in your patients. It's just that my boss said I had to go to all the gynaecology clinics and see if he'd been there.' She pulled out a photo of Jaime, 'What about him?'

The receptionist stared at the photo, then said, 'It's possible. His face is familiar. But it was a while ago.'

'Was he on his own?'

'I can't remember, but I expect he was with someone, because we don't often get a man in here alone. They are usually accompanying their girlfriend or sister.'

'Of course. Would he have been with this woman?' She placed the photograph of Annika on the desk, and watched the receptionist's reaction.

'Yes, she was definitely here. Like a film star she was.' She smiled broadly. 'I remember wondering why she'd come here and not gone to one of those really posh clinics in Madrid.'

'Was she with that man?'

'The first time she was on her own, but when she brought her sister, he came with them.'

'Her sister?'

'Yes, I think there was something wrong with her, besides being pregnant, I mean. She couldn't walk very well, and I think she was a bit backward. You know, she couldn't sign the forms or talk properly. The lady had to do it for her. It was very sad. She said her sister had been seduced by a neighbour, and she wouldn't be capable of looking after the baby, so although it pained her to do it, that was why they were here.'

'Did she give her name?' Linda asked.

The receptionist froze. 'We're not allowed to give out the names of our patients,' she said.

'That's fine. Normal procedure. I know it's important to maintain the patients' confidentiality.'

The girl nodded and smiled.

Sophie is Still Missing

'Well thank you, Maya,' Linda said, noting her name badge. 'You've been very helpful.' She felt like skipping out of the room she was so pleased with herself. So this was where Julie had her abortion. When the police knew this they could get a warrant and find the evidence they needed.

The door behind the receptionist opened and a tall man in a white coat came into the waiting room. He looked straight at Linda. She turned and headed for the exit, but not before she heard him ask the receptionist who she was. She didn't wait to hear the reply. She had to let JD know what she'd found, as soon as possible; she was the one who would be able to persuade the police to go and look at the clinic before they destroyed their records.

JD put down the telephone. She'd been talking to the headmistress of the school where Ivan's daughters were studying. At first she'd been reluctant to even speak to her without the parents' permission but when JD explained that she could call the Metropolitan Police and ask them to send someone to the school, she agreed that JD could email her a photo of Julie and Sophie to see if the girls recognised them.

'Nacho. Email the photo to the headmistress; she's agreed to ask the girls.'

'Did you explain to her what it's all about?'

'Yes, I had no option. She was going to ring the parents. I told her that these were the girls who disappeared last year and there was an outside possibility that the Lebedev children had seen them.'

'And was that enough?'

'Well I also threatened her with a visit from the police.'

'Good for you. I'll send her the photos now before she changes her mind.'

'Or alerts Ivan and his wife,' added JD.

'Maybe it's time we got the police involved,' suggested Nacho. 'What if she does ring the parents? They could do a runner and take Sophie with them.'

'But we don't know for sure that they have Sophie. It could all be circumstantial. No, we have to wait for an identification from the girls.'

'Did you hear about Valdes?' asked Nacho.

'No, what's he done now?'

'They've dropped him as a candidate for mayor.'

'That's a bit sudden. Why?'

'There was an unflattering article about him in the Voz de Málaga, suggesting he has a lot of money hidden in an offshore bank account. I think your mate, Tim might have had a hand in it. It was his type of muckraking with little substance.' Nacho didn't like Tim very much. 'You know I'm pretty sure he was the one who leaked the story about us investigating the missing girls.'

'You think so? Why would he do that? Why not write it himself?'

'Because he was fed up with you pushing him away. He wanted to punish you but if he'd written it himself, you would know.'

'Oh, Nacho, I don't think Tim is that devious. Anyway he's been very helpful in lots of ways.'

'Yes and how do you repay him? He can't even persuade you to go for a coffee with him.'

'Well that's as maybe; we haven't time to think about Tim's hurt feelings at the moment. I just hope all this press exposure isn't going to spook Ivan.' JD's phone rang. 'Hi Linda, how did it go?'

'I found the clinic, JD. Annika and Jaime took Julie for her abortion. The receptionist recognised them both, but just as I was leaving, her boss came out. He gave me a strange look and began asking the receptionist questions. I think you should get the police round there before they destroy any of Julie's records. His name is Dr Dominguez. I'll text you the address.'

'Thanks Linda. Good work.' She turned to Nacho and beamed at him. 'I think we are closing in on our Russian friend,' she said. 'Time to call in the big guns.'

'At last. You're going to ring the Captain?'

'I am. He can't ignore this now. Anything from the school?'

'Hang on. Yes, there's an email from the headmistress. According to the two girls, Julie and Sophie worked for their parents as domestic servants, but Sophie also taught the girls English. She says they were very fond of them, especially Sophie. I'd asked if the girls were ever alone with either of them, and she said the mother usually sat in on the English lessons.'

'Good, I think we can give him everything then.'

'Jaime?'

'Yes, why not? They will get more out of Jaime than we will ever be able to. Give me the file. I need to get this to Federico as soon as possible.'

She quickly dialled his number. 'Federico, it's me. We've found out where Julie had her abortion. Can you send someone round there right away? I'm worried they may destroy Julie's medical records. I'll text you the address, now.'

'I'll be right round to pick you up. You can tell me all the details while we drive there.'

'But you'll send someone round there now?'

'Yes, Jacaranda. They're on their way.'

Nacho handed her a USB stick. 'Everything's on there. I know you prefer that grubby file, but I think you'll find the Guardia Civil are digital these days. He won't thank you for that.'

'Thanks. Give me the old paper file as well. I might need it.' There was the sound of a police siren. 'That's probably him. See you later.'

CHAPTER 41

JD was in a deep sleep when her mobile rang. At first she resisted answering it, but it continued to ring and ring. '*Si, digame,*' she snapped irritably.

'Jacaranda, it's me, Federico. Sorry to wake you but I knew you'd be angry if I didn't.'

'What makes you so sure?' she asked.

'They're going to arrest Jaime. I thought you'd want to come along to the interview. You won't be able to go in the interview room, but you can watch and prompt me if you think it's important.'

Suddenly she was wide awake. At last things were moving. 'Where will you be?' she asked.

'Just get ready. I'll be at your place in five minutes.'

She threw down her phone and jumped out of bed. Just time for a quick splash of cold water and to clean her teeth and pull on some clothes. She grabbed her old tracksuit and trainers. With thirty seconds to spare she was standing in the street outside her apartment as a police car screeched to a stop beside her.

'Get in,' Federico said.

There were two other Guardia Civil officers in the back.

'Thanks for ringing me,' she said.

'Well, it's your case, really. Let's hope we can tie it up together.'

'Do we have enough proof?' she asked.

'Forensics found traces of Julie's blood in that burned out car. It was a miracle it survived the fire. It was on a piece of carpet from the boot. Quite amazing actually.'

'Do you think he'll know where Sophie is?' she asked.

'He may do. We don't know how much he is implicated in Sophie's disappearance yet. But, from the evidence you've unearthed, he was certainly involved in Julie's death. Whether he was just the fall guy who cleared up someone else's mess or he committed the murder himself, is still to be ascertained. That's why I want you to come along to the station.'

Her heart was beating wildly. This was it. If Jaime could be persuaded to talk then maybe, just maybe they'd find Sophie.

She sat in the gloom, behind a one-way mirror watching the detective interview Jaime. The chauffeur looked crushed. She could see straight away that he wasn't a bad man—she'd come across enough villains in her time to distinguish the really bad from the foolish. He seemed very religious, and Julie's accident appeared to be weighing heavily on his conscience. He didn't even try to deny that he was the one who placed Julie's body in the *Cofradía*.

'But why there?' asked the detective. 'Why not dump her in the sea?'

Jaime stared at him, horrified. 'I'm not a monster. She didn't deserve to die. She didn't deserve any of it.'

'Did you know that Julie was one of the girls who were kidnapped in 2017? From Torremolinos?'

He shook his head. 'Not at first. I just thought she was one of my employer's maids,' he replied. 'I admit, I didn't think he treated them very well but to be honest, I didn't pay much attention to either of them.'

Sophie is Still Missing

JD clicked on her speaker and said to Federico, 'He said maids. Plural. Ask him about the other one.'

Federico looked up at her and nodded.

'At first I didn't realise who she was; I had read about her and her friend in the papers at the time but it never occurred to me that she was one of the missing girls. Then one day, something my boss said made me look at her more closely. She'd changed a lot, looked older and much thinner. I felt so sorry for her.'

'But it never occurred to you to tell the police?'

'We were in Moscow. I knew they wouldn't be interested.'

'Is that why you took her to the *Cofradía*, because you felt sorry for her?'

'Yes. It was my way of offering her poor body to God. I hadn't meant to run her over. It was an accident. I wanted God to forgive me.'

'But you knew she'd be found in the *Cofradía*?'

'Yes, that was the point of it, so the poor girl's body could be returned to her family.'

'What about your boss, Ivan? Did he tell you to kill her?'

'Of course not. He just wanted me to catch her and bring her back. Julie ran out of the gate and I followed her in the car.'

'So how did the accident happen?' asked the detective.

'A deer,' he said. 'A deer ran across the road in front of the car, and I swerved to avoid it, and hit Julie. I didn't mean to.' He pulled out a handkerchief and mopped his brow. 'It was an accident,' he repeated.

'So you keep saying. Okay Jaime. I can believe it was an accident. You don't look like the sort of man who would run down an innocent girl. But you do look like the sort of man who would be ready to cover up a crime if you were given enough money to do so. We've been looking at your bank statements.

You have a very profitable taxi business there. How many taxis do you have?'

'One,' Jaime muttered, looking down at the table.

'And yet you have an income of roughly 10,000 euros every month. Now even I can't believe that one taxi would generate an income of 10,000 euros every month, so where did the rest of the money come from?'

'Well, it's like I explained, sometimes I do a bit of chauffeuring.'

'And that is what you were doing the night you ran over Julie Bennett?' He nodded. 'For Mr Lebedev?'

'Yes.'

And that's why you were at Ivan Lebedev's house that night?'

Jaime was beginning to look uncomfortable. 'I often drive him home if he's been out late,' he said. 'Not just business meetings.'

'And why do you think Julie was running out of the house that night? Was she frightened? Was she running away from someone?'

'I don't know. I'd dropped off Mr Lebedev a bit earlier and I was on my way home.'

'But you wanted to stop her?'

'Well.' He paused. 'It was very dark. We were frightened she'd get hurt. I don't know why she was running out of the gate. I didn't see her until it was too late.'

'We?'

'Mr Lebedev and I.'

'Ah, so he was there, as well.'

'No, Mr Lebedev was in Emergency. He'd had a fall and cut his head.'

'Really? So why didn't you take him to the hospital? You're his driver, aren't you?'

Jaime said nothing.

'Was she running away from him?'

Now Jaime looked really scared.

'Did Mr. Lebedev tell you to go and deal with Julie?'

'No, I told you, he was in the hospital.'

'Who took him to the hospital?'

'His wife.'

'So how did he know that Julie had run away?'

'Someone must have told him.'

'I don't believe you, Jaime. Did Mr Lebedev phone you from the hospital and tell you to deal with Julie?'

'He just wanted me to bring her back.'

'There's something about your story that I don't understand, Jaime. Why did you take Julie's body all the way to the *Cofradía*?' asked the detective. 'Why didn't you take her back to Mr Lebedev's house? After all she couldn't have run all the way to Málaga, could she? How far had she gone when your car hit her? One kilometre? Two? It would have been easier to take her body back to the house.'

'I wasn't thinking. I just put her body in the car and kept driving.'

'If, as you claim, it was an accident, why didn't you ring the police?'

Jaime turned and looked at his solicitor, then gave a deep sigh and said, 'Ivan didn't want the police involved. He told me to get rid of her, to take her into the mountains and drop her body down an old well. I started to drive inland, but I just couldn't do it. I wanted her to have a decent burial, so I turned round and headed for Málaga. She didn't deserve to be thrown down a well. Forgotten. Her body never to be found. Her

Sophie is Still Missing

parents unable to mourn her. She was a lovely girl. I couldn't do that to her.'

'So Mr Lebedev did know about Julie's death?'

Jaime nodded.

'Yes or no?'

'Yes.'

'And did he know that you disobeyed him?'

'I told him that nobody knew it was me who took her there; the place was deserted. He wasn't happy, but what could he do about it? He could hardly sack me. I knew too much.'

'We found a crucifix that seems to have belonged to you. Did you lose it or leave it there on purpose?'

'I hadn't intended to leave it there; I'm not stupid, you know.. I didn't know it was missing until I got home.'

'Earlier you mentioned "maids." Was there another girl with Julie?'

'Yes, her friend. Sophie, I think she was called.'

'So where was she when Julie ran out of the gate?'

'Inside the house I expect. I didn't see her.'

At last it was out. Jaime then went on to admit that he knew about the two girls living in the house, how they were never allowed to go out or meet anyone, how Ivan had taken a liking to Julie and raped her on a regular basis. He began to cry. 'I'm a weak man, may God forgive me. I knew what was going on and I did nothing to stop it. God forgive me.'

'It's up to God whether he forgives you or not,' said Federico. 'What I want to know, and in order for the State to offer you some little forgiveness, is where is the other girl? Where is Sophie Anderson? Is she still alive?'

'As far as I know, yes. But they are planning to leave the country. The whole family are going back to Moscow.'

'When?'

'Any day now. Ivan told my wife that he wouldn't be needing my services anymore.'

'So Sophie has been in their house in Marbella all this time?' Federico asked.

'Since they came over in the summer, yes. I imagine they will take her back with them.'

JD couldn't believe her ears. That poor girl had been an hour's drive away and they'd never known.

Federico got up. 'You continue the interview. I need to find this girl,' he told the detective.

JD grabbed her bag and rushed down to join him. 'Do you think we'll be too late?' she asked.

'It depends whether your Russian friend realises how close we are to him.'

'He's already spoken to Jaime's wife; she will have told him that we have her husband in custody.'

'True. That might be enough to spook him. We'd better hurry.'

CHAPTER 42

Ivan was in a foul mood after his conversation with Valdes. The idiot wouldn't be able to keep his mouth shut. He should never have involved him in the first place.

'What's wrong?' Annika asked.

'Get packed. We're going back to Moscow.'

'What? Right now? I can't just drop everything and leave. What would people say?'

'They'll say a lot less than if you stay and get arrested for child trafficking,' said her husband.

'Child trafficking. We had nothing to do with that. You will have to tell them; we didn't know where those girls were from. Anyway, it has nothing to do with me. You were the one who bought them. How was I to know that you'd paid for them?'

'You knew. You pretend to be the grand lady, but you know as well as I do what goes on. Did you hear me? Get packed. I won't tell you again. It won't take the police long to connect us to Jaime. And when they do, I want us to be far away. Is that understood?'

His wife picked up a vase of flowers and hurled it across the room.

'This is no time for tantrums. Save that for when the police arrest you, as well.'

'Jaime. Has he been arrested?' Annika looked worried now.

'Yes, his wife just phoned to see if I could help.'

'What did you say?'

'I said, I couldn't interfere in police matters.'

'And she didn't laugh in your face?'

'Just get ready or I'll go without you.'

'Well why don't you? I don't want to go back to Moscow. I prefer to live here. I can manage quite well without you,' his wife yelled at him.

Ivan's phone rang. 'Yes?' he said. 'Dominguez? When was that? Oh, my God. Thanks for letting us know. No, it's probably nothing. Don't worry about it. Yes, I'll let you know if anyone contacts me.'

'Who was that?'

'The gynaecologist. It seems that someone was round there just now, asking about Julie. They showed some photos to his receptionist, and the stupid girl recognised you. So now will you get packed? I don't think your posh friends will be happy to know they have been consorting with a woman who uses unpaid help in her house and whose husband gets the servant pregnant. Do you?'

If looks could kill, he'd be in the morgue by now. He'd never seen his wife so angry before. She never said a word, but slammed the door and went upstairs to her room. He could hear her banging boxes and drawers as she tried to fill her suitcase.

'Only one suitcase, mind. We'll send for the rest of your stuff, later. And before you ask, no, the dogs are not coming with us.'

At this he heard a howl of rage and anguish and something being hurled across the room. He left her to it and went into the kitchen. Igor and the housekeeper were sitting at the table, drinking tea.

'Madame and I have to go back to Moscow. We're leaving tonight. Igor I'd like you to come with us, so get packed right away. Lourdes, you will stay here and look after the house, as you usually do. In the meantime, go up to my room and pack a bag for me. Remember it's a lot colder in Moscow, so put in my boots.'

'Si, señor.'

He waited until Lourdes had left and said to Igor, 'Where is the girl?'

'On the yacht, sir. I checked on her this morning. Is she coming with us?'

Yes. We'll sail tonight. Get in touch with the captain and tell him we want to go straight to Tangier. Oh and cook one of Madame's favourites for lunch; she's in a foul mood. I don't want to have to listen to her complaining all the way to Moscow. We'll leave at ten o'clock.'

'Very well, sir. And Jaime?'

'Jaime's at the police station. He's been taken in for questioning. Don't worry; he won't say anything. He's as involved as any of us.'

'What about you and Madame?' asked Igor.

'We'll meet you there, at the yacht. I have a few things to tidy up first. Oh and send Alexie up to my study.'

'I think he's having a swim,' said Igor.

'Well tell him there's no time for that. I need him now.'

'Yes, Mr Lebedev.'

Ivan could still hear Annika banging about in the bedroom, and now she was berating poor Lourdes. He'd keep out of the way until she'd calmed down. He went into his study and shut the door to wait for Alexie. Annika would be even more angry when she knew what he was about to do. Still there was no alternative.

After a few minutes there was a knock on the door and his rather flustered accountant stood there, wrapped in a towelling robe, and with water still dripping from his long hair.

Sophie is Still Missing

'Alexie, we have an emergency. Book four tickets for Madame, Igor, the maid and me to fly to Moscow tomorrow morning. From Tangier. And I want you to go to Sussex today to collect my children from school. Book flights for the three of you to Moscow and stay with them at the house until we arrive. Is that understood?'

'Yes sir. What has happened? Is it the police?'

'Nothing has happened, yet. I'm just taking precautions. All being well I will see you in Moscow.'

'Very well Mr. Lebedev.'

'You have all our passport details?'

'Yes sir. They are in the file.'

'Good. Well get dressed and see to it straight away.'

Once Alexie had left, Ivan opened his mobile phone and dialled the number of his daughters' boarding school. 'Let me speak to the headmistress,' he said. 'It's Ivan Lebedev.' He'd never been happy about his daughters going to an English school; it had been Annika's idea. She thought an English education would make ladies of them. 'Mrs. Chalmers. It's Ivan Lebedev. I'm afraid I have some bad news. The girls must return to Moscow tomorrow; it's a family matter and I want them there. I'm sending someone to collect them.'

'This is very sudden, Mr. Lebedev. And most irregular. It's not good for your daughters to miss classes, especially at the beginning of a new school year.'

'I apologise Mrs. Chalmers, but I have no alternative. They are bright girls, I'm sure they will manage to catch up.'

'Such a shame. They had settled down so well. When will they be returning?'

'I'm not sure if they will return. I'll keep you informed.'

'He was about to end the call when the headmistress said, 'I was considering telephoning you today anyway.'

Sophie is Still Missing

'Oh, why was that? Is something wrong?'

'No, I don't think so, but it was a bit strange. I had a phone call from a private investigator in Spain asking if the girls could identify two young women.'

Ivan felt his blood chill. 'And?'

'Well it didn't seem a problem. They sent the photos and your daughters confirmed that they knew the women, and that was that.'

'What do you mean, confirmed they knew them?' His temper was rising. Was he completely surrounded by idiots?

'Your maids. The girls said it was one of them who taught them to speak English.'

'What else did this private investigator ask them?'

'Nothing. That's why I didn't ring you. It seemed very unimportant.'

'If anyone else, anyone at all, rings and asks about my daughters, I want to know right away. Is that understood?' he shouted down the telephone.

'Of course. I'm sorry if you're upset, Mr. Lebedev.'

He rang off and immediately phoned Alexie and said, 'Make that three tickets to Moscow. The maid is no longer coming with us.'

Ivan snapped his mobile shut and threw it on his desk. The sooner they got away from here, the better; that private investigator was becoming a real thorn in his side.

CHAPTER 43

When JD and Federico arrived at the Lebedev's house, all they found was the housekeeper, covering the furniture with dust sheets.

'Search the house, thoroughly,' the Captain ordered his men. 'You, leave that and come with me.' Lourdes stared at him defiantly, but nevertheless put down the dust sheets and followed him into the lounge.

'Where is everybody?' he asked.

'They've gone,' she said.

'I can see that. Where have they gone?'

The woman shrugged. 'Back to Russia, I expect. They don't live here all the time you know. This is their holiday home.'

'When did they leave?'

'A week ago.'

'We're too late,' JD wailed. 'They'll be back in Moscow by now.'

'Think again, señora. When did they leave? And this time consider your answer carefully,' said the Captain.

She hesitated then muttered, 'An hour ago.'

Just then one of the Guardia Civil officers returned and said, 'There's no-one here, Capitán. It looks as though they left in a hurry. All their clothes are still in the bedroom.'

'That's normal,' said the housekeeper. 'Madame likes to travel light. She has plenty of clothes in Moscow.'

'Capitán, look at this,' called one of the officers. 'I think someone's been sleeping in here.'

Federico went to see what he'd found. The officer was holding the door open to an under-stairs cupboard.

'My God. Is that where they slept?' said Federico, peering into the windowless space that contained a mattress and some old sheets. 'What bastards. Get the forensic team here. Let's see if we can find any of the girls' DNA.' He turned to Lourdes and glared at her. 'What do you know about this?' he asked.

She shook her head. 'What is there to know? They worked for Mrs Lebedev, the same as me.'

Instantly JD turned on her. 'They? How many were there?' She felt Federico's hand on her shoulder.

'Where are the rest of the staff? I can't believe that you ran this big house on your own?'

'Of course not. Madame likes things done properly.'

'So where are they?'

'They've been dismissed. I expect she will employ them again when they return next year.'

'I want a complete list of all the staff that were employed here. Everyone, including casual staff, and put their phone numbers as well. If I find you have left anyone off, I will charge you with perverting the course of justice.'

At last the housekeeper was beginning to look worried.

'Stay with her,' he told one of the officers. 'I don't want her disappearing as well.'

He turned to the sergeant and said, 'Check the airport. See if there any flights to Moscow. And check the train station. Alert the traffic police. I want these bastards found. They have to be somewhere.'

'But how will they get Sophie out? She'll be recognised. Her photo's been all over the news,' said JD.

Sophie is Still Missing

That morning the police had released a statement to the national press saying that the search for Sophie had been resumed and that they were hoping to find her alive.

Suddenly she remembered the magazine that Linda had brought into the office, with Lebedev and Valdes on the yacht. 'They're going by sea.'

Federico stared at her. 'By sea?'

'Yes, come on. There's no time to lose. I'll tell you on the way to Puerto Banus.'

'Capitán, here's the list.' One of his men handed him Lourdes's list.

There were eight names on it, only three were part-time. 'Here you look at this while I drive,' said Federico. They jumped into his car and with the siren blaring headed for the port.

'She's only listed one girl as a housemaid. No name, though,' JD said. 'Jaime is here, listed as a part time chauffeur. There's a chef called Igor something, Romovski, I think. An accountant, Alexie Dubrovnik, a part-time pool man and a gardener. And the housekeeper, of course.'

'Not a lot of staff for such a big house. One housemaid? That's odd. Now would you like to explain to me why we're speeding down these narrow, windy roads to Puerto Banus.'

'He owns a sea-going yacht. I think they'll go to Morocco and get a flight from there to Moscow. Nobody will question who Sophie is, there. She's unlikely to be recognised in Tangier.'

'Do you know how many yachts there are moored at Puerto Banus?' he asked.

'No. I've never been there,' she admitted. 'But this is a very big boat.' She had never had anything to do with yachts or yachting, and barely knew one end of a boat from the other.

'Oh, Jacaranda. The place is full of big expensive yachts. Don't you have a better description than that?'

'Hang on. I'll get Nacho to send me a photo.' She took out her mobile and rang her computer assistant. 'Hi, Nacho. Good morning. Is that yachting magazine still there? The one that Linda brought in?'

'Yes. Well the photo of Valdes and Lebedev is; I cut it out and stuck it on the evidence board.'

'Great. Send it to me please. And find out anything you can about the boat to help us identify it.'

'Okay JD. Where are you exactly?'

'The police are trying to arrest Ivan Lebedev but he's done a runner. I think he'll be heading for his yacht. So, hurry. We need to find it before they leave Spanish waters.'

'Okay Boss.'

Within minutes the photo arrived on her phone.

'This will help, she said.

Federico glanced at it. 'A little. A mooring would be better. We'll send the photo to the local Guardia Civil and see if they can identify it.' He made a call and then said to her, 'Forward it to this number.'

JD did as he asked. How much longer was it going to take them to get there? 'Do you think we should alert the coastal police?' she asked. 'After all they have at least an hour's head start on us. They could have already sailed.'

'Don't worry Jacaranda. We will find her. They can't get far.'

It was easy for him to say that; he didn't have to explain to Sophie's parents that they had found her and then lost her again.

Her mobile began to ring. 'Nacho?'

'I am sending you the mooring reference. It was easy to find. By the way, the yacht is registered to his wife. And, good news, it's still there. I'll send you the GPS coordinates.'

'Thanks Nacho. You're a star.'

'Good luck, JD.'

'Well?' asked Federico.

'That was Nacho. He knows where it's moored. Do you want me to forward the coordinates to the same number?'

'Yes. Right away.'

She stared out of the window. The countryside was flashing by as cars moved out of their way. JD glanced at the dashboard. He was doing 140 km an hour, but it still didn't seem fast enough for her. Her stomach was in knots. All these months and at last they were in reach of finding Sophie.

Federico's mobile rang. 'You get it, Jacaranda.'

'*Digame*,' she answered. Then her heart sank as she listened to the officer at the other end of the line.

'What? What's happened?'

'They say the yacht has left the marina. It's not there.' She held the phone up for him to hear.

'Well bloody well find it,' he shouted at the officer. 'Get the helicopters out. Contact SEMAR. We have to locate that yacht and quickly. There's an abduction in progress.'

'SEMAR?' JD asked.

'The maritime guys. They'll find it, don't worry.'

'What if they're not on the yacht? What if they're already on a flight to Moscow?'

'No, I think your hunch is right. It's the most sensible thing to do, take the yacht to Tangier and get a flight from there.' He punched a number into his phone and when they answered, he said, 'It's possible they're heading for Tangier. Make sure someone is waiting for them when they land.'

'Can they do that?' she asked.

'We have a good working relationship with Tangier. We have to,' he added.

Sophie is Still Missing

JD's stomach was churning; she thought she'd be sick. What, if after all their efforts they escaped with Sophie? Or, worse still, they dumped her overboard.

Federico's mobile rang again. 'There are three tickets booked to Moscow from Tangier airport, for first thing tomorrow. It's the only flight this week.' He waited a few minutes, then added, 'Booked in the name of Igor Romovski.'

'The chef? But why three tickets? Who else is with him?'

The phone rang again. She watched as his face became solemn. 'What is it?' she asked.

'The names of the other two passengers are Ivan Lebedev and his wife Annika. There's no mention of Sophie Anderson, or anyone else for that matter.'

JD felt like screaming. So where was she? Had they already killed her? Maybe they were going to dispose of her body in the Mediterranean.

'What do we do now?' she cried. 'Where the hell is she?'

Sophie must have fallen asleep because the next thing she knew, the sun was streaming through the porthole and shining in her eyes. Something had changed. The yacht was starting to move. And she could hear voices. Igor and another man, a Spaniard. Had Igor changed his plans? The motion of the boat became fiercer as the swell increased; they were leaving the marina. Where were they going? What was going to happen to her? Now she was too scared to cry. She lay there, shaking with fear and listened to the waves beat against the side of the boat. There was nothing she could do against these men; she was helpless. Where were they taking her?

She could hear the two men shouting but couldn't make out what they were saying. Igor sounded angry. The yacht began to increase its speed, and abruptly changed direction. Sophie was thrown off the sofa and landed on the parquet floor with a bang. She tried to sit up, but Igor had bound her too tightly. Now she beginning to feel seasick. If only she could get the tape off her mouth, but her hands were still tied behind her back. If she was sick now, she'd choke on her vomit. She swallowed and tried to control the nausea that was rising in her throat. Why didn't Igor come down to see to her? What was happening? What was he doing?

Suddenly the cabin door burst open and there he stood. But he didn't look like Igor; his normal gentle face was contorted with fear and rage, and in his hands he held a length of heavy duty rope.

CHAPTER 44

'*Si. Vale.* Yes go ahead.' Federico turned his head and beamed at her. 'SEMAR have located the yacht. They've signalled for them to stop.'

JD thought she'd be sick; she was so nervous. Please let Sophie be alive. Please God let her be there. 'What if she's not on board?' she said.

'Well we keep looking.'

'But they might already be on a flight out of the country. Maybe I was wrong about the yacht. Maybe it was a decoy.'

'No, I doubt it. The yacht seems the most likely means of escape for them. Anyway their descriptions have been issued to all the airports in the area; it's going to be very hard for them to get away.'

'I hope you're right.'

They had arrived at the marina and were parked near the empty berth; they sat there listening to the police radio and the comments from the maritime patrol. The yacht had stopped and the officers were in the process of boarding any minute. Her stomach was churning with a mixture of fear and excitement. Silently she kept repeating the mantra, 'Let her be alive, please let her be alive.'

'They're boarding now,' said Federico. He was almost as nervous as she was. '*Joder,*' he swore and slammed his hand on the dashboard.

She reached out and grabbed his arm. 'What is it? What's taking so long?'

Sophie is Still Missing

'Patience, *cariño*.'

At last she heard them on the line again. 'What are they saying? Is she there?' she cried.

Federico put up his hand to quieten her.

The radio crackled; it was hard to make out what the officer was saying. Federico put on the headphones and sat there without speaking. He didn't look very happy. What had happened? She couldn't bear the suspense.

At last he turned to her and said, 'It looks as though they've apprehended the captain, but there's another man on board. He's resisting arrest. They've opened fire.'

'What?'

Federico removed the headphones so she could hear the shouting. It sounded chaotic. Then there was more gunfire. And suddenly nothing. What was happening? They sat there in silence, waiting. JD could barely breathe. At last a faint voice came on the line. Federico snatched up the headphones again. What was happening? Was Sophie there? She watched Federico's face, hoping to glean something from his expression, but he continued to frown.

'The bastards,' he shouted.

'What is it? What have they found?' She couldn't bear the suspense any longer. 'Tell me, Federico. Is she all right? Have they found Sophie?'

'Yes, they've got her. And she's alive, but only just. The scumbag was about to throw her overboard.'

'Into the sea? Alive? Is she okay?'

'She's alive,' he repeated. 'That's all they'll say.'

'Did they shoot the man?'

'Only in the leg. He'll live, more's the pity.'

'What about the Lebedevs? Are they on the yacht?'

'There's no sign of them, only the captain and Igor, the chef. Neither of them will say anything until they have a solicitor.'

'He was going to drown her?'

'Yes. They said her legs and arms were tied and he'd weighted her down with the anchor. If we'd been any later, she'd have been gone forever.'

'How could he do that to a young girl? To anyone?' She couldn't bear to contemplate what it must have been like for Sophie to be tied up like a sack of rubbish, knowing he was going to throw her overboard. The poor girl must have been terrified. After all that she suffered, to be drowned like an unwanted puppy. JD wanted to scream with rage.

'Relax, Jacaranda. She's safe, now,' said Federico, taking her hand. 'You did it. You found her alive.'

JD couldn't believe her eyes. There was Sophie sitting on the steps of an ambulance with a paramedic by her side. She was wrapped in a blanket, and looked a lot thinner and older than in her photos, and there was a large bruise on her cheek, but it was obviously her. JD wanted to rush over and hug her, but she knew she couldn't. Forensics would want to check her out first.

She'd rung the Andersons while they were waiting for the SEMAR team to arrive, and told them the good news. Beverley had burst into tears and she could hear her saying over and over again, 'I can't believe it. I can't believe it.' Jim had been only marginally more controlled, managing at last to ask JD where they had found his daughter.

Just then she saw a tall, rather corpulent man, with blood stained trousers, being led off the yacht in handcuffs; he was limping. Igor? It had to be. So what had happened? Why were he and Sophie alone? Had Ivan abandoned them? Or was he planning to meet up with Igor once he'd got rid of the girl? The main question was, where were Igor's employers now?

'The Andersons have arrived,' said Federico. 'Would you like to see to them? Don't let them get too close to their daughter. I know they'll want to, but they just have to be patient a little longer.'

'Yes, I'll see to them.' She wasn't relishing talking to the Andersons; it was hard enough to keep her own emotions under control without witnessing theirs. 'We'd better let Fiona know, as well. I'll get Linda to go round and see her.'

'Yes, the police will want to talk to her too, to let her know we have her daughter's killer.'

JD stood there in a daze of happiness. They'd done it. They'd found Sophie, when everyone else had given her up for dead.

A white suited forensic team was boarding the yacht, and a small crowd of tourists was gathering beyond the police cordon. Now they knew beyond a shadow of doubt that Ivan and his wife were the ones who had bought Julie and Sophie and kept them as unpaid help, in other words, slaves. But the police still had to prove it; she was sure that Ivan would have the best lawyers available to defend him. They would need a waterproof case to convict them. But they had Sophie, the best witness there was. She couldn't see any way that they could wriggle out of it now. Ivan and his wife were not getting on that flight tomorrow. With any luck they wouldn't see Moscow again for a very long time.

CHAPTER 45

Federico had suggested they take Nacho and Linda out to lunch, and he'd update them on what was happening. So there they were, sitting in the autumn sunshine, watching the waves breaking on the shore, drinking some excellent wine.

'I couldn't believe it when you rang and told me you'd found her,' said Linda. 'I just burst into tears of happiness.'

'And now we've got our Russian friends in custody,' said Federico. 'Ivan tried to pull his 'diplomatic immunity' card, but the Moroccan authorities weren't having any of it.'

'So where are they now?' asked Nacho.

'In a Tangier prison. We're sending some officers to pick them up when all the paperwork has been done.'

'What about his daughters?' asked Linda.

'They've left the school. Our Russian friend wasn't leaving anything to chance. They flew out of Heathrow the same day we went to arrest their parents.'

'So the question is, how did they know you were about to arrest them?' asked JD.

'They'd have had to be deaf and blind not to realise we were getting close. We'd already questioned Valdes and the gynaecologist. I bet both of them tipped him off,' said Linda. 'That doctor looked very shifty to me.'

'Well, luckily for him, he hadn't actually broken the law. We can't prove that Julie was taken there against her will; so there's nothing to charge him with,' said Federico.

'What about Valdes?'

'Again, there's no proof he did anything wrong. We can't prove he put pressure on Comisario Sanchez to close the case, although I'm convinced that he did. But the NCP are holding an internal investigation to see if the Commissioner interfered in an investigation run by the Guardia Civil. So there will be some satisfaction in that.'

'And Malveno?' asked JD.

'A reprimand for closing the case too soon. It won't do his promotion chances much good.'

'I still can't see why the CNP would agree to close an open murder case.'

'You forget, Nacho, the CNP had already decided that the kidnapping and the murder were done by different perpetrators. They were only interested in the people trafficking side. What the Guardia Civil decided to do about the murder was up to them.'

'And Valdes, of course, can say goodbye to a career in politics. I can't see anyone touching him with a bargepole now that all that stuff's come out about him and his off-shore account,' added Linda.

'Yes, there are a lot of angry people out there,' said Nacho.

'They have opened an investigation into the construction company scam, but it could take years for anyone to get their money back,' added Federico. 'But the good news is that we had a full confession from Jaime Ortega. He has admitted to the accidental killing of Julie Bennett and is facing charges of deliberately running down Lieutenant Jose Maria Alvároz. In his defence he says that Ivan paid him to get rid of the policeman, but whether we can prove that, remains to be seen. Jaime Ortega is also charged with aiding and abetting the enforced captivity of two teenage girls.'

'Was he the one who collected Sophie and Julie after Ivan bought them online?'

'Yes, but he says he was just told that they were the new housemaids, and he was to collect them from a hotel in Tangier —not the posh one that the girls had googled, a much scruffier place. He didn't know they'd been abducted and sold. Well not at first.'

'So he's the fall guy,' said Nacho. 'Valdes and Lebedev get away with it and the chauffeur goes to prison for the best part of his life.'

'Don't worry. Ivan won't get away with it. I'm sure we have enough proof to put him away for a long time.'

'Do you really believe that?' asked JD. 'Someone like him, with so much money and plenty of influential contacts, can buy his way out of anything, even a prison sentence. Then he can set himself and his family up anywhere in the world, new identities, new friends and begin a new life.'

'No, not this time, Jacaranda. His influential friends are going to distance themselves from him, if they haven't done so already. After all, it's not just a bit of fraud we're talking about here, this is modern slavery and complicity to murder. He bought those girls and kept them locked inside his home, half starved, beaten and fearful for their lives. He repeatedly raped one of them and would probably have raped the other, if you guys hadn't uncovered what was happening. I can't see him charming his way out of that little lot.'

'And Igor?' asked Linda. 'What will happen to him?'

'All the household staff are being questioned and some will have charges to face. As for Igor, he'll be charged with abducting and holding captive a woman with the intention of murdering her. There's a stiff penalty for that.'

'So prison food for him from now on,' Linda said with a big smile. She helped herself to some clams. 'By the way, I saw Fiona. She's very happy that someone has been arrested for Julie's death, and I think she felt better when I told her it had been an accident. I didn't give her too many details, especially about the abortion; I thought that was too much at one go. There's time enough for that later. I'll go round in a couple of weeks and have a long chat to her. She says her son is coming back to Spain, so she won't be alone.'

Federico stood up and lifted his glass, saying, 'Let's have a toast. To the most annoying, stubborn and tenacious private detective in Spain, Jacaranda Dunne.'

'And don't forget her team,' said JD, with a big grin. She knew better than anyone that she couldn't have solved the case without the help of Linda and Nacho, and the support of her friends. Her phone began to ring.

'Leave it. You're off duty now,' said Federico.

'I'll only be a minute. It's Bill.' She walked away from the table so that she could hear him better. 'Hi Bill. What's up?'

'Not good news, I'm afraid, JD. Steed's disappeared. Our tail lost him. He's removed his electronic tag and now we have no idea where he is.'

'But he can't leave the UK, can he?'

'He's a wily character. You know him better than me. Anything's possible. I didn't want to worry you, JD. I just thought you should know.'

'Thanks, Bill. Ring me if you get any more news. Bye.' She leant against the wall, her legs trembling. Of course. They'd never found out who the man was that broke into her office. It was obvious now; the break-in was definitely Steed's doing. At first she'd thought it was connected to the case of the missing girls, but now she knew it was Steed. He'd known she was in

Sophie is Still Missing

Spain, all along. He wanted her to understand that he knew where she was, that he could find her. Who else would put a photo of her and Andy on her computer screen? He had taken the photo from Andy's wallet and digitised it. All the intruder had to do was upload it to her computer. This was Steed's crude attempt at intimidation. Well it wasn't going to work. If he was coming to Spain, she'd be ready for him. She looked across at the table where her friends were sitting, laughing at one of Linda's jokes. There was no point telling them about Bill's news. She didn't want to think about it today. Today was for celebrating success and friendship. But she'd have to tell them tomorrow; they could all be in danger. Steed was a cruel and cunning adversary.

Sophie is Still Missing

Thank you for taking the time to read SOPHIE IS STILL MISSING. If you enjoyed it, please consider telling your friends or posting a short review. Word of mouth is an author's best friend and much appreciated. Thank you, Joan Fallon

CONNECT WITH JOAN FALLON ONLINE AT:
http:// www.joanfallon.co.uk
https://www.facebook.com/joanfallonbooks
https://twitter.com/joan_fallon

Sophie is Still Missing

DARK HEART
A Jacaranda Dunne Mystery
by Joan Fallon

'Dark Heart' is the second book in the Jacaranda Dunne crime series.

When the naked body of a well known actor is found murdered during the Málaga Film Festival, the Guardia Civil once more turn to JD and her team for help. The murder is far from straightforward. The killer has left a trail of clues for the police to follow, but the question is why? And what is he trying to tell them? They can find no obvious motive for the murder of the actor, whose body was found in the locked basement of the Picasso Museum.

This page turning mystery takes JD and her team along a trail of dead ends and through the bloody world of terrorism, until they they discover the perpetrator was closer than they realised.